Step Into My Web

A DEATH & MOONLIGHT MYSTERY

NEW YORK TIMES & *USA TODAY* BESTSELLING AUTHOR

CYNTHIA EDEN

CHAPTER ONE

"Lady, do you have a damn death wish?" The robber shoved his gun toward the face of the woman who stood before him, her delicate shoulders squared and her spine perfectly straight.

"Not today, I don't," she assured him as the faintest trace of a British accent whispered beneath her words. The woman didn't back down. In fact, her slightly angled chin shot up into the air.

Sonofabitch. Joel Landry hadn't been looking for this shit. Truly. He'd just come in the bank to cash a check and be on his way. He'd wanted a nice, easy day. Was that too much to ask?

But...two minutes inside, and trouble had come calling.

He'd been standing behind the woman with the sleek black hair, the hair that fell in a thick curtain just below her shoulders. His gaze *may* have drifted over her body as he admired her long legs and curves, so perhaps that was why he'd been distracted. He hadn't even realized the gunman was there until the bastard had knocked out the guard, then yelled for everyone to "Freaking freeze!"

Joel had frozen. The woman in front of him hadn't.

Now he was about to have to do something incredibly stupid so she could keep on living. His typical luck. Joel sighed. Just when life had been getting back to normal. Semi-normal? Screw it. He—

"This won't end like the other times," the dark-haired woman announced.

The three bank tellers were cowering behind the counter. The bank manager was sobbing near his desk. Other than Joel and the crazy woman who didn't seem to have the sense to be scared, there were only two other customers in there. A grandmotherly type who clutched her pearls as if her life depended on it, and a young, barely eighteen-looking fellow with eyes that darted around constantly. Buckets of sweat covered the kid.

The bank manager squeaked, "Other times?" His sobs momentarily paused.

The man with the gun narrowed his eyes on the woman who faced off against him. "Who the hell are you?"

"My friends call me Chloe." A pause. "We won't be friends."

Oh, hell. Joel saw the robber's hand tighten on the gun. The man was going to fire. Joel knew it. He lunged forward, slamming his body into the woman's—

They hit the marble floor of the bank with a shuddering crash.

The gun didn't fire.

Chloe blinked, narrowing her absolutely gorgeous blue eyes. Bright blue eyes. She stared at him for a moment, with no emotion registering on her face. It was almost like—like a robot was focusing on him. She blinked once, then twice. *Click, click.*

Her hands came up and clamped around his shoulders. Her touch sent an electric surge of heat spiraling right through him. *What in the hell?*

"You're strong." Her lips tightened. "And heavy. Now, please do me the courtesy of getting *off* my person."

He'd just saved her lovely ass. Would a *thank you* be too much to ask? Joel didn't—

The gun shoved into the back of his head. Immediately, his whole body tensed.

"Trying to play the hero, are you?" The robber grunted and added, "Can't have that crap. Get up, both of you!"

Slowly, Joel lifted his body off Chloe. *Don't say anything,* he mouthed the words at her.

She frowned at him.

The bank robber shouted, "Put your hands up!"

Just one guy. Joel figured he could probably take him, but he didn't want to risk the gun going off and some innocent getting hurt.

Reluctantly, Joel lifted his hands.

Chloe lifted her hands, but she stared expectantly at Joel. As if she was waiting for him to do something. Jeez, what did the woman want, for him to take a bullet?

The robber swiped one hand over Joel's body, taking his wallet and his phone, then the guy closed in on Chloe.

"I don't have a phone on me. No ID, either," she told him, voice seemingly pleasant and helpful.

The man ignored her and patted her down, but turned up no phone. Or ID.

Joel frowned at her. Why had she been in the bank if she didn't even have her ID with her?

Her smile spread. She looked a bit smug. Sexy, yes, God, yes, he'd give her sexy points. With that dark hair, her perfect cream skin, and her red, plump lips, she was gorgeous.

But he was also starting to think the robber had been right about her. *Did* the woman have some kind of death wish?

The robber motioned with his gun. "Walk this way."

Uh, okay. Joel walked that way, but he tried to angle his body so that he was between the gorgeous, potentially death-wish-having woman and the gun.

A few moments later, they were in front of what turned out to be a storage closet. A very narrow storage closet. The robber waved them inside. It was so tight in there that Chloe's body pushed against Joel's. Every lovely inch of her. And her scent—a light raspberry? Strawberry?—teased his nose.

The robber stood in the doorway, smirking. "Won't cause any trouble in here, will you?"

Joel's stare narrowed on him. The fellow was about average height, with drooping shoulders and a slight pudge in his stomach. A weak beard covered his equally weak chin, and his grip on the gun was far too tight.

The robber started to slam the door shut—

"Harry," the woman sighed out the name. "You should've stopped while you were ahead. Had to be extra greedy, didn't you?"

"Harry" widened his eyes. "How the hell do you know my name?"

"I know lots of things," she replied demurely.

The gun was shaking in Harry's hand. Joel figured they were both about to die. Getting shot in a smelly storage closet. *That* was his end?

Only instead of firing, Harry slammed the door shut. There was a distinct *snick* as the lock turned. Abso-fucking-lutely wonderful.

Darkness covered them, the only light coming in from beneath the door. Joel remembered another time. Being trapped in the dark. The stench of blood. The feel of the heat and dirt and sweat covering his body as—

Her body pressed against his. Her arm lifted and—

A light turned on.

"I pulled the cord," she told him, again using what he was thinking of as her helpful voice. "You seemed to be suffering from some PTSD that was triggered by the dark or perhaps the close confines of the closet, so I wanted to calm you—"

"What. The. Fuck?" His heart pounded hard in his chest.

"PTSD?" Her dark brows arched. "Post-traumatic stress disorder. I can't believe you aren't familiar with the term."

He sucked in a breath. Let it out slowly. Extra slowly. "I am familiar."

A quick nod. "Oh, that's good. I was afraid that you didn't—"

"There is a bank robber out there with a *gun*."

Did she almost smile? "I noticed him."

"He could shoot us both at any moment."

Those plump lips pursed for a moment. Then…"No, I don't really think he could."

His temples throbbed. "We're lucky he didn't lock us in the damn vault." Talk about a blast straight from his nightmares. He didn't do so well in closed spaces. Side effect of being buried alive. This closet smelled of turpentine and bleach. *And strawberries—her.* But at least it wasn't some airtight bank vault that would become his coffin.

A small laugh escaped her.

An actual laugh.

What in the hell? Who laughed after being locked up by a bank robber? Was the woman truly crazy? Such a total and complete waste. Why were the sexy ones so often also the crazy-as-hell ones?

Her hand—with the softest skin on the whole planet—patted against his cheek. "That's so funny. You're quite amusing."

"Nothing about this situation is funny. Lady, are you off your meds?"

"I'm not on any medication."

"Then why are you acting so crazy? Like this is a fun, freaking game instead of a life-and-death deal!"

"First…" A soft sigh from her. "Crazy is not a clinical term, and you shouldn't just throw it out there like it is."

His temples throbbed harder.

"Second. Take some breaths. I was laughing because you thought he was going to put us in the vault."

"Yeah. How is that shit funny?"

"He's a bank *robber*. That means he is here to rob the bank of its valuables. You do know that the most valuable things are kept in the vault? Why put us in there? We'd just be in his way."

Breathe. He had to breathe. And *not* because she'd told him to take breaths.

"Harry is here for very specific items. He'll get what he needs, and then dear Harry will think that he's walking away free and clear."

She'd done it again. Referred to the bank robber by name. As if they were old buddies. His heart rate sped up even more. "How do you know his name?"

"Uh, because I was hunting him?"

Joel shook his head.

Her hand fell away. She'd still been touching him. Part of Joel, dammit, had still been liking her touch.

"Say that again." The pounding in his temples had gotten so loud that he must have misheard her.

"I was hunting him." Again, that British accent of hers slithered through. Faint, but there. Perhaps a little more pronounced than it had been before because Joel thought she might be annoyed.

Join the club, sister.

"This isn't the first bank Harry has hit," Chloe informed him crisply. "It's actually number four."

Joel stared at her. Didn't blink. Just stared.

"I was waiting for him to come in." Her smile flashed. Her voice was low, though, and he realized it had been low the whole time that they'd been in the closet. She was all whispery. Her whispery voice was...sexy. Why was he finding everything about her to be hot?

He was so messed up. Was this what got him going now? Pretty women with delusions? *Fuck me.* "And what were you going to do..." Joel drawled as he tried to get his shit together, "when he came in the bank? Chat his ear off? Become his new BFF? Because I didn't see you stopping him!"

"Well, I was about to stop him." Her lips curled down. "Then you heaved your body at me. Threw us both to the floor. And got us locked in this coffin."

Coffin.

He refused to look at the tiny walls again. Joel blew out a long breath. "I was saving your ass."

"Why?"

Ah, obviously—"Because it needed saving?"

"It didn't." She shook her head. Her hair danced over her cheek.

"Lady..."

"Chloe."

"We aren't friends. And you specifically said your friends called you that. Which probably means it's not even your real name. You have some other name that you were legally born with, and Chloe is some weird-ass alias." He'd just been making shit up because...hell, saying that stuff seemed fitting, with her. *It also seems way possible that Chloe is not her name.*

Her eyes widened. "You are interesting."

"And you're a straight-up psycho." *Breathe. Breathe.* "Sorry. I know that's not a clinical term, either. Sue me." He was about to lose *his* mind. He had to get out of that closet. He couldn't stay in that coffin another minute. "This is how things will go down. I'm going to get us out of here. I'm going to knock out the robber. And I'm going to make sure those people out there stay alive."

"Oh." She tilted back her head. Stared at him with that robotic look in her eyes again. *Click. Click.*

What was up with that?

"I didn't realize you were a superhero." She nodded. "My mistake. I guess I overlooked the cape and the awesome crime-fighting skills."

She was making a joke? Then? With her absolute dead-pan voice?

She patted his cheek once more. Let her hand linger. "I don't need saving. That will be point one."

Point one? Why was she lecturing him? They weren't in class. They were in a tiny closet. *Coffin.* They were in hell.

"As far as getting out of this coffin—"

"*Don't* call it that," he gritted out from between clenched teeth.

"Why not? It's how you keep thinking of it."

Shock rolled through him.

"As far as the coffin," Chloe continued doggedly. "I can get us out anytime we want. That's point two."

He shouldn't have come in the bank. He shouldn't have admired her ass. Or her legs. Or anything about the woman.

"Point three...Chloe is my real name. Or one of them, anyway. My birth certificate says my name is Constance Catherine Chloe Hastings. Obviously, that's just too many names, so I go with Chloe."

"Great for you. Fantastic."

"For point four, what makes you think all of those people out there need saving?" Her hand trailed down his cheek, sliding a little over the stubble he had there. So he hadn't taken the time to shave that morning. So he was wearing battered jeans and old sneakers and a t-shirt that had seen better days.

She looked like a dream.

He looked like hell.

But she was the one saying—

"Accomplice." Her hand dropped. "Obviously, one of the people out there is Harry's accomplice."

Oddly fascinated by her and this new, ever-so-unbelievable revelation, Joel had to ask, "Is that even his name? Or did you like, look at him and just think the bastard looked like a Harry?"

She smiled. A quick flash that lit her eyes. "Are you asking me if I guessed his name? I *never* guess."

Uh, huh.

"But I do make educated deductions."

Heaven help him.

Her body pressed ever closer. A certain part of Joel's anatomy appreciated that closeness. She *had* to feel that appreciation, unfortunately.

"Who do you think the accomplice is?" Chloe asked.

"Ah..." He cleared his throat. Tried to stop greedily gulping her strawberry scent. "I'm...I'm not playing your game."

"Why not? Talking to me obviously keeps you distracted so that you forget the fact you're trapped in this tiny closet. You're welcome, by the way."

"Welcome? *You expect me to thank you for trapping me?*"

"No, but you can thank me for keeping you distracted."

She...actually was. The throbbing in his temples and the fierce constriction in his chest had eased a little.

"You're very strong. Though I did notice some of the scars on your arms. Knife wounds?"

He wasn't replying.

Her sigh blew over him. "Fine. We'll talk about the scars another time."

No, they would not. There would not be another time for them. After he walked out of the bank, he planned to never, ever see her again.

"Who do you think the accomplice is?" Chloe pushed. "Come on, tell me."

"The guy came in *alone.*"

"Because his partner was already *here.*"

Their gazes held.

Her eyes widened. "You have gold in your eyes. I thought your eyes were just brown, but they're not. I don't usually miss details like that on the first glance."

"Don't beat yourself up," Joel muttered, "we all make mistakes."

Her lips parted. Red and slick and *why* was he thinking about kissing her? No, no, very much *no*.

Her smile became smug. "You don't know who the accomplice is."

Because there wasn't an accomplice—

"Fine. I'll tell you. *This* time. But I expect you to do better in the future."

They had no future together.

"It was the bank teller. The one with red hair. She dropped down too fast. I knew it had to be an inside man, so I was watching. As soon as Harry walked in the door, before he even flashed his gun, she was hitting the floor."

Was that...right? Huh. It might just be. Joel tried to replay the scene in his head.

Her tone turned slightly musing as she continued, "I'll have to get the cops to go back and talk to all the tellers involved in the previous robberies. I'm betting Harry gave a teller at each bank a slice of his haul as payment for services rendered. You know, they tell him the layout of the bank, the best time to come in, how to catch the security officer off-guard..."

"The redhead," Joel heard himself say because this *was* making sense to him. "She called out to the security guard right before Harry knocked the guy out with his gun. She had ducked behind the counter, but she screamed for security." And had he just called the robber

Harry? Like it was a thing now? What was Chloe doing to him?

But he could have sworn her blue eyes were gleaming with approval.

"Exactly. Her scream distracted the guard so that Harry could have his perfect hit." A nod. "And this is why I had to bust Harry in the act. So much easier for the cops to come in when he's working with his latest partner..."

And *this* was why he was about to bust out of the closet. "The cops aren't coming. No one had a chance to sound the alarm. If the redhead is working with him, you can bet she made sure the authorities weren't alerted."

Her hand curled around his neck. He felt her lean up against him. He bent toward her. Chloe's lips feathered over his ear as she whispered, "I sounded the alarm. I called the cops."

Why was her voice so much lower now? But, did it even matter why? Because he sure loved the feel of her mouth on his ear. So wrong. So right.

"They'll be here in five, four, three..."

She was doing a countdown. That was why she'd gotten so quiet. The cops were about to burst in and she was—

He heard an explosion. His body hurtled against hers, and they slammed into one of the shelves in the closet. Cleaning solution hit the floor. Paper towels rained down on his head. And he held her as tightly as he could.

"You okay?" Joel demanded.

"Of course."

Of—jeez. He freed her. Spun away. Kicked at the lock on the closet door. The lock and doorknob shattered, and the door flew open. He ran out and headed straight for the chaos. At least half a dozen uniformed cops swarmed the scene.

Had they blown open the entrance to the bank? SWAT members were there, wearing their distinct tactical gear, and it sure as hell looked like they'd set off a mini-bomb at the entrance. Harry was on the floor, being cuffed as he snarled and shouted. The bank manager was still sobbing near his desk. The young kid was helping the older lady rise to her feet. And the bank tellers were all being ushered toward the door by concerned cops.

"Stop the redhead!" Chloe called out as she rushed to Joel's side. "She's his accomplice!"

At Chloe's shout, the redhead whirled. She shoved the uniformed cop away from her. Fury tightened the woman's face as her hand dove into her purse, and she came up holding—

Great. A gun.

The redhead pointed the gun straight at Chloe. That was *twice* in ten minutes. She'd had two guns pointed at her within ten minutes. And for the second time, Joel leapt in to save her ass. Only this time, the gun actually fired.

The bullet blasted across his arm as he tackled Chloe once again.

CHAPTER TWO

"Your hero complex will get you killed."

The man who sat—grudgingly and grumpily—in the back of the ambulance glared at Chloe.

The scene outside of the bank was controlled chaos. Always the aftermath in situations such as this one. The would-be hero had been shot, really only a minor flesh wound, though, and the cops had grabbed the redhead before she could fire again.

"I don't think it's my hero complex," the man fired back. Handsome. In a chiseled, rugged kind of way. An accent had a faint drawl deepening his voice. *Texas accent.* "I think it's *you*. You are going to get me killed."

That was a slightly insulting thing to say. Given her line of work, it could also be true.

"My arm is fine," he snapped as he looked over at the EMT. "Barely a graze. No stitches needed. For the record, I didn't have to be carried out of the bank. Totally unnecessary."

No, he hadn't needed to be carried. But it had been a rather fun sight. All six-foot-three, two hundred pounds of him...loaded onto a stretcher against his will. Just for a little scrape.

The EMT's face took on a mutinous expression as the woman opened her mouth to reply.

"I'm a doctor," the would-be hero explained, voice softer, less I'm-out-of-all-patience. "I know a simple graze when I see one. Thank you for your help, but I'm okay."

At his softened tone, the EMT smiled. The hero smiled, too. He had a rather nice smile. A dimple flashed in his left cheek.

Then he glanced at Chloe.

His smile vanished. He went back to glaring.

Chloe rolled one shoulder. The New Orleans heat poured onto her. She hated the heat, mostly because it was constant in the South. She could feel the silk of her shirt sticking to her back. Could practically see the heat making the air thick all around her. The would-be hero climbed out of the ambulance. He straightened to his full, rather impressive height. His dark hair—a little too long—was tousled. Probably because he kept raking his fingers through it. A faint scar cut across his upper lip. It gave him a sexy, dangerous edge, but she doubted he thought of the mark in those terms.

There were other faint marks on him. On his neck. On his arms. Beneath his clothes, yes, she was sure scars were there, too. Careful, slow cuts that had been handed out by someone who knew and understood exactly how to administer pain. The cuts had been designed to torment. To break.

But she didn't think that her would-be hero had broken.

She was also just staring at him as he loomed over her. Her bad. She wasn't usually so blatant about things.

The EMT hurried away when someone else called out to her. Chloe was rather glad to see the other woman go. She wanted a moment alone with the man who'd tried to rescue her. Twice. *So cute.* And so many people said there were no gentleman left these days. Wrong.

After a tense moment, Chloe cleared her throat. Occasionally, she did try to do things the polite way. This was one of those times. One of those exceedingly rare times. "I didn't catch your name, Doctor...?"

He squinted at her. After a tense moment, his lips curled. "You know so much. I can't believe you don't already know that, too."

Well, if he wanted the truth, she *did* know. Her lips parted—

"Joel Landry." He offered his hand to her. "I'm not a practicing doctor any longer. I just said that so she'd stop poking at me."

Chloe took his hand. Felt the calluses beneath her fingers. The easy strength. "Do you miss being a doctor?"

"No." His hold tightened on her. "It wasn't for me any longer."

His grip wasn't about one of those show-of-strength situations. She'd encountered enough emotionally weak men who did that. No, it was more of...

More of an I-don't-want-to-let-you-go hold.

How strange.

Because she was tightening her hand on him the same way.

Catching herself, Chloe immediately stopped. She tugged on her hand. A beat of time passed, and he let her go. His fingers slid across her palm before his hand dropped back to his side.

Even when he let go, she could have sworn that she still felt the heat from his touch.

"Hastings! Chloe Hastings!"

She recognized the voice that was bellowing her name. Business was calling. There would be explanations to make. Paperwork to sign. Checks to collect. The usual. All in a day's work for her, really. Time to make her departure. "It was good to meet you, Dr. Landry."

"Forget the doctor part. It's just Landry." His voice was a growl. "Or Joel."

No, I don't think you are ever "just" anything. The man was unusual. He'd committed a truly fatal sin while in the bank with her. He'd made her curious.

Few things could penetrate the veil that seemed to surround her. Chloe had always known she was different from other people. She didn't respond to things the way others did. She didn't laugh often. She didn't feel the rush of emotions that others seemed to enjoy so easily.

Most days, she felt as if nothing at all touched her.

Today, Joel Landry had touched her.

"You're quite an unforgettable man," she told him with complete sincerity.

"Trust me, lady, you are—"

"Chloe! Dammit, I know you heard me calling your name!" The growling voice of Detective Cedric Coleman was coming from right behind her.

Joel had stiffened slightly when the other man approached. A small movement, but one she'd noticed. After all, she noticed everything. Part of her gift. Or curse. Or whatever the world wanted to call it. Personally, Chloe had never cared very much for labels.

Cedric's hand curled around her shoulder. "Are you okay?" His voice dropped with concern.

"I'm perfectly fine." But his concern was kind. Chloe waved toward Joel. "He's the one who was grazed by a bullet." Unnecessarily. *Hero complex.*

Cedric yanked out his ID and flashed it at Joel. "Police Detective Cedric Coleman." Both men were of similar height. But while Joel appeared decidedly rugged with his rough, good looks and the muscles that she could see straining against the old t-shirt he wore—a bloody t-shirt, now, thanks to the shooter—Cedric was far more elegant. Even at crime scenes, he dressed to impress, though she had no idea why he felt the need to do that. Cedric was one of the best cops that she'd ever met. That was the reason she kept working with him instead of moving on to another city.

Before Cedric, she *had* been moving a lot. City to city. Tracking, always tracking her elusive prey. But Cedric had asked her to stay.

So she had.

But perhaps it was time to leave again. She couldn't quite decide yet.

Cedric shoved his ID back into his pocket. His suit coat slid with the movement to reveal the holster on his hip. He quickly smoothed his coat back into position, crossed his arms over his chest, and glowered at Joel. The sun kept beating down on him, but not a drop of sweat marred Cedric's skin. How did he do that?

While he looked perfect, she was melting. Summers in England were very, very different from the sweltering days in Louisiana.

"You were shot inside the bank?" Cedric asked Joel. Cedric paced a little away from Chloe as he seemed to size up Joel.

"Grazed," Joel replied blandly. "Barely a graze."

"You're lucky. People who hang with Chloe usually get much worse."

That was rude. And uncomfortably true. Cedric had actually taken a knife to the ribs when he'd been hunting with her a few months back. "And here I thought you were concerned about me." His concern had obviously been fleeting.

"I am concerned."

She lifted her brows. He no longer sounded concerned.

"Fine, I *was* concerned, but I can see now that you're not hurt, and that's great but..." A frustrated exhale. Poor Cedric. She knew that he tended to get frustrated quite a bit when they worked together. Most people had that reaction to her. "*Chloe,* why the hell were you even working this case?" Cedric blasted as his voice rose. Definitely annoyed now. "You know that you are supposed to be—"

"Hey, buddy!" Joel's voice.

Chloe lifted a brow when Joel stepped between her and Cedric.

"How about not yelling at her?" Joel advised flatly. "She's had one hell of a morning."

The morning honestly hadn't been that unusual for her. Chloe cocked her head. She should explain a few things to Joel. "Cedric isn't your buddy. He's someone who can arrest you if you piss him off." Had he not paid attention to the ID and badge? "I wouldn't piss him off." Also, Cedric only raised his voice that way when he *was* worried. She knew he was currently under a great deal of stress. She'd promised to help him with that situation, and Chloe had every intention of keeping her promise.

Joel glanced back at her. "I piss people off all the time. Part of my charm."

Was it now? Even more interesting.

"You just caught a bank robber—two of them from where I stand—so I figure the cops should be treating you with a little more respect, and not, you know, jumping down your throat." His voice roughened. His head swung toward Cedric once more. "Maybe you and all the personnel in NOPD uniform here should take a minute to calm down and—"

Cedric stepped to the side so that he stared at Chloe once more. "Where did you find him?"

Joel had been trying to protect her. His body position and tenseness indicated that he felt she'd been threatened, so he'd moved to place himself between her and Cedric. Just as he'd tried to shield her in the bank. Fascinating.

But, oh, Cedric was waiting for a response so she would have to pause her analysis of Joel and his behavior. For the moment. "I met him in the bank." Wasn't that obvious? Cedric usually picked up on details faster than this.

"Yeah, figured that." The detective rolled his eyes. After a tense moment—she knew he was counting to ten, he always counted to ten when he was trying to remain calm—Cedric pointed a finger at Joel. "Look, *buddy*," he threw at Joel, "I get that you took a graze today and you feel all hundred feet tall and super-hero-like now, but that's the adrenaline talking. You'll come back to reality soon, and you'll be glad that I got you away from Chloe Hastings. Trust me on this." He motioned to Chloe. "Come on. We need to go. *Now.*"

She understood Cedric's irritation. She'd taken a side job, but there was other work waiting. Always.

But she saw that Joel's hands clenched into fists. He took a step toward Cedric. "This is hardly my first brush with danger, and the last thing I feel like is a superhero."

Yet he kept displaying a hero complex...

Some of the tension slid from Cedric's face as he eyed Joel with a hint of more respect. The detective clapped a hand around Joel's shoulder. "Answer the questions from the cops here, then get home. After that, take some advice from me."

Joel waited for the advice.

"Forget Chloe. You'll be a happier man for it."

That was insulting. First of all, she was unforgettable. Second, she also didn't think... "He's not happy," Chloe said.

Joel stiffened. His head angled toward her.

"You're not happy." She could see it. "You're going through the motions each day. Struggling with a past that won't let you go. It's a shame, because you truly have so much potential."

"Lady, what do *you* know about me and my past?"

So very much. She gave him a smile. "It was good to meet you, Dr. Landry. Our partnership today was more than I expected."

Joel shook his head and appeared a bit horrified. "I told you, it's just Joel. And we aren't partners! Don't know where you got that idea, but we are *not* partners. Are not, were not, and never will be."

"No?" Chloe pursed her lips. "That's too bad." She inclined her head. "Enjoy the rest of your day. I need to go with the detective."

Cedric nodded. "About time..." He quickly moved to her side. "There's been another one," he muttered.

She couldn't help but tense. This was the last news she'd wanted to hear, but it was also exactly what she'd suspected he would say. Especially given the way he'd been acting. They walked away, huddling together.

"Wait!" Joel called out. "Chloe!"

She didn't look back. Her mind was already shifting focus. Sorting through possibilities. Looking for—

"Another what?" Joel wanted to know. He'd followed after them.

Chloe stopped.

Cedric swore. "He is slowing us down. I hope this jack-off isn't going to be a problem."

She spun to face Joel. Surely, he'd taken the time to *look* at Cedric's badge and ID? He'd noticed that Cedric was a *homicide* detective?

"Been another what?" Joel asked again, his voice all deep and rumbling, as if the question had been torn from him.

"Dr. Landry...Joel." She shouldn't have to explain this, but he'd obviously not paid enough attention to Cedric's badge. He needed to be far more observant in the future. Especially if they were going to work together. "There's been another murder."

Joel's dark eyes widened. "Why the hell would that involve you? Wait, are you a cop?"

"No." If she'd been part of the New Orleans PD, she would have mentioned that fact to him when all of the other cops swarmed the scene. She was strictly freelance. "It involves me because I have to catch the bastard. Now, have a good day."

He was gaping when she left him.

And she *almost* looked back at him. Almost, but at the last moment, she realized it was better to just walk away.

***

Cedric slammed his car's passenger side door shut. He stared through the glass at Chloe's profile. As usual, no expression showed on her face. She was always so good at hiding what she felt. *If* she felt.

He hurried around the car. Opened the driver's door and slid behind the wheel. He knew he shouldn't ask but... "Are you playing some game with that guy?"

She turned to him, and her smile made his heart ice. "You know better than that, detective. I don't play games."

Hell. "What are you planning?"

"Why don't you just wait and see? Surprises can be fun."

"Not when those surprises involve you." He cranked the car. "Your surprises are pure hell."

CHAPTER THREE

The pounding at his door woke Joel in the middle of the night. The pounding ripped him from sleep—yet another nightmare that wouldn't stop plaguing him—and he shot up in bed. His heart raced in his chest, and sweat slickened his body.

The pounding came again.

Joel shoved the covers aside and leapt to his feet. He rushed to the door of his small apartment, wearing just boxer shorts and not stopping to grab other clothes. A fast and furious glance at his clock told him it was nearing one a.m. Who the hell would be at his door at one a.m.?

The pounding rattled his door once more.

He yanked it open.

Chloe Hastings stood there, clad in jeans and a flowing, red top. High heels adorned her feet, and her hand was curled and ready to pound again.

Joel had to shake his head. "You aren't real."

"Of course, I'm real." Her head cocked as she did that *click, click* type of look where she surveyed him and blinked. "Do you often have hallucinations?"

Did he often...

Joel started to swing the door shut on what he sure as hell hoped was a hallucination.

"Wait!" Her hand flew out and curled around the door. "I need your help!"

"It's one a.m."

"Yes." She nodded.

"And you're at my door, pounding," he grated, aware that his voice was rising. "You're at my door, pounding, and you expect me to—"

The door across the hall flew open. His neighbor—a guy in his late seventies with a shock of white hair and wearing a darkly stained and tattered t-shirt—snarled, "Shut the hell up! People are trying to sleep!" Carl Jones backed away, then slammed his door.

Chloe's nose wrinkled. "He drinks too much beer."

What?

"Drinking away his pain won't help. It never does."

"Lady, what is your deal?" But, because he didn't want his neighbor calling the cops, Joel grabbed Chloe's wrist and hauled her inside his place.

He shut the door. Locked it. Then flipped on the lights.

"Oh." She winced. Spun around. Stared at the thread-bare furniture. The dusty clock on what passed for a kitchen table. The pile of books in the corner. The empty walls. Walls that showed the old, peeling paint and layers of dirt. Then she looked at him again. *Click, click.* "You can afford more. You can afford just about anything. But you choose to live like this. That's interesting."

He didn't want to interest her. "How do you know what I can afford?"

"Because I reviewed your bank records."

He stood there, wearing only boxers and his temples throbbing as sweat still slickened his body. "Why would anyone give you access to my bank records?" Was he having a nightmare? One that seemed horribly real? Only instead of his normal torturer, he had...her.

She smiled at him. Appeared oddly angelic. Too freaking beautiful. "Well, in case you forgot, I did foil a bank robbery today."

"We," Joel heard himself mumble. "*We* foiled a bank robbery."

A pleased nod. "So we're a team? You're in agreement?"

"What? No!" He surged toward her. "Don't look at my bank records! Don't come to my home in the middle of the night—"

Dismissively, she fluttered her hand in the air. "This isn't a home. It's more like a hotel room. You have to put things inside to make a place a home. Things that matter." Her shoulders lifted and fell in a shrug. "At least that's what I've heard."

"How did you even know where I lived?"

"Well, the bank manager was *very* grateful..."

Joel's eyes squeezed closed. Maybe if he kept his eyes closed, she'd disappear. Maybe she'd turn out to be nothing more than another nightmare. He circled back to his original hallucination idea. Maybe she wasn't even really there. Maybe he'd finally slipped over the line and he was—

"You have more scars that I realized. I'm sorry for the pain you must have endured."

Shit. He'd forgotten. How could he have forgotten? Even for a moment? But there he was, standing in front of her, revealing far too much.

She was beautiful. Perfect skin. Probably perfect life. Some mystery woman playing a weird game with him. Jerking him around. With his eyes still closed, he ordered, "Leave."

"Did I say the wrong thing?" The floor creaked as she moved toward him. "Aren't people supposed to say they're sorry when they see evidence of someone else's pain?"

"Only if you actually *mean* you're sorry. I'm sick to death of fake words." His eyes opened.

Her lips were parted. Her eyes wide. "Me, too," she whispered. Her slender throat moved as she swallowed. For an instant, he could have sworn that he saw a flash of pain in her bright blue eyes. Then the flash was gone, and her gaze was drifting over his body. Lingering on all the scars that reminded him too much of a past that he wished he could forget.

Joel marched around her and headed into his bedroom. Where the hell had he left his t-shirt? His gaze raked the room. Not like the place was much to see. Nothing on the walls. Just two stacked mattresses on the floor. The two windows were wide open, letting the night air drift inside. Night air and bugs because there were always bugs in New Orleans. Dammit, she couldn't see this. She couldn't—

"This room is even worse."

Great. She'd followed him. Without an invitation. Surprise, surprise. "Do you always enter a man's bedroom without permission?" He spied his t-shirt on the floor. He yanked it on. Hissed out a hard breath when the wound on his arm throbbed.

"Careful, or you'll make it bleed again." Her heels tapped across the floor. "Men do usually give me permission, by the way. I've never had a problem getting into a man's bedroom before. In fact, usually the men seem quite happy to have me in their bedrooms."

He just bet they did.

Joel yanked on a pair of jeans. Then he spun to face her as he zipped up and hooked the snap.

Her chin lifted. "You may need to dress up a bit more for where we're going. That t-shirt looks far too much like the one Carl was wearing."

He gaped. "How the hell do you know my neighbor's name?"

"Because it was on the mailbox downstairs."

She'd stopped to look at the pile of battered mailboxes? What was up with Chloe? He stalked toward her. Stood toe-to-toe with his gorgeous, late-night intruder. "I am not going any place with you. You're going to get out of my home—"

Her lips parted. He knew she was about to correct him. Say this wasn't a home. Nope, not happening.

"*Home,*" he growled, beating her to the punch. "It might not be much, but it's mine, and I don't want you here. You need to leave."

Click, click. She blinked in confusion and kept studying him. "You want more than this. I know you do."

"What I want is to go back to bed." Actually, he *was* going. Screw this. Joel threw himself onto the bed—mattresses. Slammed a fist beneath his lumpy pillow. "See yourself out, would you?"

"Fine. I thought you would be interested in helping me on the case, given your past." Chloe turned away. "It's very unusual for me to be wrong. I don't think I like this feeling."

Do not ask her. Do not ask her— "What about my past?"

She was at his bedroom door. One slender hand rose and slid along the chipped wood of the frame. "You survived an attack from a serial killer."

Joel was glad that Chloe couldn't see his face. Glad her back was to him. "Read that somewhere on the Internet, did you? Or maybe you saw it on the news when the story first aired?" No matter how far you ran, sometimes you just couldn't escape your past.

Instead of answering him, she noted, "You have triple locks on your front door. Do you think the killer will find you one day?"

Joel surged out of the bed, his hands fisted at his sides. "He's *dead.* The dead won't come calling."

Now she glanced back at Joel. Most people—when they knew the truth about him—they looked at him with pity. Maybe morbid fascination. She didn't stare at him with either. She just...looked. Gazed straight into his eyes.

Joel swallowed.

Then she spoke. Her voice was low and quiet as she said, "He cut you over one hundred times, didn't he? Kept you chained up, locked away. He drugged you in your own hospital and snuck you down to the bottom level. Your friends and colleagues were right there. You thought they'd help you. You thought someone would come to save you. Only no one did."

Another lump rose in his throat. "I don't need a fucking walk down memory lane, thanks so much."

"No." She inclined her head. "Memories don't help. I thought perhaps you'd want some payback. *That* could help. But like I said before, I guess I was wrong." Another low exhale. "I won't be bothering you again. Good night, Dr. Landry."

He didn't move.

The floor creaked in the other room as she made her way to the door.

Payback? That word slithered through him. Dark. Sinister. Tempting. "*Payback?*" Joel bounded after her. She'd already undid the three locks. He caught her arm and swung her around to face him, pinning her between his body and the door. "What the hell do you mean, payback?"

"All of that rage inside of you. The pain that wants to break free. Don't you want to give it a proper outlet?"

His heart was about to burst out of his chest. "Lady…"

"You may call me Chloe. I think I told you that already. If I didn't, my apologies for not allowing the familiarity sooner."

His back teeth clenched.

Her face softened as she stared up at him. "You've seen behind the curtain. Gotten a glimpse at the real monsters out there. Other people can pretend that bad guys are just on TV shows or in movies, but you know the truth." Her gaze didn't leave his. "Dangerous people fill this world. Killers hide in the shadows, and there are freaks out there who get off on giving pain to as many people as possible."

"Lady..."

Her lips tightened.

"Chloe," he corrected. Disturbing curiosity filled him. "Just what is it that you do for a living?"

Did she smile? Maybe. A brief curl of her full lips. "I solve crimes."

"You said before that you weren't a cop."

A shake of her head. "I don't deal well with rules and regulations."

Like he hadn't already figured that out about her.

"I'm strictly freelance," she explained. "I come in when a department needs a fresh pair of eyes."

He couldn't look away from her.

"A killer is hunting in New Orleans right now. It's my job to find him. But I could use some help tonight, and that's why I came to you."

The drumming of Joel's heartbeat nearly drowned out her voice.

"So what do you say, Joel? You want a little payback for all the pain you've endured? You want a chance to help me put away a killer?"

And even before he spoke, Joel knew there would be no turning back. Because she was right. The rage and pain were tearing him apart. Payback? "Hell, yes."

***

"You brought me to a strip club?" Joel's voice was a rough growl that raked across her skin.

Chloe slid her fingers down the neck of her beer bottle, enjoying the cold sensation against her skin. Music blared around them, and one very flexible woman spun and twisted on a big pole right in the middle of the stage. "Yes, I did." Chloe took a sip of her beer. Made a face. She hated beer but she'd figured she should *try* to blend in with everyone around her. "You're welcome."

His fingers tapped on the small, round table. It immediately wobbled. "You're jerking me around."

Her gaze flew to him. "Men like strip clubs."

He stared at her.

"Women do, too." She motioned vaguely around the room. There were plenty of men *and* women in the crowd.

"Chloe."

Fine. "We're not just here for the show. We need to talk to one of the strippers."

"*Why* do we need to do that?"

"Because she's a witness." She motioned to the flexible woman on stage. "Because I didn't believe all the info that I read in the police report." She was ticking off points left and right. "Because I want to hear her responses for myself."

He drank his beer. Didn't seem to mind the taste. He hadn't bothered changing when they'd gone out. Battered shirt. Battered jeans. Sneakers. But he still looked good. Sexy, in that rough way of his.

She'd noticed other women eyeing him when they came inside the club. *Back off, ladies. I'm using him right now.* He was her ticket that night. The witness she wanted to interview—Coreen Miller—apparently had a slight issue with women. *Perhaps not so slight. Time will tell.* Time would tell her many things. In the police report, Cedric had noted that Coreen had only cooperated once he came into the conference room. Coreen had refused to talk to the female detective stationed with her.

Chloe wasn't sure why Coreen only wanted to talk to men, but Joel Landry was about to prove very useful. For a variety of reasons.

"That's our witness?" His gaze was on the stage. "Limber."

Coreen's red hair raked across the floor as she twisted on the pole.

"Very," Chloe agreed.

Dollar bills were thrown onto the stage. The music hit a big crescendo, and then Coreen was sliding off the pole. Waving. Tucking the money into itty-bitty straps on the side of her hips. Wolf whistles followed her off the stage.

"Our turn," Chloe said as she sprang to her feet. A bouncer was blocking the way backstage. A big, burly guy, but Chloe figured she could handle him.

"Wait." Joel's slightly callused fingers curled around her wrist. "You ever been to a strip club before?"

What kind of question was that? "Absolutely."

He frowned, as if her answer had surprised him.

"I was even on the stage once." She wouldn't go into details on that experience. He could take her response however he wanted.

His finger slid along her inner wrist in what might have been a caress.

A shiver slid over her. The shiver caught her off guard. What was...what was that about? It wasn't cold in the club. "Let go."

Immediately, he did. He also rose. Chloe stood at five-foot-eight, but with her heels, she was closer to his height. Not eye level or anything. But closer. Close enough that if she'd wanted to, she could have slid her hand around the back of his neck and pulled him toward her. Kissed him.

If she'd wanted to.

She didn't, of course. This was a business outing. Not a date.

"I'm betting I've been to more strip clubs than you have," Joel retorted.

Ah, he shouldn't make that bet. He shouldn't ever bet with her. He'd lose.

Joel added, "Let me handle the bouncer, all right? You want to talk to the stripper, then I've got this."

Wonderful.

She weaved through the crowd, with Joel right at her back. The bouncer caught sight of her, and one heavy brow rose.

Even though Joel had said he could handle the guy, Chloe opened her mouth to speak—

"We want a private dance with the lady who just left the stage," Joel's voice was smooth as rough silk. He shoved some money toward the bouncer. "Very private."

The money vanished. "You want Cinnamon?"

Uh, Cinnamon? They wanted Coreen...but, yes, Chloe could see where Cinnamon might be a much more appealing stage name in an establishment such as this one.

"You want her? You got her." The bouncer opened the black door that he'd been blocking. "Second entrance. She should already be in the room, waiting." A smirk. "Folks always want a private dance with Cinnamon after her big show."

That was good to know. It was nice that Cinnamon was popular. Probably led to a very good income. Chloe didn't move past the bouncer, not yet. She had a question. "If Cinnamon has a problem during one of her private dances, would she call out for you?"

His bloodshot eyes narrowed on her. "There gonna be a problem?"

Joel's fingers closed around her shoulder. "No. There won't be a problem."

The bouncer grunted. He crossed his arms over his chest, and the impressive tattoos that covered his skin seemed to dance. Chloe's eyes darted over the intricate tattoos and down to his fingers.

She could see the bruises on his knuckles.

"You need to move," Joel urged in her ear. "Private dances are only for a limited time, and something tells me the clock is already ticking on us."

She moved. Headed down the hallway. Swept her gaze to the left and right. Paused to study a dark stain on the wall.

"What in the hell are you doing?" Joel steered her forward. "This isn't freaking stare-at-the-wall night. We need to *move*." He used his left hand to rap on the door to Cinnamon's room.

A sultry voice called out, "Come in!"

They went in.

Cinnamon stood on the other side of the small room, all of her cash now hidden but she was still wearing her very tiny G-string. She also had on an elaborate bra, well, not really a bra but...something with lots of lift and sparkle.

Cinnamon smiled. "Two of you, hmm? Hope you paid Bobby extra for that."

Bobby must be the bouncer they'd passed. Chloe made a quick note of his name.

Cinnamon pointed to the wooden chair beside her. "Who wants to sit first?" She winked. "One will sit and one will watch? That how you two like it?"

"I have no idea what he likes," Chloe responded honestly. "But I can see the bruises beneath your makeup." Now that Chloe was closer to the woman, she could see the blue and black marks on her neck. Someone had tried to strangle Cinnamon.

Cinnamon stopped smiling. "I don't know where this is going, but let me tell you right now, I don't like pain. I'm not into that, no matter how much you paid."

"Good for you," Chloe said instantly.

Cinnamon's eyes were huge. Almost as huge as her impressive breasts. Her gaze jumped from Chloe to Joel. "Get your crazy girlfriend out of here."

Joel took a step forward. "She is crazy..."

That label was old. And incorrect. There was no such thing as crazy. There were delusions, there was psychosis, there was—

"But she's not my girlfriend." He motioned to the chair. "Why don't you sit down? We just want to ask you a few questions. Answer them, and we'll be gone in a flash."

Cinnamon—um, Coreen—sucked in a breath. "You more cops?"

"I'm definitely not a cop," Joel assured her. "I simply have a few questions. I want to know—"

"Donnie was a sonofabitch. He liked hurting me. And I'm glad he's dead, okay? Glad. So what if I didn't go to help him when I heard him scream? He made me scream plenty of times, and I thought it was his turn for payback."

Did Joel flinch at the word *payback?* Chloe thought he did.

"You." Cinnamon pointed at Chloe. "You and the other uppity bitches always stare at me like I'm trash. You don't believe a word I ever say."

Ah, *that* would be why Cinnamon hadn't wanted to talk to the female detective. "I don't think you're trash. I think you're very limber and quite talented at your job."

"Fuck off," Cinnamon snarled at her. She stormed for the door.

Joel glared at Chloe. "You have zero people skills."

Why did she need them? And hadn't she just complimented Cinnamon? She'd meant the compliment. The dancer was very talented and deserved all the money she earned. Chloe wished she possessed the other woman's agility and rhythm.

No matter. Time to get back on track and move things along before Cinnamon completely stopped talking. "Donnie was here last night." Donnie Adams, the victim currently at the morgue. "He got rough with you, and Bobby taught him some manners."

Cinnamon whirled toward her. "Bobby tell you that? He usually keeps his big mouth shut."

He hadn't needed to say a word, not when the proof had been on his hands. Hard to miss the bruises on his big knuckles. "He beat Donnie in the hallway outside." She'd seen the blood stain. "Then...threw him out back?"

Cinnamon shrugged.

Ah, not talking to me. Chloe glanced at Joel.

She found him frowning at her. She stared at him, then jerked her head toward Cinnamon.

Joel cast a glance toward the exotic dancer. "You...ah, heard Donnie? You heard Donnie screaming out back?"

"Yeah." She swallowed. "At first...um, I thought he was just mad at me. Screaming 'cause he was mad, you know. I was with Bobby when I heard the screams start. Bobby stormed away. Said not to let him back in because Donnie was just a drunk dick." She swiped her hand over her cheek. "Then I...I realized he wasn't just screaming because he was mad. He *hurt*."

Chloe crept closer to Cinnamon. She caught a faint, sweet scent clinging to the other woman. She filed that scent away. "You liked for Donnie to hurt because he'd hurt you."

"Yeah. Does that make me some kind of fucking bad person?"

"No." Joel shook his head. "Not even close."

Cinnamon straightened her shoulders. "When he stopped screaming, I eased open the door. Th-that was when I saw Donnie's body."

She'd just stumbled. Given a little stutter. Her gaze had jerked around the room, sliding away from Joel's before returning.

Got you. Chloe tamped down on her excitement. "You saw the killer."

"No!" Cinnamon's eyes flared wide.

"Please don't waste my time with lies."

Cinnamon's cheeks reddened.

"You saw the killer when you opened the door. He was still there." She tried to work through the puzzle. "He didn't hurt you. He just went after Donnie." Another vic who seemingly fit this particular killer's pattern. Cedric had been right on that point. It was good that he'd come to get her at the bank so they didn't waste too much time. "Why didn't you tell the cops that you saw him?"

Cinnamon had clamped her lips together.

Chloe motioned to Joel. This was his time to step up and get the woman talking.

Joel cocked his head and nodded as if he'd figured out Cinnamon. "You don't trust the cops."

"Why should I? What have they ever done for me?" She licked her lips. "You want the truth? That man in the alley...the man who killed Donnie? He did more for me than a cop ever would." She stomped forward and wrenched open the door to her room. "I didn't see his face. He had on a ski mask. I can't tell you a damn thing about him. Now get out. Your time is up."

A private dance sure didn't last long these days. Chloe headed for the door. She wanted to go into the alley and look around herself. But first... "Are you chewing gum?"

"No." Cinnamon squinted at her.

"You smell very...sweet."

A rough laugh came from Cinnamon. "That's my body butter. Bubblegum flavored. Makes me smell sweet. The customers love it."

"I'm sure they do." There were so many other things she wanted to ask Cinnamon.

But Cinnamon wasn't laughing any longer. Her gaze was locked hard on Chloe. "I didn't get your name," she suddenly said. Cinnamon's eyes were a deep, bold green.

"Chloe. Chloe Hastings."

Cinnamon's lower lip trembled. "God...he meant you..." She wheezed out a breath. "Come and get me."

"I beg your pardon?" Chloe was sure she must have misunderstood.

"He said...Killer wanted me to tell someone named H-Hastings...*Come and get me.*" Her breath panted out. "Guess he's your friend or something, huh?"

Or something, yes.

CHAPTER FOUR

"Do killers normally taunt you and ask you to hunt them down?" Joel rocked back onto his heels as he stood in the middle of a dirty, stinking alley. "Asking for a friend."

Chloe was shining her phone—or rather, her phone's light—at the back of the brick building. He could hear the distant beat of music from inside the club. "It's not the first time," she replied, sounding totally cool and collected.

He jerked to attention. "Bullshit." It had better be bullshit.

"I am quite well-known in certain circles." The light flew over the ground. "The crime scene team did a thorough job out here. I wish Cedric had contacted me before the PD sent in a clean-up crew, though."

"Oh, right, because it's always fun to find blood and guts on the ground. Best time ever."

She swung toward him. Her light hit him in the face. "You seem awfully grumpy."

Grumpy? "You have no idea." He blew out a breath and then four more. "I want to know what's happening. Every detail. Don't leave anything out."

"Why? You came along willingly enough when I told you that we were hunting a killer. I mean, you didn't even ask for specifics. Just grabbed your shoes and your motorcycle—which I really liked, by the way—and sort of bounded into action."

Adrenaline still churned in his veins. "I want to know exactly what's going on—and, dammit, will you get the light out of my face?"

The light dropped. "Fine." She shuffled closer. Probably hard to do in the dark and in those heels. "We're hunting a killer."

He would not growl at her. But he wanted to. "Does the killer have a name?"

She laughed. "That's funny. Obviously, if we knew his name, we'd have him behind bars."

He growled.

She stopped laughing. "I have his profile, so that's almost as good as a name. We're looking for a Caucasian, mid-twenties to early thirties. Fit. After all, he has to be strong if he's going to attack his victims and beat them into submission."

Holy hell.

"He attacks at night. Stalks his prey before making a move. The profile on him indicates that is because the perp wants to make sure his targets are guilty before he goes in for the kill."

His mouth had gone dry. "Did you make the profile?"

More laughter. It was...musical. Weird as all hell given their situation and location. "Of course, not. I'm no behavioral analyst. Do I look like I work for the FBI? I told you already, I'm freelance—"

"Freelance with the PD. Some mystery freelance person who has killers inviting her to hunt them down."

"According to the FBI's profile, this perp punishes those he deems bad. Donnie Adams attacked Cinnamon—ah, Coreen Miller. I checked Donnie's rap sheet before we came here. Last month, he put another dancer in the hospital, though she didn't press charges. God knows why..." A disgruntled sigh. "The FBI says our killer is taking out those who hurt others. He's had three vics at last count."

"Three?" Had he missed these stories on the news?

"Um. The perpetrator killed a suburban dad about four weeks ago. Turned out the husband was beating the crap out of his wife and kid."

Joel's hands clenched and unclenched. "So the killer is some kind of vigilante?"

"His second victim was a male who killed his wife in a drunk driving accident. The guy's alcohol level was through the roof. He walked away from the wreck, but his new wife wasn't so lucky. She was trapped in the car and died in the hour that it took the firefighters to use the Jaws of Life to get her out."

Joel shook his head. "No."

"No...what?"

"No, I'm done. I'm not..." Was that *blood* on the wall? It was. Her light had just hit it, and he could see the stain. Not red. Dark brown. And he remembered the spray of his own blood. The smell of it. The way it had soaked his body.

Rage and pain clawed at him until Joel wanted to attack everything and everyone. He wanted to fight and destroy. He wanted—

Her hand curled around his arm. "Are you with me?"

Her light was gone. She'd turned off her phone. Put it away. The moon shone down on him. He could make out her features. The soft curves of her cheeks. The plumpness of her lips. Her touch was soft and light on him, and the rage seemed to ease. He could pull in a breath. He could smell strawberries. *Her.* "I'm with you."

He thought she smiled.

Why did he like her smile? In that rotting alley, why did he like anything? "If our killer is offing bad guys, why do we want to stop him?"

"Because he's not God. He doesn't get to decide who lives or dies." Her head tilted back. "And it's the FBI behavior analyst who thinks he's only going after bad guys. I believe the killer is just doing that part to throw us off. He's no Dexter."

"Dexter?" She had not gone there. Was she seriously talking about the fictional—

"Yes, you know the character who was a serial killer but he focused on bad guys? The show was quite popular, I mean, I know it was several years ago but—"

"*I know Dexter.*" His head was throbbing again. He had the fear that it might always throb around her. "You said there were only three vics—"

"The FBI thinks there are three. I believe there are others. And, no, the vics aren't all *bad.*" Her hand slid down his arm before easing away from him. "I'll return in the daylight. See what else I can find. I think we're done for tonight."

Done? He...didn't want to be done.

But she was walking around the building, and Joel found himself hurrying to follow her. She headed for his motorcycle, but paused to look at him and say, "I think it would be better if I took a cab home."

He grabbed for a helmet, his hand clenching around it. *She's ditching me now?* "Why would the killer want you to find him?"

"Because he wants to be stopped. He knows what he's doing is wrong, but he can't help himself. That's where I come in."

She looked far too breakable to him as she stood on the edge of the sidewalk. "You stop killers."

A shrug. The loose collar on the red blouse slid down her left shoulder. Sexy as fuck. "We all need hobbies," she told him in a quiet voice, as if imparting a secret. "This one is mine. I guess crime solving is in my blood. My gift or my curse, depending on how you look at it."

He couldn't look away from her. "Will you need my help again?"

"I doubt it." She turned away. "I learned what I needed to know from Coreen." She headed across the street. Her high heels clicked on the pavement.

Right when she reached the center of the road, headlights flashed on. A car engine revved.

Everything seemed to move in slow motion after that. Chloe's head turned until she was staring at the headlights. A deer, caught too late.

The car hurtled forward. Headed straight for her.

Joel threw down his helmet. He raced toward her. But even as he was trying to run, he felt slow. *Too slow. Everything was too slow.*

Her head whipped toward him. She stared at him with wide, stark eyes.

Joel wasn't going to make it to her in time. He wasn't going to—

She flew at him, shoved him back, and they both slammed into the sidewalk.

He could smell the rubber of the tires. Could swear that he felt the heat of the engine. The screech of wheels filled his ears as the dark car rushed away.

"What in the hell were you doing?" Chloe was on top of him. Her legs straddled his hips, and her hands curled over his shoulders.

"Saving you?" Joel asked. That had been his plan.

She shook her head. "I don't think so."

He stared up at her and tried to ignore just how incredibly good she felt on top of him. This was the wrong time to be thinking about anything except surviving. The wrong time to be thinking that he wanted her. The wrong time to be thinking—

He blinked and stared up at her. Footsteps were pounding toward them. Voices were raised. Someone was talking about calling the cops.

"Why are you looking at me like that?" Chloe cocked her head. She made no move to get off him. "What is it?"

"I just realized...when I'm with you, I don't think as much about my past." The past had tried to grab him in the alley, but when she'd touched him, he'd slipped from those shadows. *I went back to her.*

No, when he was with her, things were different somehow. He thought less about the nightmare that wouldn't let go of him. And he thought about...her. He thought about hunting killers. Stopping bad guys. Questioning exotic dancers. He thought about a million things, but he stopped being a victim.

For a moment, he could've sworn a smile teased her lips.

She leaned toward him. Her lips slid near his ear. "Good. That's step one."

Then she was pulling back. Rising. Dusting herself off and appearing totally cool. Acting as if some nutjob hadn't just attempted to run her down.

And had she really whispered, *"step one"* to him? Or had that been his imagination?

If she *had* whispered it...shit, what was step two? Did he even want to know?

***

Chloe offered her hand to Joel as she stood in front of his apartment door. "Thanks for your help."

His hand closed around hers. Warmth seemed to spread from her palm all the way up her arm.

His hold tightened on her. "Is this what every night is like for you?"

More nights than he'd probably suspect. But that was good. When she was out, chasing her killers, she didn't have to stay alone in the dark and think. "Everyone needs a hobby."

"How many killers have you put away?"

"Do you truly want to know?"

"Wouldn't have asked if I didn't."

He was still holding her hand.

"Officially, only five."

His brow furrowed. "That's one hell of a lot."

"Unofficially, probably about fifteen. But I discovered early on that the local departments or the FBI hotshots like to take the big credit. I steer them where they need to go, I get the job done, and then I move on." Simple enough.

Joel stared at her.

"You're stroking my wrist. Do you realize you're doing that?"

He immediately stopped. She supposed he hadn't realized he was doing that. Cute. He let her go as if he'd been burned.

Not so cute.

It was time to leave him. "Good night, Joel. Or rather, good day." The sun would rise soon. She turned away from him.

"The driver tried to run you down."

"Maybe. Maybe it was simply an accident. A drunk guy who'd left the club and didn't realize that a woman stood in his path."

"I *saw* the car. It angled toward you."

She glanced over her shoulder at him. "I had time to get out of the way. You didn't need to try lunging after me."

A muscle flexed along the hard plane of his jaw.

"I don't need rescuing. I'm more than capable of taking care of myself. But it was a sweet gesture." She inclined her head toward him. "Until we meet again, Joel." Chloe squared her shoulders and headed toward the stairs.

"Are we going to meet again?"

Her hand curled around the old bannister. She didn't look back this time. "What do you think?"

***

He still thought she was crazy. But he also thought she was probably the most unusual woman he'd ever met in his life. Joel shut his apartment door and glanced around. Damn, the place really did look like shit.

He rolled back his shoulders. He should've been tired after the night they'd had. He wasn't. Not even a little. Adrenaline hummed through his body, and all he wanted to do was run after Chloe. What was up with that?

His body felt too heated. Like it was in overdrive. A cold shower would cool him off.

Before he could hit the shower, a knock sounded at his door.

She was back. He spun for the door. Yanked it open.

Chloe wasn't there.

Instead, he found himself staring at a man in a three-piece suit, a fellow with close-cropped, blond hair. A guy who seemed to reek money as his cold gaze swept over Joel's body. After a moment, the stranger's mouth quirked. "Expecting someone else? Or maybe, *hoping* for someone else?"

"Fuck off," Joel snarled back. He'd caught the faint British accent in the man's voice. An accent that was too similar to Chloe's.

The man laughed, not seeming to take any offense to Joel's response. But then his laughter faded. "You spent the night with my sister."

Sister? Joel's eyes narrowed. "Leave." He started to slam the door shut—

"According to my sources, you risked your life to save her. Not once, but at least two times since you met her in the bank. Three if you count the incident in the street outside of the strip club."

Joel's fingers tightened around the doorknob. "Who are your sources?"

A faint smile. Then... "I've read your background file."

What the hell? Since when did he have a background file?

"An up and coming young surgeon. You were drugged and taken from your hospital. You were tortured for hours. Then buried alive."

Joel's breath hissed in and out from between his clenched teeth. "Get your facts straight, jackass. I wasn't taken from the hospital. I was tortured *inside* the hospital." He'd only been hauled out when the killer thought he was dead.

The intent hadn't been to bury him alive. It had just been to bury him.

"My mistake." An incline of the jerk's blond head. "You dug yourself out of the grave. The man who'd tortured you was close by. *His* mistake. You beat him to death."

Such cold, calm words.

The bastard had fallen asleep in his car after he'd buried Joel. The sonofabitch had still been there. Joel had attacked—

Don't go there. Don't. "There a reason you're talking about my past right now?"

"You never returned to your work as a doctor. Instead, you started taking self-defense classes. Every class that you could find. You learned about weaponry. You learned about knives. Guns. You learned everything that was necessary in order to survive in a world gone mad."

"The world isn't mad," Joel fired back. "Just certain people are."

"True." Another smile. Joel didn't like the guy's smiles. They never reached the fellow's eyes. "That's why I need you." He lifted the briefcase in his hand. "Do you mind if I come in?"

"Yeah, I do mind. I've had a long-ass night. I'm tired, and I'm not in the mood for a guest."

The blond's smile faded. "I can pay you well."

"Money doesn't matter to me."

"What does?"

If he'd been asked the question yesterday morning, *before* he'd gone into that bank, Joel's response probably would have been...*Not much.* But this time, that wasn't his response. Instead, he had a sudden flash of Chloe's face.

"My sister is in danger," the stranger at his door continued, voice turning a bit ragged. "Chloe thinks she can handle any threat out there, but she's wrong. No one is invulnerable. She has a killer hunting her."

"I heard about that." He let go of the doorknob and rubbed the back of his neck. Tension had pooled there.

"I want to hire someone to stay close to my sister. Someone to look out for her. Someone to stand between her and danger." His lips pursed as his gaze assessed Joel once more. "Seems like you already are in the habit of doing that, after not even twenty-four hours."

"In case you missed it, your sister just left me." Though how the guy could've missed seeing her, Joel had no clue. "I doubt I'll ever see her again. I doubt—"

"I can change your life right now, Joel Landry. I can change her life. You just have to let me do it."

He felt as if he were being offered a deal from the devil. "Forget it. I'm not buying whatever you're selling."

"Okay. Let's try something different." His throat cleared. "*She* sent me."

"What?"

Once more, the blond lifted up his briefcase. "I have a contract for you to sign. A deal to make you. Chloe is outside of the building right now, waiting in the limo. She wanted to check you out first. That's what the night's adventures were about. Making sure you were the right fit. She's sure now. Chloe wants you. The question is...do you want her?"

CHAPTER FIVE

Chloe sat in the limo. Her index finger tapped slowly against her thigh. She'd ditched her heels. They were tossed haphazardly on the floorboard.

Her hand turned over, and she frowned at the scratches on her palm. She hadn't even realized she'd gotten those. Probably occurred when she'd been throwing her body at Joel so he wouldn't jump into the road. Had her palm hit the sidewalk? She replayed the scene in her mind, slowing it down, moment by moment. Yes. Her palm had scratched over the rough edges of the sidewalk. She hadn't noticed the brief sting of pain at the time. She'd been focused on other things.

Him.

"He's coming back," her driver announced.

Right on time. Punctuality was one of her brother's better assets. "Go ahead and put up the privacy screen."

It slid up with a soft hum. A moment later, the vehicle's back door opened. Reese poked his head inside. His expression appeared extra grim. "Want to guess what he told me?"

She didn't need to guess. Not when she already knew. "Fuck off."

Reese grunted as he slid into the car. The door shut behind him. She knew her driver had shut it. Marie was good. Always standing at the ready. Prepared for any eventuality.

"He's not going to take the job," Reese informed her as he pawed at his tie. Reese hated ties. He hated suits. But he'd worn one for her. "He thinks you're crazy. That I'm crazy. He thinks—"

"You told him the night was a test?"

"Yes, but...hell, was it? Who was being tested? Him? You?" He flopped back on the leather seat and closed his eyes. "I can never keep up with your games. And I *detest* it when you make me play."

She wasn't playing. Unfortunately, Reese didn't understand that.

"Why isn't the car moving yet?" He didn't crack open his eyes.

"Because we're waiting."

"On what?"

On Joel. "The witness had no reaction to him. Not to his face—"

"If the killer wore a ski mask, that makes sense—"

"And not to Joel's voice."

"Hmmm." His face scrunched up. "Maybe he was disguising his voice?" And the British accent Reese so often favored vanished instantly. He sounded as American as...he was.

"A possibility," Chloe allowed. One she'd already considered and discarded. "But I was watching closely. He didn't act as if any part of the club or as if the witness—well, Joel didn't act like anything was familiar."

"Maybe he's just *good*. A good actor. Those exist in the world, you know."

He'd have to be better than good to fool her.

A long sigh escaped from Reese. "You think the Joel Landry fellow could be a killer. That was the whole reason for this charade, wasn't it?"

There were many reasons for what she was doing. But, after everything that had happened so far... "I don't think he's *the* killer that I'm after right now."

"It drives me crazy when you're all extra careful with your words," he grumbled. "What do you *mean*? Do you believe Landry is a killer or not?"

It wasn't that simple. Yes, he was a killer. Joel had killed the man who he believed had sadistically tortured him for hours. But was Joel killing *again?* "He didn't murder Donnie Adams in that alley. It wasn't Joel."

"Then if he's not your killer, why are we still parked here?"

Why? "Because I like him."

Silence.

Reese finally opened his eyes. "Do you know how much that statement terrifies me?"

Not as much as it terrifies me. But she tried, very hard, not to lie to her brother.

"I offered him a job as your guard. He turned me down." Reese spoke very carefully as he advised, "We should drive away now."

"He didn't want to be a bodyguard. He doesn't want to stand on the sidelines." Joel wasn't the sideline type.

"It creeps me out that you already seem to know a stranger this well."

She didn't respond.

"What does he want?" The question seemed torn from Reese.

The privacy screen slid down a few inches. "He's coming," her driver announced. "And moving at a pretty good clip." Marie's voice was perfectly flat.

Just like Reese had been...Joel was right on time.

A few moments later, the back door was wrenched open. "You think you can buy me?" Joel's angry voice filled the interior of the vehicle as he surged inside. He sat right next to her. His strong thigh pressed against her as he took up far too much space. He'd left the door open, and the interior lights shone brightly inside the vehicle.

She cleared her throat and tried to be polite. Buy him? "Definitely not. I know you aren't for sale." It's not like he was some fancy trinket she'd found at the store.

Joel crowded closer to her.

"I need a drink," Reese said to anyone who might be listening. "A big one."

He was supposed to be staying away from the drinks. Especially the big ones. Because when he drank, he slipped up. She didn't want slips on this case.

"I believe that you've met my brother, Reese." She waved toward him.

Joel didn't acknowledge her brother. His dark glare stayed on Chloe. "If you want me at your side, then I'm going to be there as your partner."

She would not smile. Not yet, anyway. "I thought you told me already that we weren't partners." In fact, he'd made that point several times during their brief acquaintance.

"We weren't...then. Things have changed."

Yes, she could see that they had. His cheeks were flushed. His eyes seemed to gleam, making the gold far more apparent. He didn't look cold and grim. He seemed to pulse with life and intensity. If she'd thought he was attractive before, he was positively gorgeous now. *Sexy. Very, very sexy.*

"You sent your brother to my door. I don't know why you want me with you, but I'm ready to find out."

Looked like someone was up for another adventure. They were going to have such fun together. "There will be great risk," she warned him. "You'll be hurt. You could die."

Reese scrubbed a hand over his face. "A couple of drinks. That's what I need. A couple—"

"Will we stop a killer?" Joel cut across her brother's words. "Because if so, then the risk is worth it."

The man just did not disappoint. She'd suspected he would be this way, long before she'd ever arranged the little meet and greet between them at the bank. It was always nice when she was proven to be correct. "It will be worth it."

His stare held hers. "Then you've got yourself a partner."

Chloe offered her hand to him. "We should shake on it."

His fingers curled around hers. His grip was strong and warm and a hot spark shot through her entire hand.

Grousing, Reese reached out and shut the door that Joel had left open. The bright lights immediately died away.

His fingers slowly released hers. His index finger trailed along the inner section of her palm. That spark she'd felt before flared hotter. *Unexpected, but nothing I can't handle.* Raising her voice, she said, "Take us home, Marie."

With a hum, the privacy screen slid up again. The car pulled away from the curb.

"Uh, home?" Joel seemed wary. "I was at my home. I was—"

"If we're going to be working together, it will be easier if you stay on the grounds of my residence. Don't worry. You'll have a guest house all to yourself. You'll have plenty of privacy."

"You're in it now," Reese told him. "Welcome to her world." His British accent had returned as soon as Joel appeared. "You'd damn well better watch her ass."

"Don't worry," Joel assured him, voice dry, "I'll make sure my eyes are on her ass."

"Wait," Reese snapped. "That's not—I didn't—"

"So, Chloe, what's our first move?" Joel asked as Reese sputtered.

She'd already made the first move. She'd gotten him out of his home, into her car, and at her side. He would be with her, so he'd be protected. He could thank her later.

After they took care of solving some murders. "We hunt."

CHAPTER SIX

When the limo pulled to a stop, Joel shoved open the door and climbed out. He'd been watching through the windows and he knew that they weren't too far from Audubon Park. As they'd driven, the houses had gotten bigger and bigger. And the place they were at right now...

He whistled. "Just how rich are you?"

"You don't want to know," a voice to his right said.

His head turned. The driver had just come around the front of the parked car. Petite, her dark hair was twisted at the nape of her neck, and she wore all black.

She paused next to him. Raked him with a stare. "How long are you supposed to last?"

His brows climbed. "I'm Joel. Nice to meet you. And you are...?"

She stared back at him.

Reese climbed from the limo. Stretched. His tie hung loosely around his neck. "That's Marie Kim. Been with my sister for at least two years."

"Three," Marie said with a shake of her head. "And you know it. After all, you're the one who hired me."

Did Reese hire everyone for Chloe?

Joel glanced back in the limo. Chloe was grabbing her high heels. He hadn't even realized that she'd taken them off. He figured she'd slide them on and then exit the vehicle but—

She didn't. Just held them in one hand and popped out of the car. "Sorry I kept you out so late, Marie."

"You act like it's unusual," Marie replied. "We both know it's not."

Chloe shrugged.

"I'm crashing," Reese declared. "See you all at lunch time. A civilized hour." He headed for the giant, towering structure that passed for Chloe's house.

Marie brushed past Joel. Reese was at the house's door—holding it open for her. They whispered to each other before disappearing inside.

Chloe shut the back door of the vehicle. Stood there, still holding her shoes. She seemed lost in thought.

What in the hell have I gotten myself into? "I shouldn't have come here."

Her head turned toward him.

"We can be partners without me living at your house."

"You'll be living in the guest house. Not the main house." She turned to the left. Started walking away. Her bare feet padded over the walkway as her high heels dangled from her fingers. "Unless you'd prefer to be at the main house. There's certainly plenty of room in there."

He lumbered after her as his gaze swept to the left and the right in a vain effort to take everything in. A big, stone fence surrounded the property. Security cameras were discreetly perched along the perimeter. "Uh, Marie, she's your driver?"

"Marie does lots of things."

That was a vague answer. "She was driving tonight."

"Because I needed her to drive tonight. Someone had to drop me off at your place. And then someone had to bring Reese over later. So, tonight, she was my driver."

"You planned everything out, didn't you?" He reached for her arm.

She stilled. Looked down at his fingers, then turned toward him. They'd stopped at the edge of a massive swimming pool. Water poured from two nearby fountains, splashing into the deep pool. "I like to plan things," she confessed. "But I can see that bothers you."

"I don't like being manipulated."

"I would think most people don't." She gazed up at him.

He hated that there wasn't more light. He wanted to see into her eyes. To figure out just what was going on inside her head.

"The guest house is behind me. You will, of course, have full access to the pool and to the exercise room." Her shoulders rolled back. "You have full access to the entire property. I'll have Reese make arrangements to bring your belongings—and your motorcycle—over so that you can get comfortable."

"I can take care of moving my own damn things. *If* I stay," he added.

"You're considering not staying?"

"We can work together without living together."

She nodded. Turned and headed for the guest house. One story. Made of the same heavy, white bricks that matched the main house. She bent and pulled a key from beneath the rug in front of the door. She unlocked the door and handed him the key. "For you, in case you decide to stay."

He took the key. Just because, dammit. His fingers tangled with hers and a hot surge of attraction shot through his body. He caught the quick inhale of her breath and knew she'd felt the same thing he just had.

Only instead of saying something, she crossed the threshold, walked inside, and flipped on the lights—

"No." He wasn't playing her game. "You feel it."

"Excuse me?"

"You know I want you."

Chloe glanced over her shoulder. "You're being very honest."

"Why the hell would I lie about something like that? You're a gorgeous woman, and you know it."

"Different people have vastly different ideas of beauty."

He stalked toward her. The guest house was much bigger than it had appeared on the outside. Giant, sweeping ceiling. Windows everywhere. But he barely glanced at the surroundings. He was focused on her. "Then let me be clear. *I* find you beautiful."

She nodded.

Didn't say anything else. But she did walk toward the room on the right. The room he figured had to be the bedroom.

A rough laugh broke from him. "You feel it, too. I know you do. I can see it when we touch. You get the same surge I do."

Her head cocked as she paused in the doorway.

"And you bring me to your house. You get your brother to try and *buy* me? You think I don't see what's going on here?"

"I truly don't think you do," she murmured. "Why don't you come and take a look at the bedroom?"

He marched toward her. "You want to have sex with me. You're moving me in your place so that you have a close and convenient spot for us to have—"

"No."

No? Dammit. Had disappointment just stabbed through him?

"We could have sex at that pit you called a home. We could've had sex in the alley behind the strip club. At the strip club. In the limo. By the swimming pool. By—"

"I get the idea," Joel growled. He got the idea and all the mental images. Lots and lots of mental images that were now burned in his brain.

"The point is that if I wanted to have sex with you, bringing you to my home would be unnecessary. We could have sex at any time. In any location." Her lips pressed together, she seemed to mull something over, then Chloe added, "Unless, of course, you're shy and not much of an exhibitionist, and in that case—"

"I'm not shy! But I also don't perform for crowds. Thanks for asking."

A spark of humor made her eyes even brighter. "Are you going to look at the bedroom?"

"For someone who isn't interested in having sex with me, you're trying awfully hard to get me in the bedroom." He strode by her.

"I never said I didn't want to have sex with you."

He froze. And his eager dick surged against the front of his jeans.

"I said I wasn't moving you in here so that we could have a convenient spot for sex. You should also know that I don't need to buy lovers. That's not something I do."

He whirled toward her. "It's not something I do, either!" Was that how she thought he spent his nights?

"Good to know." She lingered in the doorway. "What do you think?"

"Of what?" Joel asked blankly because she'd totally lost him. No, he was just stuck several sentences back.

I never said I didn't want to have sex with you.

"Of the bedroom. I believe it should work well for you."

He dragged his gaze off her and finally looked around the room. The bed appeared big. Fluffy covers—he didn't care about that shit. But he realized that the entire wall near the side of the bed appeared to be made entirely of glass so that he could see outside—and he had a killer view of the pool. He walked toward the wall and he realized it wasn't a glass wall. It was two massive doors.

"You can go out to the pool whenever you feel confined."

His gut tightened at her soft words.

"I thought the view would help, too. I noticed you kept the windows in your apartment open, so maybe you'd like to just leave the doors open in here? The property is quite secure."

Joel swallowed before he turned back toward her. "You notice lots of things, don't you?"

"It's sort of...who I am." Now her head tipped back and she gazed up at the ceiling. "You can also watch the stars when you're trying to get to sleep."

He looked up. Holy shit. It wasn't an ordinary skylight. A huge section of the ceiling seemed to be made of glass.

He could stay in this room and not feel confined. Not feel like he was suffocating in the dark. Not feel like he'd been buried alive again.

And she knew that.

"You're probably tired," Chloe said. "I'll leave you to get some sleep. Once you've rested, come to the main house and we'll make plans. I want to go back and look at the crime scene in the daylight." She headed for the door.

"*Stop.*"

She did. Glanced back.

"Who lived here before me?" He was trying not to let her see how much he loved the room. It was as if it had been made for him.

"No one lived here," she told him. "I recently had the guest house added to the property."

And part of him...part of him wondered...

Did she build this for me?

But no, that wasn't possible. They'd just met at the bank. She hadn't known him before that moment. There was no way she could have gotten this place built for him. That was crazy.

"Glad you like it, Joel," she said softly. "We all need a place to call home. Maybe you can put some personal touches in here. You know...an actual photo or two." Then she walked away.

He found himself following her. "How do you know I like it?"

She slowed near the couch. "Because you aren't telling me that you're leaving any longer."

No. He wasn't. He *wanted* that room. "Am I supposed to say thank you?" Jesus, he sounded like an ass. He cleared his throat. "I'm not a charity case." Okay, dammit, that wasn't any better. He *still* hadn't managed to tell her thanks.

She opened the front door. The hinges didn't make even a whisper of sound. "I don't do charity. And thanks aren't necessary. Besides, by the time we're done with our first case, you might be cursing me. Not thanking me." She left him without looking back.

He stood there, rooted to the spot, and it took Joel a moment to realize that his right hand had clenched into a fist. He forced the fingers to open, and he peered down at the key she'd given him.

It felt like more than a key to a guest house.

It felt like a fucking key to a new life.

"Yeah," he muttered. "That's it. I've officially lost my mind."

***

"You have a tendency to pick up dangerous strays."

Chloe didn't jump when the low, feminine voice came from the darkness. She'd known that Marie would be waiting on her. She'd felt the other woman's displeasure back in the car.

Chloe turned on the lamp at the base of the stairs. The faint glow sent the shadows sliding across the floor. She looked up and found Marie on the sixth step. "I hardly think the doctor is a stray."

"But you didn't say he wasn't dangerous."

True. Marie had been with her long enough to realize that, half the time, it was the stuff Chloe didn't say that mattered the most.

"Why him?" Marie eased down to the fifth step. It creaked.

"I think he will be important to this case. You know Cedric is concerned. He thinks a lot of the FBI analysis is bullshit."

"I know Cedric is territorial. He didn't like it when the FBI Brass took over the case, so he figures you can teach them a lesson."

That might also be true, but..."I'm not here to teach anyone a lesson."

"No. You're just here because you have an obsession with death."

Chloe climbed onto the bottom stair. "And you don't?"

Marie laughed. "That's one of the reasons we get along so well, isn't it? Because we like the same things."

They did have many things in common. "There is more to Joel than meets the eye. I don't want him hurt."

Marie nodded. "Fine. Then I won't play with the new stray."

"Marie..."

"But if he bites...if he attacks *you*, he's done."

Chloe considered the matter. "That seems fair." Chloe headed past Marie as she made her way to the second level and her bedroom. She was almost at the top of the stairs when...

"Two nights ago..." Marie's voice drifted up to her. "I could have sworn that I heard a woman scream."

Chloe's hand curled around the bannister. "I had a bad dream."

"*You* don't have bad dreams, Chloe."

If only. "This time," she replied quietly. "I did."

CHAPTER SEVEN

"The Feds are about to give their updated profile and—what in the hell is he doing here?" Cedric barked when he caught sight of Joel.

Joel smiled at the homicide detective. They were in the back of the bullpen at the downtown PD. Uniformed cops were buzzing everywhere. He'd never been in a bullpen scene like this one. Kinda felt like being slammed down into the middle of some cop TV show. The air seemed to crackle with electricity. The big downside of the whole scene? The detective seemed pissed that Joel was there.

Cedric swore. Then... "Chloe, do not tell me, please, I am begging you, do *not* say—"

"Joel is my new partner. He's a former surgeon, and I think his insights on the perp we are after will prove to be extremely useful."

Joel straightened a little. She'd sounded like she meant her words. A compliment from Chloe. He'd take it.

"Right. Sure. You would think that." Cedric side-eyed Joel. "What's your excuse? I gave you good life advice, man, and you should have—"

"Detective Coleman. Why in the world is Chloe Hastings standing beside you?" A nasally voice asked that question. A voice that belonged to a tall, thin, rather pale guy who was currently glaring at Chloe.

"Agent Paul Richardson." Chloe lifted one eyebrow. "How long has it been? One year? Two? Has it—"

"It's been two fucking months, Chloe," he snarled back at her. "Two months since we last crossed paths and you damn well know it. It's been *six* months since you made me look like an ass in front of my boss."

Chloe's gaze cut to Joel. "I could have sworn it was longer."

Cedric snorted, then coughed into his hand.

Agent Richardson's pale skin mottled. "You need to get out of here. I'm about to do a profile update, and there can be *no* civilians present for—"

"The police chief said I could be here." Joel had to admire her cool and casual reply. She didn't so much as blink.

Richardson blinked. A lot. "The local police aren't in charge. The FBI is and I am telling you to get your—"

"My ass is staying put." She didn't seem even mildly intimidated. "*Your* boss also told me that he'd love any insight that I had to give on the case. He said that to me not an hour ago when I called to check in and see how his kids were doing."

Richardson's nostrils flared. The man sort of resembled a bull who was dying to charge. Joel got the feeling that Chloe was the red flag to the man's bull.

Then Richardson's angry attention shifted to him. "The new boyfriend can get the hell out."

"No. He's staying." Chloe put a hand on Joel's arm. "He's also my partner, not my—"

"I don't care what damn label you want to give him! He's out. He is—"

"*Dr.* Landry will be staying during your update. And later, he will be taking a trip to the coroner's office so that he can review the case files for all of the victims. *That* visit has also been green-lighted by your boss." She shrugged one shoulder. "By the way, everyone in the room is staring at you because your voice has gotten to be so loud. Perhaps, since you have everyone's attention, you should go ahead and deliver your report. Wasted time is an annoyance, you know. People are busy. Places to go. Killers to trap and whatnot."

Richardson's head snapped up. He looked around. Joel realized she was right. The controlled chaos in the bullpen had quieted, and everyone was staring at Chloe and Agent Richardson.

Richardson stomped his way to the little podium that had been set up in the center of the room.

Joel leaned down toward Chloe. He put his mouth to her ear and whispered, "I don't think he likes you very much." The scent of strawberries teased his nose.

Chloe turned her head toward him. She was dressed in black slacks and a white blouse. She'd slid lipstick over her plump lips and they gleamed with a warm red color. "He hates me," she retorted easily. "And, you, too, now. Welcome to the club."

"That guy is such a dick," Cedric mumbled a moment later. He was to Joel's right.

Most of the cops were frowning at Richardson as he began his talk, so Joel figured no one there felt a whole lot of love for the FBI agent. Was it a territorial thing? Or was the man truly just a dick?

"Bad deeds," Richardson announced dramatically. He lifted a small remote in his hand, and the lights dimmed. There was a massive screen behind him, and images began to appear on it. The three victims.

Three males.

"First victim," Richardson announced. "Gregory Guidry. Beaten to death at his own home. The home he shared with his wife." He changed the image with a click of the remote, and a picture of a woman with bruised eyes, cheeks, and a split lip filled the screen. "This shot was taken during one of the many times that Michelle Guidry claimed her husband abused her. She would never file charges, no matter how much friends and family members begged her to do so."

"Guidry was a real piece of shit," Cedric inserted quietly. "Know several uniforms who had to deal with him. The wife would always swear she'd fallen down. They just wanted to help her..."

Joel glanced over at Chloe. She had narrowed her eyes on the image of Michelle Guidry, and she was rubbing her fingers over her left cheek.

"Second victim..." Richardson continued in that nasally voice that was like nails on a chalkboard. "Ray Malone. He was found beaten to death inside his car. The vehicle was parked at his job. Two years ago, Ray's wife died in a car accident. It was believed that Ray was drunk at the time of the crash, but his lawyer was able to work out a deal for Ray. He never set foot in a jail."

Cedric made no comment but when Joel cut a glance at him, he saw that the detective's jaw was clenched.

"This was an image from that crash. The wife died while the firefighters were working to remove her from the vehicle. The metal had torn into her chest. She bled out."

He looked at the image. *Fuck.*

"And finally..." Richardson jutted up his chin. "We come to our most recent victim. Donnie Adams. Found beaten to death in a dirty alley. Cops interviewed folks who knew Donnie and the general consensus is that he was a drunk who liked to hurt whoever got in his way. Donnie is the third vic who fits my profile."

"His profile is bullshit," Chloe said in her ever-so-proper voice. So proper that it took Joel a moment to realize she'd even called bullshit.

And that her voice had, um, actually been quite loud.

Someone snickered.

Joel found himself smothering a laugh, too.

What the hell? When was the last time I laughed? And this sure as hell didn't seem the right time to laugh.

Richardson did *not* look amused. His eyes lasered in on Chloe. "All of the victims are approximately the same age. In their late twenties. All have a similar body type. They're big, physically imposing. Their personality traits are the same, as well. Simply put, they are bullies. They attacked the weak. They enjoyed hurting others."

There were murmurs. Agreement.

Chloe began to tap her left foot.

"Oh, damn." Cedric sighed. "Here we go. It's on now. When the foot starts tapping, she's losing patience."

"I never had patience," Chloe corrected, her voice brisk. "But I've stood here this long to be polite. I was doing that for you, Cedric. I hope you appreciate my effort."

"Consider it appreciated." Cedric winked at her.

Okay, so...Chloe and Cedric were friends. He'd wondered about their relationship at the bank. But there definitely seemed to be a bit of camaraderie going on between them. But if Cedric liked Chloe, then why had he warned Joel to stay away from her?

"These men committed bad deeds." Now Richardson looked proud. Satisfied. "And the perp who killed them, he was punishing them for their crimes. He knew what they'd done, and he was delivering justice—his justice—to them."

It almost sounded as if Richardson admired what the guy was doing.

"Payback," Richardson threw out dramatically. "It was a true bitch in these cases."

"Utter waste of valuable time." Chloe turned on her heel. "He's never going to catch the killer. Let's go."

Joel started to follow her but...

"We're looking for a very intelligent killer. Someone who stalked his prey. Who researched these men. Who waited for the perfect moment to strike. Someone who didn't mind the wait, who enjoyed it, in fact. He sees himself as an instrument of vengeance, and he is delivering justice. This man does not think he is doing anything wrong, and the people close to the victims...they are grateful to him for what he does."

Cinnamon had been grateful. She'd said as much. Joel glanced back at Richardson.

Chloe caught Joel's arm. "That man knows nothing about killers. Don't let what he is saying get in your head."

She sure seemed confident. Once more, Joel turned his head away from Richardson—

"Sorry your...ah...services won't be needed on this one, Chloe," Richardson called out. "Turns out, you aren't the only one who can figure out how a killer thinks. *Professionals* can do the job just fine without you. I have a strong profile for the Bad Deeds killer, and please, don't let the door hit you on the way out."

"He's done it now," Cedric murmured. He was almost rubbing his hands together.

"He named the killer. He gave him a moniker. What a wanker." Chloe squared her shoulders. Then she spun and marched right up to the podium.

"Uh, is she supposed to do that?" Joel asked as he sidled close to Cedric.

"I don't think Chloe ever does what she is supposed to do. One of many reasons Agent Richardson hates her."

"I am not in law enforcement," Chloe's clipped voice rang out, "but I have a PhD in psychology. Dual master's degrees in both forensic psychology and abnormal psychology..."

"She's just flexing," Cedric explained as his head angled toward Joel. "Because Richardson bugged her with something he said. Don't know exactly what set her off, but she's about to tear him a new one."

"*I* brought down the Sunshine State Strangler." Chloe's shoulders were straight. Her chin up.

The who now? Who'd she brought down? Wait, wait...*Sunshine State Strangler*. That was kinda familiar. The moniker clicked for Joel. Sunshine State—that had been the killer who'd been strangling college co-eds down in Florida a few months back.

"I'm the one who told police officers what he would look like, the type of apartment he would live in, and that he would even walk with a limp on his right side. And when that wasn't enough..." Her narrowed gaze swung to Agent Richardson... "When Agent Richardson here insisted on going by his ridiculous assumption that the man was a college professor, I'm the one who gift wrapped the perp when I set myself up as bait and lured him in."

"What the hell did she do?" Joel's breath froze in his chest. "Tell me that she did not say she became bait."

"Oh, yes, she did. That's Chloe." Cedric's words were grim. "Are you starting to see why I told you to run from her? Getting the full picture now? Wishing you'd listened?"

He wasn't running. He was watching. She waved toward the officers. "You all listened really well while Richardson was giving his spiel, and that's wonderful. But before you go searching for this perp, you need to know that his profile is flawed. Not the first time, not the last. He keeps making mistakes."

Richardson's face had gone back to being extra mottled. "You have no authority to—"

"You know me," Chloe said to the cops. "Have I led you astray before?"

"Not even once," Cedric responded. His voice was clear and certain.

Richardson fired him a dirty glare.

"Sorry," Cedric didn't sound the least bit sorry. "Thought she was waiting for a response. Don't like to leave a lady waiting. My mama raised me better than that."

Richardson turned off the screen. "If I'm so wrong, tell me what I'm missing." He crossed his arms over his chest. "Educate us all!"

Chloe's gaze darted around the room. Lingered on Joel. She swallowed.

"That's what I thought," Richardson continued. *Smug. So very smug.* "You don't have anything to add so how about you let me take over from—"

"It's not about what the men—the victims—did now. It's about what they did before. You neglected to mention that the victims knew each other. That they all shared a connection in the past."

A furrow appeared between Richardson's brows. "What the hell are you—"

"May I have the remote?" She didn't wait for him to reply. She just took it. A few moments later, she had Ray Malone's picture up on the screen. "Ignore the bloody mess that is his body," she informed the assembled men and women. Her accent thickened just a little. "Instead, focus on the ring finger on his right hand."

Joel squinted at it.

"That's a state championship ring. A football ring. Focus on it. Think about it. And now..." She pulled up the image of Gregory Guidry. "Guidry was also big guy, yes, Richardson had *that* part right. He was big guy who once played high school football and took his team all the way to a championship ring. Go Pirates." She clicked the remote a few times. Got to the shot of Gregory's Guidry's wife. "As you can see, Gregory had the same ring."

"Uh, ma'am?" One of the cops raised his hand. "I don't see that."

"*Where* are we supposed to see that?" Another officer stood up and peered at the picture. He even shuffled closer to get a better view

Chloe walked to the screen. Tapped her finger against the woman's bruised cheek. "Do you see the design there? The raised pattern? When Gregory punched his wife, he was wearing his championship ring."

"Holy fuck," Joel breathed. Now that she was tracing her finger over the spot on Michelle Guidry's cheek, he could see it, too.

"A little emblem on the top. A V for Victory. Pretty distinct." She stepped away from the screen. "If you dig into Donnie's past, you'll see that he played on that same team."

Silence.

Chloe cocked her head toward Richardson. "Though, honestly, it would have been helpful to look up their pasts *before* you did this big profile reveal. How long does it really take to see if they all went to the same high school? I'm sure you could figure that out with a few clicks on a keyboard."

He looked away.

"Ah." Chloe nodded. "You already knew they went to the same high school. But somehow, that wasn't important enough to note? What about being on the same football team? Did you know about that, too?"

"No," he gritted out. "I didn't."

"Now you do," Cedric drawled. "Good thing Chloe was here, huh?"

Joel was worried that Agent Richardson might be choking. It was not healthy to be that particular shade of red. He should probably see a doctor. One who gave a fuck.

That wouldn't be me.

"Maybe this isn't so much about a killer punishing them for bad deeds," Chloe continued as she paced back toward Joel. "Maybe it's about something that happened a long time ago. I *do* think our perp is patient. But the way he is killing, the way he is torturing those men? I don't think that has anything to do with justice."

Silence followed in her wake.

Over her shoulder, Joel saw Richardson glaring at her. He stiffened because the man was staring at her with hate plain to see in his eyes and on his face.

Not exactly what he'd expected from an FBI agent.

"This has turned out to be semi-informative for me." Chloe gave Joel a faint smile. "But it is time to go now." Her attention shifted to Cedric as her heels clicked across the floor. "We'll touch base again later?"

"Damn straight. I've got some leads I want to run down. Talk soon." His fingers brushed over her arm.

The meeting was breaking up. Cops dispersing. Chloe didn't glance back at Richardson as she walked with Joel out the front doors of the station. It was freaking hot outside. No big surprise that the city was sweltering in October, and his motorcycle waited near the sidewalk. Chloe had seemed quite thrilled to ride on the bike with him when they'd traveled to the station.

She reached for a helmet.

He snagged her wrist. "You enjoy pissing off federal agents?"

Her pulse jerked beneath his touch.

His brows rose. "Chloe?"

She tugged her hand free. "I need to get used to that."

Used to what?

"And, no, I don't enjoy pissing off all federal agents. Just annoyingly pompous, *wrong* agents who seem to be missing major points in an investigation." She stared expectantly at him.

He realized he was fighting a smile again. How did she do that? Joel didn't think she was even being funny. Not at all. But she made him want to—

"*Chloe.*" A low, rough snarl. "You are not going to screw me over again!"

Joel whirled. He saw Richardson barreling toward Chloe. The agent's rage was even more obvious now.

"You get off on trying to make me look bad in front of those cops? You think it's one of your games?" Richardson's hands flew toward Chloe as—

Joel stepped into his path. "No. Nope. Not happening."

Richardson's hands hung in the air.

"You're not touching her. You're not putting your hands on any part of her body. Got it?" Joel made sure he was blocking Chloe with *his* body. "I'm pretty sure this is not how a federal agent is supposed to act, so get your shit under control, buddy."

"Thank you, Joel," Chloe said, rather demurely, odd for her, "some people just have no self-control."

"*Chloe.*" Richardson seemed to nearly choke on her name. "You think I didn't put it together? You think I don't know who this SOB is?"

"I can see why Chloe doesn't like you." Joel nodded. "I'm pretty sure you got my name earlier, so obviously, she thought you knew who I was. We all thought that. Since she *told* it to you."

Richardson's chin angled into the air. "You're a killer."

For a moment, Joel couldn't breathe.

Chloe immediately moved to Joel's side. "He's a survivor."

"Tell that to the man he beat to death."

Joel's hands fisted. "If you know he's dead, then you know what he did to me. You know—"

Her fingers wrapped around his right fist. "Richardson understands just enough about psychology to be a true tosser. Don't let him get under your skin. Joel, *Joel*, would you look at me?"

His head jerked toward her.

"He's not worth your time. We have a case to solve."

"*My* case," Richardson fumed. "You need to stay away—"

"Sorry. The chief wants my help, so it's help I will give him. I mean, *we* will give him," Chloe corrected smoothly as she never broke eye contact with Joel. "Joel is my partner, so he'll be working with me every step of the way." Her fingers were still wrapped around Joel's.

And...her touch was calming him. As was her gaze. Her bright gaze held no judgment. No censure. He could look into her eyes and almost forget everything else.

Except, what in the hell was a tosser?

"Another mistake," Richardson warned her. "I figured you would have learned from your past.

But I guess certain women just have a type, don't they?"

Chloe tugged Joel toward the motorcycle.

Richardson's footsteps stomped away.

"That man is a prick." Chloe sounded both dismissive and annoyed. "Don't take anything that he says to heart. And, absolutely, under no circumstances, are you ever to let what he says get into your head, either." She was still touching him.

He was still liking her touch way too much.

"Joel?" Her head tilted. "He's wrong about you."

"An FBI profiler just called me a killer." His voice was rough. Hard. "And I wanted to punch him." He had been able to imagine driving his fist into Richardson's face far too easily. Over and over.

Because I am a killer. Because he was right about me.

Joel looked down at their hands. Her fingers were so small and delicate. While his...

Once upon a time, I used my hands to save people.

Until he'd used his hands to kill a man.

"This is a mistake." He pulled away from her. "I don't know what I was thinking. I should...no, *you* should stay away from me." He jumped onto the motorcycle. "I'm not some crime solver. I don't have any business being here." His fingers curled around the handlebars. "*What was I thinking*? This can't happen. You aren't safe with me. No one is safe. You are—"

She climbed onto the back of the motorcycle. Curled her hands around him. "I have my helmet on. I'm quite safe. I put it on while you were having your pity party."

"What?"

"Pity party. Don't you know what that means? If not, it's when a person is just reveling in—"

His head snapped toward her. "I know what a pity party is."

She smiled. And looked...fucking adorable in that helmet. He shook his head.

"Would you like for me to drive?" Chloe asked him. "I'm quite good on a motorcycle."

"Of course, you are. Because I'm starting to think you're some kind of secret ninja who is good at all sorts of things."

"Ninjas aren't good at all—"

He faced forward. Got the engine revving. "I'm trying to tell you...you *aren't* safe with me."

Her hold tightened on him. "Don't be ridiculous. I think I'm at my safest when I am with you. After all, you're the one with the hero complex. It makes you keep jumping in front of me at the slightest threat. You should probably stop doing that."

He didn't pull into the road, not yet. "I'm a killer." His words were low. Maybe he wanted them to be drowned out by the revving of the motorcycle. Maybe then it could be like he hadn't—

She laughed. As if he'd made a joke.

"I'm not kidding you," he fired back.

"Anyone can kill, under the right circumstances. Your circumstances were—they were very unusual. I don't feel threatened by you at all. Quite the opposite."

His circumstances, huh? "You know so much about me." Hardly seemed fair. "But I know nothing about you." The revving quieted a bit.

"Oh. Would it make you feel better if I told you that I'd killed a man, too?"

"That is not the shit that I was—"

"Because I have."

His whole body tensed.

"I guess that means we're both killers. Now, if you don't mind, we need to get to the coroner's office. I'd rather not run into Richardson while we are there, and I'm sure he'll be heading that way very soon."

I guess that means we're both killers.

He steered the motorcycle onto the road.

CHAPTER EIGHT

He'd been quiet during the entire drive. Not that it had been an overly long drive from the police station to the coroner's office but...still. Chloe had expected more.

When he pulled into the parking spot and killed the engine, Chloe didn't linger behind Joel. Mostly because she'd discovered that she rather enjoyed touching him too much. The motorcycle had vibrated between her legs, and he'd driven fast and hard to their destination. She'd found herself hugging him a little too tightly. Leaning against him a little too closely.

Getting turned on...a little too much.

An unexpected development. When she'd decided to bring him on as her partner, she'd certainly never anticipated that she'd want things to get physical, so quickly. Though, perhaps, that was her fault. She'd been aware of the attraction when they'd been pushed against each other in the tiny storage closet back at the bank. She'd attributed most of her response to adrenaline when it probably was due to—

"What are you thinking, Chloe?" Joel asked. He'd taken the helmet from her hands. Hooked it to the motorcycle. He climbed off the bike, kept his hands loose at his sides, and studied her with raised brows. "Because I can practically see the thoughts spinning through your mind."

"I'm thinking that our attraction was probably originally due to the adrenaline rush that we felt when Harry pushed us into that little closet. We were forced into close proximity, and close proximity can lead to increased physical awareness. There is no current adrenaline rush, though, and I'm not physically touching you at this moment, yet I still feel the attraction. You are an extremely handsome, fit man, so it's only natural to—"

His mouth had fallen open. He quickly snapped it closed. "Shit, I thought you were thinking about the case."

"The case? What about it?" They hadn't gone inside the coroner's office. She didn't have new information to ponder.

Joel dragged a hand over his face. "I cannot figure you out."

"Good. That means you'll never be bored by me. And, so far, you are most certainly not boring me."

His hand dropped. "You want me."

Hadn't she just said as much? "It won't get in the way of our partnership, don't worry about that. I have outstanding self-control."

"I just bet you do," he muttered.

That hadn't sounded like a compliment. "You want me, too. There's really no point in acting all shocked and maidenly."

His eyes widened. Then turned to slits. "Did you just call me maidenly?"

Her hand gestured toward his lower body. "You have this physical reaction to me. I notice—"

He spun away from her. "Fuck. Chloe, you're not supposed to point out a man's hard-on."

Yes, she knew that. But he was oddly cute when he was flustered so she'd been messing with him. "You're not doing anything about the attraction either. I thought it might be best for us to simply put things out there. This way, you won't be uncomfortable when you have a physical reaction to me again."

He swore. He had some truly inventive curses. She waited for him to get it all out and then Chloe delicately cleared her throat. "You didn't ask me."

He swung back toward her. "Ask you what?"

"Who I killed? Don't you want to know?"

"You haven't killed anyone."

"You certainly sound confident about that fact."

"You look like a strong wind would blow you over."

"To be fair, a hurricane force wind would knock anyone down."

He stared at her.

She stared back. Chatting with him this way was quite fun.

"Your brother," he rumbled.

Now you're on the right track. "What about him?"

"He wanted me to be your bodyguard."

Technically, *she'd* been the one to send Reese with that offer. Her lips parted—

"No, correction, you sent him."

Good of him to remember.

"That means you wanted protection. That means you were afraid of someone or something. If you were a cold-blooded killer, I doubt you'd want a bodyguard. You'd just go after the threat yourself."

She crept nearer to him. Saw the flare of his nostrils and the slight widening of his pupils. *He likes it when I'm close.* Only fair. Chloe had discovered that she rather enjoyed being close to him, too. "What makes you assume that every killer is cold-blooded?"

His gaze searched hers.

"When you dug yourself out of that grave…"

Joel didn't flinch. His square jaw hardened.

"And you saw the man nearby…the guy still holding the shovel that had been used to toss the dirt over your body, did you feel cold-blooded when you launched your bleeding, broken body at him?"

He wasn't speaking.

So she kept going. Her hand rose, and she slid her finger over the scar that cut across his upper lip. "He hit you in the face with the shovel. Left you with this mark. Broke your nose. So you took the shovel from him. You hit *him.* You stopped him. If you hadn't, you wouldn't be standing here right now."

"The bastard buried me." His lips moved against her finger. "He tortured me for hours, and when he thought I was dead, he dug a shallow grave and covered me with dirt."

So much pain. So much rage. "Do you see yourself as a killer because of what you did?"

A muscle flexed in that hard jaw of his.

"Because the police didn't," Chloe continued as she caressed that scar one more time, then let her hand fall. "The DA didn't. Everyone agreed it was self-defense."

"I *killed* him."

"But that doesn't make you a killer. Self-defense isn't murder."

"You think you know so much about me." He shook his head. "You got access to my files. Now you figure you're in my head."

"I am in your head." She rose onto her tiptoes. Her gaze was on the scar. No, on his mouth. She could feel the darkness surging from him, but Joel was so much more than the monster he thought he'd become. He was—

"So, Chloe, are you going to make out with the new guy or were you planning to come inside to see the dead bodies? Because I've got a date, and I can't wait on you forever."

Ruben. "Watching from the window again?"

"I was waiting for you. Then I got a little worried because things seemed all intense down here...*then* I got curious..."

She eased off her tiptoes. "I was merely talking to my new partner."

"Right. That's exactly what you were doing. Talking closely. Very, very closely."

She smoothed her hair back and waved her hand between the two men. "Dr. Ruben Minote, this is my partner—"

"Joel," he inserted. "Just Joel."

"Hello, Joel." Ruben's dark brows climbed. "Please, you must call me Ruben." His gaze slid over Joel. Warmed. "Hmm. All right, Chloe. I can see why you were distracted." He glanced back at her. "Probably are a little annoyed with me for interrupting, aren't you? My bad. How about I promise to buy you a Hurricane the next time we go to the Square to make up for things?"

"You the coroner?" Joel wanted to know.

"I'm the chief medical examiner," Ruben replied as he straightened. "The parish coroner is a whole political thing. I don't get involved in politics." He looked expectantly between them. Then sighed. "You should know, Agent Richardson called me a few minutes ago. He'll be coming over soon, and he expressly said for me *not* to share any data with you two. So, you know what that means..." He began strolling back toward the thick, squat building that waited. He dramatically announced, "It means I will be sharing every single bit of data that I have with you."

Chloe immediately fell into step behind him.

Joel curled his hand around her shoulder. "Is he breaking rules for you?"

She slanted a glance at Joel. "Yes."

"Why?"

"Because he likes me?" That could be the reason. Or maybe because she was usually the one who bribed him with Hurricanes. Hard to know for sure.

Joel's lips thinned. The little scar tightened. "You're involved with the ME?"

She looked heavenward. "We are going to work very, very hard on your observational skills. I promise, we will. By the time I'm done with you, you will notice everything." Not wanting to delay any longer, she slipped from beneath his hold and hurried after Ruben. Once inside the building, the scent of antiseptic and bleach hit her, making her nose scrunch. As they made their way back to the exam rooms, the temperature took a distinct dive. Ruben's white lab coat flapped around him as he pulled out the first body.

"Donnie Adams." A body bag covered him. Ruben's gloved fingers fluttered over the zipper. "Are you squeamish, Joel? If so, then you should—"

"Don't worry about that," Chloe assured him. "Joel's a doctor, too. He's not the least bit squeamish."

Ruben flashed a smile at Joel. "Another doctor. We will have to talk shop and—"

"I'm not a doctor any longer." Joel's voice was flat.

Ruben's smile lost a little wattage. His gaze sharpened on Joel.

Time for her to get things moving. "Even though he's not a practicing doctor right now, Joel is going to use his expertise to help me out a little. In other words, Joel would love to see the body. So if you could just pull that zipper down for us..." Chloe prompted.

Ruben frowned at her. "Are you going to faint on me again?"

That was insulting. "You had your hands on the woman's heart. What did you expect me to do? Clap for you? My response was normal."

He didn't appear convinced. "Perhaps you should let Joel and I handle things in here? Isn't that why you have a doctor as your partner?"

Ah, sneaky man. *One of the reasons I enjoy Ruben.*

Ruben's gaze was knowing as he said, "Because we both know that you have many, many wonderful strengths, my lovely Chloe..."

Joel stiffened.

"But when it comes to examining actual human bodies, when it comes to slicing into the skin and muscle, you tend to...You know..." Ruben rolled his gloved hand.

She knew exactly what she did. The fact that Joel was a doctor *had* been one of the reasons for her excitement over their partnership. Getting up close and personal with dead bodies wasn't her favorite thing in the entire world. They did make her...squeamish.

She knew why. Didn't feel like discussing it with anyone.

"I need to see his hands." She sniffed. The antiseptic smell seemed extra strong today. "Then the two of you can go over everything else."

Ruben didn't appear reassured by her response. "Okay. Joel, get close in case you have to catch Chloe. I wasn't quick enough last time, and she slammed straight into the tile."

Joel shuffled closer.

Ruben appeared to be enjoying this situation entirely too much. "I'm not going to faint. If you don't shove your hands into his chest, we'll all be fine."

The zipper slid down with a hiss.

Donnie's face seemed stained with bruises. Purple and dark blue spots stood out in stark contrast on his chalky skin.

Ruben rooted around in the body bag and pulled up... "Here you go. Right hand."

She leaned closer. Tried not to inhale. "Show me the left."

He shoved the right hand back into the bag. Pulled up the left.

Her gaze darted to Donnie's face once more. *Nope, nope. Stop it.* She dragged her gaze off his face and—

"That's a tan line," Chloe said.

Ruben pulled Donnie's rather pudgy fingers toward his eyes. "Sure is. Guy must've had a ring here. A pretty big one."

"A championship ring." She nodded. "Glory days. You keep what matters close."

Ruben lowered the hand. "Did you just solve something again?"

"No, I just confirmed something. Solving will take time." Her stomach was knotting. She'd noticed the Y incision on Donnie's exposed chest. *Oh, God.* "I'll be waiting at your desk. I have some phone calls to make so..." She spun. Almost slammed into Joel. "Oh, you are close."

"He told me to move close enough to catch you, remember?"

"I don't need catching." The knots were worse. A glass of water might be good. Deep breathing would be good. Getting out of that exam room would be good. "Come find me when you're done." Then she practically ran away.

The door swung shut behind her.

In the hallway, her eyes squeezed closed. The past tried to shove its way through her mind. The bodies...

No. She dug her nails into her palms. *I'm not losing control.* Chloe tried Cedric's technique of counting to ten. He swore that method always calmed him down. And then...

"Chloe, are you okay?"

Joel's voice. Joel had followed her out and she hadn't even heard him. Her eyes immediately opened. "I'm fine."

"You don't sound fine. And you turned very pale before you walked out." Now she could hear his steps shuffling toward her. She should have heard them before. She'd been too distracted. That couldn't happen again.

He paused behind her. She could *feel* him.

"Want to talk about it?" Joel asked.

"Talking about it is the last thing I want to do." Her spine was as stiff as she could make it. She took a determined step forward—

He caught her shoulder. Swung her around to face him. "So it's okay for you to know every single secret I possess. For you to poke and prod at all my dark places, but I don't get to know anything about you?" He bent close to her. "You share nothing with me?"

Her breath froze in her lungs. "I don't share with anyone."

His gaze searched hers. "You do now."

"Joel—"

"So...yes..." Ruben cleared his throat. Of course, he'd come to the hallway, too. "Perhaps you both missed it before when I said Richardson was coming over. I'm sure Cedric is being his usual amazing self and trying to stall the guy, but Cedric has other things to do, too. You know, detective work and all. It would be very beneficial if you and your partner focused on the matter at hand and saved the hot, intense times for later, yes?"

"This isn't a hot, intense time," Chloe responded even though she couldn't break eye contact with Joel.

"Sure appears like it is to me," Ruben threw right back.

She kept staring at Joel. "You need to go look at the body."

"Because you can't?" Joel asked. "Because that's your one weakness and something you need me for?"

"Because you're the one with the medical degree. Because I know killers. I don't know human anatomy nearly as well as you should. But if you insist on me doing this part..." She retreated a little from him and the warmth that seemed to surround him. "I'll go back in there and I'll take care of things."

"For the love of God," Ruben gasped from his position near the door, "don't let her take care of things!"

Joel shook his head. "I have this."

"Wonderful." She nodded, as if everything had been settled. "As I said before, I'll wait for you—"

"No."

"No?" Her voice rose.

"It's not wonderful. It's not even a fair exchange. Consider this a warning, Chloe. I will find out your secrets."

Laughter slipped from her. Her hand rose and lightly patted his cheek. "That is adorable." Now she pushed up close to him and brought her mouth near his ear. "Lots of people have tried. No one ever really does." She started to ease back—

His fingers circled her wrist. "I'm not other people."

True.

His finger slid along her racing pulse. "And I will find out your secrets."

She tugged her wrist free. Kept her spine straight and walked away. With every step, Chloe tried to ignore the fact that his words had sounded like a threat.

CHAPTER NINE

Ruben fanned his hand near Joel's face.

Why the hell was the man doing that?

"Hot, isn't it?" Ruben nodded. "Lots of tension there. Lots and lots."

"Screw off." He shoved open the exam room door.

"That seems like the response you'd give. You do have that whole I'm-intense-and-dangerous vibe going on. It also does seem to mesh with the type of man that Chloe usually attracts."

"You do not know me well enough for this conversation."

"True." Ruben did an about-face and headed for the exam table. "Opened up the bag a bit more while you were trying not to kiss Chloe."

"I wasn't—"

"You can see the body a lot better now. Is there something in particular that you're looking for?"

He had no freaking clue what he was looking for. "I'll know it when I see it."

Ruben laughed.

Joel frowned at him.

"Oh." Ruben pursed his lips. "You were serious. That's...um, not funny. Not a joke. I see."

"Shouldn't you have an assistant? Other staff members?"

"There are other staff members. They've gone for the day. It's Friday, you know. Some people like to head out early and enjoy the weekend." Voice lower, he said, "Some people...people like *me*, but, no, instead of being out there living my best life, here I am, being a good friend to Chloe. And hanging with the dead."

Joel reached for the file that rested near the exam table. He thumbed through the notes.

"So...what kind of doctor are you?"

Joel glanced up.

"Were you," Ruben corrected. "What kind of doctor *were* you?"

"A surgeon."

"Ohhh...Someone must be good with his hands." Ruben smirked.

Joel's gaze flickered to his own hands. He was gripping the file, but for just a moment he could almost see—

The handle of a shovel. His hands tight around it—

"Shit," he snapped and slammed down the file. This was not good.

"You think my work is shit?" Now Ruben's voice was tight. All signs of amusement were gone from his face. "You're wrong. I am the best medical examiner in the parish. If I wasn't, do you think for one moment that Chloe would trust me? She sizes people up within five minutes of meeting them. She knows if you've got a drug addiction. A sex addiction. She knows if you cheat on your significant other or on taxes. She knows—"

Joel held up one hand. "You like to talk a lot, don't you, Ruben?"

"I work with the dead. When new living people come by to visit, I get chatty. Sue me."

Joel went back to scanning the file. "He suffered severe spinal cord injuries."

"What kind of surgeon were you?" Ruben pushed.

He kept scanning. "Blunt trauma."

"You were a blunt trauma surgeon? Can't say I even knew one of those existed. Seems like a new specialty—" He broke off when Joel glanced up at him. "Right. Not funny. You're not the joking type. Got it." He coughed. "The blunt trauma the vic suffered was probably from a baseball bat. I'll turn the body over, and you can take a look at the marks yourself. Though there are plenty of pictures in the files."

He was looking at the pictures right then. "The injuries were centered in the upper spine, near the high cervical nerves?"

"Right. C1 to C8 took a battering. The worst of it was C1 to C4."

Jesus. Based on what he was reading... "Paralysis."

"Yes. If Mr. Adams had somehow survived the attack, he would have been paralyzed. Arms, hands, trunk, and legs. Based on the severity of his injuries, he would not have been able to control his own bowel or bladder movements."

"He wouldn't have even been able to breathe on his own," Joel said, voice roughening. He slapped the file back down on the tray. Quickly pulled on gloves before he reached for Donnie's left hand.

"What do you think happened to the ring?" Ruben leaned over the body. "Think the killer took it? I bet that's what Chloe suspects. A souvenir."

"You didn't recover any tissue beneath the nails."

"There was only dirt and grime beneath the victim's nails. No DNA."

Joel looked at the left arm. Then the right. "There are no defensive signs here. A guy this big, and he didn't fight back? No. No, I don't buy that." He studied the bruises on the body. Scanned the notes again. "You note a skull fracture."

"I am thorough." Ruben stiffened. "I don't tend to miss much. Again, there's a reason Chloe works with me and not with one of the other medical examiners."

"He was hit in the head first. A hard swipe to the back of the skull. It made him fall down, face first. His hands probably scraped across the dirty alley, and that's the stuff you found under his nails. He didn't get a chance to get up because the attacker then drove the bat into his back, over and over again." The bruises certainly appeared to have been caused by a baseball bat—or something like it. "The damage to his spine would have been severe and fast." He put down the file. Studied the bruises on the guy's face. "He flipped you over," Joel said, finding himself now talking to the dead man. "You couldn't roll yourself. You were helpless, and he hit you and hit you until you were dead."

Silence.

Uncomfortable. Long silence. Joel swallowed. He could feel Ruben's gaze on him.

"Chloe is the only other person I've seen who talks to the dead that way."

His stare flew to Ruben.

"She teach you that?" Ruben wanted to know.

"I want to see another body."

"Well, that's too bad because I don't have the other bodies here. They've already been buried. But I can certainly show you my files." He pointed at Joel. "Though if we are going to be working together in the future, you should know that courtesy goes a very long way with me."

"What in the hell does that mean?"

"Please. Thank you. I'm sorry. They are magic words."

"Are you shitting me?"

"Do I look like I'm shitting you?"

No. It didn't. And Joel even felt like he'd been an extra asshole. *Apologize.* "I'm sorry."

"Beautiful, magic words. Don't they feel good when you say them?"

No, they felt rusty and weird. "I don't...have good people skills."

"Yes. I noticed. Chloe shares that fault with you. Again, you and Chloe are just seeming like the perfect pair." Humming a little, Ruben strolled toward a large filing cabinet. "I have records over here. Give me a second." He'd ditched his gloves.

Joel did the same. "How long have you known Chloe?"

Ruben pulled open one of the drawers. It screeched. "Since she moved to the area."

That wasn't a clear answer.

Ruben kept humming faintly even as he strummed his fingers over the files. When Ruben didn't speak again, Joel pushed, "You're not going to tell me more?"

Ruben glanced up. "Do you want to know more?"

Fuck. "*Please,*" he gritted. The guy obviously loved those magic words.

"That sounded painful." Ruben scooped up two files. "Grating. I mean, sexy, in a Vin Diesel kind of rough and deep way, but maybe if you use that particular word with Chloe in the future, you could try to make it sound a bit softer."

"Why the hell would I use that word with Chloe?"

"I could not imagine." Ruben was back in front of him. Blinking all innocently. "Maybe when you ask her to *please* go to bed with you?"

He snatched the files. "That shit won't happen."

"Because you're not interested in Chloe."

"Because I'm working with her on a murder investigation, not trying to get her in bed."

"Like you can't multitask. You were a *surgeon.*"

He tuned Ruben out—tried to, anyway—and read through the file on Ray Malone. "You don't mention any skull fractures or contusions."

"That's because there weren't any."

"Ray Malone's blood alcohol level was sky high."

"Guess Ray never learned a lesson about drinking to excess. Even though he killed his wife when he got behind the wheel."

"If he was as drunk as this tox report says, then when the killer came for him, he wouldn't have been able to put up much of a fight."

"No, he wouldn't have. I don't even know that he was conscious when the blows occurred. No sign of defensive wounds on him, either."

"But he suffered the same rough pattern of injuries on the C1 to the C4 area of his spine."

"He did. Oh, and here is something fun. There wasn't enough blood spatter in the car to match his wounds. Cedric noticed that. I think the killer did most of the attack outside the vehicle, then he staged the body in the car."

Joel absorbed that info. He flipped open Gregory Guidry's file. "Broken jaw. Heavy facial injuries."

"Yes, he was the vic who sustained the worst injuries. No skull contusion, but—"

"He was found right inside the doorway of his house. He answered the door." Joel tried to picture the scene. "Guidry opened the door, a bat swung at him, hit him in the face, and he went down."

"Carpet fibers were discovered beneath his fingernails. If you look at the crime scene photo, it would appear he tried to crawl away from the attacker."

"Until the attacker started pounding on his back." Same freaking injury pattern. "Always at the top. C1 to C4. The bastard knows what he wants to hit. He knows why he wants to do it." The attacker wanted his victims absolutely helpless before he killed them. Damn. Joel handed the files back to Ruben. Started to walk away. Stopped. "Thank you."

Ruben beamed at him. "Was that so hard?"

"Did Chloe read all of your files?"

"Yes."

"And what did she say?"

"She's the one who told me the weapon was probably a bat."

Joel was betting Chloe knew a whole lot more than just what type of weapon had been used. "Why do you think she wanted me in here?"

"Because Chloe doesn't like dead bodies."

He thought it was more than that.

Ruben threw a quick glance at Joel. "Oh, I have to ask, have you been to the Mob Murder House yet?"

"Excuse me?"

Ruben wiggled his brows. "Chloe's place. Or...the place that her last boyfriend gave her. Whatever."

Whatever?

"That big-ass mansion near Audubon Park? You know the history of it, don't you?"

"I have no idea about the place's history." He'd just hauled his stuff there and hadn't even unpacked.

"Been owned by an infamous mob family since the early 1900s. But the last owner...word is that he just *gave* it to Chloe. They had some kind of relationship. Lasted a while. And as a thank you..." He wiggled his brows yet again. Made them practically dance. "The dude gave her the entire house. Do you know how much a place like that has to be worth?"

Her *ex* had given her the house?

"I figure it has to be worth four million." Ruben nodded. "Give or take a few hundred grand." He pursed his lips. "For a man to give a woman a place like that as a gift, she sure has to do something special. *Ahem.* Now do you see why you might want to at least practice saying please?"

CHAPTER TEN

"Are you testing me?"

Chloe didn't jump when Joel spoke. She'd heard the creak of the floor. Her gaze remained focused outside of the window. From this vantage point, she had a perfect view of the parking lot. And Joel's motorcycle.

Cedric had called her a few moments before. Richardson was on his way over.

That meant it was time to wrap things up.

"Did you finish checking out the body?" Her fingers pressed to the glass. She liked the smooth, warm feel of it beneath her hand.

"Yes. But you didn't need me to do that, did you? I bet you already have all the facts you need."

She turned toward him.

Ruben stood just behind Joel, behind and a little to the right. *Where. Did. You. Find. Him?* Ruben mouthed.

"In a bank storage closet," she replied.

Ruben's eyes widened.

"What the hell are you talking about?" Joel demanded. "No, wait. It's just a distraction. You do that. You distract me a lot. Throw out random shit to keep me off balance."

"Don't you appreciate that? Do you truly want to get lost in your past again?"

He stalked forward. Stopped only when he was right in front of her. "I don't like feeling as if you're playing with me."

"I am not playing." She grew sick of people thinking that was all she did. Did it look as if she was a child, playing with toys? "I wanted your take on the body. Wait. That's not one hundred percent true." Chloe blew out a breath. "I wanted to know what you thought of the killer."

Joel jerked his thumb over his shoulder. "Ruben conducted very thorough exams, but you know that."

"Thanks for noticing," Ruben replied, all demure-like. The man was never truly demure. "It's good to be appreciated."

She frowned at him.

He glanced away. Chloe was pretty sure he smothered a smile.

"Ruben already knows plenty about the killer," Joel continued roughly. "So...what was this? You just wanted to make sure I still understood basic human anatomy? I wasn't going to see anything he didn't. Certainly nothing you hadn't already figured out."

"I do figure out a lot," Chloe admitted.

Ruben snorted.

Joel's eyes narrowed. "Then you *were* just—"

"Ruben..." She raised her voice. "Tell me what you think about the killer and his attacks."

"Blitz attacks," Ruben replied promptly. "A powerful initial blow, one that left the vics incapacitated, then a wild surge of hits to follow that. The bodies were covered with bruises. Broken bones. I think the FBI would call him a rage killer. Unorganized and—"

Joel gave a slight, negative jerk of his head.

What she'd been hoping to see. "You don't think there was rage involved?"

"Hell, yes, there was rage. You don't beat men to death without rage." And his head inclined toward her. Voice a whisper, carrying only to her, he breathed, "Is that why you wanted me in there? Because of my personal experience? You wanted to see if I thought the guy felt the same way that I—"

Her hand rose. Her fingers pressed to his chest. Right over his heart. "It's not about how he felt. Or how you felt. It's about the attack. Do you think it was a wild surge? Bruises and broken bones just randomly everywhere on their bodies until the vics died?"

"No."

"This scene looks..." Ruben's voice seemed overly loud. "Personal. And I do have another visitor coming, so how about you two take this to a different location? Joel has some magic words he wants to try on you and—"

"Fuck off," Joel said.

She frowned at him. "That's very rude. Ruben is someone I consider a friend. You shouldn't say—"

"Ruben, please fuck off for a moment."

Ruben laughed.

She shot a quick glance at him. Why were Joel's words funny? No, no, she didn't have time for this now. Her hand pressed a little harder to

Joel's chest as she focused on him. "Wild surge or not?" she asked, her voice clipped.

"Some of it was, sure. Once he had his victims like he wanted them, the perp went crazy. Delivered as much pain and damage as he could."

Once he had his victims like he wanted them...

"But it wasn't all wild. In fact, I'd say it was pretty damn organized. In each kill, he damaged the top of the spine, C1 to C4...the section that would lead to the most extensive paralysis. He pounded and pounded there. The bruises and the bone damage are the most severe for all vics in that area. He knew exactly what he was doing. There were no bruises or damage to the spine below the C8. Because, I think, after he had delivered what he thought was enough injury to the upper spine, when his vics couldn't move, then he flipped them over. The rest of the bruises were all on the front sides of the body. The vics couldn't fight back, and he made them watch as he beat them to death."

All of the moisture had dried in her mouth.

"Brutal and sadistic." His jaw was clenched. "But that's how some people are, right? The freaks out there. The ones who like to rip your world away and give you nothing but pain and hell. Nightmares that won't stop. You can't breathe. You can't sleep. Because even after you stop them, even after you send them to hell, the memory is still there, it's—" Joel broke off. Seemed to catch himself because he knew he'd revealed too much.

Tension stretched in the room.

"I should have fucked off," Ruben finally mumbled. "You even said please. I should have walked away. Didn't mean to get in your business...But, I mean, it *is* my office. My desk right there. My window and..." His voice trailed away.

"In your professional opinion, did the killer knowingly target that particular area of the spine on all the vics?" Chloe asked Joel as she tried to get him to leave the shadows of his past and come back to her. "Was it just the swipe of a blunt instrument against the spine, or was it deliberate to—"

"It was deliberate. Deliberate and focused attacks between C1 and C4 that would result in paralysis. My belief is that the killer wanted his targets unable to fight back."

She swallowed and glanced over at Ruben. "Do you agree?"

"I...noticed the injuries to the upper spine, but I didn't realize they were so controlled. I mean, controlled considering, you know? Not until Joel started focusing so intently on them." He nodded. "Yes, I would agree. The killer knew what he was doing when he targeted the spine. It's his technique."

"His signature." She could hear the growl of an engine outside. Richardson had arrived. His car was overly loud. Probably should get a tune-up. "Feel free to share all of this information with the FBI."

"Um, you know I work for the coroner's office? You get that? It's my legal duty to share this information—any information that I have—during the course of an investigation."

"Of course, it is." She raised her brows at Joel. "Are you ready? We have other stops."

A hard nod.

"Excellent work." Chloe hurriedly advanced for the exit. "I am most—"

"You already knew all of this. I bet you knew when you first read Ruben's report. Why the hell did you go through this whole circus with me?" Joel demanded.

"Because even I can be wrong. And I wanted your opinion." She paused beside Ruben. "Thoughts?" she whispered.

He smiled at her. Leaned forward and tucked a lock of her hair behind her ear. Then he murmured, his breath brushing over the shell of her ear, "Watch yourself with him. I don't think he will play nicely."

Why was everyone so obsessed with playing? She didn't play.

"He's not the type to say please and thank you," Ruben noted softly. Then he chuckled.

She didn't get the joke, but she did get the warning. "See you on Sunday. Our usual date spot."

He nodded. "You know it."

Chloe strode briskly down the hallway. She was aware of Joel following her steps. The sooner they got away from the antiseptic and bleach and the bodies, the better she would feel. She shoved open the door and sunlight spilled onto her. Waning sunlight. She'd lost a big portion of the day to the FBI briefing and to the exam with

Ruben. She'd also slept far later than she'd intended, but her crash after the night's events had been considerable.

Richardson barreled toward her.

She gave him a friendly wave and didn't slow down. "Visiting a friend. You know how it is. Oh, wait. You don't. I don't think you have many friends."

He snarled at her.

"Watch it," Joel barked right back.

She reached the motorcycle. So did Joel. Joel towered over her. She could feel Richardson's eyes on them.

"You're gonna tell me soon why you hate him so much," Joel murmured.

She considered the matter. "I can do that." It seemed fair. Especially since Joel had shared so much with her. It wasn't as if she could tell him her real secrets, and as far her dislike of Richardson? That was certainly public knowledge.

He climbed onto the motorcycle. When she'd ridden with him before, she'd held onto him too tightly. She wouldn't make that mistake again. She'd hold herself back. There was no need to plaster her whole body against his. She could put a little space between them.

"What are you waiting for?" He offered her a helmet.

She took it. Popped it on her head. Settled in behind him.

"Your hands need to be around my waist."

She knew that. Absolutely. That hold balanced her the most, though she could always put her hands behind—

"Scared, Chloe?"

Her arms curled around his stomach. "What would I possibly fear when I'm with you?"

"You could be scared...of me."

Her head turned. She saw Richardson staring at them. No, not them. At Joel. His head was cocked, his eyes narrowed, his face tense.

"I'm not scared of you," she told Joel. "You were hired to keep me safe, weren't you?"

"And here I thought you just wanted me for my brain." He revved the motorcycle's engine.

"That, too."

"Where are we going this time?"

"Back to the strip club." She needed to see that alley before all the light was gone.

He laughed.

Richardson's frown grew worse.

"How did I know you were going to say that place?" Joel asked.

Because you're thinking like my partner.

He shot them away from the curb. She could still feel Richardson's eyes. And she didn't like the way he was watching Joel.

***

"Why the hell did you talk to Chloe Hastings?"

"Well, hello, Agent Richardson. Great to see you again. I'm good. Thanks so much for asking. Had a bit of a sinus infection earlier this week but—"

"Chloe."

"I talk to Chloe all the time. She's one of my closest friends."

"Chloe Hastings has no friends. She only has people that she uses to suit her own purposes."

"Um. I guess we can agree to disagree." He motioned toward the dead body. "Want to examine him? Or go through the other patient files? Or maybe you just want me to cut to the chase and tell you what Chloe and Joel figured out before they left? Would that help? You know, your usual routine. The one where you use the data that Chloe collects in order to make yourself look good."

Richardson's eyes became slits. "Why did she bring Dr. Landry here with her?"

Ruben rolled one shoulder in a shrug. "Because they're dating? Because the guy is hot? I don't know. Ask her."

"Did *he* look at the body?"

"Yes. A *doctor* looked at the body."

"You're compromising evidence chains. You're exposing—"

Ruben put up a hand. "Slow your roll. The police chief called and told me to cooperate with Chloe. I stayed in the exam room the entire time. Nothing was compromised, I assure you. Now, do you have questions about the vics or not?"

He snatched up the files.

"Signature," Ruben said.

Richardson's gaze shot to his.

"I'll, um, need your signature on some paperwork before you leave."

"Smartass...That's not what you meant." His jaw locked as Richardson gritted, "What did Chloe say about the killer's signature?"

"He paralyzes his victims. Focuses on the upper portion of the spine. It's only after he's completed the injuries to that portion of the anatomy that the killer goes on to—"

"Did *she* figure that out? Or was it Landry?"

There was a distinct edge to Richardson's voice. "Does it matter? They are a team."

"Who noticed the signature first?"

"I...Landry. But you know Chloe. She probably had already figured—"

"I know Chloe." A grim nod. "I know she likes to screw around with killers. One of these days, she's going to regret that tendency. You lie down with killers, you get more than blood on your hands." He stormed for the door.

"Uh...what else do you get?" Ruben called. "I mean, when you, ah, lie down with killers if you get *more* than blood on you, what else is it that you—"

"You get fucked!" The exam room door swung closed behind him.

"Always great talking with you." Ruben exhaled and the tension slid from his shoulders. "Super enlightening. Fascinating talks that we have. Please, come back again soon. Or, you know, never. Never come back. That would be awesome, too."

CHAPTER ELEVEN

"Are you sleeping with Ruben?"

Chloe didn't look up at Joel's question. She kept her head down, her dark hair falling forward to hide her face, as she poked around the alley. "No."

"Why not?" Ruben had sure implied that they were very, very close.

"You need to be more observant."

"So you keep telling me." Sweat trickled down his back.

"I'm not his type."

"You're every guy's fucking type."

She ceased poking at the ground. Her head tilted back, sending her hair sliding over her shoulders. Her bright gaze darted to him. "Did you just give me a compliment?"

"I mean...don't get me wrong, you have these very, very disturbing moments...like when you're in a bank and you're taunting robbers..." He found himself edging closer to her. *Like a moth to a flame.* What. The. Hell? He caught himself. Stopped. "But you know you're beautiful."

"Beauty is subjective. What one person thinks is a treasure, another thinks is trash."

"You're not trash," he growled.

She waved her hand around the alley, and a faint smile tugged at her lips. "I just like digging in it."

He shook his head. She wasn't going to tell him about Ruben. He got it. The woman could lock down or evade like a master.

But he wasn't giving up. "Richardson."

She went back to examining an area near the dumpster. "I'm definitely not sleeping with him. He's not *my* type."

"Good to damn well know." A surge of anger had slipped through him. Chloe and Richardson? That image had blasted into his head and he'd like to never imagine it again. "I meant, though, why do you hate him?"

"Because of his incompetence, two women died in Florida. I kept telling him that he was incorrect in his assumptions. Over and over again. He wouldn't listen to me. I wanted him to send out a warning. I knew the killer would attack again. Richardson had this whole theory about a cooling off period. Said the perp wasn't going to deviate from the pattern."

"He was wrong."

"Richardson was angling for a big promotion. The man had his face on every news channel. He wanted to be seen as the next big expert on serial killers. He had his eyes on behavioral analysis stardom." Her lips curled down. "But he overlooked important details. People died. Instead of learning from that mistake, he appears to have merely doubled down on his ignorance."

"Doubled down?" His eyebrows climbed. But then he became distracted by the fact that Chloe was leaning onto her tiptoes and trying to peer into the large, green and incredibly disgusting dumpster near her. "You're not planning on climbing in there, are you?"

"I'm just taking a look." She put a foot on the side of the dumpster. Grabbed the top. Heaved herself up.

He locked his arms around her waist. "Crawling inside a dumpster is not a good idea." Words that he never, ever thought he'd have to say to a woman.

"I wasn't crawling inside. I was taking a look. By the way, you're very strong."

His fingers were holding her a little too tightly. He needed to put her down—

"No, no, you're moving me the wrong way," Chloe chided. "Instead of putting me down, can you lift me up?"

"Are you serious right now?"

Her fingers brushed over his. "You're not even straining. Impressive. Lift me up a bit more, will you?"

Grudgingly, he obliged. "Tell me that you don't dumpster dive for fun on the weekend."

"I have dived into a dumpster before, but I assure you, the situation called for the action. It wasn't merely for fun."

He gaped at her. But she was focused on the dumpster not him, so she missed his expression. Probably for the best.

"You can lower me."

He let her feet touch the ground. His fingers...lingered. "What were you hoping to find? Let me guess, was it the murder weapon?"

She turned toward him. "Of course not." A quick smile. "Besides, Cedric was in charge of the crime scene. I know he had the dumpster searched *before* it was emptied yesterday. I just wanted a visual. Trying to see if there was an easy way *out* of the dumpster."

"A way out?" When she'd turned, his fingers had loosened their hold. But they were still around her waist.

"Um. Yes. I'm working out semantics. Trying to figure out where everyone was. And, well, it would have been helpful if perhaps the cops *had* overlooked a small clue or two somewhere around this scene. Not like a bat. Hard to overlook that. But a ring? Much easier to miss." A pause. "May I ask you a question now?"

"Fire away."

"Why are you still holding me?"

His fingers flexed. "I have no idea."

The strip club's back door swung open. There was a startled gasp. Then... "Wh-what are you two doing here?"

There was no surprise on Chloe's face. Her pupils didn't flare and she didn't give any jerk of surprise or anything like that. Come to think of it, she was never surprised anytime they got interrupted. He was starting to think she might be psychic or something.

Smooth as could be, Chloe said, "Cinnamon, I was hoping we could talk again."

With those words, Joel got the sudden impression that Chloe had just been biding her time out back while she waited for Cinnamon to appear.

"I want you to stay away from me!" Cinnamon began to back away. She grabbed for the door. Started to swing it closed.

But Chloe caught the edge of the door. "Wait! Don't go back inside, not—" Then she stopped and frowned at the side of the door. Squinted.

Cinnamon jerked harder. She was obviously stronger than Chloe and that door would be smashing Chloe's delicate fingers in the next few seconds—*shit*.

She's not getting hurt on my watch.

He grabbed the door. Curled his fingers around the edge. "Just give us two minutes, would you?"

Cinnamon glared at him.

"Please," he gritted out.

She licked her lips. "Fine."

Well, hell. Ruben had been right. Certain words could be magic.

"Two minutes," Cinnamon continued grudgingly, "and then that's it. You leave me the hell alone." She stopped trying to jerk the door closed.

Joel released his hold, too.

Chloe kept squinting at the side of the wood. "I'm pretty sure this is blood spatter."

He craned his head to see. "How can you tell? It just looks like grime to me."

"The angle," Chloe explained. "If you look here at the drops—"

"Your two minutes are ticking down," Cinnamon huffed. "I came out here to toss away the trash and not to waste any time with you."

Chloe gave a hard nod. "Fine. Let's cut straight to the chase. Where is Donnie's ring?"

Cinnamon's gaze whipped away from hers. "His what?"

"The championship ring that Donnie wore. It's missing. Where is it?" Chloe asked patiently.

Cinnamon's cheeks flushed. "You think I stole it?"

"I never said you stole it. I just asked where it was."

"How the hell would I know?" Cinnamon stepped back.

"Because you do. Because Donnie told everyone that you were his girl. Because even though you hated him, he...had an attachment to you."

"Sonofabitch wouldn't let me go." Pain and rage tore in Cinnamon's words.

"I'm sorry," Chloe's voice was softer. "I think knowing the location of the ring might help us to find his killer."

Cinnamon's eyelids flickered. "Oh. Is that what you think?" She rocked back onto her heels. "You know, I do remember now. He used it to pay a debt in a card game recently. Donnie liked to play his cards. Pity he lost more than he won."

A card game? "Where was the game? At one of the casinos?" Joel figured that had to be the—

"Nah. He got barred from them long ago. It was an off-the-books game. Invite only. Donnie knew someone who got him in a few times. But...come to think of it..." A nod. "He lost heavily during his last run. Very heavily. That's why he was so mad." Her fingers fluttered near the bruises on her neck. Bruises she hadn't yet covered with makeup. "He wanted that ring back. Said it meant something to him. I bet he was gonna try and get it back."

Joel figured they needed to talk to the man who ran the card game. "Where's the game?"

"At the Serpent."

He had zero clue what the hell that was. Chloe nodded, though. Like it was a thing she completely understood.

"But you got to know someone to get in," Cinnamon rushed to add. "Not like just anyone from the street can head in for a game."

"Don't worry. I know someone." Chloe smiled at her. "Thank you."

Cinnamon whirled away.

"What color were his eyes?" Chloe inquired quietly.

Cinnamon stiffened. "What are you talking about?"

"The man in the ski mask. What color were his eyes?"

Cinnamon turned back toward her. "I didn't see his eyes."

"But there *were* eye holes in the mask?"

"I don't know. I was too busy looking at Donnie's body to pay attention!" Her voice broke. "Your two minutes are up. Leave me alone. I mean it. Stay away." This time, she grabbed once more for the door handle, obviously intending to shut them out. And probably then *lock* them out.

"What about the baseball bat?" Joel heard himself ask.

A tremble worked over Cinnamon's body.

"Did you get a good look at that?" he pushed.

"I didn't get a good look at anything." She wrenched the door shut.

He exhaled and tried to ignore the fact that the alley smelled way too much like piss. "She's lying."

"Yes. She didn't have a garbage bag with her. She wasn't coming out to dispose of the trash."

"No, no, I mean...she saw the baseball bat."

"Well, certainly she did." But Chloe didn't look at him. She was peering at the wall near the door. "More flecks. There's so much crap out here that I bet the crime scene techs didn't notice it all."

"Why did she lie about the baseball bat?"

"Because she doesn't want us to know what she saw. She's scared. Scared people lie." Said very matter-of-factly.

"Don't you want her to tell us the truth?"

"She did. Partly. We'll go to the Serpent and learn more."

"What in the hell is the Serpent?" And how did Chloe know about the place?

"When the door opened, I had to stand right...here." She waved her hand. "And if you were to hit me from behind, the blood spatter from my head wound—if I were about seven inches taller, you know, Donnie's height—the spatter would fly so that a portion of it hit the side of the door. The side, and the interior section. The interior was cleaned. The side wasn't. That's why I could still see some drops. When the door is shut, you forget to clean the side." A brisk nod. "I'll have to make sure Cedric knows this."

"Wait." He curled his hand around her shoulder.

She shivered.

It was sweltering out there. She *couldn't* be cold.

Her head turned toward him. Her gaze seemed very, very intent.

"Chloe?"

"The blood spatter indicates the door was open. But Cinnamon told us she peeked out *after* she heard the screams. Her story isn't matching with the evidence." A sigh. "She's not just lying to us. She'd hiding something very big."

"Why?"

"Probably because she's terrified. We'll find a way to make her talk, don't worry. Meanwhile, Cedric can work his magic here." Her gaze darted to his hand. "Do you know that you're still touching me?"

"Do *you* know that you shiver when I touch you?"

"Yes, I do. It's because I feel like an electric current travels through my whole body when you put your hand on me. Very unsettling."

What. The. Actual. F—

"It won't distract me, though. Don't worry about that."

"I was not even a little bit worried about that." Damn. They were in a stinking alley, and he was thinking about tugging her closer. Seeing if he could turn her shiver into something much, much more. "The Serpent."

She pulled away from him. Sent off a text on her phone. No doubt to Cedric. Then she walked toward the mouth of the alley with her head down.

"Are you going to tell me what the Serpent is?" Joel demanded as he trailed behind her. "Or do I just get to guess?"

"It's a club. With a special room reserved for VIPs." She frowned down at the phone and paused before exiting the alley. "Cedric will have a team here within the hour."

"That's great news." He moved to her side. "How will you get us in the VIP room?"

"I know the owner of the club."

"How?"

She stepped forward.

He reached out and circled his hand around her arm. *Will she shiver a second—*

"He owes me a favor. He's the kind of man who pays his debts. He'll see us. Don't worry about that."

Now he had to wonder just what sort of favor she'd done for the guy.

"The club won't be letting visitors in tonight, though, so you can consider yourself off for the rest of the evening." She strolled toward the motorcycle as if she didn't have a care in the world. But then she paused. Frowned.

He realized that something was on the seat of the bike. He hurried forward and saw— "What in the hell is that?"

"A tarot card."

"It's a freaking devil." A weird-looking guy with horns and the big, clear words...*The Devil* written in heavy font across the bottom of the card. Joel's head whipped up. He glanced to the left. To the right. There was no one close by. No stranger milling in the area and eyeing his bike.

"Someone is sending us a message," Chloe said as she picked up the card.

"What the hell are you doing?"

She arched one delicate eyebrow.

"That could have prints on it!"

Her lips curled. "You've been watching a lot of *CSI*. Like crime shows, hmm?"

When he'd been in his dump of an apartment, he'd watched too much TV...that was, when he hadn't been out, running on the streets again and again. "Prints," he pointed out to her. But she should not need the reminder. "Cedric can—"

"It's a card that was left on a motorcycle. Cedric isn't going to care about it. And I can guarantee you that Richardson won't think it's related to the case."

"*Is* it related to the case?" He figured it had to be, seeing as how it had been placed on his bike while they were checking out the crime scene.

"No. It's a warning, but I don't think it came from the killer we're after."

She didn't *think* it had? "What kind of warning?"

Chloe slid the card into the motorcycle's saddlebag. "What do you know about tarot cards?"

"Absolutely nothing." What was he supposed to know?

She eased onto the bike. "Would you like for me to drive this time? I think you'll be most impressed by my skills—"

"I'll drive." He straddled the bike. He was pretty sure her skills would terrify him. But before he got the motorcycle moving, Joel wanted to know, "What does the devil card mean?" Because he was sure she knew. The woman seemed to have random knowledge about everything.

"Many things." Her arms slid around him. "Bondage. Enslavement." A pause. "Fear. It refers to feeling trapped..."

Sonofabitch. Ever since his attack, Joel's greatest fear was being trapped. Locked up. *Buried alive.* "That message is for me. Not you."

"That was my original thought. But you don't have enemies in this town, do you, Joel?" Her voice was soft. Careful. "You only arrived here six months ago."

It figured that she'd know when he arrived. "I came back six months ago," he corrected. "I lived here a long, long time ago." Another life. "And, no, I don't have enemies."

"Not that you know about." Her hold tightened on him. "Here's the thing. We can all have enemies. Even if you haven't done anything to stir up rage, sometimes, an enemy can be out there. Some of the most dangerous people hide how they really feel about us. They act like they are our friends. They aren't."

He didn't like just sitting there in the open. Last night, Chloe had almost been run down on that street. And now—the creepy card.

The jackass who'd left the card could still be close by.

Someone wanted me to know...some bastard is out there and he understands what I fear.

Joel hurtled away from the curb on the motorcycle and twisted and turned through the streets of New Orleans. The motorcycle growled and vibrated beneath him. Chloe's body pressed tightly against his. He could feel her. Was hyperaware of every single thing about her. That was becoming a problem for him. The longer he was with her, the more he reacted. The *stronger* his reaction.

He drove through the gates of her home, then brought the bike to a stop near the guest house. The engine idled a moment before he killed it and kicked down the stand.

Chloe didn't immediately release her hold on him. "There's another meaning to the card."

He looked over his shoulder at her. She still wore her helmet. Looked gorgeous because she always did.

He held her gaze. Waited.

Chloe slowly pulled away. She handed him the helmet and climbed from the bike.

He sat there, watching her. "You can't leave me in suspense."

She stilled.

"What's the other meaning?"

Chloe bit her lower lip. "The card is also about seduction."

"That freaky goat guy on the card is about seduction?"

"The devil is always about seduction. Physical pleasure. The card isn't necessarily a dark warning. It can just be a message of what's coming."

He should get off the motorcycle. "Physical pleasure. Someone wanted us to know that physical pleasure was waiting for us?"

"Don't you like that meaning better?" Chloe asked as she swung away. "I do. It's much better than thinking that someone just threatened us with bondage and enslavement."

He watched her as she headed for the main house. Joel considered the situation. Yeah, if he had to pick, he'd choose physical pleasure over being trapped and locked away any day of the week.

Been there, done that. And he had the scars to prove it.

CHAPTER TWELVE

There was a sharp knock on his door. Joel frowned at his computer screen. He'd been doing research and time had gotten away from him. He realized now that it was nearing midnight. And who the hell would be coming to see him at midnight?

Only one person came to mind.

Chloe.

Joel shot out of his chair and stalked for the door.

More knocking. A little more demanding this time.

"I'm coming. Hold on, just—" Joel yanked open the door.

Not Chloe.

A glaring Marie stood on the threshold. She was holding a big, black, zippered garment bag. "This is for you." She thrust it toward him.

"Thanks?" Yes, he knew his response sounded like a question.

"Clothes for tomorrow night. Chloe said you needed them. Whatever you're doing with her, she wants you to dress the part."

"Uh, yeah, I do have clothes of my own."

"Not like those." She crossed her arms over her chest. Glared more.

He lifted his brows. "Is there a reason you seem to dislike me?" Because her disdain was more than apparent. "I can't remember pissing you off, but if there's something I've done—"

"You're not tough enough."

Laughter spilled out. "You have no idea."

"You killed one person. Big deal. Like that makes you some kind of stud."

"Excuse me?" He must have misheard. It was late. He was tired.

"Chloe helped me. She pulled me out of the darkest time of my life."

And she came into my life when I didn't think anything could get darker. When he'd thought there was nothing else to lose.

Marie surged toward him. "Do you have any idea how many enemies she has?"

He blinked.

"How many people would like to see her vanish? And she gets *you* for protection? Day one, and all you want to do is get in her pants."

Yes, dammit, guilty. He did want to get in her pants. But that was his business. His and Chloe's. "Okay, you need to back off—"

"*You* need to stay on guard," she ordered as if he hadn't spoken. "Everyone you meet has a secret agenda. People who pretend to be nice? They are the worst ones. Look deeper. See the truth. Maybe you'll last longer than her last wanna-be partner did." A hard nod.

"What in the hell happened to her last partner?"

But Marie clamped her lips together.

Oh, now she stopped talking.

He lifted the garment bag. "Thanks for this."

"Whatever." She spun on her heel.

"Where's Chloe?"

"Think she's on a date." She didn't glance back. "Don't expect her back anytime soon."

A date? "Chloe goes on dates?" Was that jealousy slipping its way through him?

"Sure, she does. You got a problem with that?"

Maybe I do. Only there was no *maybe* about it.

But Marie wasn't sticking around to tell him anything else. He stood there, holding the garment bag, and feeling a knot of tension swirling in his gut. *Chloe was on a date.*

He shut the door. Dropped the garment bag without glancing inside it. Then went back to his seat in front of the laptop. He'd been digging up information on Chloe for most of the night. He'd found references to her in dozens of criminal investigations.

It wasn't her crime solving that interested him the most, though. Chloe knew his secrets. He figured it was only fair for him to learn hers.

So he had to go back deeper and deeper. He thought that he'd finally hit pay dirt.

Heartbreak in London. The Hastings' Murders Horrify City.

The headlines had him leaning forward even more.

The picture of Chloe—a young, thirteen-year-old Chloe—made his throat tighten. Her parents had been murdered by a masked intruder at their estate. The intruder had broken in during the middle of the night. He'd killed them, but Chloe had been unharmed.

She'd found their bodies when she woke the next morning.

The reporter said that Chloe had tried to revive them. Their blood had covered her night gown. Soaked her skin.

The mysterious killer had never been found.

Never been brought to justice.

But...just one year after her parents had died, there was another headline...

Hastings' heir returns. What? He shook his head. Tapped on the keyboard. The reports were from some old paper in England. The website was shit, and half of the articles were cut off because they were so old and—

Another knock at his door.

His shoulders tensed. This time, when he walked to the door, he wasn't expecting Chloe to be waiting for him. How could she be? *Chloe was on her date.* He curled his hand around the doorknob and hauled open the door. "Look, Marie, I'm not in the mood for more—"

Reese blinked at him.

"What the hell is this?" Joel demanded. "Unwanted visitor night?"

Reese held up beer. "I know how fond you Americans are of your six packs." He grinned. "After your first day of working with my sister, I thought you might want to unwind a bit."

Joel stared at the beer. Then at Reese. "All right. You can stay." He hurried back to the desk.

He needed to shut down his laptop before Reese could see—

"Researching us, are you?" Reese called out cheerfully. He didn't seem even mildly upset. "Chloe said you'd do that."

"Chloe likes to think that she knows everything that's happening. And that she knows everyone." He snapped shut the laptop. Turned around.

Reese tossed him a beer. "She usually does know everyone. Always been good at figuring out what makes people tick."

"She doesn't know me."

Reese took a beer for himself and put the others on the coffee table. He popped the top and enjoyed a very, very long pull. "You'd be surprised." He threw himself down on the couch. "But how about you tell me what you've discovered so far? I can let you know if you're going in the right direction or just reading some tabloid bullshit." Another long pull on the beer and then, "That site you were just on? That would be tabloid bullshit, in case you were wondering."

What he was wondering..."Did Chloe send you out here? She wanted to see what I was digging up on her or something?"

"Looked to me like you were digging up info on me, not her." Reese tilted his head. "And I haven't seen Chloe tonight. I think she's gone out."

"On a date," Joel growled. He popped the top on his beer. Chugged it all down and crushed the can.

"Chloe isn't dating anyone. Don't know where you got that idea."

Joel stared at the smashed can. "Marie."

Soft laughter.

He looked up.

"She was messing with you. Probably wanted to see your reaction. Marie has this idea that you're infatuated with my sister."

"Infatuated? Who uses that word?" He trashed the can. "I need another beer."

"Have at them. And I use that word. I was trying to be polite but if you'd rather…"

Joel lifted the second beer can toward his mouth…

"I could just say that Marie is convinced you want to shag my sister."

"Shag your sister." He almost choked on the drink. "That's not much better than infatuated."

"You're not denying either charge."

"I just met your sister."

"Yet you're already living here and getting possessive when you find out that she might be with another man."

"I don't get possessive." With the beer can, he pointed toward Reese. "I know what you're doing."

Reese pursed his lips. "I completely suspect that you do not."

Joel had to laugh. "God, you sounded exactly like her for a moment there."

Reese's face darkened as he drained his beer.

Joel took the seat near him. Kept a loose grip on his beer. "You're trying to distract me. But you're the one who told me that you'd let me know if I was heading in the right direction or not."

"And I will tell you. But for every question I answer, you have to answer one for me, too."

"Whatever. Sounds fair."

Reese put down his beer. "Want to go first?"

"Why weren't you in the house when Chloe's parents were killed?"

Reese's eyes widened. "No beating around with you, eh? Straight to the heart."

Joel shrugged. "Thought it was better than wasting time."

"You obviously were reading the tabloid rag about how the heir returned a year after the murders. So you already know I wasn't in the house when it happened."

Joel studied him in silence. Then... "Is that a question? Are you asking me if I already know you weren't there? Fine, let's say that *is* a question. And my answer, is...yes. I read enough to tell me that you weren't there. According to the story I was scanning before you arrived with your beer, Chloe's brother went missing when he was fourteen years old. She was five. They were walking together along the lake at their country estate. He vanished and was presumed dead."

Reese glanced at the floor. "That was the story."

"Only you turned up nine years later. Chloe was fourteen. Her grandfather—who'd been raising her in the year since her parents' deaths—had just been buried. She had no other family. You swooped in. The long-lost brother..."

"Such an informative rag you were reading. How long did it take you to stumble across this gossip? Have to say, I find myself impressed."

"It took a while," Joel allowed. He'd gotten lost at the laptop as he scanned and scanned for information. "But I'm persistent."

"Good to know."

"Her grandfather had left everything to Chloe, assuming you were long dead. So, technically, I guess you weren't the heir, after all. She was the heir to it all."

"The money was in a trust for Chloe. Her guardian would control it until she turned twenty-one."

"*You* became her guardian."

Reese was still staring at the floor. "Chloe insisted. There was...one of grandfather's friends was supposed to become her legal guardian. Chloe didn't want that. She wanted me. I wasn't going to leave her again."

"Again?" Joel locked onto that word. "Is that what happened when you were fourteen? You ran away and left Chloe behind? Because when I was reading, there were several theories about what happened to you. Some said you ran away. Spoiled, rich kid just cut out on his family. Other stories said you were kidnapped. Held for a ransom, but your parents didn't pay."

"Tabloid rags. Can't believe everything." Now he looked up. "A week after my disappearance, I was found wandering in the woods. I was a kid. Lost. No memory of what had happened to me." His hand lifted and rubbed along the back of his head. "I'd hit my head. Fallen. The people who found me had no idea who I was. You see, I'd wandered very, very far from the lake. Miles and miles. They led a quiet, sheltered life. To them, it seemed as if I'd been hurt. They thought I'd been abused, so they weren't going to turn me over to the people who'd injured me so badly."

"You mean...to your parents? To your real parents?"

"I never said my real parents abused me. I said the people who found me—they assumed I'd been abused. My memory didn't return for years. When it did come back, I went straight to Chloe."

An interesting story. One filled with so many holes. Too many to be real.

"My turn," Reese declared. "Though, I have to confess, no, I wasn't really counting the number of questions you asked me. How about we go with five? It's a good, sturdy number."

He'd gotten nothing useful out of Reese. But Joel gave a grim nod.

"Why did you accept this job?"

"Because I didn't have anything else to do."

Reese's gaze sharpened. "You're a doctor. A surgeon. Why in the world would you turn your back on a career that you worked so very hard to get?"

"A surgeon uses a scalpel to cut into the skin of his patients. I used my hands to slice them open." He could feel the darkness pushing in his mind. "The SOB who tortured me for hours sliced *me* open. Every single time I think of picking up a scalpel to use again, I think of him."

"Chloe would say..." Reese cleared his throat. "She'd say you think you *are* him."

"That isn't a question."

"No, no, just an observation." A long exhale. "I think we could use something stronger than beers."

Damn straight.

"Question three." Reese scraped his fingers over his jaw. "Why are you in New Orleans? You were living in Dallas. Had family there. Friends. A girlfriend. A—"

"My girlfriend left as soon as she caught a look at all the marks on me. I was in a hospital bed. She couldn't even meet my eyes. Just said she was sorry and ran away."

Reese cursed. "Chloe would never do something like that."

"No, I don't think she would." *Chloe wouldn't leave.* He had a hard time imaging her running from anything. "As for my friends, they didn't know what to say to me. Most of them worked in the hospital with me. They thought I blamed them because the bastard tortured me *inside* the hospital and no one came to help me."

"Did you blame them?"

"That's question four. And I don't know. Maybe." He only knew he hadn't been able to talk to them. They hadn't understood him any longer. No one had. "I was adopted when I was a kid. My biological mother lived here in New Orleans. I lived with her until she passed away." Then he'd gone into the system. Bounced around in some foster homes and gotten very lucky. The couple who'd adopted him had been willing to open their hearts to a surly, distrustful kid. They'd taken good care of him. But they were dead now, too, and after Joel's attack... "I had some good memories here. So I thought, since my life in Dallas wasn't working, I'd try new scenery."

A moment of silence as Reese seemed to absorb that explanation. He shifted a little against the couch cushions. "And are things working for you here?"

"I met your sister. You tell me. Is that something good? Or something bad?"

Reese opened his mouth, as if he'd answer, then he caught himself. More silence ticked past.

"Sorry about your parents," Joel murmured.

"And I'm sorry about what happened to you." Reese eyed the remaining beer. "There's a whiskey room in the main house. Left by the previous owner. Chloe hates whiskey, so she told me I could do whatever I wanted with it. Want to go and pop open a twenty-year Pappy with me?"

"Hell, yes."

"Excellent." Reese gave an abrupt nod and rose to his feet. "I hate drinking alone."

Joel uncurled much more slowly. "Did you know the previous owner?"

"No, he was some friend of Chloe's."

"I heard he was a mobster."

Reese laughed. "Sounds right."

That shit is not funny.

CHAPTER THIRTEEN

He was swimming.

Chloe paused along the pathway that led to the swimming pool. Technically, the pathway branched. If she went to the right, she would head to the main house. It was close to two a.m., and she was exhausted. She could slip inside and crash in the big bed that waited for her.

Or she could go to the left. She could follow the faint sounds of splashing. She could go to Joel.

She found herself turning to the left.

The pool lights glowed a dark, deep turquoise from beneath the surface, and she watched as Joel's powerful arms circled into the water again and again as he made laps around the pool. He was quite good. Quite fast.

Very focused for a man who'd been drinking whiskey.

She kicked off her high heels. Headed to the side of the pool. She slipped down until she was sitting on the edge, she hiked up her dress, and she let her feet dangle in the water.

Her head cocked as she watched him. Chloe was fairly certain that Joel wasn't wearing swim trunks. He was moving very quickly, but from what she could see—

"*Chloe.*" He'd stopped on the opposite end of the pool. His breath sawed in and out as he lifted a hand and shoved wet hair off his forehead. "How long have you been here?"

"Just a few minutes." Her feet moved lazily in the water. "You're an extremely good swimmer."

He pushed away from the wall and swam toward her. She couldn't help but tense as he approached. There was something about the way he was moving through the water and keeping his focus locked on her. He rather reminded her of a shark.

Is he coming to take a bite?

When he reached her, his hands rose and curled along the pool edge on either side of her body. She knew the water was about five feet deep in that area, so he stood easily.

"You remind me of a shark, swimming after prey." Chloe wasn't sure why she'd admitted that. But it was true.

When did I become his prey?

"Did you have fun tonight?" Joel asked her.

Fun? "Not particularly."

Water trailed down his chest. "Marie said you were on a date."

"No."

"Your brother told me you weren't dating anyone."

"I'm not." She couldn't look away from him. She'd known that Joel was strong. But, seeing him this way...the man was cut. He must exercise like a fiend.

"I'm sure there are plenty of men who would want to date you."

"That's kind of you to say, but to be honest, I tend to scare off a lot of men."

"You?"

"Yes. Remember when you first met me?" Of course, he'd remember. Their acquaintance was still new. "You couldn't wait to get away, either."

More water trickled down his chest. "That's not true. I thought you might have a death wish, but getting away wasn't what I wanted." He moved even closer to her. "Why aren't you dating anyone, Chloe?"

"Does whiskey make you ask personal questions?"

His gaze searched hers. "How do you know I had whiskey?"

"Because my brother called me. Told me you'd helped him to empty a bottle. He sounded rather drunk."

"Oh, I assure you, he *is* quite drunk."

"He swore you helped him empty the bottle, so when I heard splashing, I thought perhaps you'd fallen in as you staggered back to your place. Instead, I found you appearing all fit."

His right hand inched closer to her leg. "I didn't drink as much as your brother."

"So I'm realizing."

"Your brother talks a lot when he drinks."

"Does he now?" *Tell me something I don't know.*

"We had a deal. Each time I answered a question for him, he'd answer a question for me. Except once he got into the expensive whiskey..." One bare shoulder moved in a casual roll. More water dripped down his body.

"Let me guess." She knew how this story would end. "He stopped asking questions and just answered them for you?"

She caught the flash of Joel's smile and was reminded, once more, of a shark.

"Drinking makes Reese chatty."

"I've warned him about that trait in the past." Her heart was beating a little faster. She kept her voice steady, though, as she said, "You were getting my brother drunk so that you could ask him questions about me?"

"I was."

She tut-tutted. "That doesn't seem like a nice thing to do."

His fingers brushed against her thigh. "I don't remember saying I was a nice man."

His touch seemed to burn her. Her breath came a little faster. "Did you learn anything interesting?"

"I learned lots of interesting things."

"Like what?"

"Like when your brother drinks too much, he loses his accent."

She shoved away from the wall and sank into the pool. Chloe let her body slide into the water right in front of him. He backed up, just a bit, just enough to make room for her.

"Chloe!"

She was shorter than him, so the five feet of water came much higher on her. His hands closed around her hips and he lifted her up. Held her in the water so that her feet could kick slowly under the surface.

"What are you doing?" Joel demanded.

"You made the water look good. I thought I'd join you." *Lie.*

"You're wearing a dress."

The dress was currently floating around her. Or, at least, the bottom of the dress was. "Noted. I am wearing a dress, and I don't think you're wearing anything."

"Didn't have swim trunks. Figured it was only me out here. Why not ditch the clothes and jump in?"

Why not indeed? "You don't have to hold me. I'm a very good swimmer."

"Maybe I like holding you."

Her hands rose and curled around his broad shoulders. She knew what he was doing. Part of her was even impressed. "You think you're learning all my secrets."

"No, tonight, I think I was learning your brother's secrets. Though I have doubts about him actually being related to you."

Their wet bodies brushed. "What else did you learn?"

He didn't answer her.

She became aware of just how close they were. And when their bodies had brushed a moment before... "Oh." He was aroused. The thick, long length of his cock was unmistakable.

"You're the one who jumped in with me. Can't help the response I have. I happen to think you're sexy as hell."

Why was her breath coming so fast?

"What did I learn? Let's see..." His voice was deep. Rumbling. Sexy. "I learned that you were in a bad relationship. Reese said you've been avoiding any serious ties since then. He said that was the reason you weren't dating."

Bad didn't begin to come close to describing her last relationship.

"Scared, Chloe?" Joel breathed against her mouth. "Did you get burned before?"

"I did." He seemed to surround her. "But I'm not afraid of you."

"No, I don't think you are."

With every breath that she took, Chloe could swear that she tasted him. "What are you waiting for?"

"Chloe?"

"You don't want a relationship." With his past, she knew that was the last thing he wanted. Chloe rushed to explain, "I don't, either. But you can still kiss me. I'm not asking you to fall in love with me or anything like that. I'm merely asking—"

"You want my mouth?"

"Yes." Hadn't she just said as—

Joel pressed his lips to hers. Her mouth was open and when he kissed her, when he thrust his tongue past her lips and tasted her...

Heat. Intensity. Desire.

Her hands tightened on his shoulders. Her lips parted even more. Her tongue met his.

He kissed her harder. Deeper. A growl built in his throat.

Her legs rose and locked around his hips. The skirt of her dress caught between them, but she could still feel the hard length of his cock thrusting against her.

He wanted her. No lies. No tricks. Just need.

When she'd originally jumped in the pool, her intent had been to distract him. He'd been far too observant regarding Reese. A problem. So she'd been trying to stop his line of inquiry. But then...

Then desire had pulsed through her blood. They'd kissed. She'd wanted him. Far more than she'd expected.

Far more than I've wanted anyone else?

His fingers slid along her waist. Dropped lower and touched her thigh as he slid his hand under the fabric of her skirt. His touch was careful and rough at the same time. A combination that made no sense but was turning her on like mad.

She pushed closer to him as a moan built in her throat. He was kissing her with a raw, desperate hunger. Distant alarm bells rang in her head. With every touch of his lips and tongue, the desire she felt for him grew stronger. *Didn't count on this. Didn't plan for this.*

But she certainly wanted this. Wanted him.

Her hips arched against him. The water made it so easy to move. To rub against the length of his cock. To push her sex against him. To *ride* over his cock when she shifted her body just the slightest bit and—

Joel tore his mouth from hers.

No, don't stop. I like this too much.

But he wasn't stopping. He was moving his mouth. Putting his lips on her throat. Licking. Kissing. Lightly biting.

And his fingers...

His fingers had slid between their bodies. His fingers pressed over her panties. Pressed, then pulled, and the wet fabric tore for him.

"Joel?" Chloe gasped out his name.

His head lifted. He stared into her eyes. His face had turned savage, almost primal, with passion. "Do you want me to stop?"

She shook her head.

"Good." His fingers slid over her sex.

She bit her lip to hold back a moan. He pushed one long finger into her, working it in deep, then thrusting a second into her.

She stopped biting her lip. Her head turned—

His thumb rubbed over her clit. He rubbed and thrust his fingers into her. Worked her into a hungry frenzy.

This time, she didn't bite her lip. She bit him. Her teeth sank into his shoulder.

"Fuck, yes, you are sexy as hell." His fingers moved faster. Stroked all of her. Explored every inch of her sex as if he had a right to her.

Her heart beat faster and faster. She arched into his touch. Rode his hand. Loved the way he seemed to know exactly how to touch her. How hard. How fast. How—

"Chloe?"

Oh, God. Pleasure was erupting. Blasting through every cell of her body.

"Not fucking now, Reece," Joel growled.

His fingers are still inside me.

Her sex was squeezing him tightly as she came.

"Is...is my sister in the pool with you?" Reese's voice slurred on the question.

"Yes, she slipped and I caught her." Joel's voice was guttural. "Go back inside."

"But...Chloe—"

"You're drunk." Now Joel's voice was even rougher.

His fingers are still moving in me.

"Go inside," Joel ordered again. "You don't want to slip and fall like Chloe did. *I've got her.*"

"Night," Reese mumbled. He shuffled away.

Chloe had squeezed her eyes shut when the orgasm hit her. Her mouth was still pressed to Joel's shoulder. She lifted her head. Opened her eyes.

The blue light from the pool sent shadows dancing over his face. He looked so rough. Dangerous.

And his fingers were inside her.

"His timing was shit," Joel rumbled. His fingers began to withdraw.

An aftershock of pleasure rushed through her and her sex squeezed around him.

"Fucking hell." He heaved out a rough breath. "You need to get out of this pool and get away from me."

His fingers were gone. Her legs were wrapped around his waist. She lowered them. Let go of him and grabbed the pool wall.

Joel turned and dove for the opposite end of the pool. He swam hard. Fast.

Angrily.

Chloe pulled herself out of the pool. She heaved up and stood and realized that her knees felt shaky. The fabric of her dress had billowed in the pool, but now it clung to her far too tightly. The panties he'd torn fell onto the stone patio. She stood there, dripping, quivering, and wondering what would be happening right now if Reese hadn't appeared.

Joel was swimming laps again. Rough, fast laps. His arms slammed into the water. His legs kicked with fury. She waited until he came back to her side of the pool and asked, "Does this mean you don't want to talk about it?"

He threw out one hand and grabbed the edge of the pool wall. His head angled back. "Talk?" he gritted. "No, can't say I want to talk."

"Then what—"

"Fuck. I'd like to fuck, but I think that's off the table, isn't it?"

Why would you think that?

"Go to bed, Chloe."

She stood there. Kept dripping. A shiver swept over her.

"Or is fucking part of the job description?" His voice was even rougher.

Now her chin lifted. "That was mean."

"Yes, well, I can be a mean bastard." He shoved away from the wall. Headed for the other side of the pool.

She waited.

Dripped.

When he came back, Chloe crisply informed him, "It's not part of the job description."

He looked up at her.

"What happens between us—personally—has nothing to do with the job. I wanted you tonight. I thought you wanted me." The signs had been pretty unmistakable. "I apologize if I was wrong." With that, she scooped up her heels and her torn panties and strode for the main house.

"Chloe!"

She didn't stop even though she heard the sound of water sloshing behind her.

"Chloe, dammit, wait!"

She didn't want to wait. Her chest felt funny. An ache. *Hurt?* Joel wasn't supposed to hurt her. Nothing about this situation was supposed to hurt her.

And yet...

His hand locked around her shoulder. "Stop."

They were almost at the main house.

"You're naked," she said without looking back. "Reese is probably still up. Marie might be, too. You should go back to your place and get dressed. Or maybe just turn in for the night."

"Why aren't you looking at me?"

She pulled in a breath. Schooled her expression. And glanced back at him.

The faint glow from the nearby gas lantern provided illumination, but not, she hoped, enough light for him to see her eyes too clearly. "I'm looking at you now."

"What happened in the pool?"

You gave me a fantastic orgasm. "I think you know what happened."

"I know I felt you come against my hand. Are you going to deny that?"

Chloe shook her head.

"You think it was a mistake? You want to forget—"

She wrapped her hand around the back of his neck. Yanked him down toward her and pressed a kiss to his lips. Her mouth was open, so was his, and her tongue dipped inside. She loved the way he tasted.

And the way he made her feel?

Completely unexpected. "I don't want to forget anything," she whispered. "You're the one who told me fucking was off the table."

He flinched. "Chloe..."

"Figure out what you want. Sex has nothing to do with our partnership. It only has to do with pleasure. I don't want strings. I'm not looking for some kind of forever." She didn't believe in that. "Figure it out," she said again. "You know where I am."

With that, she let him go and moved toward the door. "And don't forget that you're naked," Chloe called over her shoulder.

She went into the main house.

Shut the door behind her.

Chloe dripped her way up the stairs.

***

Fucking hell.

Joel watched her until she vanished. Stood there freaking naked as she left him. With a hard-on that ached for her.

I could feel it when she came around my fingers.

She'd been incredible. And if her brother hadn't interrupted them...

I'd have her now.

He'd been a total ass when he threw out that bit about fucking being a part of the job description. He hadn't meant it.

He just...He hadn't intended to want her so much. To need her.

He tried to turn the doorknob, but it was locked. His hand lifted to pound—

The door opened.

"Here's a towel." Reese tossed it at him. Appeared and sounded decidedly *less* drunk. "No need for you to come in here tonight and fetch one."

Joel looped the towel over his hips. "Chloe."

"She's gone to bed. I suggest you do the same." His words only slurred a little.

"I want to talk to her."

"I don't think that's what you want. I believe you have another four-letter word in mind. Good night." Reese slammed the door shut.

The guy had been right. Talking wasn't what Joel wanted. Joel swung around. He took a step forward even as he wished that he'd kept his fool mouth shut in the pool.

Joel stopped. More like froze.

The light from the nearby lantern was falling directly on him. He noticed the marks on his arms. His chest. *The scars.* When he'd been in the pool with Chloe, he'd forgotten all about them.

The pool had been lit with lights that shined from under the water. All of his scars would have been visible. Every single horrible one.

But...

She hadn't *looked* at them. She'd held onto him fiercely. She'd locked her legs around him. She'd kissed him. She'd let him touch her, finger fuck her...

And she hadn't been repulsed. Hadn't shuddered at the sight of him.

She hadn't *cared*.

Slowly now, considering, he made his way to the guest house.

Chloe doesn't care how I look.

And...

I will have her.

CHAPTER FOURTEEN

"Don't you look dashing?" Reese lifted his brows as he made that...question? Statement? "I dare say, that suit fits you far better than it ever fit me."

With an effort, Joel kept his body relaxed as he stood in the foyer. He'd just entered the house and found Reese waiting for him. "Chloe is supposed to meet me." He'd gotten a text earlier that day with meeting—and dress—instructions from Chloe. He hadn't seen her since the previous night, and here it was...eight p.m. Sharp.

What had she done that day?

And why the hell had he felt as if he...missed her? Ridiculous.

"Ah, yes. I believe you have your big date at the Serpent tonight, yes?" Reese rocked forward. "She'll be down in a moment." He stared expectantly at Joel.

Joel stared back.

"Had the strangest dream last night," Reese finally announced.

"Did you now." Not a question. More of a...*I don't want to hear about it.*

"You were in the pool. So was my sister. She'd fallen in." His eyes went all wide. Fake innocence.

"Only instead of helping her *out* of the pool, you were taking advantage of her."

Taking advantage, huh? "I had a weird dream, too," Joel drawled.

"Do tell."

"I was drinking with this British guy only...after the third, no, fourth glass of whiskey, I swear, the man started sounding as American as, well...I am."

Reese swallowed. "Funny dream."

"Wasn't it?"

"I—"

"Joel, you're right on time." Chloe's voice sounded pleased.

His head automatically turned at her words and—

Fuck me.

He found himself hurrying toward her. She stood at the top of the staircase, and she was gorgeous. She wore a black dress that clung to every curve on her body. High heels made her arched feet look both incredibly dainty and sexy. *Screw me shoes.* He'd heard the term a time or ten before but never, ever had he wanted to screw so very—

"Is everything all right?" Her fingers trailed over the wooden bannister. "You have quite a perplexed look on your face."

Perplexed was the last thing he felt.

Her heels tapped gently down the steps. He should say something. Compliment her. Joel's mouth opened—

"You look gorgeous, love," Reese declared. "Absolutely exquisite."

"Yeah." Joel cleared his throat. "Killer."

She hesitated, ever so briefly, before continuing her journey down the stairs. She paused on the second step from the bottom, a step that put her near eye level with Joel. "Killer is exactly what I was going for, thank you so much." She sent him a brief smile. "You look dashing."

Reese laughed. "Told him the same thing."

"But it sounds different coming from her." Joel took her hand. Curled his fingers carefully around hers.

Her lips were painted a sleek red. She'd lined her eyes with black liner and put smoky shadow on her eyelids. The result was that her eyes seemed even sexier. Mysterious and enchanting, and he was not the kind of man normally to be enchanted.

She finished descending the stairs and stood at his side.

He kept his hold on her hand. "What's the plan for tonight?"

"We go in. Question the owner of the Serpent. Talk up the patrons. See what we notice."

"Simple enough plan."

"It's the people we have to watch. The reactions they make. How they respond to us." Her voice was very serious. "Everyone has secrets, but I've found that most people hate keeping those secrets. They do things to let the truth slip all the time. The trick is to just watch for those slips. To understand them."

He'd done more digging on Chloe and her secrets during the long hours of the day. But every time he thought that he'd uncovered something he could use, more questions appeared instead of answers.

"I don't think we should take the motorcycle tonight. As much as I love your ride, I feel like we'd be better served with another vehicle."

"*That means I'm driving.*" Marie's voice.

He glanced to the side and saw her standing near the entranceway. "Of course, you are." How could it be a party without Marie and her glares?

She waved a hand vaguely in the air. "I'll stay close in case there is trouble." Her eyes were on Chloe. "You need me, all you have to do is call."

"Hopefully, that won't be necessary." She looked over at Reese. "You'll be good tonight?"

"Good enough. Don't worry about me."

With a nod, Chloe pulled her fingers from Joel's grip. "Then let's get moving."

He fell into step behind her—

"Take care of my sister," Reese fired out.

Joel inclined his head. That was his job, wasn't it?

The night air was warm and heavy against them. All too soon, they were in the back of the limo and heading for their destination. Marie had the privacy screen up as she drove.

Joel waited for Chloe to speak.

She didn't.

He waited a little longer. Still nothing. Hell. "I'm an asshole."

"Are you now?" Her stare was directed out of the nearby window. She was staring at the buildings as they drove past them.

"I wanted you fucking badly, and stopping like that—I said stuff I didn't mean. I..." She wasn't looking at him. "I'm trying to apologize here."

"Is that what you're doing? Are you certain?"

"Yes."

Her head finally turned toward him. "Usually, when people apologize, they say things like, 'I'm sorry.' I didn't hear that."

"I'm sorry," he rasped.

"Your apology isn't necessary. And again, I'm not so sure that's what you're really doing."

"Then what is it that you think I'm doing?"

"Trying to figure out a way to say that you still want to sleep with me."

He leaned toward her. She smelled delicious. "I don't want to sleep with you." Faint illumination came from the soft lights in the back of the limo, so he could see her face as he flatly said, "I want to fuck you. Sleep doesn't exactly come into play in the equation."

Her tongue swiped over her lower lip. "I see."

"You think we can do it?" He wanted to touch her skin. Slide his fingers over the curve of her cheek.

"Yes, yes, I think it should be quite possible. Why wouldn't it be? Unless you have some sort of anatomical anomaly that—"

A surprised laugh burst from him.

What the hell? Did I just laugh?

Before Chloe, he hadn't laughed, not in months. But...A smile pulled at his lips. "I assure you that, anatomically, I'm more than up for the job."

Her brows climbed. "I thought so, given what I could feel last night. And what I could see."

About that... "You didn't say a word about my scars."

"Why would I?"

"They don't bother you?"

"They aren't my scars. They're yours. Why would they bother me?"

"Because they make me look like a freak. Because my body was sliced to hell and back, and I'm covered in white ridges that will never go away."

Her hand lifted. Her fingers touched his mouth. No, the scar that cut across his lip. The only scar on his face.

"You mean scars like this one?" Chloe asked softly.

He wanted to lick her finger. To pull it into his mouth.

Why the hell am I in some kind of sexual overdrive with her?

He'd only fucked one woman since his attack. He'd picked her up in a bar, kept the lights off so she wouldn't see his body, but when she'd turned the lights on and gotten a look at him...

She'd run as fast as his girlfriend had when she'd fled the hospital.

Chloe wasn't running. She was leaning toward him, looking like the sexiest dream of his life, and her finger was sensually sliding over his lip.

"Yeah," he forced himself to say. And his tongue did slip over her index finger. "Scars like this one." Only the other scars were much worse than that little one.

A shiver slid over her at the touch of his tongue. Because he was watching her so closely, he caught the faint movement. Only he knew she wasn't shivering because of revulsion.

Desire.

"I won't lie to you and say that I don't notice the scars. They mark you." She lightly traced the scar on his lip. "But they do nothing to detract from you. I don't know why you would think they do. If anything, they make you sexier." Her hand fell away.

He shook his head. "There is no way they make me—"

"They show how strong you are. They show that you're a fighter. I happen to find strength and determination to be extremely sexually attractive."

Joel couldn't believe what he was hearing. "Then if each scar is a sign of strength...hell, you must be *extremely* sexually attracted me." Because he had scars to spare and—

"Yes, I am." Chloe spoke so calmly. So clearly. With no hesitation or subterfuge whatsoever.

"I do not understand you," he whispered. *But I want to.*

"Most people don't. I've gotten used to that." What could have been a hint of sadness drifted through her voice. "So, are we reaching some sort of sexual deal?"

His heart shoved into his chest even as his dick shoved hard against the front of his pants. "I work as your partner on the case..."

"Partner. Protector. Whatever term you prefer."

He wanted her mouth.

"But," Chloe continued, "that's unrelated to anything physical that happens between us."

His gaze was still on her mouth. "Completely unrelated."

"Can you compartmentalize that way? You won't...just because we have sex, you won't lose your objectivity?"

He forced his stare to rise so that he could stare her straight in the eyes. "Are you asking me if I'm going to fall in love with you?"

Chloe's head moved in a small, negative shake. "I asked if you would maintain your objectivity."

"Will you maintain yours?" Joel pushed back.

"You should carefully consider this." Her voice had turned husky. *Like a stroke right over my cock.* "Because maybe...perhaps you could be my partner, but not my lover. Or my lover, but not my partner."

Now he had to touch her. Because...*I will be both*. His hand curled under her chin. "Do you know what most people say about surgeons?"

"That they're very good with their hands? And I must say, you certainly proved that last night."

She delivered those words in her cool and easy British accent, and it actually took them a moment to register in his mind. When they did, Joel found himself smiling again. "Did you just give me props for my sexual skills?"

"You know you brought me pleasure. I was merely stating a fact. But if you want to take the words as a compliment, please feel free."

"Thanks." He leaned even closer. "Surgeons do have good hands, but people also say that a high number of surgeons are psychopaths."

"Yes. I have heard that." She didn't seem even mildly fazed. "Surgeons, CEOs, politicians. People with very high stress jobs—like surgeons—have to be able to emotionally distance from the work they are doing. If you couldn't distance or detach yourself, then every single time you cut into a patient, your fingers wouldn't be as steady. You'd be more likely to make a fatal mistake."

Every single time you cut into a patient.

He looked at the fingers he'd curled around her chin. Her delicate jaw. He immediately released her and eased back.

"Did I say something to upset you?" Chloe asked.

He flexed and clenched his fingers. "You don't seem overly concerned that a psychopath might be touching you...and planning to fuck you."

"Three points. First, all psychopaths aren't killers, and all killers are most definitely not psychopaths. Just because you can maintain an emotional distance doesn't mean you're some cold-blooded murderer. There are plenty of people who fit the psychopathic personality definition who lead full, productive lives."

"Good to know." He could *never* predict what the woman was going to say. Never. "What's point two?"

"I actually don't think you possess many psychopathic personality traits. At least not any of the ones that would trigger alarm bells. While I think you can be charming when the situation calls for it, I haven't exactly seen a ton of superficial charm floating from you."

She'd just said he was a dick. He was sure of it. She'd used Chloe-speak to do it.

"Although you *did* manipulate Reese last night when you plied him with whiskey. And people with psychopathic personality traits are very adept at manipulation."

"Hey, he's the one who brought up drinking the whiskey. I just decided to be a pal and drink a little with him."

The car was slowing down. Were they already at their destination? Joel squinted as he peered through the tinted rear windows to try and see where they were.

"I think you have empathy. You attempt to hide it. You *do* try to act as if you don't care, but the empathy is there. It slips through your cracks. I could see it when you talked to Cinnamon. Deep down, you care about people. I suspect that caring is what drove you to become a surgeon in the first place. You didn't do it because you wanted a high-paying job or social esteem. You did it to help people."

"Surgeons are arrogant assholes. Ask anyone. Trust me, I can fit that bill perfectly." He flattened his hands over his thighs. "What was point three?"

The limo's rear door opened. "We're here," Marie said. "And there's already a line."

Chloe started to slide from the limo.

He caught her wrist. "Point three."

"Right. Point three." She looked down at his hand. "You wouldn't be the first psychopath I'd slept with."

Well, fuck.

His hold tightened on her. "Got an ex you hate, huh?"

"You have no idea."

It must be the guy who'd burned her. "Want me to kick his ass for you?"

She sucked in a sharp breath. "No. Quite the contrary. I want you to stay as far away from him as you possibly can." She tugged her hand free. "Let's do a test run. Tonight, it might be appropriate for our two roles to blur."

"I don't get exactly what that means."

"It means that we're partners, but I need for you to act as if we're already lovers."

Before he could reply, she slipped out of the car. He followed. Realized they were a few streets away from the Square. And that Marie had been right. A line did circle the building. A line of richly dressed men and women were vying to get in the place. Two big bouncers waited near the entrance. Over the heads of the bouncers, a glowing snake appeared and disappeared—with a red tongue flickering out—on the side of the two-story structure.

"I'll stay close," Marie murmured. "Remember, if there's trouble, I can be here in a flash."

He looked at the throng of cars lining the road. "Doubt it."

"You shouldn't doubt my skills," she immediately retorted. "I never say anything I don't mean."

Okay.

Marie jabbed him in the chest. "You gonna take care of her?"

Damn straight. "She won't leave my sight."

She grunted—what he took as a pleased sound. Then Marie hopped back into the vehicle. As she drove away, Joel eyed the line. It kinda looked like a long, twisting snake. If they waited in that thing, it would take forever to—

He realized Chloe had left him. *So much for not letting her out of my sight!* Chloe was walking straight toward the bouncers. They immediately waved her forward and even lifted the little red rope that blocked the entrance for everyone else.

He rushed to catch up with her. "Chloe—"

One bouncer immediately lowered the red rope.

The other shoved his hand against Joel's chest. "I don't think so, buddy," he snarled. "Take your ass to the end of the line."

Joel looked down at the hand, then back up at the guy who had at least three inches and fifty pounds on him. Joel smiled. "You'll want to stop touching me."

Laughter.

"Before I have to kick your ass," Joel finished.

"I'd like to see you try." The guy shoved harder. "I would like—"

Joel caught his hand. Twisted. Applied the right amount of pressure on the bouncer's wrist. Not enough to break it. Just enough to send pain radiating all the way through the fellow's arm.

"Oh, for goodness sake." Chloe's heels tapped toward him. She unhooked the red rope. "Joel, I want you to release Wedge at once."

Wedge?

Joel let him go. "He was being handsy."

Wedge lunged toward him.

Chloe stepped between them. "Wedge, stop. He's with me."

Every single muscle in Joel's body had locked down. Fury burned within him.

Wedge's fist was raised. His face twisted into a snarl.

"Lower the fist," Joel ordered. "Get it the hell away from Chloe's face. *Now.*"

Wedge blinked. "I'd never hurt her."

Joel grabbed Chloe's hand. Yanked her behind him.

Wedge had lowered his fist.

"He's with me," Chloe repeated quietly. "Sorry. I thought you saw us exit the limo together."

Joel glared into Wedge's beady eyes. "He did see it," Joel assured her. "But he thought he'd have some fun." Joel leaned toward Wedge. "Not with me, you won't. And if you ever raise your hand near her again, I'll make sure you lose those fingers."

"I wouldn't hurt Chloe," Wedge grunted. His lips twisted. "But you on the other hand..."

"Bring it, big guy," Joel taunted. *You raised your fist to her? I will make you—*

"Stop this nonsense!" Chloe elbowed Joel. "This is a waste of time. Wedge, we're going inside. Kingston is here, I assume."

"On the second floor. Though he might be...occupied."

"Well, I'd be surprised if he wasn't. Don't worry. I'm sure we can catch his attention." She glanced at Joel. "Are we quite ready now?"

He was ready to pound the hell out of Wedge, but...later. For the moment, he gave a curt nod and followed Chloe inside.

He expected pounding music. Gyrating dancers. This was a club, right?

But...

Joel didn't get what he expected.

Classical music drifted in the air. Diamonds dangled from wrists and ears and necklaces as champagne exploded from bottle after bottle. No wonder Chloe had insisted that he dress up. Each man there was wearing a suit that screamed of money. And the women? Dressed to tempt. To make a man beg.

"This doesn't exactly seem like the place I expected to find Donnie Adams," he muttered.

"Appearances can be deceiving." Her eyes slowly swept the club.

One woman strolled by with a roll of her hips. She was wearing a ruby big enough to choke a small child. Joel whistled. "Donnie seemed to be a thug. An asshole who hurt dancers. How the hell would he have the money to fit in here?"

"Let's find out how." She took a determined step forward.

He immediately pulled her back. "Not so fast." A dark corner waited to the side. He guided her there, then pinned her between his body and the wall. "Ground rules. Now. Before anything else happens."

"Whatever are you talking about?"

"I'm supposed to be the protection, right?"

"Is that why you were flexing with Wedge? You wanted me to see that you were capable of being...fierce? Unnecessary, I assure you. I already know you are—"

"I wasn't flexing." Jeez. Insulting. "I was stopping the dick from pushing me around." He brought his body even closer to her. "He could've hit you."

"He wouldn't have done that. Wedge doesn't—"

"You stepped between him and me. He wanted to pound his fist into my face. When you moved between us, that beefy fist of his could have hit *you*." Joel huffed out a breath. "Then I would have needed to kill him."

She stared into his eyes. Seemed to search his gaze. *Click, click.* "No."

"What?"

"No. You wouldn't kill him. You might hurt him rather severely if he'd punched me, but you wouldn't kill him."

"What are you—"

"However, the point is moot because Wedge wouldn't hurt me. Wedge would never hurt any woman. His father abused his mother while he was growing up. He was a big man, much like Wedge. He hurt her over and over, until Wedge got big enough to stop him."

"How do you know this?"

She shrugged. "I have my ways."

So he was learning.

"Men are fair game for Wedge. But he would never, ever hurt a woman."

It was fabulous that she was so confident but... "Accidents can happen. If someone wants to take a swing at me, you do not step in the way to protect me, got it? I protect you. Not the other way around."

"My mistake. Sorry."

"You don't sound sorry."

She smiled.

His heart lurched hard in his chest. God, when she smiled that way...*absolutely beautiful.*

"Excuse me." A husky, feminine voice intruded from close by. "The game is about to start. Kingston wanted to make sure you were ready."

Chloe hadn't shown so much as a flicker of surprise when the other woman spoke, so Joel knew she hadn't been caught off-guard by the interruption. *As per usual with Chloe.* But he on the other hand...

What game?

"We are most definitely ready. I thought Kingston might be busy upstairs, so we were just waiting for the invitation," Chloe replied smoothly. "Thank you."

The woman—a blond wearing all black—gave a quick nod before she backed away.

Joel glanced up and his gaze trekked to the second level of the club. He saw a man up there—clad in a black suit—staring down at them. A redhead had her hand on the man's arm, but he didn't seem to be focusing on her at all. Instead, his gaze was on Joel and Chloe.

"Guessing that's Kingston?" Joel asked.

"Most people call him King. I think I may be one of the few he lets call him Kingston."

Lets?

"I probably should have asked sooner, but how are you at poker?"

Joel's head swiveled back to her.

"Can you bluff well?" Chloe wanted to know. Then, before he could respond, she added, "No worries if you can't. Losing will work just as well for us as winning."

"We're here to play poker?"

"Lower your voice," she urged him. "Not exactly one of the sanctioned games, if you know what I mean."

Sure, he got it. This was an illegal game. Otherwise it would probably be held in a casino, not in the VIP area of a club.

"Stakes are high. And unusual," she explained quickly. "So don't go doing anything crazy like betting yourself, okay?"

What?

"And don't bet me. Seriously. I am not in the mood to screw a stranger tonight."

He still had her trapped against the wall. "Damn right you're not."

That smile of hers flashed again. "I was joking. Sexual favors aren't traded here. Kingston wouldn't allow that."

He didn't smile back at her. "We don't joke about you sleeping with strangers." A possessive edge had entered his voice. "We don't joke about that shit at all."

"Oh. Are you—are you already getting into character?"

He remembered what she'd said right before she'd exited the limo. *We're partners, but we need to pretend that we're already lovers.* "Sure," he growled. "That's what I'm doing. Just call me a method actor."

Her hand patted his chest. "I didn't expect the possessive side, but I think it will play well."

I am not playing.

"We should go." She nodded.

Did she have any idea that her hand seemed to be scorching him? Probably not.

"Kingston doesn't like to wait."

Like I give a shit.

But he slowly backed away.

"If you'd like, you can wrap your arm around my waist. That will make it look as if we're inseparable. That you like touching me. Keeping me close."

I do.

They began walking for the stairs. He wrapped his arm around her waist. Pulled her close.

"You should know that there will probably be some people up there who won't be overly thrilled to see me." Her voice was low.

He slanted a glance at her. "Why is that?"

"Oh, various reasons."

He just bet. "Why aren't *you* the one who is playing poker tonight? How'd I get to be the lucky one?" They were almost at the top of the stairs. More bouncers waited up there.

"I'm not allowed to play here any longer."

Allowed?

His lips parted, but before he could respond—

"What the fuck is she doing here?" An angry voice bellowed. "There is no damn way I am playing with *her!*"

A guy with a fat neck, beefy hands, and a blood-red face barreled toward Chloe.

Sighing, Joel stepped in front of her.

He had the feeling this was going to be a very long night.

CHAPTER FIFTEEN

"Relax, Morris," Chloe instructed the red-faced fellow as she curled her hand over Joel's shoulder and moved up to his side. "I'm not here to play."

Morris huffed out a breath and his nostrils flared. "Damn straight, you're not. You're *barred* from these games. Cheaters aren't allowed!"

The cheating title chafed, but the man wasn't entirely wrong.

"Cheating?" Joel angled his head toward her. She could have sworn that a gleam of humor appeared in his eyes. "You were cheating in a backroom card game?"

Um... "As to that," she began.

"Counting cards," Kingston Broussard clarified as he sauntered toward them. The redhead who'd been at his side earlier had vanished. "Our lovely Chloe has a delightful knack for card counting."

"Delightful, my ass," Morris snapped back. "It's cheating. Cheating is fucking cheating, and if she's here, then I am not playing tonight—"

"Watch the tone," Joel cut in, and *his* tone was low and lethal. "Because you're about to piss me off. That's not something you want."

Morris shrugged his rounded shoulders. "Why the hell do I care if you're pissed? I don't know you. You don't mean dick to me."

Joel smiled at him. Chloe craned her head a bit to better see that smile. *Chilling*.

"You will care," Joel promised silkily. Then his arm lifted and curled around Chloe's shoulders. He pulled her against him. "Chloe isn't here to play tonight. She's with me. I'll be the one playing."

Morris grunted. "Nope. Not happening. The woman will still count the cards. She does it like some freaky robot. She'll do it and she'll send you some secret message and then you'll take all my money just like she did."

Was he still mad about that? Someone could certainly hold a grudge.

"I don't appreciate the way you're talking about her." Again, Joel used the low and lethal tone that made goosebumps rise onto her arms. "This will be your last warning."

"Oh, really?" Morris laughed. "What are you gonna do about it?"

And, once more, Joel smiled.

Morris backed up.

"*Enough.*" Kingston's order. He'd been watching—observing and evaluating Joel she knew—and now he was ready to step into the fray. "This is my club. My game. *My* rules." He waved a hand toward Morris. "You don't like the people here, then you can drag your ass out."

"No one will play if she's here!" Spittle flew from Morris's mouth. "No one will sit at the table with her. They will—"

"Blindfold me," Chloe said as she focused on Kingston. "I'm sure there are plenty of available blindfolds in this place." Knowing his kink as she did. "If my eyes are covered, I can't count anything." But she could still hear everything that was going on. And sometimes what you could hear was as important as what you could see.

Even more so.

"Sounds like a perfect solution." Kingston nodded. "But, Morris, if you don't agree, I think I already told you what to do."

Drag your ass out.

"Blindfold. That will work. But *I* put it on her." With that, Morris stomped for the black door that waited about five feet away.

"Pleasant fellow," Joel mused.

"Sure." Kingston sauntered closer. "Just the kind of guy who makes you want to kick his ass." He smiled at her. "Hello, Chloe. I didn't think you'd ever be back in my place again." His voice was low, carrying only to her and Joel.

"I needed information."

"Um." His attention slid to Joel. "And who do we have here? Details on your companion were pretty sketchy."

"I'm a sketchy guy," Joel returned.

"Those are the types of friends that Chloe likes to attract." Kingston tilted his dark head. He seemed to take Joel's measure. "It's your first time at my table, so listen closely to the rules. I don't repeat myself. No weapons are allowed. Ten thousand dollar buy-in. If you can't settle your debt at the end of the night, it will be settled for you." His bright gaze cut to Chloe. "No cheating allowed. If you're caught cheating, I choose the punishment."

Joel still had an arm wrapped around Chloe. At Kingston's words, his hold tightened even more.

"Name's King, by the way," Kingston said smoothly. "And once you cross that threshold..." He indicated the waiting door. "You're in my world."

"Well, that certainly sounds ominous as hell," Joel replied. "Am I supposed to be intimidated or impressed?"

Kingston smiled. "If you're smart, you'll be neither." He turned away.

"Ten thousand dollar buy-in..." Joel called after him. "How the hell would a guy like Donnie Adams manage to get that much cash in order to enter your game?"

Kingston looked back. "Where he gets the cash from doesn't matter to me. He has to show it in order to step up to the plate. He had enough to show in order to get a seat at my table."

"If he had ten Gs, then why'd he end up paying with a high school ring?"

"I don't have his ring. Already told Chloe that." Kingston waved his hand toward the door. A bouncer immediately opened it for him.

Joel blew out a low breath. "You knew he didn't have the ring," he whispered as he angled his head toward her. "And yet we're still here?"

"Kingston doesn't have it. Someone else in that room does." That was why they had to get inside.

"And the ten thousand dollars? The dress you're wearing is pretty tight, so I think I'd notice if you had that much cash strapped to you. You don't have a bag. You don't have—"

"You think my dress is too tight?" She was momentarily distracted.

"I think your dress is perfect." He sidled ever closer. She thought he was going to press a kiss to her cheek, but instead, he whispered in her ear, "What are we doing about the money? Do I need to put down—"

"You don't have to pay anything. I already transferred the money. We're good." She licked her lower lip. "You have to be my eyes."

He pulled back a little. Frowned at her.

"When we go inside, Morris will blindfold me. You have to watch closely. Look for small tells. Ask about Donnie, but don't be obvious."

"Are you coaching me right now?"

That was exactly what she was doing, yes. "If you have the chance to prove yourself, do it."

"Prove myself? What in the hell does that mean?"

"Favors go a long way in this world."

"I have no idea what you—"

"Game is starting," a bouncer called. "The door is about to close. You in?"

Chloe stared up into Joel's swirling gaze. "He's in." She grabbed his hand and led him into the VIP room. As soon as she swept inside, her gaze assessed the players.

Morris—she knew him already. Wyatt Morris owned a chain of grocery stores. Had a big gambling addiction. Lots of criminal ties.

To his right, there was a newcomer. An elegant woman with glass-sharp cheekbones. Her hair was pulled up in a twist, and diamonds glittered on every finger.

An almost ridiculously handsome man sat beside the woman. The top few buttons of his shirt were undone, and his posture appeared relaxed as he lounged in his chair. Late twenties, maybe early thirties, he had golden skin and deep green eyes. He flashed a grin at her.

The ring on his finger glinted. Just one ring. The one she'd been hoping to see.

Bingo.

"Here's the blindfold." Morris waved it toward her. "I'll put it on and—"

"I'll do it. My game. My rules, remember?" Kingston snatched it away. He motioned to a chair that was a few feet behind the table. "Sorry, love, but to make everyone more comfortable, you have to sit back there."

Because just being close to the table—while wearing a blindfold—somehow made it possible for her to read their cards? Whatever.

Before she sat down, Chloe made note of the others in the room. The dealer—that was the redhead who'd been with Kingston before. Chloe knew Kingston would also be playing at the table. Also seated was a man with silver-tipped hair and another fellow with a day's worth of stubble on his jaw.

She eased into the chair. Crossed her legs.

Joel was still holding her hand. She thought he was doing it deliberately. Letting others know that she belonged with him. Such a nice touch. Chloe was impressed.

"Just like old times, hmmm?" Kingston asked as he bent toward her.

She caught the flash of fury on Joel's face right before Kingston slid the blindfold over her eyes.

Then...there was darkness.

"Happy now?" Kingston asked. Presumably, the question was for Morris.

A grunt was the reply.

She still held Joel's hand. She squeezed it to get his attention. She caught his crisp, masculine scent as he leaned closer to her. Her head turned toward him. She pressed a kiss to his cheek.

Heard him suck in a breath.

"Check out the ring at the table," Chloe breathed.

She felt his nod. Then he slid back. Stopped touching her. Odd, but she immediately missed his warmth. She heard the squeak of his chair as he settled in.

No one was wasting time with chit-chat. Not this group. They were all ready to get right down to business. Chloe pulled in a deep breath. Slowly released it. She did that a few times to center herself. To push away tension. She became aware of the perfume that hung in the air. Recognized the expensive, French scent. Knew it had to come from the redhead. Kingston always gave his lovers that same scent. She took another careful inhale.

Cigar smoke. No one was smoking in that room, Kingston wouldn't allow it, but someone had smoked right before coming inside. A Cuban cigar. Expensive.

Her nostrils flared again. She tried to pull in more scents. Looked for something that would perhaps be familiar to her.

A scent nagged at her. Not close enough to fully detect. Not yet.

It teased...

A smooth female voice asked, "Players, are you ready?"

There was a murmur of agreements.

"Then let's begin."

Chloe heard the flutter of cards as they were dealt.

***

Over one hundred grand was on the table in front of him. Joel cast a quick glance at his cards, realized he had jack shit, but didn't let that slow him down as he tossed more cash into the pile. Then he looked over his shoulder at Chloe. Her chair had been positioned a few feet behind his.

She sat with her back perfectly straight. Her legs were crossed, but she didn't idly kick her foot or anything like that. Chloe was completely still. Her face was expressionless. The black blindfold covered her eyes and skimmed her cheeks.

"Yeah, I get that she's fucking gorgeous," the man across from Joel tossed more chips onto the table. "But how about you try focusing on the game?"

Joel gave the jerk a slow smile. He'd already noticed the ring on his finger. "I am focused, champ."

The man grunted. "What's that supposed to mean?"

"You're a champ, aren't you? That's a championship football ring on your finger." He leaned forward for a better look. "High school. Let me guess...big man on campus back in the day?"

The fellow laughed. His fingers tapped against his cards. "Not my ring. It's a trophy."

Killers keep trophies. "Good for you." Joel knew he sounded bored.

There had been no introductions at the table. Joel got that this wasn't exactly the kind of place where names were exchanged. So he had no idea who the fellow currently tapping away at the cards actually was.

A pretty boy. With a bored air. And a trophy on his finger.

A killer? Maybe.

"I'm out." This was from Morris. At least, Joel knew *his* name. Morris had been steadily losing all night.

Joel had won and lost. He was actually up about fifteen grand overall.

Three hours had passed.

Chloe hadn't spoken a word. How could she stay so still? Once more, he looked back at—

Her finger was tapping. Just like the guy across from—

"Look, if you want a break to screw her," the pretty boy snarled, "then just—"

Joel lunged across the table. He locked his fingers around the pretty boy's throat. "Cheating isn't tolerated at the table."

Joel sure as fuck hoped that was the message that Chloe had been sending him. If not...*Too late.* He'd been acting on instinct.

The guy gasped—and then he shoved a knife toward Joel. The knife slid right out of the pretty boy's sleeve. Like some kind of freaking magic trick. Joel jumped back just in time to avoid the slice of that blade. "Got enough cuts," he grunted. "But thanks so much."

The SOB was now on his feet and brandishing his knife. Except when he'd stood up, two playing cards had slipped from his sleeve. So the knife hadn't been the only thing he'd been hiding.

How the hell had Chloe known?

"You brought a weapon to my game?" Kingston's voice was ice cold. "And you cheated at *my* table?"

"I—" Fury flashed on his face. The fury gave way to fear. The man ran for the door. A bouncer got in his path, and he stabbed down with the knife. The blade sank into the bouncer's forearm.

The bouncer's fist plowed into his attacker's face. Joel heard bones crunch even as the cheater fell to the floor, screaming in pain.

The others at the table jumped to their feet. Gaped.

"I am done with these games, King," Morris declared. "Done. Shit always goes wrong here."

Kingston's face twisted with fury. "Eli, you dumb prick. You just made the worst mistake of your life."

Joel didn't look over at Eli. His gaze had returned to the bouncer. The guy with the knife shoved into his arm. "Listen, you don't want to take that out—"

Too late. The bouncer yanked at the blade. Blood immediately soaked his arm. *Hell.*

"Um...excuse me?" Chloe's voice. As smooth and easy as could be. "May I remove the blindfold? Is the game finished?"

Joel closed in on the bouncer. "Let me see your arm."

The bouncer slapped a hand over the wound. The blood seeped through his fingers. "Screw off."

Eli was on the floor. Whimpering and holding his nose.

"The game is over," Kingston said flatly. "But no one is leaving the building."

"I think your bouncer is losing a lot of blood." Again, Chloe's voice was mild. "He should go to the hospital."

"N-no...h-hospital," the bouncer croaked. His complexion was turning ashy.

"Then Joel can fix him," Chloe continued crisply.

The blindfold still covered her eyes. How the hell did she even know about the amount of blood loss?

"He's a doctor," Chloe continued while everyone else seemed frozen. "Let Joel help Jimmy."

Jimmy? Was that the bouncer's name? *There are two bouncers or guards—or what-the-hellever they need to be called—in the room.* How had she known which one was injured?

"You a doctor?" Kingston demanded as his gaze raked Joel.

"I was." His jaw hardened. "He should have left the knife in."

"Well, it's out. Take care of him, and I'll owe you."

Chloe's voice seemed to whisper through his mind. *If you have a chance to prove yourself, do it.*

Joel stared down at his fingers.

Favors go a long way in this world.

"I haven't worked on a patient in a long time." There was a faint tremble in his fingertips. "He should go to the hospital."

"Jimmy is wanted by the cops. He's not stepping foot in a hospital. If you're a doc, fix him. Now."

A quick look showed that more blood poured from Jimmy's wound. *Fuck.*

"Chloe, your doc boyfriend isn't moving. Motivate him." Kingston's order was angry. Hard.

Joel rolled back his shoulders. *I can do this.* Maybe. Probably. He felt a light touch on his arm and flinched.

"It's okay," Chloe told him softly. She'd taken off the blindfold. She leaned onto her toes and pulled his head toward her mouth. "I can take care of him. You don't have to do anything you don't want to do."

"Thought you fainted at the sight of blood," he rasped.

"No, it's only bloody dead bodies that get to me. I can stitch him up. You don't have to do this."

"I-I think I'm going to pass out," Jimmy croaked, sounding shocked. His big body began to sway.

Hell.

Joel surged forward and caught him. "I need room to work. *Now*."

CHAPTER SIXTEEN

Blood covered Joel's hands. Or rather, blood covered the gloves that he wore as he stitched up Jimmy Trainor. Chloe tilted her head and watched him work. Fast. Steady.

Kingston had plenty of medical supplies that he'd made available to Joel. The back room on the club's first floor was *almost* an OR. Mostly because this wasn't the first time that an attack had occurred on the premises. And since Kingston and his employees didn't exactly like to report workplace injuries, he'd made a habit of keeping medical gear on hand for emergency situations.

"You heard I lost my last doc, didn't you?" Kingston murmured as they watched Joel meticulously pull up another stitch.

"You mean the resident that you were slipping cash to treat your crew? I did hear he'd gone to Florida." She pursed her lips. "That bit of gossip might have reached my ears."

"That why you brought the new doc with you tonight? You looking to loan him out to me?"

She focused on Kingston. "Joel is not up for loan. He's my partner."

A nod. "You just brought him here then...so, what? I'd owe you?"

Yes, actually. One of the reasons.

"How'd you know we'd need his services tonight?"

She had to laugh at his question. "You always wind up needing a doctor at one of your card games."

Joel's head whipped toward them. He stared at her. Then his gaze drifted to Kingston.

"I don't think that your *partner* likes it when someone else makes you laugh," Kingston told her.

"That's a strange thing to say."

"Is it? Laughter can be a very personal, intimate thing. Especially with a woman like you."

Joel had gone back to work.

Chloe considered the situation. "I don't see laughter as intimate at all."

"In order to laugh, you have to let someone close enough to be able to amuse you. You don't let many people that close, Chloe."

"Neither do you."

"True."

They watched in silence as Joel finished his stitches. He yanked off the bloody gloves. Tossed them in the trash then leaned down to say something to Jimmy. She couldn't see his lips so Chloe wasn't sure what Joel had said, but a moment later, he was striding toward her.

"All done?" Kingston asked. "I'll assume my employee is no longer in danger of bleeding out?"

"He was never in danger of bleeding out. It looked one hell of a lot worse than it was." Joel's hands were fisted at his sides. "Told the asshole he'd better not do anything to rip out my stitches or I'd be pissed as hell."

"Um, yes, can't have stitches ripping." Kingston turned on his heel. "I take it you're now ready for payment?"

"I don't want your money—"

Chloe put her hand on Joel's chest. "He's not talking about money."

Joel's gaze zeroed in on her.

"And, yes," she continued when Joel didn't speak up, "we are ready for payment."

"Then follow me. He's waiting for you."

She started to follow—

Joel snagged her wrist. "He?"

"Yes. I expect the payment we're about to get is the card cheater. And it's perfect because he's the man we needed to interrogate."

Joel shook his head. "How are you so calm? Is this a typical Saturday night for you or something?"

"Yes."

He blinked.

"We should hurry. I'm not certain how long we'll have with our suspect before he passes out."

A muscle jerked along Joel's clenched jaw. "Why the hell would he pass out?"

Chloe winced. "Because he broke Kingston's rules."

***

The club was a freaking maze. Joel followed Chloe and Kingston down a dimly lit hallway, and the next thing he knew...

What. In. The. Hell?

He was in another back room. Only this one wasn't nearly as clean as his make-shift operating room had been. This place was covered in dust and heavy boxes lined the walls. Right in the middle of the room, sagging in a chair that sat beneath one overly bright light, was the man Kingston had called Eli.

But Eli wasn't just sporting a broken nose any longer. His eyes were both black. His jaw was swollen. And blood dripped from his busted lip.

"Dammit," Joel snarled. "Am I supposed to patch him up, too?" He took a step forward.

Kingston lifted a hand and blocked his path. "You have five minutes to talk to him." His stare remained on Eli. "You will answer their questions honestly. If you lie, Chloe will know. She'll tell me. I'll hurt you."

Eli cracked open his eyes. The narrow slits glared at Joel. "How'd you...know...what I was..."

"I knew you were cheating." Chloe's heels tapped across the floor. "Because you were winning more hands than was statistically possible."

"Bitch...could h-have been...having good n-night..."

"When you lost, it was on a pattern. Too predictable. And you always lost on the smallest pots."

"Y-you were...g-guessing..."

"I don't guess," Chloe informed him. The woman even sounded a little insulted by the accusation. "You had cards up your sleeve. You also had a knife. I heard it tap the table when you collected your winnings."

Well, damn.

Joel looked over and saw Kingston lift a brow at Chloe's explanation. The other man looked impressed.

"This doesn't count as part of our five minutes, does it?" Chloe asked Kingston. "Because he's been asking questions. Joel and I haven't."

Kingston glanced at his watch. "Start now."

"Where'd you get the ring?" Chloe asked.

His busted lips pulled into a smile. "What ring?"

Kingston pulled a bloody ring out of his pocket. "This one."

Chloe sighed. "Your prints are on it now. That is going to make things harder for me."

He frowned at the ring. "I can wipe them off."

"You'll wipe off other evidence, too. Please, *don't.*" Chloe closed in on the man in the chair.

"Ahem." Joel cleared his throat. Loudly.

Her head swiveled toward him.

"Eli there isn't restrained. How about you don't get too close to him?"

"Eli isn't going to attack," Kingston assured him. "Are you, Eli?"

Eli shook his head. "All...mistake..."

"Jimmy is my nephew." Kingston's eyes glittered. "Driving a knife into his arm was most definitely a mistake. One you'll regret for a long time."

"You're taking up my five minutes." Chloe didn't move any closer to Eli. "How'd you get the ring? Did you kill Donnie Adams?"

"What? Hell, no."

"Then how did you get the ring?" she repeated.

"Donnie lost my money, so he had to pay up." Eli licked his bloody lower lip. "Got him in a few times. One of those you-scratch-my back, I-scratch-yours type of situations."

"What did Donnie scratch for you?"

"He...could get a good supply."

"Drugs?"

A jerky nod. "So, I got him in. He was riding high. First time, he doubled his money. Dude thought he couldn't lose."

"Everyone can lose," Joel said. Simple fact.

"Eventually, Donnie lost all that he'd ever won, then more. I covered him, but I made him give me the payment back. Didn't have it all in cash, so he had to give me things to make up for it."

"Things." Chloe appeared to accept that explanation. "List them."

"He gave me the ring. Some jewelry. Sh-shit was probably hot. Got a car."

"I'm assuming that was, ah, hot, too?" Chloe wanted to know.

"The rest of what he owed me—he got the cash from that stripper girlfriend of his. Five grand. With the 5K and the other stuff, he paid the debt to me in full. I-I had no reason to kill him."

"Yet you came here tonight, flashing his ring."

"I...liked it."

Joel didn't buy that explanation.

Neither, apparently, did Chloe. "You were wearing it as a message, weren't you? No one can screw you over without paying."

Eli didn't respond.

"Um, Joel?" Chloe called out. "I'm sorry, but I do need to get just a little closer, if you don't mind."

"I mind." He immediately moved toward her.

"Don't worry." Kingston took up a position behind Eli. He shoved his hands down on the man's shoulders. "I'll make sure he doesn't move."

Chloe looked expectantly at Joel. "Good?"

No. "Nothing here is good. We need to get the hell out of this place." The sooner, the better in his book.

"Hurtful," Kingston stated. "Ever so hurtful."

Chloe nodded. "That was harsh. I thought the music on the first floor was really quite lovely."

"Thank you, Chloe." Kingston tightened his grip on Eli. "Knew you'd appreciate it."

She held Joel's stare. "I need to get closer. Just for a moment."

"Why?"

"So I can smell him."

His eyes closed. "Of course, that's why. Should have realized it sooner. You need to smell him." He prayed for patience, then opened his eyes. "Do it."

She did. A quick sniff. And... "Cinnamon."

The jackass smelled like Cinnamon? Joel leaned in close, too, but, no. "That's not

Cinnamon." It was a smell from his childhood. "That's—"

"It's bubblegum body butter. Cinnamon had it on when we went in for the private dance with her."

Kingston's brows shot up.

"Wasn't a private dance," Joel clarified. "We were questioning her."

"I even saw the container of the body butter near her bag. Sure, there are probably plenty of other people who use the same lotion but...this is an interesting development, don't you think?"

He did. Joel focused on their prey. "You know Cinnamon."

Eli's gaze darted away.

"You know Donnie's girlfriend. Know her well enough that the scent of her lotion is clinging to you right now."

Eli tried to shrug, but couldn't due to Kingston's grip. "I got a private dance tonight. Guess we all like them, huh? Where's the crime?"

"You look guilty." Chloe backed away from him. "You have the dead man's ring. I strongly suspect you had sex with the dead man's girlfriend. And you pulled a knife tonight, showing us all that you are extremely prone to violence. Kingston, I think you should turn him over to the cops."

Kingston's face hardened. "You know I don't like cops, Chloe."

"Yes, but I followed the trail and came here, and they will, too. If you cooperate, they'll dig into your business less. They'll just rip apart *his* life." She pointed at Eli.

Horror flashed on Eli's battered face. "No!"

"I assume you have businesses you don't want the cops to know about?" Chloe didn't seem overly sympathetic. "That's unfortunate."

"I didn't kill Donnie—*I swear!* Yes, I know Cinnamon. She called me after she found the body. She was freaking out! We'd hooked up a few times, and she knew I could handle trouble."

"You can't handle shit," Kingston fired at him.

Joel was in agreement with that assessment.

"I have an alibi! I can prove I didn't do it! As for the ring...I had it *before* he died, okay? I can prove that, too!"

"You will need to prove that," Chloe said in her cool British accent. "So be prepared to do so. Now if you will tell me—"

"Time's up," Kingston interrupted.

Her head whipped up. "But—"

"Your time is up. Take your doc and head out. Trust me on this, you'll want to be clear of the Serpent very, very soon." Kingston's expression was unyielding.

"Fine." She sure didn't sound as if anything was actually *fine* with her. But she headed for Joel. He thought she seemed a little pale. "He means trouble is coming," she whispered. "We need to get the hell out of here, *now*."

"What kind of trouble?"

"Let's not find out." She curled her fingers with his and pulled him back through the dimly lit hallway. She walked quickly, unerringly, as if she'd been there dozens of times before. They didn't speak again until they'd exited the club. Sure enough, even though hours had passed, there was still a long line of eager people waiting to get inside.

"Not going to happen tonight." She shook her head. Pulled out her phone and fired off a quick text. "Told Marie to pick us up on Decatur, near the Square. We can't wait around here." Her heels were clicking again as she hurried.

"Just what is going down here?" He wanted to know.

She didn't speak.

"Chloe."

"We need to be farther away. The Square is supposed to be closed at sundown, but I know a way we can cut through it and come out on Decatur. We'll want to stay to the shadows that the Square will give us."

Joel glanced over his shoulder. Didn't see anyone following them or even looking their way, so why was she hauling ass so much and worrying about staying in the shadows? Her heels clicked faster as he kept pace with her, and when they neared the Square and a streetlamp sent light spilling onto their path, Joel reached the end of his patience. *"Enough."* He closed his hand around her arm and pulled her to a stop. He turned her around to face him. "Don't you think I deserve an explanation?"

"Probably several." She rose onto her toes and looked over his shoulder.

"No one is back there. No one is coming after us. Your boyfriend Kingston probably told them to stay away from you."

"He's not my boyfriend." She was still looking over his shoulder. "And I'm certain that I am under an order of protection from him, but I doubt he extended the same courtesy to you."

"Sure. Right. No courtesy to me. Didn't expect that to happen. So what if I helped his cousin?"

"Nephew."

He waited for her gaze to come back to him.

She kept looking over his shoulder.

"I'm angry with you," he growled. "You made me cross a line I never wanted to cross."

Her gaze flew to his. "I did?"

"Don't play innocent. We both know that's not something you are."

She bit her lower lip.

"You knew I didn't want to sew up that guy."

"Yes, but you have the skills so why let them go to waste?"

"Because it reminds me too much of—" He stopped. Let her go. "Screw it. Let's go meet up with Marie. No, you meet up with her. I need space."

Her hand rose and pressed to his cheek. "You can't let what happened in the past force you to give up something you love. You aren't a killer, Joel."

Wasn't he? "Tell that to the bastard I beat to death."

She didn't even flinch. "How many lives have you saved since you became a doctor?"

"What is this? Some kind of balancing the scales bit? Life doesn't work that way."

"No, it doesn't. But you can't let one horrific thing destroy you. That's not how life works, either. If that were the case..." Her hand pulled away. She turned her back on him. "I would have been destroyed years ago." Her steps weren't as fast now. But they were just as certain. "Splitting up is fine. Especially if you feel the urge to get...space, I believe you said...from me. I can handle myself for the rest of the night. You go your way. I'll go mine."

He stood there with his hands fisted at his sides, and he felt like an absolute asshole. Why? Because he was pretty sure he'd hurt her feelings. She'd pushed him into doing the one thing he'd dreaded most...

Blood on my fingers. Skin sliced open...

But...

But I did it. He'd sewn up the guy and hadn't lost his mind. Hadn't gotten trapped in a terrible flashback or blacked out or even hurt the vic like he'd feared. Like a shrink had once told him would happen.

I did it.

Chloe was slipping underneath some heavy tree that hung over the edge of the thick, wrought iron fence that surrounded this portion of Jackson Square. Joel sucked in a deep breath. One that did nothing to calm him as he watched her. Did she seriously think he was just going to leave her alone?

No. I would never leave her unprotected.

Joel bounded forward, ducking under the broad limbs of that tree—and found her...

Scaling the fence?

In her high heels?

She was a shadowy form clinging to the limb of a tree and half-hauling herself over the top of the fence.

Some of the tension that had filled him since the knife attack eased. "I expected you to be a secret acrobat. Figured you'd just do some fancy roll over the fence." He crossed his arms over his chest and studied her. His vision had adjusted a bit more to the darkness there and he was pretty sure he was on eye level with her ass.

"I could use a boost. If you don't mind." Her voice was ever so prim and proper.

"And where should I put my hands for that boost? Not a lot of options are available at the moment, and it seems like I have to—"

"Oh, for God's sake, Joel. Just put your hand on my ass and push me over!"

A half-grin slid across his mouth. "Yes, ma'am." He put his hand on the rounded curve of her ass and gave her a quick push.

She seemed to shoot over the fence.

Too hard.

"Chloe!" He grabbed the branch and his foot shoved against the wall. In the next breath, his feet were slamming into the ground on the opposite side of the fence. "Chloe, are you—"

She was brushing off her dress. "I'm perfectly fine." The moon shone down on them. "You didn't have to follow me. I thought we were splitting up."

"Changed my mind." He moved closer to her. "Is this a safe place?"

"Safe is a relative term."

"Why the hell did we need to run from the Serpent?"

"Because the cops are going to be swarming the club any moment."

As if on cue, he heard the shriek of sirens. "*Why* are cops going there?"

"Because someone called them."

"It's like pulling teeth. Very slowly and painfully." Joel sawed a hand over his face and the stubble that covered his jaw. "*Who* called the cops?"

"Can I trust you?"

"I'm your partner! If you can't trust me, who can you trust?"

"Kingston."

His hand slammed down to his side. "You think you can trust that jerk? He's the one who battered Eli's face to hell and back."

"No."

He waited. She didn't speak. "More, Chloe," he ordered, demanded, pleaded—almost all the same thing with her.

"No, Kingston is not the one who hit Eli. There weren't any marks on Kingston's knuckles. If he'd been the one to punch Eli so hard, then his knuckles would have been bruised and scraped."

"Fine. So he got one of his flunkies to do the job."

"That's entirely possible."

"And you still trust *him?* What kind of relationship do the two of you have?"

She turned away. Began walking slowly through the Square. Now that they were inside the walls, she didn't seem as worried about rushing through the night. "We don't have a personal relationship. We have a business arrangement. He comes to me when he needs certain insights, and I go to him when I want to experience a better understanding of the criminal world."

"How many times has he put a blindfold on you?" Now where the hell had that question come from? Joel was sure there had been something else he meant to ask.

She stopped walking. "You sound jealous." Chloe peered over her shoulder. "There is no need for that. I've never slept with Kingston. I don't intend to do so."

Good to know. Better than good. Yet he still had so many damn questions. "So you just let the guy blindfold you in the past because...?"

"He was taking me to see a certain portion of his business. The location of that business was confidential. He thought the blindfold would stop me from being able to ever get there again on my own."

A sigh slipped from him. The scream of sirens was even louder now. "Let me guess, he was wrong."

"Absolutely." She skirted around a fountain. Headed toward a bench and a stone walkway. "I could find my way back there anytime I wanted."

There was a lamp shining over the bench. The light fell on her. Made her dark hair gleam.

"You still didn't tell me who called the cops. Did you do it?" He'd made it to her side.

She peered over at him. "I did tell you."

"No, sweet—" He caught himself at her frown. Had he been about to call her sweetheart? Joel cleared his throat. "You didn't tell me."

"Sure, I did. Kingston."

He blinked.

She kept staring steadily at him. Joel quickly replayed their conversation in his mind...

"Who called the cops?" His question.

"Can I trust you?" Her ever-so-cautious reply.

"I'm your partner! If you can't trust me, who can you trust?" His grating demand.

"Kingston."

Well, damn. She hadn't been saying that she trusted Kingston. She'd been saying he called the cops. "Why would a guy like him alert the cops?" Before they'd left the club, Joel thought Kingston had made his opinion of law enforcement—and their involvement—pretty clear.

She leaned toward him. Put her hands on his chest. Brought her face in all close to him. "Because," she whispered, "he is a cop."

Joel shook his head.

"Undercover. Actually, more FBI than NOPD." She was still close. "But please keep that information strictly confidential, would you?"

That jerk...that arrogant SOB had been undercover?

"Don't worry. It will appear that someone else called the cops. The blame will be placed on one of the players at his VIP game. Maybe it will even be placed on you or me." A shrug. "But Eli will be questioned by the FBI. And I imagine that Kingston will manage to maintain his cover."

"You can't do this."

"Do what?"

"Keep me in the dark. I need to know important shit like this. Before we went in the Serpent, I should have known the truth about him."

"But if I'd told you all of this before, your reaction to Kingston would have been different. You needed to treat him with suspicion. You needed to act as if he was the enemy."

"It's called trust," he forced from between clenched teeth. "I believe we addressed it before and—" He broke off. Chloe wasn't listening to him.

Her head had angled toward the bench. "Something is there."

He frowned at the bench. "Looks like someone just left a piece of paper on the bench. No big deal."

But she was pulling away from him. Creeping toward the bench.

Fine. If she was going to look, he'd play along. The closer he got to the bench, the better he could see—

It was a card. Not some piece of paper.

Death.

A curse broke from Joel as he realized that he was looking at another one of those cards, a tarot card. Beneath the light, he could see that a black knight was riding on a white horse, and under the horse's hooves, the word Death was clearly written.

Wonderful. Fantastic.

He lifted up the card, holding it only by the right edge, and as he angled it beneath the light, he realized that the knight's face? It was a skeleton. "Yeah, this shit isn't good." His head snapped up as he studied the darkness around him. "*Who the hell is there?*" Joel called out.

"We should leave." Chloe bumped into him.

He didn't see anyone in the dark. Didn't hear anything. "Maybe this was left by one of the people who set up a table in the Square during the day." He'd passed by before and seen plenty of psychics and fortune tellers working with tourists. Could have just accidentally been left by one of them, but...

But we found the other tarot card in the alley behind the strip club. What were the odds of them randomly finding *two* of those cards? He'd bet astronomically low.

The shadows didn't move.

"If you want to threaten us, show yourself!" Joel blasted. "Don't just leave some random-ass card for us to find. Don't taunt us with the Death card!"

"We need to go. I don't think he's here any longer."

He?

"Come on. Marie should be waiting."

He pocketed the card. Stayed close to her as they got the hell out of there. When they exited near Decatur Street, sure enough, Marie and the limo were waiting. She had the back door open.

"Trouble?" Marie asked as she caught a look at their faces.

"Nothing too major," Chloe replied as she slid in the back.

Marie pinned Joel with a hard glance.

"Oh, right, definitely, not major." His jaw hardened. "Unless you count a knife fight and some asshole in the Square threatening us with Death as *not* major."

"Get in," she urged.

Like he needed to be told twice.

The door slammed behind him. Moments later, the limo raced away.

CHAPTER SEVENTEEN

"It wasn't a death threat." Chloe smoothed her hands over the sides of her dress. "That wasn't the intention of the card."

"It's a card with a skeleton on it, and the word *Death* is big and bold at the bottom." Joel was sprawled on the seat across from her. "Seems like a pretty clear threat to me."

On the surface, certainly. "Last night, I went to see an acquaintance who has expertise with tarot cards. I'd done research with her a while back, and I wanted to make certain I still had a proper understanding of the cards. While I do possess some knowledge about tarot, I wanted to know more."

"*That's* where you were last night?"

"Yes." The cards were a taunt. Not a threat. Or at least...not a threat, yet. Perhaps. *I don't want to be wrong on this.* "What you see is not what you get with a tarot card. The Death card doesn't actually translate to a real, physical death. I suppose it could in certain instances, but it is very unlikely—"

"You believe in this psychic stuff?"

"I believe in many things. However, I don't think anything psychic is at play here. Someone is using the tarot as calling cards. Someone is sending us messages."

"The Bad Deeds killer?" His fingers drummed against the leather.

She swallowed. "A possibility." She truly hated that name for the perpetrator.

"More like a probability, don't you mean? Seeing as how the first card was found at the strip club? The Devil card that he left for *me*."

"You assumed it was for you."

"Because you told me it means feeling trapped, enslavement—and, yes, with my past, that certainly fits the bill for me." His voice was dark and grim. "But that would mean the perp out there knows about me."

The car drove slowly through the city. "I also told you the Devil card could be about seduction."

"Yeah, that was the part I liked."

"Sometimes, though, seduction can have a darker edge. The interpretation can differ from the meaning of the Devil card that I told you."

"How does this not surprise me?"

"I wanted to be sure. That's why I checked with an expert."

"Keep talking, sweetheart."

"Sweetheart?"

"Slip of the tongue," he muttered. "Just keep going."

"The card may not have been for you. The message could have been for me. For us both. Depending on who is getting the card—the message is different."

"Cut to the chase. What's the full message?"

"Cards are always about interpretation. In this case, I was told we could interpret it to be about...temptation."

The tension in the car—already high—seemed to notch up even more.

"Temptation," he repeated.

"It can be a card that references seduction. Seduced by material items, yes, but also...physical pleasures."

He surged toward her.

She couldn't help but tense.

"You're telling me that card is some kind of warning about the attraction I feel for you? It's saying I'm being tempted?"

She wet her lips. "We're being tempted."

"So some all-knowing jackass out there realizes I want you?"

That we want each other. She held that response back. "It's possible it could have been a warning not to act on our attraction." She was using some of what she knew—suspected—for this assessment. *Not just the card.*

"So someone wants me to keep my hands off you?" His hand rose. Curled along the nape of her neck. "Am I supposed to listen to the warning?"

"That is your choice."

He didn't lower his hand. He did begin to sensually knead the tense muscles in her neck. Odd, she hadn't even realized how tense they were until he'd begun stroking her.

"What's the meaning of the Death card?" Joel asked. "You said it's not always about someone dying?"

"That would be quite literal. The cards don't usually work that way." She found herself arching into his touch. "It is about an ending though. It could be the end to a particular chapter in a person's life. The end to a relationship. Big, important change."

"Anything else?" His fingers kept up their careful work.

"The card symbolizes letting go of attachments. Severing the ties that you had in place."

"So someone is severing ties with you...or with me. If you want to get all symbolic."

"Yes." Her voice was husky.

Joel edged nearer. "Or maybe we just have a crazy killer on our hands. Some guy who has been watching you way too much. He's playing a game with you. He told Cinnamon that he wanted you to come and get him. The very fact that he left the card in the Square—don't you see? He had to be there. Hiding in the shadows. He was watching you. Stalking you." His words deepened. Roughened. "Then he left the Death card. To me, it's not about symbols. It's about that prick saying that he's coming...and he's coming to kill you."

***

The night had certainly not gone as planned. The card in the Square had not been expected. Mostly because she didn't think the man who'd left it *had* been in the Square when she'd been there. She thought he'd been there before her.

That he'd left the card, knowing she'd take that escape route. Knowing that she'd find the card.

If that was the case, he was anticipating her movements.

Which meant he was far more clever and dangerous than she'd realized.

It also meant there wasn't time to waste.

So at three a.m., she found herself standing in front of Joel's door. When they'd returned to the property, he'd left her without a word. Not that she could blame him for his anger. She *had* manipulated him. She'd pushed him to treat Jimmy's wound. She'd thought it would help Joel. Sometimes, the only way to confront a demon was to face him head on. But...

Not her call. Not her choice.

So she was going to do something that she rarely ever did.

Her hand lifted. She rapped gently on the door.

He could be sleeping. She should have considered that possibility before she'd crept all the way over to his place. He was probably exhausted, but adrenaline had kept her up so she'd assumed that he would also be—

The door flew open. "You do not want to be here right now." A low, angry growl.

Her hand was still in the air. Curved in a little fist that hovered near his chest. The lights were on behind him, so she could easily see that he wore only a pair of faded jeans that clung loosely to his hips. His chest was bare. Muscled. Flexing. A faint gleam of sweat covered his shoulders and she wondered what he'd been doing—

"Thought the scars didn't matter to you." Deep and dark.

"What scars?" Chloe asked absently because she'd just been counting that wonderful six pack of his and— "Oh, right. Yes, what about them?" Her gaze flew up to meet his.

A muscle twitched in his ever-so-clenched jaw. "Leave, Chloe." He started to shove the door closed.

"But I came to say I'm sorry, and I don't say that very often." She caught the edge of the door. "I apologize, Joel." He'd apologized to her earlier, and now it was her turn. Tit for tat, as the saying went. A real partnership.

His head tilted. "Just what is it that you are apologizing for?"

"You didn't want to work on Jimmy's wound. I pushed you. In my defense, I thought I was helping, but you didn't ask for my help, and I had no right to put you in that situation."

He laughed, but the sound was far from humorous. "This may be the worst apology that I've ever heard."

"Truly?" She tucked a lock of hair behind her ear. "I thought I was doing fairly well. All things considered."

"Go to bed, Chloe." His stare raked over her. Then his eyes squeezed shut. "I am not up for this right now."

She looked down at herself. She'd pulled on shorts. A tank top. Hadn't bothered with much else. But he was half-dressed as well, so why judge her? She dismissed that worry and decided to get to the heart of the matter as she looked back up at him. "Are you going to leave me?"

His eyes opened. "Is that why you apologized? You thought I had gotten so tired of being played by you that I was going to leave at dawn?"

She might have experienced a concern or two. "I'm not playing with you."

He moved toward her, getting very, very close in her space as he towered over her. "I get the feeling," he seemed to breathe the words against her, "that you play with everyone you meet. Maybe it's second nature to you. Maybe your mind just runs so fast that you think no one can keep up with you—"

"That's not what I—"

"But it won't work like that with me. I don't go anywhere without knowing the full truth. There is no walking blindly into situations. There is no you holding back on me because you want my reactions to be real."

She swallowed. "You're still angry."

That muscle twitched along his jaw again. "*Angry as fuck.* Eli had a knife, Chloe. What if he'd used it on you?"

"That wasn't going to happen."

"You don't know that. You can't predict everything. You're walking a very dangerous tightrope. One day, that rope is going to shake or break completely. You're going to fall. What the hell will you do if no one is there to catch you?"

A tremble slid along her body. This wasn't going at all the way she'd—

He spun away. Stalked back inside.

Slammed the door.

She didn't move, not at first. Chloe stared at the door. He hadn't told her if he would still be there in the morning. His fury had all but vibrated in the air around her. Her arms rose and curled around her stomach. She knew she should go back to the main house.

But...

Anger began to churn inside of her, too. It was hot. Tight. Unfamiliar. Her emotions were normally in such careful check. She didn't have to worry about things like this but...

Her left hand shot out to bang against the door.

It flew open immediately, as if he'd just been standing there and waiting for her. "Seriously?" Joel snarled.

"Seriously," she snapped right back. "You asked me a question. I should get to answer."

His brows lowered.

"*You.*"

"Excuse me?"

"My answer is...*you* are supposed to be there to catch me. You asked me what I'd do if no one was there. You were hired to be my partner. That means *you* will be there."

He leaned one shoulder against the doorframe.

"It means I can count on you to help me, just as I would help *you*, and if you're already backing out on basically day one—"

"I think it might be day two, or maybe even day three, if you count our bank robbery experience as day one—"

"If you're backing out already, then do me the courtesy of telling me to my face. I think I deserve that." Her chest was heaving. Her cheeks felt quite flushed.

"Happy now? Glad you got all of that off your chest?"

"No. I am not happy." Did she look happy? Sound happy? "You're angry. You're—"

"Aroused as hell."

She stopped. Blinked. Tilted her head. Studied him again.

"Do you know you do that?" Joel asked, voice almost curious.

"Do what?"

"When you're trying to figure someone or something out, you stop, stare, and it's almost like I hear a little *click, click* going on in your head as you try to evaluate the situation."

Click, click. Her body straightened. "Good night, Joel." She immediately spun and darted away from him. Her steps were fast as she surged toward escape.

"Chloe?"

She went faster. She edged around the side of the pool.

"Chloe, stop!"

She wasn't ready to stop. He'd been the one to tell her to go away and now—

He grabbed her arm. Whirled her to face him. "What the hell is wrong?"

"*I'm not a robot!*" The words emerged far too much like a scream.

"I never said you were! Hold on! I never said—"

"*Click, click,*" Chloe reminded him. "I'm sorry that my mind doesn't work the way you think it should." *Look, another apology!* Maybe she was on some kind of terrible roll. "I'm sorry that I'm not human enough for you." *Third apology!* Going for a record.

"You're human. Look, I didn't mean—"

She yanked against his hold. He held tight, and her reflexes kicked in. The training she'd had over and over again while she was growing up.

Don't be taken. Never be helpless. Don't let him hurt you.

Her leg swept out as she unbalanced Joel, then she turned with her body and hurtled him toward—

The gleaming water of the pool.

Except Joel didn't go down alone. He had never let go of her wrist and when he toppled into the pool, he was still chained to her. He pulled her with him, and they both crashed into the water. She sank fast and came up kicking, sputtering, and, with her left hand, shoving water out of her eyes.

He was beside her. Against her. Still holding her right hand. Water dripped down his face. His chest. They'd fallen into the deep end, and her feet didn't touch the bottom. She was treading water as she brushed against him.

"Did you just push me into the pool?" Joel demanded in his deep, dark voice.

Why did she like that voice? "Yes, I did. I thought you looked like you could use some cooling off."

"I'm not cooling off."

Her legs kicked in the water. "Let me go."

His fingers smoothed along her wrist. A careful caress. Then he released her.

Swim away. An internal order.

Instead, she kept treading water and staying exactly where she was. "I'm not a robot," Chloe said again. "I feel and I need just like everyone else."

"What do you need right now?"

That voice... She wouldn't answer him. She couldn't open herself up that way.

"Because I can tell you what I need, Chloe. I can tell you what I've been wanting ever since I came home tonight."

Home. Did he even realize that he'd just used that word? Probably not. Probably didn't matter. Just a slip of—

"You."

Her feet stopped kicking. She would have slipped right beneath the surface of the water, but her hands flew out and latched onto his shoulders. She held him tightly as her body pressed against his.

"I was in my bed, thinking about you. Wanting you. Then you showed up at my door with your half-assed apology."

"It wasn't half-assed." Her voice had gone husky. "I meant it."

"You showed up in the shirt that showed your tight little nipples. A top that told me quite clearly that you weren't wearing a bra."

"In the interest of honesty, I'm not wearing panties, either."

His hands wrapped around her waist. His cock shoved against her.

"You looked at me like you wanted to eat me alive, Chloe."

"I was distracted by your six pack..." Twelve pack?

"You don't care about my scars."

She stared into his eyes. The blue light of the pool was all around them. "Do you care about mine?" Her question slipped out.

"You don't have any scars, Chloe. I've never seen a single one on your body."

That was because the scars weren't on the outside.

A furrow appeared between his brows. "What do you mean about your—"

She stopped his question by kissing him. She pressed her mouth to his. Opened her lips. Darted her tongue into his mouth.

If possible, his hold on her became even harder. Even more unbreakable. He kissed her back slowly. Carefully. As if he was afraid he'd scare her off if he used too much force.

She wasn't the type to be scared. She wanted force. Passion. Power. She wanted everything that he had to give her. In return, she'd give him all that she had.

His tongue met hers. He tasted her. Took. He deepened the kiss. Let more of his hunger out to play. She loved that, and a moan trembled in her throat.

Her legs were curling around his hips. Her body arching into his.

But—

He tore his mouth from hers. "Not here. The last thing I want is your brother interrupting again."

He kept his hold on her and swam with her toward the stairs that led out of the pool. They walked up together. Her knees felt a little shaky. She stood there, dripping onto the stones of the patio.

He held out his hand to her. "This has nothing to do with our partnership."

She reached for his fingers. "Absolutely nothing."

She started walking with Joel toward his place—

Or maybe she ran with him to his home. It was a little hard to tell. All she knew was that seemingly in the next moment, they were inside the guest house. He'd slammed the door shut, and she was pinned against it. He was in front of her. All big, hot, and sexy, and his mouth was on hers. He was kissing her with the raw power she'd so craved moments before. Kissing her as if nothing mattered more.

Desire exploded within her. Her nails raked over his chest. She wanted to feel every inch of him against her body. Skin to skin. But her wet clothes were in the way.

He pulled back.

"The clothes have to come off," she panted. "I need—"

He was staring down at her chest. His expression could only be termed savage.

She looked down. Her wet clothes clung to her like a second skin. Her nipples were shoving forward against the fabric. "Um..."

He bent his head. Took one nipple—and her wet shirt—into his mouth. She gasped at the contact and arched closer to him. Her hips rocked restlessly because she needed him. Wanted him *inside* her. "Joel! You're making me go wild!"

"Good." A deep rumble. "That's the way I've been since I met you." He scooped her into his arms. Carried her into the bedroom. He dropped her on the bed, and she sank into the soft mattress.

"I'm going to get everything wet..." Her words trailed away at the look in his eyes.

"I want you wet. Wet and ready." He leaned over the bed—over her—like some kind of hungry lion.

I think he's going to eat me up.

His fingers curled around her shorts. He yanked them down. Stared at her. "No panties."

"I told you I wasn't wearing them. I wasn't lying—"

His fingers went between her legs. Pushed into her sex. Two long, strong fingers and a quick cry of pleasure escaped her. He pulled his thrusting fingers back. Pressed his thumb to her clit. Began to stroke her faster and harder.

Then he stopped.

Just...*stopped.* "Joel!" He'd taken his fingers away. Why had—

His hands were now on her thighs. He shoved them farther apart. He bent down and put his mouth on her.

She grabbed the covers. Held tight. His wicked tongue felt so good. Rough and warm and the way he was lapping at her...Licking. Stroking. Tasting her so completely...

She came. Cried out his name.

He kept tasting her. Her legs were splayed over his shoulders, and she didn't even remember putting them up there. Maybe he had. Maybe...

Who cares?

He lifted his head. Joel stared at her with a dark gaze that burned straight to her soul.

Her breath heaved out even as her heart raced. She was still gripping the covers. His hands curled around her legs. Lowered them to the bed. Aftershocks of pleasure hummed through her, and she watched—silently—as he eased away from her and moved toward the nightstand.

He was still wearing his jeans.

Those needed to go.

He opened the nightstand. Pulled out a foil packet. Gripped it. Glanced at her.

"What exactly are you waiting for?" Chloe asked him as she pushed onto her elbows. "Some fancy invitation? If so, consider that invitation sent. It was sent several moments ago when I was chanting your name."

A faint smile curved his lips as he turned back toward her.

She sat up and reached for his jeans. "These are entirely in the way." She unhooked the button, pulled down the zipper, and his cock sprang toward her. Heavy, full. Her fingers tightened around him. She squeezed and stroked. Enjoyed the way he felt. So hot and hard beneath her grip.

So she squeezed again. Stroked more. Leaned even closer to him.

"Baby, if I don't come in you right now, I will lose my mind."

"Can't have that." She blew lightly over his cock. "I rather enjoy your mind."

Things happened very quickly after that. His jeans vanished. He sheathed his dick in the condom, and she found herself beneath him on the bed. He pushed at the entrance of her body. She was slick and ready, but ever so sensitive from her recent orgasm, and when he thrust inside of her, Chloe's whole body tensed.

"You...okay? Chloe?"

"Far better than okay." She scraped her nails down his back. "Don't stop. Don't you dare stop."

Laughter. Rough. Ragged. "Wasn't planning on it."

Great. Wonderful.

He withdrew. Thrust deep. Their bodies heaved together and there was no more talking or laughing. There was panting. Moaning. Her head tipped back against the pillow as she tightened her sex around him. Squeezed hard.

Fucking perfect.

The second orgasm blasted through her body. Even longer and stronger than the first. She was shuddering and gasping and probably doing some serious damage with her nails, but there was no control. She couldn't pull herself back.

And she didn't want to pull back.

He was with her. His hands gripped her hips. Joel's hold was strong. Possessive. He lifted her up. Positioned her so that he could plunge as deep and hard into her as he wanted.

As she wanted.

She was staring into his eyes when the release hit him. She saw the faint gold in his eyes burn ever hotter with pleasure. Primal satisfaction hardened his features. She couldn't look away. She could feel the tremors in his body. The jerk of his cock inside of her.

Her hand lifted. Touched his cheek. Her fingers slid toward his mouth. Lightly traced the faint scar that sliced his lip.

"Kiss me," she whispered.

His head lowered. His mouth brushed over hers.

Even as she felt a teardrop slide down her cheek.

CHAPTER EIGHTEEN

"Running away?" Joel asked without opening his eyes. He'd been aware of her careful movements. Sleep hadn't been a possibility for him. He'd been too focused on her. On the insane pleasure they'd had together.

In the aftermath, he'd ditched the condom. Come back to the bed. Pulled her into his arms. He wanted to go again. Over and over. But pushing for that hadn't seemed...hell, he didn't know what it had seemed. *Gentlemanly?* Since when was he a fucking gentleman? Or maybe pushing to go again had seemed too savage. Too hungry.

When it came to Chloe, he was finding that he was rather savage. *I need her.*

He hadn't pushed. He'd just held her a moment. Her breathing had eased. Her hand had pressed to his chest, over the scars as if they weren't even there.

She doesn't care.

He'd been sure that she'd drifted to sleep. Holding her that way, it had seemed almost soothing for him. He hadn't actually *slept* with anyone since his attack. His eyes had slid closed, and he'd been more relaxed than he could remember...

Until she started to slip away.

"Hardly running," Chloe replied. "I was more planning on tip-toeing in the hopes that I wouldn't wake you."

His eyes opened. His head turned toward her. He'd left the bedside lamp on, and he could see her clearly.

Fuck. She was standing naked near the side of the bed.

"Just getting my clothes. Dressing. Going back to my room." She scooped up her shirt. Frowned at it. "Still wet. Do you mind if I just borrow one of your shirts?"

She was beautiful. Perfect. *Those breasts. The flare of her hips.*

"Joel? Do you mind if I use one of your shirts?"

He'd prefer she stay naked but... "Help yourself."

She dug in a nearby drawer and pulled out one of his old college shirts. When she put it on, the shirt swallowed her, falling way past mid-thigh and scooping off one shoulder.

The shirt shouldn't have been sexy. It was old and faded. Had a few holes in it. But on her...*Better than any negligee.*

What was up with him having that thought? But there was just something about seeing her in *his* shirt.

"Why are you looking at me like that?" Her head tilted. She studied him and for one second—

Click, click—

He stopped. Shut down the thought. She was damn well no robot. She'd burned hell-hot in his arms, and he wanted her, again and again.

"I'm looking at you like this..." Joel explained in a voice deepened by need, "because I want you again."

She bit her lower lip.

"And you're running away. So..."

"I'm not running away. I was going back to my room. I wasn't sure how you'd feel about someone sleeping in the bed with you all night. And sleeping is...personal."

Joel laughed. "But fucking isn't?"

She looked down.

Shit. Had he just hurt her feelings? "Chloe, I didn't mean—"

"Sometimes, I have nightmares. They can be pretty intense. I've even been known to...hit or attack the person with me."

His brows climbed.

"I thought it would be better if I slipped away. You seemed so peaceful that I thought you were asleep and you wouldn't even notice that I'd left."

He had been feeling peaceful. Not because he'd been asleep, though, but because she'd been in his arms. Now he sat up. The sheets bunched around his waist.

"Didn't think you'd enjoy getting a fist to the face." A shrug from Chloe as her gaze slowly rose. "Trying to leave on a high note, as it were."

"What do you have nightmares about?"

Her long lashes flickered. "Is this the part where I'm supposed to say...tell me yours, and I will tell you mine?"

"Chloe..." He didn't talk about his nightmares. Sure, he'd gone to see a shrink after the attack and killing. But he'd gotten nothing from good old Gordo.

Nothing good. *Only more bad.* But, no, he didn't want to think about that part. About how Gordo thought he was some kind of ticking time bomb. *When you're pushed too hard, your psyche will break. You will break.*

"I think we may be more alike than you initially realized, Joel. We both like to keep things inside." She returned to the bed. Stared down at him. "It's late. We should both get some sleep."

"I'll walk you back."

"You don't have to—"

He climbed out of the bed. She backed up. He stood toe-to-toe with her. "If you're not staying in my bed, the least I can do is walk you home."

"I live on the same property with you. It's less than a three-minute walk."

"Humor me."

"Because you're being...a gentleman? Seeing the lady home?"

"You actually think I'm a gentleman?" His words mocked her.

"I think you're something quite extraordinary."

"What?"

She looked away. "Your jeans are wet."

"I'll wear sweats." He grabbed a pair. Didn't bother with a shirt. Odd, because he used to stay covered up almost fanatically. Not wanting anyone to see the scars and stare at him. Not wanting people to ask what happened. Not wanting pity or horror but—

Chloe didn't care about the scars.

So why the hell should he? And if other people didn't like them...*screw off*. Those other people and their reactions didn't matter. Not like they were Chloe. She mattered. She—

Whoa. Down boy. Slow your roll. It was one bout of crazy-good sex. Settle. Down.

She hurried out of his home. Her steps were silent over the stone pathway. He trailed her, but wasn't sure what he was supposed to say. *Let's do that again? Over and over until neither of us can move?* Did that sound desperate? Or demanding?

Both?

The night was quiet. Still. Hot.

His gaze flickered toward the pool. A smile tugged at his lips when he thought of her pushing him in. Her attack had actually been pretty good. No, better than good. It had been... "Fuck me."

"Again? Right here?" She spun toward him. "We're a little close to the house, and Marie is quite the night owl so—"

"You've had training."

"Can you be more specific? Are you talking about sexual training? Because I did once learn the art of the strip tease but it was for a case that I was working."

He filed that fun tidbit away in his brain under the section for *Will Definitely Pull Up Later*, and focused—tried to focus—on the matter at hand. "You said you hired me for protection. But you know self-defense moves."

"I think it is important for every woman to know some basic self-defense. The world we live in is very dangerous."

He eliminated the distance between them. Seemed to always be doing that. *Because I like being close to her too much.* "You know more than basic moves."

She didn't deny those words. She also didn't confirm them.

"If you can handle yourself, why do you need a bodyguard?"

"Extra assistance is always valuable. And I need you for more than just bodyguard work. Your medical knowledge has proven quite valuable so far."

"Bullshit. I get the feeling you can figure out pretty much everything on your own." He had to be missing something.

"You have skills that I value." Her head tilted back. Shadows surrounded them, so he couldn't make out her expression. "After your attack, you picked up all sorts of fun talents. Krav Maga, Brazilian Jiu Jitsu, Combat Sambo, Kickboxing, the Keysi Fighting Method—"

"It worries me when you know so much about me."

"It shouldn't. I have no intention of ever using anything I know against you. Please believe that."

Okay. So that statement had been odd. Yet for some reason, he did believe her. "And I won't use anything I learn against you."

Her lips parted. "Promise?" A whisper.

The air was tense. Her voice had broken just a little with her whisper. "Yes, baby." His head bent and his lips brushed over hers. "I promise."

Her fingers curled over his shoulders. She leaned into him. Met his tongue with her own in a careful, sensual caress.

Then she slowly eased back. "What do you think we should do tomorrow? Regarding the case?"

Okay, that was a one-eighty. So much for his hope that they'd be hitting the sheets again.

She was straightening her shoulders. Lifting her chin. Trying to get back to business? She should get that was an impossible task when she stood before him, clad in his shirt and not wearing underwear.

But...perhaps he'd play along. Because there had been a note of vulnerability in her voice that he hadn't expected. Something that nagged at him.

When she turned and began walking to the main house once more, Joel fell into step beside her. "I think we're focusing on the present too much."

"Do you?"

"These vics are all linked by what happened in the past, aren't they? So why aren't we looking at that?"

He thought he caught the flash of her smile as she glanced away. Then Chloe said, "I certainly hope the special agent has contacted the old football coach who knew the vics. Surely, he'd have insight to offer."

"Oh, yes, the coach would know his players." He paused. "But I'm certain other people would know them, too."

They were in front of the main house. She hesitated at the door. "Tomorrow is a Sunday. Their old high school won't be open, but I suspect we could manage to pay a visit to someone else who might be able to shed light on the past for us."

"You already have something lined up, don't you?" Sure, she did.

"I might." She faced him. "Turns out, the retired librarian from that high school lives about thirty minutes away. Maybe we could join her for a spot of tea."

"People in England have a spot of tea. People down here have sweet tea served in pitchers, often with lots and lots of sugar added. Iced tea. Cold and delicious."

"Then we should join her for one of those pitchers of the cold tea."

God, she made him want to smile. He rubbed his chest. "Say...noon?"

"That's precisely what I was thinking. Though we should plan to leave so that we can *arrive* at the librarian's house at noon."

Holy hell. She'd already scheduled the meeting. "Did you just test me? Like, you already had all of this in your head, and you just wanted to see if I could come to the same conclusion that you did?"

"If it was a test, you passed."

Well, happy day.

She reached for the door. It opened before she could curl her fingers around the doorknob.

"Thought I heard someone," Reese announced blandly. "I was going for a drink of water. Figured I'd better check to make sure thieves weren't afoot." His gaze trailed over Chloe. His eyebrows shot up. "Interesting fashion choice."

"Thank you. I do feel quite comfortable."

No embarrassment at all. That was his Chloe. *Wait. Back up...mine?*

She offered him a faint smile. "Good night, Joel. Let's plan to meet around eleven, shall we?"

He nodded. "See you then."

She brushed past her brother.

Reese stared at him. He didn't look very happy.

Too bad. For the first time in a very long while, Joel felt happy. *Because of her.*

Reese waited a little, probably long enough for Chloe to head upstairs, then he stepped forward, coming outside fully. He shut the door behind him. "I don't like the way you're looking at my sister."

Ah, the faint British accent was in full effect. "Exactly how am I looking at her?"

"You know how you're looking at her," he snapped back.

Joel nodded. "She's an adult. I'm an adult. Don't really see how this is your business."

"She is my *sister.*"

"Is she?" Now he was truly curious. "There doesn't seem to be much of a family resemblance between you. And you know what?" He leaned conspiratorially close to Reese. "When you drink enough, you lose your inhibitions...and your accent."

Reese swallowed. "Chloe is my family. I value her more than I value anyone else in this world."

The guy sounded one hundred percent sincere. Interesting.

"I would do anything to protect her. You need to understand that from the get-go. She may think you're not dangerous, but she's been wrong before." A rough laugh rumbled from Reese. "Sure, Chloe hates to admit when she's wrong. But it happens. I had to pick up the pieces last time. I had to see her pain. I won't let her go through that again."

"I'm very curious now." He was. "A few days ago, you were the one offering me a job. Now— and correct me if I'm wrong here—you're the one threatening me? What do you want, for me to leave Chloe? Because that's—" Joel stopped before he said...*Not ever going to happen.*

Whoa. Way whoa. They'd had sex one time. Only one. They'd known each other for a few days. This was hardly some permanent relationship.

"Of course, I don't want you to leave her." Reese squinted at him. "Why the hell would you think that?"

His temples were starting to throb. "Because you're warning me away from her?"

"I'm telling you not to hurt her, jackass! I happen to love that woman. I don't love many things in this world, but I love her. She saved me. So if she's wrong about you, if you turn out to be some crazed, out-of-your-head, psycho killer, then I will end you. Do you understand me?"

"I think you are being exceptionally clear." Truly. Clear and loud. "And you know what? If I do turn out to be some crazed, out-of-my-head, psycho killer...you need to come for me."

"What?"

"Stop me. Come and—" *Shit*. His breath heaved out.

"You okay, man?" Reese asked. "You just...your face just went all weird."

"Come and get me," Joel rasped.

"Yes, damn straight I will. Didn't you hear what I said to you like thirty seconds ago?"

"No, that's what the killer we're after—the perp we're hunting—he left that message for Chloe."

Reese gaped. "When? Where? What the hell are you even talking about?"

"The Bad Deeds killer." His hands were clenching and releasing. "He told the witness who saw him...he told her to tell Hastings... *'Come and get me.'*"

Reese rubbed the back of his neck. "I don't like that. Chloe didn't mention that part to me."

"I thought he was taunting her. Like some kind of challenge. But maybe it's more." He turned away. Shuffled back toward the guest house.

"More like what, Joel? Don't leave me hanging!"

"More like..." He looked over his shoulder. "He's a crazed, out-of-his-head, psycho killer who can't stop himself, and he needs her to do it."

Reese flinched. "Do not leave her." A rough warning.

"I wasn't planning to."

"You were hired to protect her. No matter what happens—personally—between the two of you, swear to me that you'll keep her safe."

That was easy enough. "I swear, I will keep her safe."

Reese's head moved in a jerky nod. He turned and fumbled with the door handle.

Joel felt rooted to the spot. "You're not her biological brother, are you?"

"Don't know what you're talking about. I'm her brother, and I would do anything for her." He had the door open.

"And I'm not the enemy. If I'm supposed to protect her from every threat out there, don't you think I shouldn't be wasting time wandering around in the dark? Don't you think you all need to trust me with the secrets you carry?"

Reese hadn't stormed inside. He was lingering. Hesitating. So Joel pushed his point. "I can protect her better when I know everything. If you really want her safe, if you really love her—"

"Morgan Fletcher."

"Who in the hell is that?"

"The man she almost married. Make sure he never, ever comes close to her again." Reese rushed inside. Shut the door. A little too hard.

For a moment, Joel didn't move at all.

The man she almost married. Tension knotted his muscles. His temples throbbed a little harder. Chloe had nearly married someone?

He stalked back to his place. Threw open the door. Started to head back to the bedroom. Stopped.

His laptop was still on the desk. It would take like...two minutes to do a quick search on Morgan Fletcher. He could spare two minutes.

He yanked open the laptop. His fingers flew over the keypad.

So, yes, this is what jealousy feels like. A hot, angry knot in his stomach.

There were probably lots of Morgan Fletchers in the world. Tons of them. What had he been thinking? It would probably take longer than two minutes to find Chloe's Morgan.

Not her Morgan.

But...

It didn't take long. Not long at all. Less than two minutes, in fact. Because the first result that popped up in his search...

Criminal defense lawyer Morgan Fletcher is presumed dead after his yacht capsized off the Boston coast.

Joel swallowed. Read a few more articles. Even managed to find...

Morgan Fletcher had been scheduled to sail with his fiancée, Chloe Hastings, but due to a family emergency, she was unable to venture out with him. Authorities believe an electrical malfunction caused the yacht to...

More articles and then...

After an exhaustive five-day search, the Coast Guard suspended the search for Morgan Fletcher. The family is asking for privacy at this time as...

There was a picture with that story. A photo of a handsome man with sun-streaked, blond hair. Dark eyes. Wide, charming smile. He had his arms around a dark-haired woman. She was staring up at him ever so solemnly even as he looked at the camera, so only her profile was available. But it was a profile that Joel would have recognized anywhere.

Chloe.

CHAPTER NINETEEN

"You seem oddly quiet today." Chloe climbed off the motorcycle and toyed with the helmet. "Is something wrong?"

Joel took the helmet from her. Rolled back his shoulders and stood at her side. "Hard to talk when we're driving so fast."

"Yes, certainly, but..." Something was off. She could see the tension in the tightness of his jaw. "What happened?"

Joel glanced toward the tidy, brick house that waited behind two oak trees. The giant trees were heavy with swaying Spanish moss. "Nothing happened. What was the librarian's name again?"

"Judith Key."

He advanced for the house.

She grabbed his arm. "If you regret what happened between us last night, then it will not happen again." She spoke quickly, wanting to get this out fast. "You needn't worry about—"

He spun toward her.

Oh.

That wasn't regret in his stare. She hadn't been able to see his eyes during their tense ride. But now that she was staring straight at him, she could plainly see the heat staring back at her.

"It will definitely happen again," Joel assured her.

"That's good to know." Chloe licked her lower lip. "So...what's the problem today?"

"There is no problem."

Frustration surged through her. "When you hold back, it makes things harder between us." She let him go. Strode determinedly for the house.

The sound of his laughter stopped her. "You are not serious."

She did a quick about-face. "I absolutely am."

"You're the queen of holding back."

Her spine snapped straight. "That is just insulting."

"You know about all the broken pieces that I have. You know what happened to me, how I spiraled, hell, you know that my girlfriend couldn't handle the sight of me...somehow, you know it all, don't you?"

Yes. "Does it matter?"

"Morgan Fletcher."

She didn't flinch. Didn't gasp dramatically. Didn't move at all.

And that seemed to frustrate him because his lips thinned. His nostrils flared.

Then he was the one closing in and reaching out to her. Except his hold wasn't rough. Despite the heat blazing in his eyes, his touch was careful. Gentle.

Confused, she frowned at him.

"You can let me in," he told her as his hand slid down to circle her wrist. "You can do that. I understand, okay? You lost someone close to you. It hurt. You were going to marry him, and now you've put up these walls because you are afraid of being hurt again."

She looked down at his hand. He was rubbing his thumb along her pulse. "I'm confused. Your eyes look angry, but your touch is...comforting?"

"Yes," he gritted out.

"Why are you comforting me?"

"Because you lost someone you loved."

"I see. And the anger? Why are you so angry?"

His jaw hardened. "I think I'm jealous."

"Excuse me?"

"Forget it."

She wouldn't. She didn't forget anything. "You don't need to comfort me, but it is a kind gesture."

His thumb stopped sliding over her wrist. "Because...you didn't love him?"

She pulled away. Turned away. "Because I didn't lose him. Morgan isn't dead." Her gaze was on the front of the house. She took another step toward it. Narrowed her eyes. "Oh, dear."

"What the hell do you mean, he's not dead?"

"The door is ajar."

He rushed forward. Stopped. Stared. "So? Maybe Judith Key left it open while she went out to do some yard work or something."

"Perhaps." She crept closer to the house.

"You don't think it's something innocent and easy, do you?"

"No, I do not." In her experience, doors left ajar were rarely ever a good sign. People had become very vigilant in this day and age. The era of leaving your doors open? Gone. The news had seen to that. The news screamed that threats were everywhere, even right next door.

When they reached the front porch, her suspicions were confirmed. The doorknob and lock had both been smashed. A heavy weight settled along her shoulders.

"We should call the cops." Joel's voice was low.

"Yes." She nodded. And used her elbow to push the door open.

"Chloe!" A strained whisper from Joel. "Stop!"

Too late. She was already inside. She could see the smashed furniture. The broken lamps. The chaos.

Joel grabbed her arm. "What are you doing? You can't—"

"Do you smell that?" She did another deep inhale. "It's blood."

"All the more reason for us to get out—"

"What if she's still alive?"

His eyes glittered at her.

Then...she heard a moan. Faint. So weak. Coming from the right. Down the hallway? Maybe...in a bedroom? She lunged in the direction of the sound.

Joel grabbed her, locked his arm around her stomach, and hauled her back. "Oh, hell, no."

"Joel! Someone is hurt!"

"Or it's a trap. The way this weekend is going, anything can happen. You *stay* here, understand? I'll check it out. That's why I got brought into the picture, remember? To protect your lovely ass." He pushed her behind him. "Stay here."

He rushed down the hallway. She had to admit, his rush was very quiet. Sneaky. Chloe craned her head and saw him slip into an open doorway.

She pulled out her phone. Typed *SOS* and the location. Sent the text to Cedric.

She didn't hear anything. Not from Joel. Not any other moans from their would-be victim. Joel had told her to stay put but...

When he got to know her better, he'd realize that was never an option.

She crept down the hallway. She also made sure to pull her gun out of her bag. She kept it down near her side as she edged toward the open doorway. And then...

Joel. He was on his knees. His hands were covered in blood.

A woman with salt and pepper hair sprawled before him. Her face was chalk white. Her lips were parted, and she struggled to speak. Another weak moan came from her.

"Call nine-one-one," Joel barked at Chloe. "And don't you *dare* leave this room!"

She shoved the gun back into her purse even as she grabbed for the phone. "Why can't I leave?"

"Because she's still alive. Because I'm holding my fucking fingers inside her to stop her from bleeding out. Because the attack happened just *minutes* ago. If it had happened longer than that, she would already be dead. That means the bastard is still here."

Chloe took a step toward the doorway even as she dialed nine-one-one.

"*Don't,*" Joel snarled at her. "Don't you face him alone. *Stay* with me. Don't make me choose between protecting you and saving her."

She put the phone to her ear. "I thought we agreed last night that I could protect myself..."

"Chloe..." Joel warned.

"*Nine-one-one, what is the nature of your emergency?*"

The killer was out there. Could be close. Had to be close. *Dammit.* Chloe slammed the bedroom door. Locked it. Secured herself in that room with Joel and the victim. "A woman has been stabbed."

"Barely missed her heart," Joel called out. "Profuse bleeding. Victim is in shock. Pulse rate is—"

"She's very bad," Chloe added. "There's a lot of blood and we think the attacker is still somewhere close by. So if you could please send help very, very quickly, that would be appreciated." She rattled off the address. "Thank you." She swung back around toward Joel.

The woman—Judith—stared at up him. Tears streamed on her cheeks.

"Stay with me," Joel urged Judith. "You're going to be fine, you understand me? *Stay with me.*"

Blood was on his hands. His wrists. His forearms. The blood was everywhere.

Chloe swayed. Her breath panted out.

The blood was everywhere because Joel had put his fingers into the vicious stab wounds on Judith's chest.

Wake up, wake up! A scream echoed in Chloe's mind. *It was a mistake! I want to take it back. I want to—*

"Chloe!" Joel thundered. "Chloe, I need you!"

She blinked.

Joel was there. Joel and all the blood.

"Wh-what can I do?" Chloe managed to ask.

CHAPTER TWENTY

The stretcher burst out of the house.

Cedric grabbed Chloe and hauled her to the side. Judith was on the stretcher. Joel was straddled on top of her—working furiously and calling out orders to the paramedics as they wheeled Judith and Joel toward the back of the waiting ambulance.

Chloe's breath came faster as she stared at Joel. She tried to ignore the stickiness on her fingers. The blood that wasn't dry on her yet.

The back doors of the ambulance were slammed shut. The siren screamed.

The ambulance raced away.

"Why were you here?" Cedric asked softly.

Another car had just arrived on the scene. A way too obvious black SUV. Surprise, surprise, Agent Richardson shoved open the driver's side door.

Someone was always late to the party.

"Chloe."

She glanced at Cedric.

"You're very pale. You're not going to pass out on me or anything, are you?"

Her chin notched up. "Absolutely not. I can't believe you'd even suggest such a thing."

"Right." He paused a beat. "Why were you here?"

"We were following a lead."

Richardson was slithering closer.

"What kind of lead?" Cedric wanted to know. He caught sight of Richardson and shifted a bit closer to Chloe.

"Judith was a former librarian for—"

"She was the high school librarian for the championship winning Pirates, right, Chloe?" Richardson inserted, voice as nasally as ever. "And you thought she could tell you about the men who've been killed."

"The thought did cross my mind, yes."

"You're slow." He shook his head at her. "I was here yesterday talking to her, and, hate to break it to you, but she had nothing to add to our investigation. The dead men didn't exactly hang out in her library."

"Well, considering that someone came in today and tried to shove a knife in her heart," Chloe returned as frost slid in her voice, "someone must have thought that she *did* have something to add." She raised one eyebrow. "Perhaps you simply didn't ask her the correct questions. You've done that before, you know. Asked the wrong questions. Made the wrong assumptions. And innocent people paid the price."

Cedric whistled.

She knew that whistle was a warning to her. He was trying to tell her to watch herself before she went too far. But she wasn't in the mood to heed warnings. Blood was on her hands. It was sticky and cold now, and it reminded her far too much of things that were better left forgotten.

"Ah, Chloe..." Cedric had pulled out his trusty notepad. "Did you see the attacker?"

"No. Joel wouldn't let me chase him, so...no."

"Wouldn't *let* you?" Cedric stared at her as if she'd just grown two heads.

Her breath huffed out. "He had his fingers in the woman's chest. He was spouting off about how he couldn't save her and protect me and even though he said the perp had attacked only moments before, he insisted that I stay close by. *In* the room." She lifted her fingers. "I helped him. We saved that woman."

"She's probably going to die." A casual observation from one of the crime scene techs who walked past. "I mean, did you *see* the size of that blood pool in there?"

Cedric squinted his eyes as his gaze raked over Chloe. "Are you cold?"

She looked down. Goosebumps covered her arms.

The always dapper Cedric shouldered out of his pressed coat and put it around her shoulders.

It was still warm from his body. She gave him a grateful smile.

"Maybe you want her to die."

At that dark statement, her gaze jumped to Richardson.

"If Judith Key dies, then she won't be able to point the finger at the person who attacked her."

Don't let him get beneath your skin. Do not. "The police officers that you see around us are currently scouting the area for clues. Hopefully, they'll find something that will lead us to her attacker. *And* she will—hopefully—survive the attack. After all, she had a highly trained doctor at her side within moments, and he just left in the ambulance with her. Joel wasn't going to abandon her."

Richardson pursed his lips. "That what he was doing? Saving her? Heard some chatter about him on the radio."

She didn't like the way his face tightened when he talked about Joel. Oh, who was she kidding? There was very little she did like about the man.

"Chloe." Cedric's voice was warm. Gentle.

She returned her attention to him.

"I just have to get all of this down, then you can go to the hospital, too."

Yes, she wanted to go there.

"You had the idea to come and talk to Judith today because you thought she could give you insight on the case?"

Her breathing hitched the faintest bit. "We had an appointment at noon to talk with Judith. Someone beat us here."

"You sent me an SOS text before you called nine-one-one," Cedric noted.

"The front lock was broken. As soon as I saw it, I texted you."

"*And you still went inside?*" Richardson's voice rose even more at her. "Even knowing you were entering a crime scene?"

"We went inside and helped a victim. I'm sure it's quite appropriate to do something like that." She needed to get the blood off her fingers. "Do you mind if I go back inside? I need to wash this blood away."

"I do mind." Richardson stepped into her path. "It's a crime scene. You don't get to waltz back inside."

"You should let me in there. I might see something that your people miss."

Oh, he didn't like that. Not one bit. *If looks could kill...*

"What were you going to ask her?" Richardson suddenly wanted to know.

"I *will* ask her...when I see her at the hospital...if anything unusual happened at the school during that championship year. If anyone was killed, died in an accident, went missing—"

Now he laughed. "You honestly think I haven't checked all of that? I'm not a moron, Chloe. I've pulled up records. I talked to the coach. I talked to *her* because the coach told me that she had old yearbooks I could look at to see the whole class since that shit isn't online."

She didn't bat an eyelash. "Did you see the yearbooks?"

"All but the year I needed. When I was here yesterday, she said she'd misplaced that one. She was going to look and find it for me."

"Her home is trashed." Chloe considered the ramifications of that chaos. "Perhaps the attacker was looking for the yearbook, too. Assuming, that is, her attacker is the same perp that we're after from the Bad Deeds murders. And if it's him, he'd have to be watching you. If he's a smart killer, that's what he should be doing. Keeping an eye on the lead investigator. Watching what he does.

Who he talks to." She surveyed the scene. The thick foliage. The heavy oaks. "Maybe he saw you leave here empty handed. Maybe you brought him right to her."

"Are you saying her attack is my fault?"

"I'm saying that you need to make certain you're not being watched. And, hopefully, Judith will fully recover and be able identify her attacker for us. Now, I'm sorry, but I don't have more to add. I want to get to the hospital so unless you have more questions for me..." She directed her attention at Cedric, not Richardson.

"I'll call you," Cedric promised. "If I need to follow-up."

"Thank you." She was more than ready to leave.

But Richardson kept getting in her way. He smiled at her. "Just how did you arrive here, Chloe? I only see a motorcycle. I don't see your typical—"

She lifted her bloody fingers—and the keys that Joel had given her while they were in the house. "I'll be taking the motorcycle, but thank you for the kind offer of a ride."

"I didn't offer—" Richardson blustered as his cheeks went red.

Cedric was called away.

Richardson immediately sidled even closer to her. "You need to watch yourself."

Curiosity compelled her to ask, "Are you threatening me?"

"No, I'm trying to give you advice. Ever since you came strolling in with Dr. Landry, I've been checking up on him. He's bad news."

"I find him to be delightful news."

"No, you don't. You find few things in life to be delightful. You're not wired that way. If you're with him, it's because you're working an agenda. Either you think you can use him or..." He searched her eyes. "Maybe you even think he's the killer you're after. I *talked* to his shrink from Dallas. Got the guy to give me his take on the dangerous doctor."

She eased out a soft breath. "That sounds very much like something the shrink should not have revealed. Patient-client confidentiality and all. He'd better be careful or Dr. Jennings will find himself without a license."

Oh, no.

"Got you." Richardson grinned at her.

"You do?" Her voice was perfectly calm even as her heart raced. "I didn't realize you were touching me."

"I never told you the shrink's name. You knew it already. That means you've been digging into Joel's past, haven't you?" The agent's eyes gleamed. "You don't trust him, not for a second. Keep your friends close but your enemies closer, am I right? So tell me...the real reason you didn't go rushing to look for a suspect in the attack here today—it's because you had a suspect in your sights, didn't you? You thought Joel *was* the attacker. Did he get here before you? Or maybe— hell, was *he* the one who came up with the idea to come out here?" His words tumbled out, faster and faster. "Maybe he was doing some big theater piece in front of you. Acting like he was saving the woman when really, he was just finishing her off.

You stayed with them because you wanted to make sure she lived. Because at your core, you're not as crazy as some people say. You're—"

"Crazy isn't a clinical term. It's highly overused. I get tired of reminding people about that. And if you must know, I keep my friends close because they matter to me. I am very protective of them. As far as Dr. Jennings is concerned, I knew his name because Joel told me his name." The lie was smooth and easy. "And since Joel has *saved* Judith's life, you can come to the hospital and ask her about the attacker yourself. I'm sure she'll clear Joel."

"Too late, Chloe. Too late. You screwed up. I saw it in your eyes. It was only there for a second, but you wished you could take the words back. As soon as you said the doctor's name, you realized what you'd done."

"You have no idea what I wish. Don't delude yourself into thinking that you do." She stepped around him. "I have places to go. Crimes to solve. You should try that sometime. You know, the crime solving part."

"Joel Landry is dangerous!"

"Anyone can be dangerous. It's all about the circumstances. How far an individual can be pushed..."

Before he or she breaks.

***

She rode away on the motorcycle as if she drove motorcycles every single day. Revved the engine and shot away like she was about to win some race.

But she'd shown her hand. She didn't often make mistakes, he'd give Chloe Hastings that, but this time, she'd screwed up. And as he'd hoped and prayed, he'd been there to see it happen.

Paul Richardson put his phone to his ear. "Get Dr. Gordon Jennings on a plane. I want him here, as fast as possible."

Chloe never did anything without a reason. Getting close to Joel on *this* case? Their sudden acquaintance meant the former surgeon *had* to be connected to the killings.

And Dr. Gordon Jennings was going to help Paul figure out that connection.

***

Hospitals were too bright. The overhead lights often made her head ache. The scent of antiseptic burned her nose, and the clean floors squeaked too much beneath her feet. The temperature was always too cold for her, and the constant pages that sounded over the intercom distracted her.

She couldn't afford more distractions. She'd already screwed up once that day.

Chloe had gotten the blood off her hands, but each time she looked down at her fingers, she swore she could still feel the stickiness on her skin.

She hated that stickiness.

"Chloe?"

She looked up. She'd been sitting in a very uncomfortable chair—one with a long tear along the seat that exposed the cushion and rubbed against the back of her thigh.

"Chloe?" The man in the white lab coat took a few quick steps toward her. "What's happened? Is everything okay?" A stethoscope dangled around his neck.

"Dane." She stood. Her knees felt a little shaky. *Unacceptable.* "I didn't realize you were still here. I-I was told that you'd transferred down to Florida."

"Yes, well, that's because I *was* offered a job down there after I finished my residency." He closed in on her. "The position was in Miami. Seemed perfect. I even tried things out for a few weeks, but it just wasn't home. Came back here a few days ago when the hospital director called me. There was an opening for an ER doc. I took it." His gaze assessed her. "Do you know that you have blood on your shirt?"

"Better than having blood on my hands."

He backed up a step. "Uh...yes? It is?"

"You're working the ER here." He'd been a resident before, but he'd finished up that work. Then gone to Miami. *Now Dane is back...*

"Yes, yes, that's what I just said. My shift started a few minutes—"

"I need you to check on a patient for me. The lady at the front desk was extremely unhelpful."

Surprise flashed across his handsome features. "Sally? Everyone loves her. She's—"

"I would love to hear a list of Sally's many virtues, but could you tell me about them after you check on the patient? Her name is Judith Key. She's a stabbing victim. She was brought in a little while ago and—"

"She's in recovery. I just heard about her, actually. Seems some doctor was on scene and he was able to keep her alive. Guy's being called a hero."

As if on cue, Joel pushed open the ER's swinging doors. He paused to talk with some man in a suit. A man with glasses and an attitude of authority. The fellow slapped his hand on Joel's shoulder.

Joel's head turned. He looked around the waiting area as if he was searching for—

Me.

His stare locked on her.

She could almost feel him exhale. Or maybe she was the one doing that because relief burst through her.

"Chloe?" Dane put his hands on her shoulders. "Are you all right? Do I need to check you out? You're very pale. I know you have that blood issue and judging by your shirt, you are *not* having a good day."

"Could be a much worse day. You could have told me that Judith was dead."

Joel stalked toward them. Someone had given him a pair of green scrubs to wear. His hands were clean—no blood on him—and his eyes seemed to shine with flecks of gold. "She made it," Joel announced.

Was he aware of how he sounded? Excited? *Happy?*

Chloe smiled at him. "That's just what Dane was telling me."

Dane let go of her shoulders and turned toward Joel.

Time for fast introductions. "Dr. Dane Ambrose, this is Joel Landry. Dr. Joel Landry. He's the hero you were telling me about."

Dane flashed a warm smile at Joel and offered his hand. "You're already a legend." He laughed. "Got to ask, did you really keep your fingers in her chest during the entire ambulance ride?"

"I'm not a legend. I'm just someone who is very glad that Judith is okay." He shook Dane's hand. His gaze assessed Chloe. "You're too pale."

"People keep telling me that. It is starting to become insulting."

"Oh, Chloe, you're still gorgeous," Dane assured her. "But you look as if you might faint at any moment. Want me to check you out?"

"No. I'm good." The last thing she wanted was to be checked out by Dane. "How is Judith?" Chloe asked Joel. "Did she say anything about her attacker?"

"The lady isn't exactly talking." He crossed his arms over his chest. "And she's also sporting a concussion on the back of her head. My guess is the attacker hit from behind to take her down. Then he stabbed her. She might not have ever seen him." His attention shifted between Chloe and Dane. "How do you two know each other?"

"Uh…" Dane coughed. "I need to finish my rounds. Chloe, we'll catch up soon." He hurried away.

She didn't pay him any attention. Her focus was on Joel. "Are you upset?"

His eyes narrowed. "Because the young doc wanted to check you out? Mildly annoyed, not—"

"Because you crossed the line again. You say you don't want to be helping people, saving them, but you just did it again with Judith. Only, unlike your experience with Jimmy, you don't appear particularly shaken in the aftermath."

His hands dropped to his sides. "I was not shaken when I stitched up Jimmy."

"Fine. Choose another word." She inched closer to him. "You're different."

"I-I didn't think about it. I just did it. Hell, maybe it was easier because of what happened with Jimmy. I just..." He trailed away. "Can we get out of here?"

Brilliant idea. "Yes. Let's. I have never been a major hospital fan." She immediately turned on her heel and hurried through the waiting area. She sniffed when she passed the unhelpful Sally. Then they were outside. The motorcycle waited, gleaming in the light.

"Uh, did you drive that here?"

"No, it drove itself here." She straddled the bike. Gave him an expectant look.

His lips curved. "I like it when you're sarcastic."

"No, you just like me." She actually meant those words to be sarcastic.

But Joel nodded and appeared all solemn. "Yes, I do." He bent and brushed his lips against hers.

Her fingers clutched the front of his scrubs. *Scrubs?* "Joel..." Chloe murmured against his mouth. "Where are your clothes?"

"In a garbage can someplace. They were covered in blood." He feathered another kiss over her lips. "I'm so fucking glad she made it." A shudder worked over his body. His forehead pressed to hers.

"She made it because of you. If I'd been there without you, I wouldn't have been able to save her. You made a difference."

He didn't move away from her. "Maybe we do make a pretty good team."

Yes, she was starting to think the exact same thing.

***

She needed to get the hell out of town. Cinnamon stared at her reflection. She hadn't put on makeup yet. Her eyes were too big. Her lips devoid of color. She hadn't been sleeping well. Not since Donnie's death. Him dying should have made everything easier for her.

But every time she closed her eyes, nightmares came.

I saw him.

She'd lied to Chloe Hastings. Lied to the cops. Lies were pretty easy for her. Mostly because they were a matter of survival. She'd figured that Donnie had deserved exactly what he got. So she shouldn't have felt guilty.

But in her nightmares, she was the one swinging the bat at him.

Her image became blurry. Shit. Why was she crying?

Cinnamon wiped away the tears. Stupid, useless tears. She needed to get out of this town. Start a new life. Stop being Cinnamon. Maybe she could go back to being Coreen Miller.

Only...it was hard to remember her. The young girl with all the big dreams. She seemed so very, very far away.

Her phone rang. Cinnamon knew by the ring tone who was calling. She almost didn't answer it. But if she didn't answer, what would he do?

Her fingers were shaking as she reached for the phone. "H-hello?"

"I want you to do a favor for me."

"I already did," she heard herself whisper back.

"One more. It will be the last favor I ask."

I don't believe you.

"And I will make it worth your while, Coreen."

Coreen. "I want to leave town," she heard herself say. "Help me get enough money to leave, and I'll do whatever you want. I need to forget this place. This life—everything."

"And everyone?" His voice was low. Dangerous.

"I will forget you," she promised. It was what he wanted, wasn't it?

"One favor."

"One favor," she agreed.

CHAPTER TWENTY-ONE

"I guess you're some big hero now."

Joel had just walked into the kitchen at the main house. He'd showered, put on fresh clothes, then gone hunting Chloe. Instead of finding her, he found Marie waiting for him. She was sitting on the counter, her legs dangling in front of her, and an apple gripped in her right hand.

"Hardly would say that." He crossed his arms over his chest. "You still hate me, huh?"

"Not hate. That takes too much energy. I don't like wasting energy." Marie picked up the knife from the counter beside her. She began to slice into the apple, never taking her eyes off him.

"You should be careful," he warned. "You don't want to cut yourself."

Humor sparked in her eyes, for only a moment. "I'm good."

"Okay." He glanced around. "You seen Chloe?"

"She was showering. She had blood on her when she arrived. Surprised she kept her shit together knowing blood was on her body. Normally, she would have lost her mind about that. It's her one thing, but I'm sure you already realized that."

"Excuse me?"

"It's why she likes to have a doctor dodging her steps. Not like you're the first." She brought the knife to her lips. There was a slice of apple on the blade. She ate it. Watched him.

And he tried to follow along. "Chloe has worked with other partners who are doctors?"

She winked.

"Chloe didn't mention any other—"

"What Chloe doesn't say is often more important than what she does."

What the hell did that even mean?

"I'm sure you noticed that she doesn't like it when things get bloody."

"I might have noticed," Joel allowed. "But the issue seems to be more for dead bodies. At least, that's what she told me. The vic today wasn't dead."

"Because of the hero, rushing in to save the day." She brought the knife to her lips once more. Took another bite. "But you still managed to get blood all over Chloe. Managed to make her face one of her own worst nightmares. Guess that doesn't matter to you, does it? You're walking around here, all cocky and smug, because *you* had a fucking good day. La, dee, dah."

Now tension knotted in his shoulders.

"But did you ever once stop to ask her how she was doing?" Marie asked.

A throat cleared.

Marie swore. "*Chloe.* You know I hate it when you sneak up on me."

"No. You only hate it when I catch you sharing secrets." Chloe stood near the open kitchen door.

"Joel was busy putting his hands inside Judith's chest and stopping her from bleeding out. He didn't have a chance to sit and hold *my* hand and make sure I wasn't going to get all weepy on him."

Marie laughed. Her legs kicked out. "You never get weepy."

Joel headed straight for Chloe. Her hair was back in a little bun, still damp, and she'd dressed in jeans and a loose top. Flats covered her feet. "Are you okay?"

"I'm absolutely fine. Why wouldn't I be?"

A snort from Marie. "Liar, liar."

Chloe didn't glance at the other woman. "Don't I look fine?"

She looked fantastic. Good enough to eat. Joel reached for her hand.

"What are you doing?" She frowned at him.

"I'm holding your hand now. What's your worst nightmare?" But Joel thought he knew. After the digging he'd done on her, the pieces were slipping into place for him.

But she tugged her hand and tried to pull it free of his grip. "This isn't the time to talk about nightmares."

"I think it is."

She shot a hot glance at Marie. "Do you see what you did?"

"I see. And I'm impressed. Props to you, doc, for stepping up." She jumped off the counter. "Maybe you'll last longer than I thought."

"Marie, you are not helping," Chloe told her.

"I absolutely am." A soft response. "You're the one who throws up walls. Self-sabotage, isn't that the fancy name you threw at me once? Now I'm throwing it back at you. Because we both know we're too much alike." She was still holding her knife as she slipped from the kitchen.

"Interesting woman," Joel noted.

"Yes, Marie is the most lethal lady I've ever met. Never go against her when she's holding a knife." Chloe sounded completely serious. As if she'd just delivered a warning Joel should never forget.

"You say a whole lot of scary shit to me."

"Do I? Then prepare yourself. Because something else scary is about to come out of my mouth."

He waited. Was she about to tell him her worst night—

"You and I are going to find a body."

"Say again?"

"You and I. Us. We're getting on your motorcycle and we're heading for a big park. A quite scenic, lovely park. Once we get there, we'll take a walk and perhaps find a body. If we get lucky."

"Sure. Right. Because what else would you do in the afternoon? I mean, especially if you spent your morning covered in blood and at a crime scene. You should then definitely spend the afternoon and evening locating a dead body."

"Precisely." She gave him a quick nod. Even a cautious smile. "May I have my hand back?"

"No. Not until you answer my question."

"Excuse me?" Her smile dimmed.

"It's because of your parents, isn't it? I read about them. About you. You were in the house with them. You found their bodies. Did their blood get on you? Is that why you can't stand the sight—"

"You can't rely on everything that you read. Most stories are a mix of truth and lies." She wasn't trying to tug her hand free any longer. "But, yes, my blood...issue developed when I was younger. When they died. I don't like seeing the dead cut open, but honestly, who does? I'm sure many people feel the same way. As for the unease I experience when blood gets on my skin, it's a visceral memory. Their blood was on me. It was a very long time before I could get it off. The stickiness and the smell today at the crime scene put me back in a bad moment from my past, and I-I don't like going back there."

God. She spoke so flatly. So carefully. But he could feel her pain. All carefully held back. What had Marie said? That she put up a wall? Hell, yes, Chloe did. He could practically see it. When he thought of what she must have gone through as a kid...to see her parents that way... "Baby, did you see them die?"

"You keep using terms of endearment with me. I don't know if you mean them or not."

"*You* keep trying to distract me. It won't work."

She shrugged.

"You must have been in the house," he rasped.

"It was an estate. Quite large. Had been in the family for a long time. It could be quite possible to be in one wing of the house and have no idea what was happening in another location. You could even scream until you were hoarse from one room, and the people having a party downstairs would never hear you."

His heart slammed into his chest. "Did you ever scream like that?" *Tell me no. I need you to tell me—*

Her long lashes lowered. "Why would I have screamed?" Once more, she pulled at his grip.

This time, he let her go. "Did..." He stopped. Tried again. "Did your parents have a lot of parties?"

"Every weekend. They enjoyed them." She turned away. "I've never particularly enjoyed parties."

"No, I don't see where you'd like them." He followed her out of the kitchen. Caught sight of Reese ducking into—was that a library? The place came with its own library? Sure. Why the hell not? "Give me one minute, would you, Chloe?"

"You haven't even asked me whose dead body we're trying to find. That seems odd."

He paused. Realized he probably should have at least wondered. Instead, he'd found himself in a whole mindset of...*Why-the-hell-not* with her. "Whose body are we trying to find?"

"Promise you won't get mad."

"I will make no such promise." Now he felt alarmed.

"In the interest of full disclosure, I had these items *before* you asked me to stop holding back on you. And I fully intended to tell you everything when we met with Judith. It was absolutely, one hundred percent on my to-do list. Know that."

"God, I have a bad feeling in my gut." Knots, lots of twisted knots. "You may be giving me an ulcer."

"You should see a doctor about that," Chloe returned without missing a beat.

He would not smile at her. He would also not let her distract him.

"Oh, Joel, you were just so excited when you seemed to have the idea of talking to the librarian. I hated to tell you that I had already talked with her."

Silence. No, not silence. At least, not total silence. He could hear the ticking of the grandfather clock that stood near the entrance to the library. "You already talked to Judith."

"Are you mad?"

"*When* did you talk to Judith?"

"Before we met, actually. So you shouldn't feel like I didn't include you in the question session. Our paths hadn't crossed at that point."

"Uh, huh." He ran through scenarios in his head. Scenes. "Wait, back up. So you'd already made the connection with the high school football team *before* that whole bit at the police station? When you stared at their ring fingers and acted like you'd reached some major conclusion, you already knew that shit?" He almost laughed. "And here I thought you were hyper observant."

"I am hyper observant. And I have an eidetic memory."

Reese strolled out of the library. "Someone is bragging."

She shot him an infuriated glance. "I am not!"

He smiled. Saluted and headed for the stairs—

"No." Joel grabbed his arm. "Back to the library. You and I need to talk."

"What? Why? Look, I just heard Chloe. You have a dead body to dig up."

"We're talking." He pushed Reese toward the library.

Chloe sniffed. "Why do you need to talk to him?"

"Why did *you* go visit Judith?"

"Because of the first victim. As part of my investigation, I always dig into a victim's past. I use the victim to help me find the killer. That's how I work. Gregory Guidry. Recent police reports told me that he'd been abusive to his wife, but I'm always curious..."

"Here we go," Reese muttered from the library's doorway.

"What makes someone start attacking the ones they love?" Chloe mused. "Was Gregory always a bully? Did he hurt others before his wife? I wanted to know so..."

"So you dug into his high school life," Joel concluded. "Got you."

"Judith didn't remember much about Gregory. But she let me see some of the old yearbooks that she'd kept as mementos. I actually have two of the yearbooks. Gregory's senior year and his junior year."

Joel closed the distance between them.

She tipped back her head to stare at him.

"You *have* two of the yearbooks?"

"Yes." She winced. "I suspect all the wreckage at Judith's house was caused due to the perp looking for those books. Particularly Gregory's senior yearbook. She had two copies of his junior year—I have no idea why—but only one copy of the senior year. When I left her, she still had a full set of all the school yearbooks from her thirty years as a librarian, all the years except..."

"Senior year, right. Got it. And just exactly *where* do you have the yearbooks?"

"In my bedroom."

His breath froze in his lungs.

"Are you all right?"

"Fantastic. Best ever." He heaved out a breath. "Someone attacked Judith because that person wanted the yearbook."

A nod. "And he or she probably didn't want Judith talking. But she'd already talked to me."

"You have the yearbook upstairs."

"I have two yearbooks upstairs, I told you—"

Joel glanced over at Reese. "When we leave, make damn sure all of the alarms are set at this place."

Reese bobbed his head in agreement. "Count on it. I'll also stay extra close to Marie. She can keep me safe."

"Marie's boyfriend won't like that," Chloe returned with a little wince. "Keep your hands to yourself or you'll get cut."

"I was going to keep my hands to myself," he muttered. "That was the plan. Don't know why you would have thought otherwise."

Joel focused on Chloe. "What did you find in the yearbooks?"

"I made the connection with the rings *because* of the yearbooks. I remembered seeing Gregory with his team. A close-up shot of his championship ring. I'd only thumbed through the pages but because of my—"

"She's gonna mention her memory again," Reese rumbled.

"That *did* help me to connect the men," Chloe plowed on. "They were all on the same team their senior year. So when the other two became victims, I knew it was tied to their shared past on that team."

"Why'd you take the junior yearbook, too?" He was trying to follow along.

"Because Judith told me that no one went missing that senior year. That no one vanished. That there was no traumatic event at the school." A vague expression of guilt crossed her face. "By the way, I told Agent Richardson that I was going to ask Judith questions about what happened during that year. Oh, and did you know...he went to see Judith, too?"

"How the hell would I have known that?"

"She told him she couldn't find the yearbook for Gregory's senior year. Said she'd misplaced it. I...may have asked her to keep our visit private."

"Of course, you did."

"So when Richardson finds out, he won't be happy." Chloe didn't seem bothered by that prospect. "Are we ready to search for the body now?"

"No, we're ready for you to back up and tell me *why* we have Gregory's junior and senior freaking yearbooks! Why did you want them both?"

"So I could look and compare the students in the classes. I wanted to see if anyone was there for junior year but gone for Gregory's senior year."

"People transfer, Chloe. They switch schools all the time." Didn't mean something bad had happened.

She gazed steadily back at him. Right. Yes. This was Chloe. She'd probably already figured something bad *had* happened. "Tell me," he said.

"There were five people who were in the junior class, but not the senior one. I got a friend at the FBI to look into missing persons' cases. He didn't turn up anything. No matches to those individuals. He even tracked them down for me. To be thorough, you know."

Joel waited.

"Or, he *was* tracking them down. I received my last update from him as soon as I returned here today. Before I hopped in the shower. One woman wasn't located. She was never reported as missing. She had a foster family, he said."

Joel's shoulders straightened.

"She was eighteen, and she'd threatened to run away a lot. She *had* run away from other homes. So her foster family thought she'd just hitched a ride with someone and never looked back. Her case worker should have known about what happened, should have checked on her disappearance, but it didn't happen. She vanished, and it was as if no one noticed."

"Who was she?"

Watching him closely, Chloe said, "Portia Strong."

His brows climbed. "Is that name supposed to mean something to me?"

"Does it?"

"Not a damn thing."

"Okay." Chloe nodded. "I think I know where she is."

"Sure, you do. You found out that she was missing like...what, thirty minutes ago? And now you know where she is. The cops haven't found her in years—"

"They didn't know to look for her. No one noticed that she was gone. How can you find someone if you aren't looking for the person?"

"And you're just going to magically walk right to her body?"

"Of course, not."

Okay. Fair enough.

"Magic won't be involved. A cadaver-sniffing dog will be."

He squeezed his eyes shut. "Give me five minutes alone with your brother."

"Fine. I need to check in with Cedric anyway." She turned smartly on her heel and paced toward the kitchen. As she headed away from him, he saw her raise her phone to her ear.

"At least the cops will be involved," Reese noticed from the position he still held in the library's doorway. "The last time my sister found a dead body, they thought she'd killed the bloke."

"Drop the English accent. It gets on my nerves."

"You get on my nerves," Reese fired back.

Joel grabbed him, half-dragged him inside, then slammed the library door shut.

"You have a dead body to find," Reese mumbled. "Don't let me delay you."

"Who was her partner before me?"

"Like...sexually?" A wince. "I am super not comfortable with this whole conversation." Reese shook his head. "Her sex life is her sex life and I do not—"

"I don't want to know about her past lovers." Didn't want to even think about those jackasses. "I mean—whatever this shit is that we do. Crime solving. Killer hunting. Who helped her before me?"

A quick laugh. "She doesn't need help on that end, if you know what I'm saying—"

"She prefers doctors because she can't stand the sight of blood. When you're tracking down bastards who murder, blood is typically involved. She has to have someone on hand for that part of the job." *And that's why I'm really here.* "Who was it?"

Reese scrunched up his face. "She was hanging around with a guy a few months back. But he wasn't like you. She didn't move him in and offer him an actual job. That's something she's only done with you."

He filed that important point away. "Was he a doctor?"

"I *think* he was wearing scrubs once? Younger guy. Younger than you, anyway."

Joel took a stab in the dark. Because he'd recently seen Chloe being chummy with one other doctor. "Let me guess. Black hair. Green eyes. About two inches shorter than me?"

"If you know him, then why are you asking me about the fellow?"

Because I didn't know him. Not until that day. "Why'd she stop working with him?"

"Ask her. I have no clue." Reese reached for the doorknob. He started to open the door—

Joel pushed it closed. "Chloe was there when her parents were killed."

"That doesn't sound like a question."

"She hates the sight of blood because she got their blood on her."

Reese swallowed. "This all seems like stuff you should be talking to her about. Why are you coming to me?"

"You're supposed to be her brother—"

"I *am* her damn brother!"

"Her brother disappeared. Ran away when he was fourteen. I don't believe for one single moment that someone like Chloe wouldn't have hunted for him."

Reese glanced at the floor. "She was a kid when I vanished. Super smart. Always was. Used to scare our parents because she was so smart. Parents aren't supposed to be scared of their kids." That last line...it was different. Deeper. It held the ring of truth.

Joel latched onto what Reese had finally revealed. "They were afraid of Chloe? Because she was smart? That doesn't make any sense."

"It does if they were doing something they shouldn't have been doing. If they thought Chloe would figure them out." Reese's voice turned raspy. "They'd leave her alone so much. Shut her away. I know they could hear her calling for them."

Chloe's voice whispered through Joel's mind. *"It was an estate. Quite large. Had been in the family for a long time. It could be quite possible to be in one wing of the house and have no idea what was happening in another location. You could even scream until you were hoarse from one room, and the people having a party downstairs would never hear you."*

Joel's heart ached. "Their killers were never caught."

Reese looked up at him.

"Chloe solves murders all the time," Joel continued, voice roughening. "But she didn't find the person who killed her parents?" *I don't buy it. She would have hunted him. Would have searched until she found the killer.*

"Some cases are harder than others."

He stared into Reese's eyes and searched for the truth. "Do you know who killed them?"

Reese licked his lips. "I'm not as smart as she is when it comes to killers."

"That's not what I—"

"But I know what you're thinking. I know why you wanted to see me alone. I know what you suspect."

What he suspected...what was curling in his gut like a snake getting ready to strike...

"Chloe isn't like that." Reese shook his head. "She didn't take a knife and hack her parents to pieces. She didn't slice them over and over until blood soaked her skin. That's not what happened that night."

"But you weren't there," Joel said softly. "So how do you really know?"

Reese didn't reach for the doorknob any longer. He squared his shoulders and kept staring Joel dead in the eyes. "If you honestly think that shit about my sister, then get the hell out of our house, right now. Get the hell out and stay away. She doesn't need you. You aren't good enough for her. You aren't worth her. You aren't—"

A rap at the door. "Joel? I hate to rush you, but we need to get going. We only have so much daylight left, and Cedric said he'd meet us for the search. If you're occupied with Reese, then I can certainly do this without you."

"You're not going anywhere without me," he called back. His eyes pinned Reese.

"She tried to save them," Reese whispered. "They'd been terrible to her. But she still tried. That's what she does. She's not the monster. I don't care what you hear. I don't care what lies you're told. That's not her. Back then, she'd been reading anatomy books. Fucking anatomy. She tried to put them back together. Tried to stop the blood loss. That's why she was soaked when the cops arrived."

Joel thought of what he'd done that day. Of the way he'd insisted Chloe stay with him in that room with Judith. She'd wanted to leave.

But she hadn't.

"Fuck me." Now he was the one grabbing for the door.

"Be good to her," Reese snapped behind him. "Or I will kick your ass."

Joel threw a frown at him.

"Fine. I'll get Marie to kick your ass. And you will be so sorry because she happens to be fantastic at ass kicking."

Joel yanked open the door.

Chloe was glancing at an empty drinking glass in her hand. "All done?" She didn't look up. "Finish interrogating him about my parents' murder?"

"You knew I—"

"I was listening at the door," she confessed quietly. Chloe raised her eyes. "I went to the kitchen just to get the glass. Old school, but effective, I assure you."

"You listen at a lot of doors?" Joel asked to buy himself time. Time to figure out how to say...*I'm sorry.*

"More than one would expect." Her spine seemed very straight. She put the glass down on a nearby table. "We should hurry. Cedric is sending teams to the five locations I've suggested—"

"Five?"

"Well, it's not like I know the exact spot for the body. But five locations are most likely. We'll start at the top of the list and work our way down. That's why we have to hurry. Losing daylight and all that."

She made her way to the door. Her steps seemed a little fast. And that spine of hers? Still stiff and straight.

"You hurt her."

Jesus. Joel spun around. "Reese, don't skulk up behind me."

"You need to apologize."

"Yeah, I get that shit."

"Chloe didn't kill our parents."

"I never said she did." He made his way for the door.

"Oh, yeah? Then what was that whole interrogation scene about—"

"I thought you'd killed them." He looked back because he wanted to see Reese's reaction.

And he saw it. Would have been impossible to miss the other man's flinch.

But Reese snapped, "I *didn't.*"

No, but maybe her real brother did. Chloe wasn't waiting, so he followed her outside. He pulled on sunglasses as he saw her going straight for the motorcycle. She climbed onto the bike. Didn't put on the helmet. She gripped it tightly in her hands.

With silent steps, he closed in on her. "I'm an asshole."

"No, I don't think that you are."

"You should think that I am." His fingers slid carefully under her chin so that he could tilt her face up toward him. "At Judith's place...staying in that room with me must have been hell for you."

"It certainly was not an experience that is going on my highlight reel."

"Why did you do it?"

"Because if I'd gone out of the room, I was afraid you'd follow. Then that woman would have died. You did an amazing job of saving her. I wish that I'd had your skills...back then."

He knew she meant when her parents had been attacked. Voice gruff, he said, "You were a damn kid, baby."

Tears gleamed in her eyes. "I was the only one there. They only had me. No matter how hard I tired, I couldn't put them back together again."

"*I am so sorry.*"

"It wasn't your fault. You didn't kill them. You didn't leave me in that house with them."

He wanted to pull her into his arms and never let go. "I'm sorry that I didn't understand you better from the beginning." He could see the truth now.

Her gaze focused on him. Sharpened. Not *click, click.* Not some robotic study. Never that. He'd read her all wrong. When she stared so hard, she was seeing past the surface. Trying to understand him—as he should have been doing with her.

"You're not cold," he told her, voice still gruff. The sight of those tears in her eyes was wrecking him. "You're not detached."

"Is that what you thought I was?"

"Hunting killers isn't some sort of game for you."

"P-please stop touching me."

*That tremble in her voice...*He removed his hand. "I'm sorry, Chloe."

"You thought I was playing a game? That I'm cold?"

"At the beginning, yes."

She flinched.

God, I don't want to hurt her. "I'm telling you everything. That's our new deal, isn't it? Full truth? I'm telling you what I thought. And how completely wrong I've been about you." *I will never be wrong again.*

Her gaze cut from his. "I want to protect you."

"And I damn well want to do the same for you." Protecting her was his priority. Making sure that she never, ever got hurt again. Not by any of the perps out there. *Not by my own careless words.* "You hit my life like a hurricane. Spinning and storming and I didn't know what to do or think. I just got bits and pieces of you and I tried to force all of them to make sense."

She wasn't looking at him.

"I'm sorry," Joel said again, and he meant those words. He sure as hell hoped that Ruben— the ever helpful medical examiner—had been right and they could truly be magic words. "I hurt you. When I was questioning your brother, he had it wrong. I didn't think you killed your parents. I wanted to know more about *you.* If I know more, then I can make sure that I don't hurt you again. Hurting you is the last thing I want to do."

A jerky nod. "I don't particularly want to be hurt. Sometimes, it is unavoidable."

He didn't speak. He waited. Waited...

Her gaze reluctantly slid back to him.

"I will avoid it," Joel promised. "I can do that. You're changing me. I feel like I've been sleeping. Or, hell, maybe I just haven't been living. Ever since that bastard put me in the ground, I haven't been the same. Nothing mattered. I dug myself out of the grave, but I felt like I was still buried. The days just passed and passed..."

"We should go—"

"Then I met you. *You* matter, Chloe. *You* matter." She'd changed everything for him.

She was searching his eyes. Searching—

"Joel?"

"Yeah, baby?"

"Please touch me again."

Please. A fucking magic word. He slid his hand under her chin.

"Lean toward me."

He leaned close.

Her lips pressed to his. A soft, tender kiss. "You matter, too."

CHAPTER TWENTY-TWO

They found her at the third park.

Portia Strong had been a runner. In the yearbook—during Portia's junior year—she'd been on the cross-country team. Smiling from ear to ear as she stood with her arms thrown around her team-mates.

By senior year, Portia was gone.

After her FBI contact had notified Chloe that Portia hadn't been seen in years, she'd immediately contacted Portia's former foster mother. The call had been brief. Chloe had identified herself and said she was working in conjunction with the NOPD on a missing person's case regarding Portia Strong.

The foster mother had immediately hung up on her. *That* was why the call had been brief.

Chloe had called a second time. Told the woman she wasn't interested in any illegal payments that the foster mother had received while pretending to "care" for a missing girl. Chloe had just asked when the woman had last seen Portia. What Portia had been wearing at the time.

The foster mother hadn't remembered the exact date. She did remember, though, that Portia had left early because she liked to get in her runs before school. She'd been wearing jogging shorts. A t-shirt. Red running shoes. Red had been Portia's favorite color.

With that info, it had been easy to map out the most likely places that Portia would have used for her morning runs. After she'd done that, Chloe had called in a favor. Gotten the cadaver dog and—

"Cujo says this is the spot."

The German shepherd wasn't straining against his leash or doing anything dramatic like you'd see on a TV show. He'd simply run through the parks, one after the other. He'd sniffed the ground. He'd hunted.

When he found the right spot, Cujo stopped. Sat. Waited like a good boy.

"Cujo?" Joel queried from beside her.

Cedric nodded and waved toward the dog's handler. "Mickey here is a bit of a Stephen King fan."

Chloe stared at the ground beneath Cujo. "You need to get an entire crew out here, Cedric."

"I was afraid you'd say that." He put his hands on his hips. "You're seriously telling me that some poor girl has been under the ground for ten years?"

"The vegetation is denser beneath Cujo. The grass thicker in that area. The earth likes the nutrients."

Cedric gaped at her. "Do not tell me more. I don't like to hear that stuff." He pointed at Mickey. "Your dog is sure?"

Cujo whined. Pawed once at the ground.

"Dead certain," Mickey assured him.

***

Radar was brought in. It showed the body. Or, what was left of the body. The retrieval process was slow. Painstaking. The crime scene techs didn't want to destroy even one bit of evidence. Chloe watched them from a distance.

Joel stayed at her side.

He hadn't said much during the long hours, and she understood. This...this was one of the parts she hated, too. And for Joel, seeing a body unearthed had to be a reminder of his own hell.

One of the techs yelled out, "We've got her!"

Chloe found herself moving closer to Joel. Her hand reached for his. "Every bit of evidence we find brings us closer. We'll stop the man who did this."

He looked at her hand. Curled his fingers around hers. Slowly raised his head. "Damn straight we will."

She had to swallow as she stared into his eyes. This whole arrangement with Joel was so different from what she'd expected. With every moment that they spent together, she felt as if he was truly getting to know her. Looking past the surface. Just as she was doing with him. She liked who Joel was beneath his surface. There was so much more to him than met the eye.

"Chloe!" Cedric's deep voice rang out. "You're gonna want to see this!"

She released a quick breath, nodded, but didn't let go of Joel. "You don't need to come with me." She was afraid for him to get too close. "I know this is a nightmare scene for you." *A grave.* He'd been buried alive, and now he was watching a young victim being uncovered. "You can stay over here, or if you'd like, you can even go back home. I can catch a taxi ride."

"Where you go, I go." Grim. Determined.

That was Joel. Determined to his core. She squeezed his hand. If they were doing this together, there was no way she'd let go of him. She wanted him to know that she would be there for him, every single moment.

They slipped under the yellow crime scene tape and darted under the lights that had been set up. When they neared the uncovered remains, Chloe made sure to stand a safe distance back. *No contamination.*

"Check out the jacket," Cedric directed.

She could see the victim's lower body. The running shoes that had been uncovered. Red shoes. She forced her gaze up and realized...a jacket had been placed over the victim's face and chest. Not just any jacket, though. "That's a letterman jacket."

"That's a letterman jacket for the *Pirates*," Cedric corrected as he crouched near the victim. "The kind of jacket that a football player would wear."

"He covered her face." A sign of remorse? Most psychologists would say so. But...it could also be that the perp had covered her face because...

He doesn't want her to see what he did. He doesn't want her looking at him.

"How does she fit into the Bad Deeds case?" Joel asked.

"I think she started it all." A crime from years ago had led to multiple murders now.

A black SUV rushed to the scene. The brakes squealed. A moment later, the driver's side door was thrown open.

"Great. Here we go." Cedric rose to his full height. "Someone finally dragged his head out of his ass and joined the party."

Paul Richardson jumped out of the vehicle. "Get them away from there!"

She glanced heavenward. "You're welcome," she told the agent. "Don't worry, Richardson. I assure you that Cedric, Joel, Mickey, Cujo, and I were all happy to assist you in finding this murder victim."

"Get away from there!"

Hmm. His response didn't sound like a thank you.

She stepped back. Reluctantly. Joel moved in unison with her. Just as reluctantly.

Richardson spared a fast glance for the uncovered grave before he turned his back on the vic. "Two dead bodies, today, huh? Guess you're rolling high."

"Two?" Chloe repeated. What was he talking about? They'd only uncovered one dead body.

"This vic...and Judith Key. Two dead bodies." When Richardson made that stark announcement, he stared straight at Joel.

"Judith isn't dead," Joel snapped back. "I saved her. Get your facts straight. She's in the hospital. She's stable. She was doing just fine when I—"

"She died thirty minutes ago. That means you did *not* save her."

Pain. Chloe saw it flash on Joel's face. He took one fast step back, and his retreat made her heart ache. She knew how much he'd wanted Judith to survive. How hard he'd worked to save her.

"That's not possible," he said, his confusion clear. "I...her vitals were good. She was in recovery."

"She didn't recover. She died. And you know what, Joel? I think this is a good time for you to come down to the station with me."

"How is this possibly a good time for that?" Chloe asked.

At the same time, Joel barked, "Why the hell would I come to the station with you?"

Richardson appeared smug. Never a good sign.

"No." Chloe shook her head even as dread settled around her. "Joel doesn't have to go to the station with you."

Richardson sent her a sideways glance. "Sure, he doesn't *have* to do it. I'm not arresting him...*yet*."

"Arresting me?" Joel laughed, a rough and humorless sound. "Damn straight you're not."

"But if Joel doesn't come to the station—willingly—it will look suspicious, and I'll have to write that in my files."

She didn't like where this was going.

"Chloe can tell you," Richardson added, all oily smooth, "if you cooperate, it goes better for you. You come down to the station, you answer my questions, and hey, maybe it ends right there. Maybe you set me straight."

Joel looked at Chloe. "What's happening here?"

She was still holding his hand. An open grave waited a few feet away—his worst nightmare. She knew that Richardson had picked this moment, this spot, deliberately. He'd wanted to hit Joel when he thought the other man was weak.

Your mistake. He's not weak.

What was happening? Easy. "Richardson is trying to rattle you. He somehow has it in his mind that you might be a suspect in this case."

Once more, Joel laughed.

Chloe didn't.

Neither did Richardson.

Joel's head swung back toward the agent. "That's ridiculous."

"Is it? Then come with me to the station. Answer my questions. Show me how ridiculous it truly is..."

"I'm not a killer!" Joel snarled.

Richardson glanced back at the grave. "Are you sure? Because I believe you once killed a man, at a scene much like this one."

Joel pulled his hand from Chloe's hold and lunged for Richardson.

Chloe grabbed his back and held on tight. "Don't." She pressed her body to his. "Don't let him get in your head."

"Oh, I don't have to do that." Even his voice had turned smug. "Dr. Gordon Jennings has already done that."

Joel stiffened.

No, no, no.

"He's waiting down at the station, Joel," Richardson added. "He had so very much to say about you. He was quite concerned when I told him what was happening down here. He insisted on flying in from Dallas."

Lie. She'd bet that Richardson had been the one to arrange the man's flight.

"Dr. Jennings thinks that you're a dangerous man. After talking with him, do you know what I realized?"

Chloe eased her hold on Joel. Moved to his side. "You realized that everyone in the world is more competent than you are?"

He shot her a dirty glare. "No."

"Oh. It's okay. One day, you'll realize it. Keep trying. Never give up."

His lips thinned. "You fit my profile," Richardson told Joel. "Remember that wonderful profile I delivered to the NOPD? It fits you to a T."

She squeezed Joel's arm. "Remember what *I* told you about his profile." *That it was utter bullshit.* "I stand by my words. Mean them now more than ever, I assure you."

Richardson plowed on even as Cedric closed in, frowning. Richardson said, "We are looking for a very intelligent killer. There is no doubt, *Doctor* Landry, that you are highly intelligent. We are looking for an individual who stalked his prey and waited for the perfect moment to strike because this man saw himself as an instrument of vengeance. This man thought he was delivering justice." Richardson waved toward the open grave. "Odd, isn't it? That we find this victim buried in a grave...much like the grave *you* were buried in?"

"The killer was hiding her body," Chloe retorted. "Nothing odd about that. Predictable. Typical. You hide a body by burying it."

Richardson raked her with his stare. "You're good, but you're not *this* good. You didn't just wake up today and randomly find this body."

"There's nothing random about anything I do."

"Joel led you to this body, didn't he?"

"No," she shot back. "He—"

"Explain it all to me at the station," Richardson ordered. He pointed at Joel. "Come willingly now or not so willingly later, Dr. Landry."

Joel didn't speak. Chloe was still holding tightly to his arm.

After a tense moment, Joel swallowed. Glanced her way. "I remember what you said about his profile."

She nodded.

"You knew this would happen, didn't you?" Joel's voice was low.

But she knew Richardson heard him. Richardson was so close, he'd have to hear.

"I remember what *you* said, too, Chloe," Joel told her. His expression was far too somber. "You warned me not to let what he was saying get in my head. You warned me because you knew his profile fit me. I didn't realize it back then, but I get it now."

"You aren't the killer we're after. I *know* that." Her heart was racing. "And *you* need to remember what else I said. In case you forgot, let me say it again. Loud and clear." But she looked at Richardson when she delivered her next words. Looked him dead in the eyes and said, "That man knows nothing about killers."

Richardson glared at her.

"I'll go to the station," Joel agreed. "Because you're right, Chloe, he doesn't know a damn thing, at least not about *me*."

"Because you're not a typical killer?" Richardson demanded.

Joel began to reply—

"Don't worry. I've already figured that out." Richardson brushed past Joel. "Nothing typical about the way you kill. Most people don't paralyze their victims. But since you're a doctor, you knew just where to strike, didn't you?" He paused. "Hmm." He half-turned and studied the grave. "If she's really tied to this case, think we're gonna find her with a messed-up spine, too?"

"C1 to C4," Joel gritted out. "Those were the injured—"

"Yes, I know. And the fact that *you* figured that stuff out so quickly on your visit to the ME? Sure makes you look extra guilty to me. After all, it's easy to find the pattern in the kills...if you're the one doing the killing."

CHAPTER TWENTY-THREE

"Chloe doesn't need to be in the room." Richardson waved dismissively toward her. "I asked you to come down to the station, Joel. I didn't ask Chloe for a meet and greet." He raised his brows. "Or is she somehow magically a lawyer, too? Did I miss that part on her resume?"

Joel turned his head toward Chloe. She was seated right beside him while Richardson had taken up a spot on the other side of the table. Consideringly, Joel told her, "I totally get why you dislike him."

Chloe nodded. "He does make it easy, doesn't he?"

Richardson cleared his throat. "So that's how it's gonna be? You two are gonna work this partner bullshit and try to cut me out? Hate to break it to you, but that's not happening."

Joel's heart drummed fast in his chest. He couldn't believe he was actually in interrogation—or that Richardson suspected him of murder. Trying to keep his voice flat and calm he said, "Chloe is here because I want her to be with me. As for a lawyer, I don't need one. I'm not guilty of anything."

"I happen to think you are," Richardson returned. "And I'm not the only one."

"Oh, really?" *How the hell is this happening?* "Then why don't you stop playing games and tell me who else thinks that I'm somehow the *killer* that Chloe and I have been working so hard to catch."

Richardson smiled at him. Joel hated the agent's smile.

"A witness has come forward."

From the corner of his eye, Joel saw Chloe tense.

"This witness says you were in the alley with Donnie Adams. The witness saw you swinging a baseball bat at him. And you know what? When we went to your apartment, guess what we found hidden in the back of your closet?"

Bam. Bam. Bam. Joel's heartbeat suddenly seemed to be beating so hard he felt as if his whole chest had to be shaking. "Bullshit." His immediate response.

"No. I'm afraid it's quite true. The bat is being run for prints and evidence collection as we speak. I can assure you—"

"I can assure *you*..." Chloe cut in with a voice that sounded completely steady. Almost bored. "Joel's prints will not be found on that baseball bat. The true killer planted that bat in his apartment, probably after Joel moved out. It would certainly have been easy enough to do. Child's play. Joel's neighbor—when Joel *lived* at that location, by the way, because that is his former address—his neighbor spent most of his nights chugging beers until he passed out. His wife died two years ago, and the poor man hasn't been the same since."

How did she—no. Joel wasn't even going down that road.

"The perp knew that Joel had moved. So he thought it would be easy to stash that baseball bat in Joel's former home. He thought—"

"There was blood on the bat." Richardson drummed his fingers on the table. "Did I forget to mention that part sooner? Whoops."

"You didn't forget," Chloe assured him. "You were just being a dick."

She said it so easily. So properly in that accent of hers. Joel almost smiled.

Then he remembered he was in freaking interrogation and that the agent thought he was a killer. Smiling felt very wrong.

"Wonder if the blood on that bat will belong to poor Judith Key?" Richardson's lips pulled down in a sad frown. "I heard you rammed the bat into the back of her head before you stabbed her."

"*I didn't!*" Joel's hands fisted on top of the table. "Look, I tried to save her—"

"Tried and failed."

"I—"

Chloe curled her hand over one of his fists. Immediately, Joel took a breath. A deep, slow breath.

"Oh, Agent Richardson, even a man as dense as you should see that this is a setup. A bat in an empty apartment. Woo." Again, Chloe sounded bored. "I'm disappointed that you had Joel come down for this. We just found a body, after all. If you'd given us a few more hours, we probably would have gotten your killer for you, too. What a waste of time and energy."

Richardson had his attention locked on Joel. "I've got my killer. Like I said, it wasn't just the bat. It was the witness."

"Who is the witness?" Joel demanded.

"You want a name? Why? So you can go out and slam a baseball bat into—"

"I want a name because I want to know who is lying about me." Chloe's hand was still wrapped around his. Just her touch was helping him to stay focused. To breathe.

Chloe was there. They were going to figure this mess out.

I didn't kill Donnie Adams.

"It's not a lie if it's the truth," Richardson fired back.

"It's. A. Lie." From Chloe. Clipped.

"And how do you know that?" Now Richardson turned his head toward her. "How do you know that this witness—who *swears* that Joel was the one swinging the bat at Donnie Adams— is not telling the truth?"

Joel glanced at her. Chloe's profile was perfectly smooth. Expressionless.

"That's what I thought," Richardson said. He nodded. "That's what I—"

"Joel couldn't have been in that alley. Because that night..."

The night before Joel had met Chloe at the bank... *Shit. I don't have an alibi for that night.* He'd just realized...*I was running around the city. Jogging aimlessly because the apartment was closing in on me. I ran and ran and can't even remember all the streets I took. I can't—*

"That night," Chloe continued in her ever-so-cool voice, "Joel was with me."

Richardson opened his mouth. Gave a little jerk. "What?"

"If you will recall, the very next day, Joel and I were at the bank together. We stopped the bank robber. Caught him in the act." Her head turned toward Joel. "Our first case together right, darling?"

Darling?

"Our first case, but hardly the first time we met." Now her head angled back in the agent's direction. "You see, Joel was with me the previous night. The night that some mystery witness swears she saw Joel swinging a bat? *Impossible.*"

"She saw him." Richardson's face was going splotchy.

"*She* saw him only if Joel was in two places at once. I hardly think that is possible. He was with me," Chloe repeated with a roll of her shoulders. "We were having sex. It lasted for a very long time."

Joel could not take his eyes off her.

"He's an incredible lover." A faint smile. "When we were finished—or pausing, if you will— we slept in each other's arms. Then we woke up, went to the bank, and foiled a robbery. A big day. Oh, sure, if you check the security cameras at the bank, it will appear that we arrived separately, but that was planned. Deliberate on our part. We wanted to throw off Harry's accomplice."

"You're lying," Richardson accused.

"Am I?" Her fingers were warm and soft around Joel's. "Prove it. Give me a lie detector test. I guarantee you, I'll pass it in an instant."

Holy shit. Holy…

Joel tried to keep his breathing as easy and steady as Chloe's. Hard when he felt as if he were hyperventilating. She was claiming to tell the truth, but she wasn't. She'd just lied for him. Given him an alibi. Protected him. Now Richardson was staring at them both with angry suspicion. The agent was going to dig and dig and dig, and Joel knew he'd figure out that Chloe was lying and—

"Don't believe me? My friend Marie saw Joel in the house with me. She can back up the story. So can my brother Reese. So that's three witnesses who will say Joel was not attacking Donnie Adams with a bat. Three…to your one." Her head cocked. "Who do you suppose a jury will believe?"

Richardson leapt to his feet. "Don't even think of leaving!" He stomped toward the door. Threw it open. When it slammed shut, the walls seemed to shake.

At first, Joel didn't move at all. She'd…she'd covered for him. He swallowed. "Chloe—"

Her hand rose. Her index finger pressed to his lips. "You don't have to say a word, my love. I know you wanted to keep our personal relationship a secret, but I couldn't let him throw suspicion on you."

Uh, okay. He hadn't really cared about keeping—

She pulled him in for a tight hug. While hugging him, Chloe brought her lips to his ear.

"He has eyes on this room. He's recording everything we say and do." Barely a whisper. "Back me up, no matter what happens next."

What in the hell else could happen? Some witness was out there, accusing him of murder, and Chloe had just lied to a federal agent in order to protect him. What could possibly happen next?

The door opened. Swung open so hard that it thudded into the wall.

Chloe gave a little jerk of surprise. Joel had the feeling her jerk was faked.

"Thought it would be helpful if I brought in someone who had expertise when it comes to you, Joel." Richardson was back to being an arrogant prick. "He's also someone I thought might be able to give me a better read on you, Chloe."

Chloe slowly pulled away from Joel. She looked toward the doorway. He followed her glance and shock rolled through Joel.

Yep, right. Almost forgot about him. So this is the shit that comes next.

"I believe I told you that Dr. Gordon Jennings was waiting at the station." Richardson motioned toward the man in the brown suit with the carefully cropped beard and watchful eyes. "It was time for him to stop waiting."

Tension knotted Joel's muscles.

"Joel." Gordon's voice was low. Probably meant to be soothing. It was the same low, *I-care* voice he'd used in their few sessions back in Texas. "I'm here because I'm worried about what you've done."

What you've done.

Gordon advanced on him. "Is being trapped in this small room difficult for you? You haven't been in here long but I know how small spaces stress you."

He hadn't even realized it was a small space. Chloe had been touching him, and he'd been focused on other things—*like proving my innocence*—so he hadn't even noticed that Richardson had put them in what had to be the smallest interrogation room in the whole world. Hell, it was barely bigger than—

"But if you go to prison, you will be in a cell for a very, very long time." Gordon's expression turned sad. "I warned you about that. Warned you about how tiny those cells would be. I told you that you had to control your rage and not strike out but you—"

"Oh, for God's sake..." Chloe's British accent was stronger than ever. "Can your license just be stripped away right now? Must we go through the whole process where Joel and I file a formal complaint against you?"

Gordon's gaze shifted to her.

"Dr. Jennings..." Richardson's voice was smooth as silk. No doubt because the jerk was confident once more. "I believe you know Chloe Hastings?"

Wait...how would his former shrink know—

Gordon blinked. "No, I don't know her. Haven't ever met the woman in my life. Why would you think that I knew her?"

"Don't be concerned about the matter, Dr. Jennings." Chloe shook her head. "The agent thinks many incorrect things. It's simply what he does."

Richardson's gaze was jumping back and forth between Chloe and Gordon. "But you..." He pointed to Chloe. "You slipped up. When we were talking at Judith's place, you mentioned him. You knew—"

"I knew about Joel's shrink because he told me the man's foolish diagnosis."

No, I didn't. Joel's gut clenched. Went ice cold.

Chloe rubbed her hand down his arm. "Didn't you, Joel? Didn't you tell me about him?"

He nodded. Joel didn't speak. He was afraid he wasn't as good as she was at telling lies. He'd just realized that Chloe was very, very good.

Her expression didn't change. Her breathing didn't accelerate. Her voice stayed perfectly normal.

He had no doubt that she could pass any lie detector test with flying colors.

And he also realized...

Chloe has lied to me.

Because it was obvious that she knew a great deal about him. Things that she'd never said.

Richardson stalked around the table. He yanked out his chair and took up his seat once more. Gordon headed for the table, too, but he didn't sit. Kind of just lingered. Looked. Studied.

"If standing up makes you feel more superior, by all means, do continue to stand," Chloe instructed. "Pomp and circumstance are important to people with low self-esteem."

Gordon's chest puffed up. "I assure you, I am—"

"Wrong. That's what you are. Your assessment of Joel was wrong from day one. You put him on a dangerous path. Instead of supporting him, you tried to rip him apart. And now, here you are breaking the standards of your profession because you want to reveal confidential information about a patient."

"People are dying," Gordon told her. His *I-care* voice had cracked. It was more of an *I'm-getting-angry* voice. "And the man that you are touching so familiarly—the man you are obviously romantically involved with—he *threatened* to commit murder in our sessions. I know things about him that I cannot keep quiet. If you think a patient will commit a crime, it is a doctor's duty to—"

"Whatever. You believe you're going to get a book deal or something out of this whole situation. Be on every TV news show. I've seen it before. With him." She nodded toward Richardson. "Selling out the innocent to benefit yourself."

The two men both glared at her.

She's doing this deliberately. Trying to draw their attention away from me. Trying to make them angry with her. Because she was...protecting Joel?

"And, yes, I am romantically involved with Joel," Chloe admitted easily. "Dr. Jennings, you wanted Joel to think he was a monster, a man that had to remain separate from the world, but that's not who he is."

Gordon's hands slapped onto the table. He leaned toward Chloe. "Let me tell you who he is..."

Chloe's hand caught Joel's. Twined again with his fingers. "I don't need you to do that. I already know exactly who he is."

"You know who he was before he was cut open with that knife. You don't know the man who crawled out of the grave."

Joel was staring at Chloe. Looking at her profile because he didn't want to look at Gordon any longer. That bastard—Joel had gone to him after the attack. Only to be told...

You'll never be normal again.

Chloe angled her head so that she was staring back at Joel. "I like the man who crawled out of the grave."

His breath seemed to freeze.

"Then you're making a lethal mistake." Gordon's voice was rougher. "He came out of that grave with nothing but rage and hate burning inside of him like a raging wildfire. Joel was an injured animal. He attacked and slaughtered the first person he saw."

"You mean the man who buried him. Joel attacked the man who put him in the ground." She continued to hold Joel's stare. She didn't flinch and glance away. Just looked straight at him.

And Gordon continued his attack. "You know the cops found him walking in the middle of the street, don't you? Bloody and wild? He attacked them. *They* didn't bury him."

"And *he* didn't kill them." Her stare didn't waver.

"In our sessions, all he could talk about was his rage..."

"I'd be angry, too, if someone tortured me and left me to die. Seems like the right reaction."

"Is wanting to go out and *kill* the right reaction? Because that was what he confessed to me. What he said he wanted to do. Joel wanted payback."

He...flinched. Joel couldn't help it. Because he remembered when Chloe had come to his apartment door and asked if he would like to go out with her...to go to that club...she'd offered him...

Payback.

He tried to pull his hand back. *God, Chloe, you knew. You knew it all back then.* Because she must have gotten access to his psych files. She'd been manipulating him every step of the way.

While he'd...

What in the hell had he been doing?

Falling in love with her?

He shut down the thought. Shut it down fast and hard. Brutally hard.

Chloe tightened her hold on his fingers.

"In our sessions, I noted that Joel's affect was off. His girlfriend at the time had left him. He couldn't talk with friends or old associates. He couldn't connect with anyone."

"He connects just fine with me," Chloe replied. She shrugged. "Don't know why those people had problems. Maybe their affect was off."

"Joel talked about punishing the guilty. About how the killers out there had to be stopped. That the world wasn't a safe place."

Still gazing into Joel's eyes, Chloe said, "It's not." Then her head turned as she studied the shrink. "Everything Joel has said certainly seems rational to me. Killers do need to be stopped. The guilty should be punished. Correct me if I'm wrong, but I do believe that's the basic tenet of the American criminal justice system?"

"You don't understand twisted minds," Gordon charged. "You don't—"

Chloe laughed. *Laughed.* "Oh, my, but you are certainly wrong. About Joel and me. I understand twisted minds perfectly. Mostly because I have one." She stood. "And because I have one, I know that Joel doesn't. He isn't a murderer. He's a protector. You feared that he'd lose his control and act on those impulses he told you about in your precious sessions?"

"Only a matter of time." Gordon nodded his head. Stroked that stupid beard. "I saw it coming. That's why when the FBI agent called me, I—"

"I don't think you can see anything at all, and you're not even wearing a blindfold." She tugged Joel to his feet using her hold on his hand. "You told Joel that he would lose all sense of right and wrong. That he would grip a scalpel, that he would try to operate on a patient, and he'd suddenly be back in his worst nightmare."

Gordon's eyes widened. "That's right. I did tell him all of that. He...shared it with you?"

Nope. Joel hadn't shared a damn thing.

"Obviously," Chloe said.

"I warned Joel that he would disassociate. Advised him that he should never practice medicine again. Unfortunate, but—"

"Untrue. It was a load of absolute horse shit. I've seen him practice medicine. Seen him save lives. And his fingers didn't even shake. He's the steadiest, strongest man I know, and *you* did him a disservice when you pushed your own agenda with him, Dr. Jennings. You saw what you wanted. Not what was there. He isn't the monster. You are." She nodded toward Gordon, then Richardson. "Joel isn't under arrest. He was polite and answered your questions, and now we're leaving."

Sounded like a killer idea.

They headed for the door.

"He hasn't *saved* any lives," Richardson pointed out. "Judith Key is dead."

Chloe stopped in front of the door. "He didn't just work on Judith. He saved another man, too. Joel has nights that are quite busy." She glanced back at the agent. "And you should have already realized that he *did* save Judith. Then someone else went into that hospital—someone who didn't want Judith to talk—and that person killed her. Probably put an air bubble into her IV or something that he thought would be untraceable like that. Why don't you try being an actual crime solver and go pull security footage from the hospital? Or you know, talk to the staff? When you see that I'm right, you should come and apologize to Joel."

Joel wasn't gonna hold his breath for an apology.

"Judith's death puts a whole new light on the crimes for me. I think we're looking for a medical professional."

"Yeah...like Doctor Landry there—"

She continued, as if Richardson hadn't spoken, "Someone who works at the hospital where Judith was being treated. Someone who could slip inside easily and would know how to kill a patient without arousing suspicion. With that much knowledge, we have to be looking for a nurse. A doctor. And considering the targeted nature of the attack on the three male victims, it does stand to reason that the perpetrator knows human anatomy. He knew which areas of the spine to target—

"All of this points to Landry."

"Except for the fact that he has an airtight alibi." Her chin lifted. "He has me."

"You're not saying anything," Richardson snarled at Joel. "You gonna let her do all the talking for you? Can't you defend yourself?"

Joel laughed. The reaction seemed to be the last thing that Richardson expected. Good. Joel faced him and Gordon. "You think that taunt will injure my pride? Chloe is more than welcome to defend me any time she wants. But sure, I can defend myself, too. I didn't kill Donnie Adams. I haven't killed anyone in New Orleans."

"And you have an alibi for the night of Donnie's murder? You were with her?" Richardson wasn't giving up.

"You heard Chloe. She said I was with her." How about that? Those words hadn't been an actual lie. More like a twist of the truth. Joel recalled something that Marie had once told him about Chloe...

What she doesn't say is often more important than what she does.

Damn. He'd started acting like Chloe did. Using her tricks.

Tricks she used on me from day one.

The anger was there, swirling inside him. The burn of betrayal. But he couldn't let his control waver. Not yet. Not while they had an audience.

"I think we're done now," Joel said. "So how about you two…"

"Piss off," Chloe told them politely.

Joel brought her hand to his lips. Pressed a kiss to her knuckles. "I was going to say fuck off, but pissing off works, too."

CHAPTER TWENTY-FOUR

"I know you're angry." Chloe stood beside the motorcycle. The light from the moon fell down onto her as she twisted her hands in front of her body. She was trying hard not to reach out to him. Mostly because she was afraid he'd reject her touch.

He didn't get off the bike. He'd brought her home in silence. She'd felt the tension in his body. The anger that bubbled beneath the surface.

"Angry?" Joel seemed to taste the word. "Is that what I am?"

"Joel—"

"You lied, Chloe."

Yes. More times than she could count. "I did it to protect you." As if that would somehow make it better.

"You mean in the interrogation room? I'm not talking about when you stared straight at the FBI agent and lied about us having sex the night Donnie died. I'm talking about other times. Times you lied to me. All of the times...*to me.*"

"So am I," she whispered miserably.

"What?"

"I was trying to protect you." Over and over. "I know you don't believe me or understand—"

"Because you've been keeping me in the dark!"

"Shortly after I met you, I realized Gordon was wrong about you, but if I just went straight up to you and told you that tosser was an idiot, you wouldn't have believed me. I had to show you he was wrong."

"Because Chloe knows best. Because Chloe has to be the puppet master who manipulates everyone around her."

Chloe's shoulders stiffened. "I'm sorry."

"How did you get my psych file? Wait, *when* did you get it?"

"I received it about a month ago. As to how, I have a friend who is good at hacking. He got into Gordon's system."

Joel swore. "A month? A whole fucking month? *Why?*"

"I don't want to hurt you."

"Too fucking late for that." His voice was raw. Savage.

She flinched.

"Why? Why me, Chloe? Why the hell did you pull me into your web?"

"I originally wanted to see your file because I was doing research on people in the area..." *Tell him.* "Who might fit the profile of the killer."

"The Bad Deeds Killer."

She nodded. "I saw you the day I learned of Gregory Guidry's murder. You were running down the street. I was at the crime scene, and you just—you ran right past me."

"I don't remember that."

"You run a lot, Joel. You never remember where you go. You're too busy trying to escape. But I saw you and—"

"And you notice everything, don't you? Every fucking thing. You saw me, probably recognized my face, and you decided to rip my life apart."

She couldn't let him see how much his words hurt her. She'd learned to never let anyone see when she hurt. Some people liked pain far too much. "You were at the crime scene. When I saw you, I remembered what had happened to you."

"Sure, you did. What with that great eidetic memory and all."

She would not flinch. "I use the victims to help me find the killers. I work backwards. I was building an idea in my head based on Gregory of what the perp might be like. And all of a sudden, you were there, running right past me, and after what you'd done to the man who you believed hurt you—"

"Believed? I damn well know what that bastard did to me! You weren't there! You don't know! You don't know how he laughed when I bled. How he smiled when he cut deeper and deeper. How he told me no one would ever come. No one would find me, no one would—" Joel stopped. Exhaled.

She reached up to touch him because she hated his pain. She wanted to take it away and make it better for him—

"Don't." He jerked away.

She was the one to suck in a deep breath. Pain knifed through her and Chloe had to hurriedly lower her lashes so that he wouldn't notice the tears that filled her eyes.

"You set me up from the beginning, didn't you?" His voice was angry, but cold. Very cold. "All some giant test. A game you were playing."

"I don't play games." Her voice was rough. Too ragged. "People always say that, but I don't."

"*Look at me.*"

Her head snapped up. A tear slid down her cheek.

He swallowed. His hand lifted toward her, but it stopped. Fisted. Fell back to his side. "It wasn't coincidence that we met in that bank, was it?"

Slowly, she shook her head.

"How the fuck did you arrange that?"

"I...I knew Harry's pattern. The trick was getting you in the bank on the right day. I made sure a check was sent to you from your lawyer's Dallas office and I—"

"God, you are a piece of work."

Chloe pressed her lips together.

"You manipulated me from day one. Nothing was real, was it?" Both of his hands locked around the handlebars. Tightened fiercely. "I'm just someone else for you to mind fuck—"

"*No!*" The snarl tore from her and everything—

The walls came crashing down.

Her heartbeat seemed too fast. Her breathing too fast. Her body too hot. Everything was too much. "I'm not mind fucking you. I've been trying to *help* you! Yes, I set up the meeting in the bank. All I had to go by on you were Gordon's notes. I don't trust the assessment of other people. I needed to interact with you myself! And within five minutes of meeting you, I knew how wrong he was. But *you* didn't. You were living in a grave that he'd created for you. Believing the lies he'd told you, and I had to help you to break free. So I gave you opportunities. Choices. *You* made those decisions. You chose to move here. You chose to be my partner. *You* chose to be my lover." She didn't swipe away the tears on her cheeks. She didn't care about them.

I care about him. Why couldn't he see that?

"I knew you weren't the killer, Joel. You weren't the man I was after. But you were the man I needed. I wanted you to stay with me. I still want you to stay with me." She'd never been this open with anyone in her life.

Maybe because no one had ever mattered this much?

"You don't let me in, Chloe." His voice seemed as ragged as her own. Not as cold any longer. Rough and gruff. "I don't know any of your secrets, yet you know everything that makes me bleed. How the hell is that fair?"

It wasn't. "Joel…" She almost reached for him again.

But he had the motorcycle roaring to life. "I can't watch you cry," he rasped. "I can't fucking do it."

She couldn't stop crying. She hadn't cried in so long, but the tears were coming now because he was hurt. She'd done this. "The more time I spent with you, the more I wanted to help."

"I'm not a freaking fixer-upper project! I'm a person, I'm—"

"I think I love you, Joel."

He stared at her. The motorcycle growled.

A tremble shook her body.

"I can't tell," he said.

"What?" She didn't understand.

"I can't tell when you are lying or when you're telling me the truth."

A chill swept over her body. "I see."

"*What do you want me to do?*"

Chloe choked down the lump in her throat. *Put the walls back up. Get your control back, Chloe.* "I want you to figure out if I'm lying or telling the truth. When you do, come back to me." She turned away. Made herself put one foot in front of the other. She'd get inside. Shut the door. Get herself together.

"Chloe!"

She didn't stop walking. "You haven't figured out anything yet, Joel. Come back to me when you do." Because...as she'd told him before...

It had always been his choice. His decision. Every step of the way.

The motorcycle roared down the road.

When she opened the door of the house, Marie was waiting for her near the foot of the stairs. A brown envelope was gripped in her hands. "Did he really need to rev the bike that way?" Marie asked with a wince. "Loud as hell. Annoying."

"I think he really needed to rev the bike that way," Chloe replied woodenly.

Marie advanced on her. Narrowed her eyes. "Why the hell do you have tear tracks on your cheeks?"

"Because I hurt him."

"No, no, *bullshit.* You have tear tracks on your cheeks because he hurt you." She shoved the envelope into Chloe's hands and pulled out one of her knives in the next moment. Marie always had a knife hidden somewhere. "I'm going after him," she fumed. "I will make him sorry, don't you worry about that for a second, I will—"

"Where did this envelope come from?"

"It was on the doorstep. Had your name on it. Figured it was for one of your weird cases."

She flipped over the envelope. Saw her name. Recognized the familiar scrawl. A fist squeezed her heart as she ripped open the envelope. The tarot card spilled into her hand. Yellow background. A man with his hand in the air, standing near a powerful altar. A man who was...

The Magician.

Her head whipped right back up. "Go after Joel."

"Oh, I'm going after him. I will make him so sorry, I will—"

"Protect him. Please. He doesn't want to be around me now, and I need you to go. Stay with him. Make sure he's safe."

Marie hesitated. Worry flashed in her eyes. "Someone is after Joel?"

"I trust you, Marie. You're the best, most skilled—"

"Assassin you know?" Marie finished darkly. She looked down at the knife in her hand. "Just like my father." Grim. Sad.

"No. *No.*"

Marie peered up at her.

"You're nothing like him. You're the best, most skilled hunter I know. You can find anyone, and we both know it. Yes, your father trained you how to track prey just like he did..." *To track and then to kill.* "But you didn't cross the line. You never have. You never will. You can find anyone, at any time. I know you can find Joel. I need you to find him. Then make sure he stays safe. Please," Chloe pleaded again. She could hear the desperation in her own voice.

Marie held her gaze. "We both know the only reason I didn't cross the line was because you stopped me when I was in the middle of my first kill."

"Me being there wasn't the reason you didn't finish the job. If you'd really wanted to do it, you would have just taken your knife and shoved it in my throat. *Then* done the job and gotten paid."

Marie licked her lower lip. "I...didn't want to kill you."

"You didn't want to kill anyone," Chloe corrected.

"You know how many people my dad killed. You know what he—"

"I know you're not your dad. I'm not my father, either. We're our own people. We make our choices. That's what matters."

"You always say that." She squared her shoulders.

"Because it's always true."

"Say it enough and one day, I might believe you." Marie yanked open the door. "I'll find your lost partner, don't worry. I might hurt him a little, but I'll be sure he stays alive—"

"You already do believe me. That's why you're going after Joel. And thank you."

Marie disappeared into the night.

Chloe looked back down at the card. Then at the envelope. That familiar scrawl. She'd feared it was him. Had known, deep down, all along, that it had to be.

The stairs creaked. The fifth stair, to be exact. She raised her eyes. Found Reese staring at her.

"What's happening?" he asked. Like Marie, he had worry in his eyes.

"A dead man is in town." Her hold tightened on the card and envelope. "And I think he's about to be a problem."

CHAPTER TWENTY-FIVE

Joel lifted the shot glass to his lips. Drained it fast. Didn't even feel the burn as the whiskey slid down his throat. He immediately motioned for another.

He was in the loudest, roughest bar he could find. And everywhere he looked, Joel saw...her. Chloe. With tears on her cheeks. Tears he'd made her shed.

I am such a bastard.

When he'd seen her tears, all he'd wanted to do was wipe them away. Kiss them way. Pull her into his arms. Tell her everything was okay.

I think I love you, Joel.

The whole world had stopped when she'd said those words. And he'd wanted—so very badly—to believe her. But Chloe had been playing him from the beginning. What if she was still playing him? *What if I want her so much that it doesn't even matter?*

Was he that desperate? That far gone? That *in* love with Chloe Hastings?

"Oh, wow, I've seen that look before." A guy slid onto the barstool next to him. "Woman trouble, am I right?"

"You have no idea." Joel slanted him a quick glance.

"You'd be surprised." The man smiled at him. His gray eyes swept over Joel. "I've had my heart broken before. Shattered beneath the heel of a sexy high-heeled shoe." He motioned to the bartender. "I'll take what he's got."

Wonderful. A stranger trying to be chummy. "Look, buddy, I am not in the mood to commiserate. And trust me, you've got no idea what my life is like."

"Oh, I'm not here to commiserate. Just to get drunk off my ass." He took the shot glass that had been placed in front of him. Lifted it toward Joel in a salute. "Cheers." He drained it in one gulp. "Another!" he called.

Joel studied the refilled shot glass in front of him. The amber liquid. He remembered the last time he'd had whiskey. With Reese. And the guy's accent had vanished. "Can't believe anything with them." He reached for the glass. Held it too tightly because...

I want to believe her. I want to believe she loves me.

He'd been staring into her eyes. Those tears...

He let go of the glass. Rubbed his chest. It ached.

"Nope. You can't believe a word some women tell you. They're just trying to get in your head. Trying to mess you up. That's what my fiancée did to me." The chatty stranger drained the second glass. "But I have plans. I'm not out yet."

Joel found himself peering at the fellow once more. Dark hair. Wide shoulders. T-shirt. Jeans.

The man caught his glance. Flashed another smile.

Oh, fuck. Joel knew that smile. The man's eyes were a different color. The hair was a different cut and color, too. But the smile was the same. The exact same.

"You all right?" He slapped Joel on the shoulder. "Because it looks like you've just seen a ghost."

He had. Joel was staring at a ghost. "Get your hand off me."

"Okay." He removed the hand. "Settle down. Obviously, you're not the kind of man who makes friends easily." The man tossed some cash on the bar. "See you around." He pushed off the stool. Slipped into the crowd.

Hell, no. *Hell. No.* Joel yanked out his wallet and threw money down as he surged after the guy.

"Hey!" The bartender's shout followed him. "You didn't even touch your second drink!"

Joel ignored the call and rushed out of the bar. He looked to the left. *Not there.* Turned his head to the right. *There.* The man was ducking into an alley. "Stop!" Joel shouted.

He didn't.

"*Morgan, stop!*" He used the name deliberately. The name of the man who'd planned to marry Chloe. Morgan Fletcher.

For just a moment, the man stopped. Then he darted into the alley.

Joel raced into that alley right after him. His feet flew over the cracked pavement as he turned the corner and hurried inside and—

A hard hand grabbed him and slammed him into the alley's brick wall. "Don't you know better," the man who *had* to be Morgan Fletcher asked, "than to go running into dark alleys? Has Chloe taught you nothing?"

Morgan's elbow was jammed against Joel's throat. Was he supposed to be impressed by that shit? He wasn't. Joel drove his knee into the fellow's dick, as hard as he could. Morgan gasped and eased his grip. Joel used that opportunity to yank down Morgan's hand, to head butt the bastard, and to drive a fist straight into Morgan's stomach.

Morgan groaned as he doubled over. "Je...sus..." he panted. "Just...messing with you."

Joel kept his hands loose at his sides. "I'm not in the mood to be messed with."

Morgan put his hands on his knees. Sucked in a couple of deep breaths. "Dirty move. My dick may never be the same."

"I don't think the world will mind."

Morgan tilted up his head. "But will Chloe?" A taunting smile curled his lips. "I think she—"

"I don't think Chloe gives a damn what happens to you or your dick. She's with me now." Even as he said those words, even as he heard the possessive growl in his own voice, Joel realized...

I mean it. Chloe is mine. I'm hers. Because they were partners. Good. Bad. All the stuff in between—they were partners.

"Is she?" Morgan taunted. His hands were still braced on his knees. "Then how come I don't see her with you? How come I found you all alone, drinking ever so sadly in a rundown bar?"

He shrugged. "Because I like drinking in rundown bars?"

Morgan continued to hunch over and that bothered Joel. He tensed because he expected—

Morgan surged up, and when his arms rose, he clutched a gun in his right hand. *Damn. He'd dragged that out of thin air.* Or maybe...he'd probably had it hidden under his shirt. Morgan brought the gun up and at Joel, but—too late. Joel had sensed the attack. He kicked at Morgan's wrist and hand. Some bones snapped, and the gun went flying.

Morgan didn't cry out in pain. Just hissed out a breath. "I can see why you appealed to her. Chloe likes a bit of danger. Turns her on."

"And I can see why she told me that she'd once had sex with a psycho."

Morgan threw back his head and laughed.

"I wasn't making a joke." The gun waited a few feet away. "You faked your own death, didn't you? Why the hell would you do that?"

"Chloe hasn't told you?" Morgan flexed the gloved fingers of his right hand. Winced. "Oh, that's right. Chloe doesn't tell anyone her secrets." As if imparting a very special piece of knowledge, he lowered his voice and revealed, "That's how you can tell that she doesn't love you. Not truly. Because if she did, she'd tell you everything."

"She didn't tell you jack shit about herself," Joel threw back at the bastard. "Is that how you knew she didn't love you?"

Morgan wasn't laughing now. The faint light from a nearby window trickled into the alley. "She told me plenty."

"I don't think so. Turns out, I can play poker pretty well. I know a bluff when I see one."

"Not when Chloe is the one bluffing. No one can tell when Chloe bluffs. Lies or truth, you never know with her."

Fuck me. Hadn't Joel told her...*I can't tell when you are lying or when you're telling me the truth?* He'd just told her that, and this prick seemed to know those exact words. "Have you been watching us?"

Another flex of his fingers. "You don't overly concern me."

"I'll take that as a yes."

"Chloe is quite something, isn't she? Know how I'd describe her?"

"I don't particularly give a shit how you would—"

"Death and moonlight." Whispered. Said almost tenderly. "That's what she is. Chloe will always be drawn to death. To the darkness that waits in the world. She can't help herself. It's almost an addiction. And she's moonlight. You think you can catch her. You *want* to catch her because she's so beautiful, but like moonlight, she just slips through your fingers." He peered at his fingers. "I think you broke two of them. Maybe fractured my wrist. That wasn't very nice."

"Coming at me with a gun wasn't *nice,* either."

"I wasn't going to shoot you. Just testing your skills."

"Bullshit." Like he'd believe anything this asshole said.

"Do you know who killed Chloe's parents?"

The one-eighty question made Joel tense even more.

"I do. Chloe does, too. If she honestly cared for you, wouldn't she tell you the truth? She told me."

Joel braced his feet apart. Got ready for the attack he knew was coming. And he decided to use some of the tools Chloe had given him. His plan was to attempt to handle this...shit, like she would have done. "You wanted her on the yacht with you."

Silence.

Yeah. I can throw out my one-eighty shit, too. "But Chloe knew what you were. Oh, sure, perhaps you fooled her at first, but she eventually saw through you. She always sees through the monsters, doesn't she? She found evidence that proved what you really were. A criminal defense attorney...who *was* a criminal."

Again, more silence. So Joel plowed on. He took what he'd learned and pushed. "If Chloe had wanted to be on that yacht, she would have been. You knew when she canceled, that all of your plans were about to fall apart. She had incriminating evidence on you. Enough to ruin your life."

"I didn't leave evidence behind," Morgan snapped out. Definitely not sounding so controlled any longer. "Chloe had her guesses. That's all."

Joel smiled. "Chloe doesn't guess, and we both know it. So when she wasn't there, you knew that you had to disappear. Faked your death. Got to say, that seems rather dramatic."

"You have no idea who you are dealing with. You're an amateur. A fool who got lucky because he didn't die when he was tossed in a grave. You don't understand Chloe, and you will never understand me."

"No? Well, news flash. I don't give a shit about understanding you." He'd be happy to never see the man again. "But when it comes to Chloe, I think I'm starting to figure things out. And if you were listening to us tonight—the way I suspect you were—then you know that Chloe loves me. That pushed *your* buttons, didn't it? It's what drove you to seek me out. It—"

"You left her crying. Chloe cries for no one."

Her tears. His chest burned once more.

"She didn't even cry when she killed her own brother," Morgan said. "Didn't shed a tear."

His heartbeat was too loud.

"You won't last." Morgan took a slow step back. "I'll make sure of that."

Joel thought the bastard was going to dive for the gun. He surged toward it, too—

But instead of going for the gun, Morgan yanked out a knife. He lifted it up high with his left hand and brought it down toward Joel's body as—

Another knife flew from the darkness. Spun end over end until it lodged in Morgan's shoulder. He dropped the blade he'd been holding. It clattered to the alley's floor.

Joel's head immediately whipped toward the thick darkness at the end of the alley.

Morgan barreled past him. Bleeding, swearing...

Joel wanted to rush after him, but what other threat waited in the alley? Had that knife been meant for Morgan or for him and what did—

Footsteps crunched over loose gravel. Marie strolled out of the darkness. "I was aiming for him, in case you were worried."

The gun was near his foot. Joel started to pick it up—

"Nope. You should leave it there. Knowing Morgan, it was probably used in a crime and if you touch it and get your fingerprints on it, then you'll be hauled to jail." She waved a hand vaguely around the alley. "This whole scene is probably a setup. He wanted the cops to catch you assaulting him, so it's a good thing you decided to let the jerk get out of here."

It didn't feel like a good thing. It felt like a terrible mistake. "The bastard faked his own death. I'm sure the cops would like to know he was here. *Why* he faked it. And—"

"He'll have a complete new identity. Chloe told me once that no one would ever be able to prove who he really is. So if Morgan was out, in public, and he was luring you to this alley, it was all so he could spring a trap on you."

As if on cue, a police siren screamed.

"We should leave," Marie advised. "I think they're coming here." She took his elbow. Tucked her arm through the crook. "Looks like we're a couple this way." They walked out of the alley, arm-in-arm, all casual-like. "Nope. Not going for your ride." She steered him away from the motorcycle. "Morgan probably said the guy who assaulted him was riding that beast."

"When would he have said that? He just ran out. He didn't have time to call the cops—"

"I'm sure he alerted them before he ever said hello to you. Then his entire exchange with you was calculated. Designed to draw you out and get you exactly where he wanted you. Chloe told me that he was always very good at predicting behavior."

"Chloe didn't tell me jack shit about him." Well, except for the fact that he'd been psycho. *True. He seemed to be.*

"Chloe was probably trying not to scare you. You're kinda dealing with enough stuff already. Turn here. My car is just around the corner."

A police cruiser was rushing toward them.

They kept strolling, nice and slow.

The vehicle passed them.

"I'm not scared of that asshole."

"Good."

"Why are you here?" Joel asked her.

"Because Chloe sent me to protect you. I was wondering why she didn't come herself—she said something about you not wanting to be around her."

I left her. I shouldn't have left.

"Then I heard that little convo between you and Morgan. Cleared some things up."

A red sports car waited a few feet away. She directed him straight to it.

"I didn't need protecting," Joel pointed out.

She let him go. Beamed at him. "You know, I have to say, your skills impressed me. You might be able to keep up with Chloe, after all."

"You're being nice to me. It worries me." That bright smile made him nervous.

Her laughter rang out. "You just had an alley face-off with Chloe's crazy ex, and I'm the one who worries you?"

"How did you know where I was? And how are you so good with knives?"

She pointed to the car. "Get in."

He didn't want to get in. He wanted to tear off and search for Morgan. *Fucking jerk came at me with a gun.* Morgan was obviously obsessed with Chloe. Hell, no wonder Reese *and* Marie had warned Joel that he needed to keep Chloe safe.

And I left her alone.

Now Morgan was on the streets and Chloe...

He yanked open the passenger door. "Get me back to Chloe."

"Great life choice there, doc." She slid behind the wheel. Turned the car on and had soft blue lighting filling the interior. Rock music blasted as she got them on the road and maneuvered through the city.

Joel stared out of the window and thought about Chloe. *If that bastard is going after her...*

"I was going to be just like him." Marie's voice was soft. Joel could barely hear it over the pounding radio. "I didn't want to be. But I'd grown up only with him. He trained me. He taught me. He groomed me to take his place."

His head turned toward her. "Who did?"

"My father. He killed one hundred men."

Holy—

"He was a hitman. Knives were his specialty. He wanted them to be mine, too." She stopped at a red light. Her hands tightened around the wheel. "I was on my first job. I knew what to do. How to do it. It would have been easy. Killing was the only thing I'd ever been taught to do."

"Marie..."

The light changed—a moment *before* it changed, she was already surging forward. "Chloe found me. She walked right up to me. I was like two minutes away from completing the kill. She came to me. Said there was still time. Different options were out there."

"She found you at your darkest time," he mumbled. "You...told me that once."

"I thought she was crazy."

Despite what she was telling him, he *almost* smiled. "So did I, the first time we met."

"Told her to get away from me. Told her...there was nothing different. I had no idea how to do anything else. No idea of anything else I could be." Her attention stayed focused on the road even as she kept talking in her low, soft voice. "And Chloe, she told me...said I could stay with her while I figured it all out. She'd give me a job. I would be safe. All I had to do was just make the call."

Another turn. The music kept blaring.

"I've been with her since then. Want to hear the wildest part? I even started taking cooking classes last fall."

They were almost home.

Home.

"Turns out," Marie murmured, "you can use knives for more than just killing. And I'm very, very good with my knives."

"I can attest to that."

She didn't speak again. Not until they were back on the property. Her finger pressed the button to turn off the radio. "Aren't you going to ask why I shared all that?"

"I'm guessing Chloe told you to tell me the truth?"

"No. Chloe doesn't tell her friends what to do. That's not who she is. Haven't you figured that shit out yet? Stop being slow." Her head angled toward him.

"Why did you tell me?"

"Because Chloe loves you. If she said it, she meant it. And you're here right now—instead of running in the opposite direction after meeting that freak Morgan—and I think *I* know what that means." A pause. "Do you?"

"I don't want him to hurt her."

"I don't think he ever would. He has an attachment to her."

"Yeah, fucking noticed."

"That attachment is love to him. Not to everyone else. But, it's as close as he can get." She toyed with her keys. "Tell me, how close to love can you get?"

His breath sawed out. "It's only been a few days. She's only been in my life *a few days*."

"Came in with hurricane force, didn't she?"

Damn straight she did.

Marie slid out of the car.

He followed quickly. He needed to find Chloe. He needed—

Marie put her hand out, blocking his path when he headed for the main house. "She was with Morgan for six months. He asked her to marry him. Morgan is very good at saying the right things. At doing the right things. If he doesn't want you to see the monster inside, you don't. Even Chloe was fooled for a while. She doesn't like being wrong."

"I noticed that trait."

"In that whole six months, she never told Morgan that she loved him."

She told me. "She lied to me."

"I tried to warn you about that. Even gave you clues. Said that with Chloe, what she says—"

"Isn't as important as what she doesn't say. Check. Got it now."

"So why don't you go figure out all of the things she hasn't said? Go see her for who she really is. And if you're not going to be here for the long haul, then do us all a favor, would you?" Her hand dropped. "Be gone by the time the sun rises. Don't ever drag your ass back." With that, she began walking away. Toward the main house.

He started to follow.

"Chloe won't be in there." She didn't look back.

"Then were the hell is she?"

"If she was worried about you, don't you think she'd be waiting in your place?"

He whirled around.

"Don't forget. Be gone by—"

"I'm not going anywhere," he shouted back. "Except straight to Chloe."

CHAPTER TWENTY-SIX

She was sitting on the couch when he opened the door. Chloe's spine was perfectly straight, her hands were folded in her lap, and her chin was up. She wore loose, cotton jogging shorts and a blue top. Her feet were bare, and he noticed that her toes were curling against the floor.

Her only sign of nerves.

At least, the only sign Joel could see.

He shut the door. Flipped the lock. Leaned his shoulders back against the wood and tried to figure out where to start—

"I hope you don't mind that I was waiting inside. I'm sure this is me overstepping, but..." Her voice trailed away.

"You're not overstepping. You own the property." Some gift deal that he'd never figured out.

"But this is your home, and you shouldn't invade someone's home."

"Why the hell not?" He couldn't take his eyes off her. "You invaded every other part of my life."

She sucked in a breath.

Wrong thing to say. Came out wrong. "Chloe—"

"I only came inside because I wanted to make certain you were safe. After I received the card from Morgan, I was afraid he might try to wait for you in here. I sent Marie to look for you, and I came here." She rose. "Morgan isn't here, obviously, so I'll get out of your way." She headed for the door.

Morgan. He didn't like hearing the bastard's name on her lips. "You're not going anywhere, sweetheart."

Her hair slid over her shoulders.

"Met the ex tonight," he drawled. "Got to say, he strikes me as a real prick."

"You have no idea."

His posture was relaxed but tension knifed through his entire body. "Because *you* didn't tell me about him."

"Yes, well, it is hard to drop certain points in a conversation. You don't get to just say lines like... 'Oh, by the way, I have an ex-fiancé out there who faked his own murder. He has extreme issues letting go, so I worry that he might be stalking me.'"

"Is that what he's doing? Stalking you?" *The sonofabitch.*

"Morgan does many things."

"Like pretend to be dead."

A nod.

"Why?" But he had his suspicions, as he'd said to the bastard in the alley. Joel wanted to see if he was right.

"I'm different."

That hadn't been the response he'd expected from her.

"I've been different my whole life. I don't think like everyone else. I can't. I see people, and I'm constantly trying to figure out what's driving them. I always tend to favor darker motives. I understand those motives. I understand darkness. All of the bad impulses that people have. The impulses that drive them to hurt and kill." She wrapped her arms around her stomach. Bowed her head.

She's death and moonlight.

"Morgan Fletcher was a criminal defense attorney. He took the biggest cases, the most sensational ones. His clients—they were some of the worst killers out there. The first time we met, I was sure I wouldn't like him at all. How could I? He defended the people I wanted to put away." Her hair had slid over her face. "But when we talked, he understood me. No, he understood *them.*"

Yeah. The jealousy is back. I know the guy is a straight-up bastard, and I'm still jealous. How rational was that? Not at all. But who cared? With Chloe, Joel was far past the point of being rational.

"We could talk about killers for hours. About what drove people to commit horrible crimes. About the demons inside of us all. He could figure out what was happening at a crime scene as quickly as I could. He didn't mind when I got lost in my own head. He didn't mind when I spent days hunting a murderer. He liked to hear every detail about what I was doing. And I didn't realize, until too late, that he liked it all too much."

"The sonofabitch pulled a gun on me tonight, Chloe."

Her head whipped up.

"And I broke his hand. A few fingers. Maybe his wrist. I also gave him a few other mementos to remember me by."

"Did you call the police?"

"Marie said he had probably already called them. That he'd arranged the whole scene so it would look as if I'd assaulted him—and, yeah, guilty, but only because he made the first move and I was defending myself."

"I've never seen anyone as good at manipulation as Morgan. He could have a jury believing a mass murderer was a choir boy. He could have *me* believing that the devil was prince charming."

Joel wished he'd given the dick a few more mementos. "When did you realize the truth?"

"The night before I was supposed to go out on that yacht with him. Everything he said and did was perfect—when he was with me. Like each response was designed to please me. To match me. But no one is perfect, and it was that very perfection that made me so nervous. I started digging into his past. At first, everything was fine. So I had to look deeper and deeper. I had to go back more and more. It was only when I went back to his time in high school that I found my answer."

"And you found it the night before the yacht trip?"

"His high school girlfriend vanished. Just disappeared one day. No trace of her was ever found."

"How do you know he was involved? How'd you get proof?" A rough bark of laughter escaped him. "Another cadaver-sniffing dog—"

"I didn't get proof. I *had* no proof. I had nothing but every instinct I possessed telling me that I had been wrong about him." She was still hugging herself. "I don't like to be wrong."

"I have noticed that, sweetheart."

She flinched. "She looked like me."

"What?"

"Dark hair, blue eyes, similar build. She looked like me."

He shoved away from the door. He wanted to pull her into his arms—

"I had no proof. No option. Just...fine, for the first time, I *guessed*. I called him. I told Morgan— I *lied* to him and said I knew what he'd done. One of my tests. Always testing people, yes? That's me." Chloe rocked back onto the balls of her feet. "I said I had proof. I said her name. I wanted his reaction." Her breath had turned ragged.

"And what was his reaction?"

"Morgan said that the moment he met me, he knew I'd be the one."

"The one fucking what?"

"The one who would understand him. The one who would see every part of him and understand what he was."

I should have never let him get away. "So he admitted—"

"No, he never came out and admitted anything. But the next day, his yacht sank, and he was supposedly dead. I went to the police. Told them what I suspected, but his family was well connected in the area. He was well respected. Money and power can turn the tide on most stories." A bitter laugh. "I've certainly seen that happen more than once in my life."

"Wait." His mind was spinning. "You said you got a card from him tonight—when I first came in, *that's* what you said."

"Yes." She reached into the loose pocket of her shorts. Pulled out a tarot card.

The Magician.

"He wrote my name on the envelope that contained the card. I recognized his handwriting. I'd suspected he was the one leaving the cards all along. This case—something about it drew him out."

Joel wasn't so sure it was the case. "He wants you."

She met his gaze. "When he left the Death card, I thought it meant we were done. That he was severing ties to me."

"I don't think that's what it meant." He took the Magician card from her. Their fingers brushed. He didn't even try to ignore the lick of electricity that shot through his blood. "What does this mean?"

"Depends on the way the card is positioned. If the Magician is upright, it can refer to a determined, powerful man."

A stalker dick of an ex.

"If the Magician is inverted, the card is about confusion and deceit."

"Was the card upright or inverted?"

"I have no idea. Marie found the envelope."

"Marie…" A whole new topic. "That's an interesting friend you have."

"How so?" A cautious response.

"She told me, Chloe. About her past."

Her eyes widened. "That means she trusts you."

He looked down at the Magician card. Ripped that bitch in half and tossed it away. "She does, so why don't you?"

"I do. I—"

His hand slid under her chin. "I'm not going to run because you have some crazed ex out there who should be rotting in a jail cell."

"I-I can't prove what he did. And Morgan will have changed his identity so thoroughly that no cop will believe he's the man I say. I didn't have proof before. I guessed, I—"

"Baby, you don't guess." He lowered his head. Brushed his lips over hers. "You make educated deductions."

"Y-you remembered I said that."

"I remember everything you tell me." Another slow kiss. "I'm not scared of your ex," he breathed against her mouth. "He needs to be scared of me. I'm not going to let him get anywhere near you. And you and I—we will find a way to get his ass locked up."

"He's probably long gone now. He wanted to see you. To get close to you. But if you broke his hand, he will run. He'll plan for another time and—"

"And we'll be ready for him. But the prick needs to get in line. We already have one killer to catch."

Her hands rose. Curled around his shoulders. "You're not...leaving?"

"Not ever the hell again," he swore. "But things are going to change." His hand slipped around to the nape of her neck. Sank beneath the thickness of her hair. "New deal. From here on out, I know everything."

"Everything?"

"That's a pretty fucking important point. Non-negotiable. I don't want lies."

"And I don't want to hurt you." Her gaze searched his. "Can't you see that?"

"I see that you try to protect everyone else, but, sweetheart, you seem to forget, I was the one hired to protect *you*."

"Joel..."

He couldn't hold back any longer. He'd been desperate to return to her. Desperate to see her. To hold her.

His mouth took hers once more, but this kiss wasn't slow or gentle. It should have been. *He* should have been. But he wasn't.

Her lips were open. His tongue thrust inside her mouth. She met him eagerly, hotly, and her body pressed to his. She kissed him with the same hunger that he felt. A hunger Joel knew would never end.

He wasn't going to magically get enough of her. One time in bed—a dozen times in bed—

wouldn't be enough. With Chloe, he'd never have enough.

"I won't lose you," he said before he scooped her into his arms. He'd finally found someone who mattered to him. She'd gotten into his heart, and when he'd stood in that alley facing off with Morgan, Joel had come to several important conclusions.

First, Chloe was his. Lies, truths—whatever she'd given him in the past—she was still *his*.

Second, he would kill to protect her. No one would hurt Chloe, not on his watch. *And I will never hurt her again.*

Because the third thing that had burned through him? It was the realization that Joel couldn't handle Chloe's tears. They'd wrecked him.

He carried her back into his bedroom, kissing her while he walked. He loved her taste. Loved the way she responded to him. The heat of her body. The eagerness of her touch.

He lowered her onto the bed. His dick was hard and eager as it thrust against the front of his pants. He wanted inside of her. Right the hell then. No preliminaries. No waiting. He just wanted to sink into her as deep as he could. Wanted to mark her.

Possess her. Completely. Always.

But he wasn't that uncivilized. At least, not yet.

He grabbed the edges of her shorts. Yanked them down—the shorts and the small pair of panties that she'd worn. Her bare sex met his hot stare. "Have I told you..." He hardly recognized his own voice. "How good you taste?"

"Joel..."

He spread her legs. Put his mouth on her. He wanted her to come against his mouth. He wanted her to go wild so that he could let his last bit of control go. His tongue lapped at her. Licked. Stroked. His fingers slid into her core.

Her fingers shoved into his hair even as her hips rocked up against him. "Joel!"

Her taste was making him drunk. Her thighs were trembling around him. Her body quaking.

And she was coming... against his mouth, his tongue, just like he'd wanted.

Yes.

He eased back, grabbed a condom, and returned to her as fast as possible. She was slick and eager, and when he put his cock at the entrance to her body, Chloe immediately arched toward him. She took him in, all the way, and he was lost.

No holding back. No being gentle.

Only frantic thrusts. He gripped her hips. Held her too tightly. Thrust and withdrew. Sank into heaven again and again. She was moaning. He growled her name. She was so hot around him. Squeezing so perfectly that he thought he'd lose his mind. He was probably bruising her. He shouldn't bruise her. He...

She bit his shoulder.

God, that was sexy.

He bit her. A sensual bite on the curve of her shoulder, and she came. He felt the contractions of her sex around him, and he followed her into oblivion. Joel sank into her one more time and exploded as the pleasure consumed him.

***

Cinnamon's bags were packed and waiting in the trunk of her old car. She'd come back to the club just so that she could get her stash of cash. Sure, she'd been promised payment for the job that she'd done, but unease had settled heavily within her.

I can't trust him.

She'd done what he'd ordered. Followed his directions exactly. She should have been able to trust him. He was supposed to be one of the good guys, after all. She'd even thought of him as her hero once.

But now I'm not so sure.

So she'd come back to the club. Snuck in the back door and gone for her room. One of the old planks in her floor was loose. She'd discovered that plank during her first week of work. So she'd lifted it up and made herself a little hiding spot. Whenever customers had given her a big tip, she'd put some of the money in that little hole. The club's owner believed in taking half of her tips. *Half.* She'd decided to cut him out of the mix. Just a little.

She scooped up the cash. Shoved it in her purse. Then slammed that chunk of wood back into place. It was time to go.

Cinnamon was dying tonight.

The persona was gonna vanish. She'd be Coreen or maybe even someone brand new. She crept down the hallway and went straight for the back door. Cops had been there earlier, getting blood samples and other creepy shit. All because of Chloe Hastings and her partner.

They were trouble.

I don't want any trouble.

She opened the door. The hot air hit her. *Freedom.* No one would ever know she'd come back to the club. She'd take her stash and get out of town.

He wouldn't have to know. He could just keep the money he'd promised her. She didn't need it. Didn't need him.

She rushed forward.

"Hello, Coreen."

Her breath caught. He was there. Near the dumpster. Waiting. Her heart fluttered in her chest even as she had the sudden flash of a frightened bird. Wings flapping too fast. That was her heart. Flapping.

"I have something for you," he said in his warm, kind voice.

The flapping eased. He had her payment. He was keeping up his end of the deal. She hurried toward him. Her high heels wobbled. "I will never tell anyone."

"I know. I'm going to make sure of it."

Too late...she realized he wasn't holding her money. That wasn't the *something* he had. She tried to turn her head away.

Even as she felt the blow hit above her ear.

CHAPTER TWENTY-SEVEN

"My brother didn't go missing when he was fourteen. He was sent away."

Chloe had her hand on Joel's chest. His heartbeat raced beneath her fingers. Her breathing was still unsteady because she was just recovering from the pleasure he'd given her—the pleasure they'd given each other.

The bedroom was in darkness, but moonlight spilled through the glass over the top of the bed. That wonderful glass section of the ceiling that she had gotten installed just for Joel. She'd have to tell him that story soon. Have to tell him so many things.

But she'd start with her past. Because she needed Joel to see that she did trust him.

"Who sent him away?" Joel asked.

Her fingers slid over his chest. She could feel the patchwork of scars on his skin, and when she thought of the pain he'd endured, tears burned her eyes. She always used the victims to help her hunt the killers. But Joel wasn't a typical victim. He was hers. "My parents did. They knew what he was becoming, and they wanted to stop him."

"I don't understand."

"No." She knew he didn't. Not yet. "Because when you did your research, this part wasn't in the stories you found. This part wasn't anywhere. They made sure of it." Maybe they'd still be alive if they hadn't tried to cover everything up.

Maybe not.

"What was he becoming?"

"Have you ever heard of the Macdonald triad?"

"No."

"It basically says there are three indicators that a person may grow up to engage in violent behavior. Or to become a serial killer." She carefully traced another scar. "My brother killed my cat in front of me. Took a knife and—" She stopped. "That's sign number one. Being abusive to animals, especially pets."

Joel's body had gone tense. "Sonofabitch."

Yes, he would see where she was going with this story. "Arson is the second part of the triad. My brother set fire to the barn. Animals were inside—I supposed that would be circling back to sign number one—but...my mother was also inside."

"Oh, my God." He caught her hand as she traced his scars. Held tight.

"She got out. Two of the horses didn't. You know, sometimes, I can still hear their screams." That last part had slipped out. Something she hadn't told anyone before. Their cries haunted her. She'd tried to go in and save them, but she'd been so little. Her father had held her back. His hold had been unbreakable. Tears had slid down her cheeks.

I didn't cry much after that.

"I'm so sorry, baby."

"The third indicator is bed wetting. I know, seems mild compared to the others, doesn't it? Sort of an odd add-along. Honestly, if you've got the other two, they seem far more worrisome to me." She swallowed. The sheet covered most of her body, but it didn't give her any warmth. The warmth came from Joel as she pressed against him. As he held her hand. "My brother met all of the requirements in the triad. When he was fourteen, he took things a step further. He snuck into his best friend's house and put a knife to the boy's throat."

"Fuck."

"His best friend fought him off. My parents managed to stop the family from pressing charges. They were good at keeping things quiet. Hidden. Always so good. They promised to take care of my brother. Swore he wouldn't hurt anyone else. A few days later, the tabloids started reporting that my brother had disappeared."

"Are you telling me they *faked* a whole missing person's case with your brother? Chloe, that's not normal."

"My family was far from normal." She was pretty sure he understood that by now. "They sent him to a psychiatric facility. They thought he might get help. Or, at least, that's what I heard them say to my grandfather one day. I think...I suspect they just wanted my brother locked up so that he couldn't hurt anyone else."

"And what about you, Chloe?"

Her head shifted on the pillow so that she was staring at him. "What do you mean?"

"What did they do to you?"

She licked her lips. "I didn't show the signs of the triad."

"Baby, I never thought you did." He pressed a kiss to her forehead. "What did they do to you? Why were they afraid of you?"

The breath she took seemed to chill her insides. "Who told you they were afraid?"

"Reese."

She nodded against the pillow. "I didn't show the signs of the triad but as I got older—as I noticed more things...as I understood more—I realized that one of them did."

He pulled her closer. Not just holding her hand now. Holding her tightly.

"It's not just the triad signs that should worry you. There are other signs. I was always so curious. Always reading and studying everything, and I learned that there were other signs that you needed to look out for that could predict violent behavior in adults. I was reading so much because—" But Chloe stopped.

"You don't need to hold back. I want to hear everything."

"I was researching so much because I thought I might be able to help my brother. By then, I was this thirteen-year-old kid, and I thought I'd find some miracle to help him. To change him. To stop him from becoming what I heard them whisper about."

"You didn't find a miracle." Sad. Soft.

No. She hadn't. "So many signs can warn of trouble. Showing no remorse. No empathy. Repeated lying. They're all signs. God, I'm guilty of the lies, aren't I? But it's because I learned from the best."

"Chloe?"

"Manipulation. Another sign. Always using others to get what you want. Having no regard for rules. Narcissism. Being so fast to anger. To fly into a rage. But also appearing charming. So charming. You can charm anyone, but if things don't go your way, then the truth will show. The monster will show." Her lips pressed together. "I saw her monster."

"Her?" Joel's question was hesitant, and she realized...he'd figured it out.

"My mother. She was the one who wanted my brother locked away because she knew what he'd become. It was something she already was. I was putting the pieces together. I was realizing the truth about her. And I even discovered that two of her friends had died within the last year. Violent, mysterious deaths. My mother was visiting both of them when they died. How could the cops not see that pattern? How could they not care? Could her money really just keep hiding everything? I knew I had to stop her. I knew I had to do something. I *knew*." Pain roughened her voice. "I asked her if she was guilty, and she told me that those women hadn't been good friends to her. That was her answer. No guilt. No sadness. And then she went and threw another party." She'd thought it would be easier to tell him everything while she was in his arms. But...

It somehow felt wrong. Like she was bringing the dirty, darkest parts of her life into a place that should have been special. Safe.

That was how she felt when she was in Joel's arms.

Safe. Special.

She pulled away from him. Tugged one of the sheets with her and wrapped it around her body as she stood by the side of the bed.

Slowly, he sat up. "Why did you leave me?"

"Because when you hold me, I wish that everything had been different."

"You didn't kill them, baby. Morgan told me— I already know that your brother did."

Shock rolled through her. "I never told Morgan about my parents. Or about who killed them." If he knew the identity of their killer…

"What?"

"If he knew, then he figured it out on his own." Just as she'd figured out his past. He knew about the lies that surrounded her. And she knew his. *Mutual destruction.* Hadn't he promised her that once? "I've never trusted anyone enough with the full story."

"But you're telling me." He climbed from the bed. Yanked on his pants. Didn't button them all the way as he closed in on her. "Is it because you think you have to do it? Because you don't." His hands closed around her shoulders. "It's hurting you to go back there. I can see it. I don't want your pain." His voice was gruff. Ragged. "That is the last thing I want. I should never have made you tell me. I should never have pushed. Baby, you can stop. You don't have to—"

"My brother *did* kill them. He escaped from the psychiatric facility. He came back to the house. He snuck inside. And first, he went for my mother. I know because of the security footage I saw later."

"There was security footage? Shit."

"My grandfather made sure it vanished."

"Of course, he fucking did." His hold tightened.

"He went for my mother, but my father woke up. So my brother stabbed him. Over and over. My mother tried to run. She never stopped to help my father. She just ran. She screamed at my brother and told him that I was in the house. I suspect she wanted him to go after me. She probably thought it might give her time to escape." Chloe bit her lower lip. She'd found those videos in her grandfather's study months later. Until then, she hadn't known that her mother had tried to make her a victim, too, and that her brother hadn't gone after Chloe.

"But he stayed focused on her," Chloe continued woodenly. "He stabbed her in the back. She fell." She'd seen every moment in the footage. "Then he flipped her over and stabbed her four more times. And then I found him, standing over her body."

"*Baby.* Tell me you ran. Tell me you got the hell out of there!"

She looked into his eyes. "He could have killed me. He didn't. He took the knife from our mother's body. Told me he was sorry, and he shoved it into his chest."

"*Fuck.*"

Her family's story wasn't some warm, fuzzy memory. It was a nightmare that never stopped. That replayed in her head late at night.

"He wasn't dead. I ran to him." Not from him. "He was still alive. I grabbed the handle of the knife because I was going to pull it out. I was going to save him. I didn't even register what he'd done. He was just...he was my brother. But he said..." She was choking. Suddenly so far in the past that she could barely breathe. "*P-please*...He said please. My hands were around the handle of the knife, and he was saying please and he was staring up at me and asking me to kill him. His fingers curled around mine, squeezed, and the knife..." A tear leaked from her eye. "I shoved it deeper into him. I killed my brother."

CHAPTER TWENTY-EIGHT

Joel yanked her against him. He pulled her into his arms and held her as tightly as he could. So tight. *I never want to let go.* She shuddered against him. Seemed to go boneless as she hung in his arms. And he didn't speak. What the hell was he supposed to say? He wanted to make things better for her, but there was no way to change the past.

I wish I could. I wish I could have been there. To help thirteen-year-old Chloe.

Was it any wonder she shut people out? That she studied everyone so carefully? That she was so obsessed with discovering the secrets that everyone possessed? He understood so much about her now. Could see so much.

She'd trusted him with her darkest moments. Trusted him because Chloe loved him?

I will never betray her trust. I will never betray her.

He kept holding her. Pressed kisses to her hair. Sheltered her in his embrace. Until she drew a shuddering breath. Then her head lifted. "The cook was the first person to arrive the next day. When she...found everything..." Chloe's voice sounded detached. Weak. "She called my grandfather. Not the authorities. Him. And he called his very good friend, the chief inspector."

"They covered it up."

A nod. "It was better for my grandfather. Better if a random stranger committed such terrible acts instead of the world thinking his grandson had been a twisted monster. The chief inspector knew it was wrong, but he—I watched as he got rid of my brother's body. Dragged him out. Made him disappear. There was never even a funeral for him and I..." Her eyes squeezed shut. "I've had a lifetime of lies. I try not to lie outright. I swear, I do. So I just—I leave things out because I don't want to be like them, but it's so hard."

"Look at me."

Slowly, her eyes opened.

"You are nothing like them."

She started to shake her head.

"*Nothing.*" He bent his head and brushed his lips across her mouth. "You are the strongest, most determined woman I have ever met. You want to stop monsters. You don't want to make them. You are good. You're nothing like them."

"When my grandfather died, guess who was supposed to become my guardian?"

He tried to remember the articles he'd read. *Truth and lies, blended together.* "It was a family friend." But Joel couldn't remember the name. Didn't think it had been reported.

"The chief inspector. The man who'd buried my brother in an unmarked grave somewhere. I wasn't going to live with him. So I found another solution."

Holy shit. "You found Reese, didn't you?" Only Reese wasn't the man's real name. Joel wondered what was. *Who* the guy truly was.

"I found him. He found me. We fit each other."

She'd found Reese. The same way she'd found Marie? *The same way she'd found me?*

"His life wasn't easy. He grew up hard and rough. He tried to find a new life. He heard about my brother's disappearance. Did some research and realized that he bore a physical resemblance to the man the world had known as Charleston Reese Hastings."

"He's a good actor," Joel said, thinking of the accent that *could* be perfect. "That's what he did. He pretended to be your long-lost brother."

"I knew he couldn't be my brother, of course."

Sure, she'd known. She'd watched her brother die. *I'm so sorry, baby.*

"And the chief inspector knew. But it was certainly not like he could say anything to reveal what had really happened."

"You could have stopped the charade, though. You could have—"

"I told you, I found him. He found me. He wasn't just trying to get money. He wanted a life. A family. I gave him that. He did the same for me."

There was more, he knew it. So much more to the story. But Chloe's shoulders were sagging. Shadows lined her eyes, and he realized she had to be exhausted. Talking about her past had sent her back to the darkest time in her life. She'd faced her nightmares...

For me.

He tucked a lock of hair behind her ear. "I love you, Chloe Hastings."

She gave him a tired smile. "Not yet, but I think you will."

What?

"I'm going to shower. After I'm done, we have to talk about your lying witness." She slipped from his arms.

He opened his mouth. Started to tell her that he absolutely *did* love her, but she'd just distracted him. Deliberately because that was her way. "You know who the witness is?"

"Of course," Chloe replied as she dropped the sheet and gave him a view of her perfect ass. "Richardson slipped up when he used the 'she' pronoun with us. Obviously, it's Cinnamon. She's the only woman who would benefit from lying about you. At least, the only one I've been able to figure out."

"Why would she lie?" He was still staring at her ass. Absolutely beautiful in the glow of the moonlight.

"Because she knows who the real killer is. She's known all along. She's protecting him by throwing you at the police. But don't worry, we aren't going to let her get away with that trick." She was at the threshold to the bathroom. "My brother is out looking for her now. It was a truly divide and conquer night. I stayed here, hoping Morgan wouldn't show, but being on guard, just in case. Marie went for you, and I trusted Reese to find our witness." Chloe looked back at him. "We're all a team, don't you see?"

Yes, he did. He was finally seeing everything clearly.

Chloe shut the bathroom door.

He knew why she'd just done that. *I see it all.*

She'd shut the door because Chloe was crying again. He'd pushed her, she'd revealed all the broken parts of her past, and now she was hiding her pain from him.

She didn't need to hide a damn thing.

He stalked for the door. Didn't knock. Just grabbed the knob and threw the door open.

She was already in the shower. The water was pouring on her and there were tears on her cheeks.

"I know you hate to be wrong," Joel told her as he kicked out of his pants. "But this time, you are."

Her eyes widened.

He climbed into the shower with her. Let the water pound into her. "I said I was in love with you.

A cautious nod.

"You said I *will* be. As in, one day, I might love you. Baby, you are so wrong." He kissed her. Thrust his tongue into her mouth and savored her.

Her body shuddered against his.

"I *am* in love with you and I swear, part of me thinks I fell in love with you when we were in that freaking bank closet. *I. Love. You.*"

CHAPTER TWENTY-NINE

I love you. Those were beautiful words. Deep and rough. Seeming to come straight out of Joel's very soul. Chloe wanted them to be true. So badly but...

It was so soon. They were so soon.

"Ah, sweetheart, you think it's okay for you to love me already, but I can't love you yet?" He feathered kisses over her cheek. "Try again."

Her eyes closed. He was kissing her tears away. No one had ever done that. When she'd been a child, her mother had hated it when she cried. She'd said tears were useless. That they should never be shed.

She didn't have empathy. She never cried. She never felt anyone else's pain.

Had her brother been born like their mother? Or had she made him into a monster?

And what did she make me?

Joel pressed another tender kiss on her cheek.

"Say it again," Chloe demanded. But the demand came out more like a plea.

"I love you."

She could hear it a thousand times. Morgan had said he loved her, too, but that had been different. His words had never made her feel this way. When Joel said it—

"I love you, Chloe."

She felt good. Warm. Safe. He could always seem to make her feel safe.

She looped her arms around his neck. Pressed her wet body tightly to his and kissed him with a frantic abandon. His cock pushed against her belly. There was no mistaking his arousal. He wanted her. She was aching for him. When they came together, when their bodies were connected, she stopped being so alone.

Joel did that. *He* made her feel like she wasn't detached from the rest of the world.

She pulled her mouth from his. Her breath heaved as she told him, "I'm on birth control. I do not have any sexually transmitted diseases."

"I...neither do I."

"Then make love to me. Right now." She sounded desperate. She was. "Skin to skin. I want only you. Nothing between us."

"You don't have to ask twice." He curled his hands around her waist. Lifted her up. Pushed her back against the cold, tiled shower wall.

His cock brushed at the entrance to her body. But he didn't enter her yet. He probably thought she wasn't ready. That she needed more foreplay. More time.

She only needed him. Chloe arched her hips against that thick length and took him all inside.

"*Fuck me,*" Joel groaned.

"That's exactly what I'm doing." Her nails dug into his shoulders.

Joel held her stare. She saw the gold blaze in his eyes even as she watched his control shatter.

The water pounded down on them. He pounded into her. Flesh to flesh. She could feel every single inch of him. She'd never gone without protection with a lover. Never told someone so much about her life. Never been so open. Never trusted anyone so completely.

"Joel!" Her body felt stretched tight. Too sensitive. Hyper aware. Every glide and retreat of his cock had her longing for more. So much more. She'd just come a little while ago, but she was desperate for him again.

The pleasure they gave each other was overwhelming. Shattering. Addictive.

She'd never found such a powerful release with anyone else. She knew she never would.

His hand eased between their bodies. He stroked in just the right spot, touching her in just the right way, as if they'd made love dozens of times, and the climax hit her. Stole her breath even as it blazed through her entire body.

He came right after her. She could feel the jerks of his release. The hot warmth. She clung to him even tighter.

Joel.

He'd been so much more than she'd expected. He'd changed her whole life. Did he realize that?

His breath was panting. Her heart was pounding. Racing so fast. Or maybe that was his. They were entwined so closely together that it was hard to tell.

She pressed a kiss to his shoulder. The water was still pouring on them.

Her mother had once told her that a good shower could wash away all the sins of the world.

Her mother had been such a liar.

**

"Look, man," Reese straightened to his full height, but the bouncer hardly seemed intimidated. "What was your name, Benjamin? Bob—"

"Bobby," he snapped.

"That's what I was saying." He sniffed. And waved a twenty at the fellow. "I saw Cinnamon's car outside. I just want to go back and have a little dance with her."

"Cinnamon's not working tonight."

"But her car is out—"

Bobby swiped the twenty. "Not working, dumbass. She must have left the car here last night and took a ride home with one of the other dancers." A grimace or smile or something slid across his wide face. "But if you want to give me more money to hear me tell you the same thing over and over again, knock yourself out."

Reese wanted his twenty back. "I don't like you."

Bobby shrugged.

Huffing out a breath, Reese stormed out of the strip club. The woman had most certainly *not* left her car there overnight. Before chatting it up with Bobby the bouncer, Reese had put his hand on the vehicle's hood and it had still been warm.

He poked around a bit outside, then saw the alley. A trickle of unease slid over him because

Chloe had told him that Donnie Adams had died in that alley.

He crept toward the entrance. *Chloe is counting on me.* "Listen!" Reese called out. "If there are any vengeful spirits or other dark shit waiting in here, I didn't do anything to you! I'm just looking for a dancer!"

Something...moaned.

Reese swallowed. Chloe was the brave one. He was more the not brave one. But he inched forward. A small inch.

Another moan.

The sound seemed to come from the darkness near the back of the club.

Yeah, this looks like the perfect spot for an attack. Anyone could be waiting in that darkness. And he was not the hero type. That wasn't his gig. He was as far from a hero as it was possible to be.

"*H-help...*"

A woman's voice.

Reese's feet were moving toward the darkness before he could stop himself. He pulled out his phone. Used the flashlight to shine in that dark corner and he saw what looked like a broken—

Oh, God. That's a woman.

A woman trying to reach a hand out to him. Blood covered the side of her face and head. Soaked her hair.

"*Help...*" she gasped out again.

He wasn't a hero, but he was the only person she had. He dialed nine-one-one even as he sank to his knees beside her. So much blood. What in the hell was he supposed to do?

***

A phone was ringing. *Her* phone was ringing. As Chloe towel-dried her hair, she followed the sound of the rings back into Joel's den. Her phone was on the couch. She didn't even remember leaving it there. She scooped it up and her fingers slid over Reese's image as she took his call. "Did you find her?"

"*There's so much blood, Chloe!*"

Her heart stopped. "Reese, did someone hurt you?" Her hold nearly shattered the phone.

"Not me, her! I found her, Chloe! I'm in the alley, behind the strip club. There's blood all in her hair. On her face. She was asking for help, but she's not speaking at all now. I don't know what to do. Chloe, you always tell me...what do I do? Tell me what do to!"

"Did you call nine-one-one?"

"Yes, yes, they're coming."

"Good, Reese. That's great. Talk to her. Try to get her to speak with you again."

"Chloe...I don't want this woman dying in my arms."

She whirled around. Joel was walking toward her. A smile was on his face, but when he saw her expression, his smile faltered.

"What is it?" Joel asked. "What happened?"

She turned the phone on speaker. "Cinnamon was hurt," she explained to Joel. "Please, tell Reese how to help her."

"Her head was smashed in!" Reese's accent was gone. His voice shaking. "So much blood!"

"Reese, listen to me," Joel's voice was calm. Even. "I want you to do exactly as I say..."

***

They burst through the doors of the hospital. Joel and Chloe had dressed quickly and hauled ass to meet Reese. Joel had stayed on the line with Reese until the ambulance arrived. He'd done his best to give Reese instructions but...

Reese whirled away from the registration desk. The front of his shirt was covered in blood. "Chloe!" He ran right for her.

He ran right for his sister.

Joel watched as Reese threw his arms around Chloe and held on tight. The man's body shuddered.

"It's okay," Chloe told him. "You did great, Reese. You did great."

There was a lot Joel didn't understand about those two. Definitely not blood related, but he could *see* now that they were family. Chloe thought of the guy as her brother, and his love for her was plain to see.

Just hugging Chloe seemed to make the other man stronger.

Reese nodded a few times, then slowly let her go. His spine was straight as he glanced over at Joel. "Thank you."

"You don't need to thank me for anything."

Reese's Adam's apple bobbed. He kept standing close to Chloe.

"Reese, I need you to tell me everything that you saw in that alley." Her words were low. "Every single detail, okay?"

"Okay." He blew out a breath. "Chloe, do you think...did I save her? Did I save someone?" His voice was high, hopeful, almost like a little boy who was scared to ask a question because he wanted the answer to be positive so very badly.

"You did." She nodded. "See, I always told you that you were going to do great things, Reese."

"I was scared out of my fucking mind," he admitted. The cracking, hopeful voice had faded.

"But you still helped her. That's what matters."

The emergency room was bustling with patients. Kids, adults. Every single chair was full. The staff at the check-in table had a ragged air about them as they handed out charts.

They needed information, and he was going to get it. "I'm heading to the exam area. I'll see what I can find out about Cinnamon."

"Wait!" Reese grabbed his arm. "You can't just walk back there, can you?" He blinked. Let go of Joel.

"I'm a doctor. I won't be lying if I tell anyone that. Maybe I'll get lucky and the admin fellow who wanted to give me a job the other day will be in the back—I'll get him to help me out."

Chloe's head cocked. "You didn't tell me that you were offered a job here."

"That's because I'm not taking it." He stared into her eyes. "I'm not leaving you." He waited for that message to sink in. *I won't ever leave you.* Then he turned and headed for the swaying doors that would take him back to the patients. He'd learned long ago that—in a hospital—if you just walked with determination and acted like you knew where you were going, no one tended to get in your way.

"Uh, he *is* leaving you," Reese's overly loud voice followed him. "He gets that, doesn't he? He's literally walking away right now."

"He'll be back." Chloe sounded confident. *"Now tell me what you saw."*

Joel kept walking until he reached the double doors that led back to the ER. He shoved his hand up and headed straight inside.

He'd only taken two steps when—

"Hey!" A sharp voice. "You're not supposed to be back here!" A nurse with graying hair and wide eyes bustled toward him. "Turn around and get right back outside!"

Well, so much for walking with determination. Joel opened his mouth—

"Nancy, he's a doctor. Don't you recognize him?" A man in scrubs and with a face mask dangling around his neck stepped from an exam area. "That's the hero." He motioned toward Joel. "He was the doc in here who fought so hard to save that stabbing victim. Remember? He rode with her in the ambulance. Kept his hand in her chest."

"Oh." Nancy's expression softened. "I heard about you." She advanced and patted Joel's arm. "Sometimes, they just don't make it. No matter what we do."

But I thought she was going to make it.

Nancy's brows lowered. "Did you join the staff?"

"I—"

"He's with me," the man in scrubs responded.

"Oh, okay, Dr. Ambrose." She gave them a nod and made her way to a waiting patient.

Dr. Ambrose. Dr. Dane Ambrose. The doctor who'd been so chummy with Chloe before. Joel had recognized him instantly. "Glad you were here," Joel said.

"Consider it your lucky night," Dane returned. He moved closer to Joel and lowered his voice as he said, "Guessing Chloe sent you back here, huh? Is this about that woman who was just brought in with the head injury?"

"Yes. It's about her. How'd you know?" His voice was just as low as Dane's had been.

"Because I saw Reese with her. I know Chloe's brother." He stepped to the side and motioned for Joel to follow him. "She's not conscious. Her skull was fractured."

"Any chance I could see the X-rays?"

"What? Why?"

"I'd like to figure out what kind of weapon was used on her."

"It looked as if someone took a bat to her head," Dane whispered back. "Poor woman." He peered down the hallway. "I will get in serious trouble if anyone sees us...but, I owe Chloe."

"Everybody seems to."

"She showed me how to go after what I want. Until I started watching her, seeing what she could do, I was afraid to take some chances, you know what I mean? But sometimes, you just have to do it. Have to go for what you want."

"This seems like a great time to take a chance." *Make the move, doc.* "Let me see the X-rays. Then take me to the patient."

Dane's gaze was unblinking. He seemed to be trying to decide...

Do it.

Abruptly, Dane nodded. "Come with me."

***

"She had money in her bag, Chloe. It wasn't a robbery. Someone just hit her in the side of the head. *Hard.* Then left her sprawled on the ground. If I hadn't heard her moaning and calling for help, I don't know what would have happened to her."

"There were no stab wounds on her?"

"No, none."

"Any defensive marks that you saw?"

"No. It just looked like she'd been standing close to the dumpster one moment, and someone hit her in the head in the next minute. Hit her right here." His hand raised and he touched Chloe about an inch over her right ear.

Chloe stared at him. Narrowed her eyes.

"You're not seeing me right now, are you?" Reese asked her. "You're like in the alley or something."

"No signs of struggle. That means she got close to him. She knew him. She chose to get close to him. Then he lifted the weapon. She saw it too late. Tried to turn away, and it hit her in the side of the head."

"There was so much blood." He shuddered. "It's all over me."

"Head wounds bleed a lot. But she was moaning. You said she called out for help." Chloe ignored the voices and people around them. "He knew she was still alive. She was weak. She wouldn't have been able to fight back. Why didn't he finish her?"

Another shudder. "That sounds cold. Scary cold. Can you word that differently or something?"

Why didn't he finish her? That one question was burning through her mind. *I thought he might be in the medical field. A doctor. A nurse. Cinnamon was attacked, but left alive. And what happens to vics who are hurt? Where do they go?*

To the same place Judith had gone.

"Chloe!" The sharp call jolted her to awareness. That had been Cedric's voice.

"Oh, great." Reese peered over her shoulder. "It's the cops. The one we like, and the one you don't."

She didn't have to glance over her shoulder to know who he meant. And, sure enough, the bark of her name came again. Only this time, it wasn't coming from Cedric.

"Chloe!" Agent Richardson snapped. He grabbed her arm. "What are you doing here? How the hell did you know about the victim?"

She glanced down at his fingers. Then back up at his face. "My brother Reese is the one who found her in the alley."

Richardson's face twisted. "Found her or tried to shut her up? You knew she was the witness who'd turned on Joel. You knew—"

"I know that you need to get your hand off me, Richardson." Chloe's order was flat.

For a moment, his hold tightened.

"Mister..." Reese began angrily.

Richardson let her go. He pointed at Reese and his bloody shirt. "You're coming with me. Right now. We're having a private talk and you are going to tell me everything you saw in the alley."

"Funny." Reese's smile was cold. "I just told my sister *everything*. Seems right that you get to come in second again, doesn't it? Because I know all about you, Agent Richardson."

"Reese," Chloe warned. "Be careful with him. He's looking for a reason to arrest Joel and probably you, too, now."

More agents were filing in. Two men in dark suits. When Richardson motioned with his hand, they immediately took up positions next to Reese.

"Let's take this outside," Richardson directed.

"Sure." Reese was all cool. *On the outside*. She knew it was a front. The man was a very good actor, after all. "I could use with a bit of a fresh air." His British accent was in full effect.

He sauntered away. Richardson and the FBI agents dodged his steps.

Cedric stayed with her. She raised her brows at him. "Did he give you orders to watch me?"

"Absolutely."

She shook her head.

"But I'm here because I wanted to update you on Ruben's findings. By the way, he was upset about this week's beignet date being canceled. Told me to say you'd owe him a double order next time."

"I'll get him as many beignets as he can eat." She moved with Cedric to stand behind a tall, potted plant. "What did he discover?"

"He was examining the remains we found, and, yes, dental records did ID the vic as Portia Strong. But that's not a big surprise, is it?"

"No." Not even a small surprise. *I'm sorry you stayed in the ground so long. I wish you'd been found long ago.*

"What was interesting—at least to Ruben—is the fact that Portia had suffered severe damage to her spinal column. He said to tell you...C1 to C4."

"Oh, no." Her gaze darted to the busy ER. All of the people in uniforms. Scrubs.

He cleared his throat. "I was hoping for a better reaction. You know, like that was some big puzzle piece that we needed to put things together."

"It is a big piece." She kept staring at the crowd. "Why are we here?" Her gaze darted to the doors that led back to the exam and operating area of the ER.

"Uh...because Coreen Miller was attacked? Because she was brought to the ER for treatment."

"She wasn't killed." Chloe began walking toward those doors.

"Judith Key was left alive, too. Well, mostly alive." He kept step with her. "She only died here and—"

Chloe stopped. "She died here."

"Uh, yes, you know that. We both know that. Everyone knows that."

Her head swiveled toward him. "You need to get a cop in Coreen's room. Now."

"Chloe?" His face hardened. "This is the reaction I wanted, but I need you to tell me what's happening."

"Keep someone with her at all times. And we have to find Joel."

"Wait...Joel, as in...Richardson's chief suspect?"

A hurried nod.

"As in...the man I *know* you lied to protect?"

About that... "Cedric, I can explain."

"Yeah, you'd better. Because as soon as I heard what went down in that interrogation room, I knew you were lying. Chloe, I was with you at the bank. You weren't partnering with him already. The guy was as thrown off balance as could be by you. I even warned him to stay away. Not that the fool listened." The faint lines near his mouth deepened. "You lied to protect him, and now you tell me that he's somewhere here, running around in the same hospital where the injured witness is who can ID him?"

"Yes, but Joel didn't attack her. I swear it! He really was having sex with me at the time. I mean, tonight."

Cedric's mouth opened. Closed. "Then maybe your brother attacked her." Grim. Hard. "That's sure what Richardson was thinking. It's why he had Reese go outside for questioning. Maybe you had your brother go take out the witness because you wanted to protect your lover."

"You've got good instincts, Cedric. You're the best cop I've ever met. You want to help people, and it always shows." Her heart raced too fast. She had to find Joel. "What do you think is going on here? Do you think I'm protecting a killer or that I'm trying to stop one?"

***

"The lab's down this way," Dane said as he threw open a door. "Shortcut. You know how hospitals snake all around the place. This corridor will take us to the ground floor lab. Her X-rays are in there. You can scan them, but like I said, I swear, I think the woman was hit with a freaking baseball bat. I've seen injuries like that one before. Had a poor kid in a few weeks ago. He wasn't wearing his batting helmet, and he knocked himself good." A grimace as he held open the door for Joel. "Or, bad, you know?"

Joel slipped by him. "A baseball bat as the weapon would sure fit with what Chloe and I—"

Something slammed into the back of his head.

Joel fell down. His face hit the floor.

CHAPTER THIRTY

"Don't panic. There's no need to struggle."

Joel's eyes had just flown open. He found himself sprawled on an exam table. *Strapped down.* Something was shoved into his mouth. Something—tape?—had been placed over his lips.

Dane's head popped into his line of vision. "There's no need to struggle," he said again. "Because you're not going to get out of the restraints."

Joel's head throbbed. Waves of nausea rolled through him. He blinked a few times as he tried to figure out what in the hell—

"This is probably invoking quite a bit of déjà vu in you, isn't it? When I saw you and Chloe, of course, I immediately recognized you. Then I had the idea for what to do *with* you."

He tried to talk. A rag rolled around on his tongue. Joel nearly choked.

"I had read about what happened to you. Hard to forget that story. You were taken in your own hospital. Hidden there while you were tortured, and no one ever found you." Sadness tinged his voice. Only to vanish as Dane laughed. "Brilliant! I realized if I could get you in the hospital again, I could make you disappear! There are so many unused rooms and forgotten corridors in hospitals. Wings that are being remodeled or closed down. I mean, they didn't find you before. Why find you this time?"

Joel jerked at the restraints. They were so tight they cut into his chest and legs. His stomach. His—

"This is nothing personal, I assure you of that. It's necessary, though. Someone has to take the fall for the murders, and it's not going to be me. I don't want to be locked up. I'm doing the world a service." A nod. "I'm taking out the trash."

Joel's eyes narrowed on the bastard.

"No? Don't believe me? I find that hard to buy. I mean, I suspect a part of you can even agree with me. A part down deep inside." His hand pushed over Joel's chest. "We both know that the monsters in the world need to be taken out. They shouldn't be here. If they hurt others, they have to be stopped."

You hurt others, you bastard! Joel was staring at a monster.

"Stop looking at me like that. I'm not going to torture you. That's not what I do. Besides, you're not one of my targets. You're just necessary. I need someone else to look guilty. I thought that FBI agent would lock you up when he found the bat at your old place." A sigh. "But somehow, Chloe got you out of that predicament. The woman can work miracles, can't she?" Admiration glowed in his eyes.

Stay the fuck away from Chloe! He bit on the rag as he tried to yell that order.

Dane leaned over him. "I have a few friends at the PD. Okay, maybe not actual friends, but guys who owe me. See, I know what they did at the Serpent. I was there for a while. Saw all kinds of things going on. Legal. Not legal. Whatever. Those...acquaintances...kept me updated on the case. That's how I knew to plant the evidence implicating you. I even got Cinnamon to point the finger at you."

Joel heaved against the restraints. Immediately, pain blasted through his brain.

"You've got a concussion. Probably a fractured skull. Had to knock you out for a moment." His hand was still on Joel's chest. "I hit Cinnamon a whole lot harder, but that was also necessary. I knew that if she was injured, she'd be brought here. This hospital is the closest one to the club where she works. And if she came here, I figured you and Chloe wouldn't be far behind." He finally lifted his hand. "It was all about getting you here, then separating you from Chloe. Pretty good plan, don't you think?"

If you touch Chloe...Joel snarled behind the tape. Chomped on the rag in his mouth.

"Settle down." Dane didn't appear impressed. "You're not going to do anything to me. And, hey, if it makes you feel better, I have no intention of hurting Cinnamon again. When she wakes up, she'll go along with my story that *you* did it. You don't have an alibi for her attack, you see. You'll be the one the cops think hit Cinnamon. You'll be—why the hell are you shaking your head?"

Joel kept right on shaking his head.

"You don't have an alibi," Dane told him. "I was watching Chloe's place. I saw you leave *alone*. You were having a fight. Arrived just in time for the tail end of it. Saw you speed away. That's why I went after Cinnamon then. I used the perfect time to attack—"

Joel kept shaking his head.

Dane ripped off the tape. Tore out the rag. "*What?*"

Shit. The bastard had taken some skin with the tape. "Have...alibi..." Joel gasped out. "Went...back to Chloe."

"No."

"Y-yes..."

"I saw you leave. You were mad as hell. I even followed you to that bar. You went in and I knew you'd get drunk off your ass—"

Joel smiled.

Dane's face twisted. "You went back to her?"

"I'll...always...g-go back to...Chloe."

"Not anymore, you fucking won't." He shoved the tape back over Joel's mouth. The tape, but no rag, and since the tape had already been removed once, it didn't stick down as hard. Dane whirled away. Began to pace.

Joel craned his head so he could see the small room. Peeling paint. Bare light bulb. Exam tray with...

Scalpel.

The shiny scalpel was the only thing that looked new in the old room.

"You're going to disappear." Dane kept pacing. "No one will find you. I know where to put your body. Even Chloe won't find you. The cops think you're guilty. They'll go with that story even if Chloe doesn't. And if I can't convince her to change her mind..." He stopped. "Then I'll kill Chloe."

"No!" Only his scream came out as more of a growl. Muffled behind the tape.

Dane fired a glance at him. "Your fault. You shouldn't have gone back to her." He crept toward the exam tray. Stared at the scalpel. "I'm going to make it quick. I promise. I couldn't kill you in that corridor because I couldn't have too much blood there. Too much blood would take too much time to hide. I cleaned up the spatter from your head wound. No one will notice anything left. Since no one uses that corridor, there's no security camera in the area. See, I thought of everything." His fingers curled around the scalpel. "This is what will happen. In a while, I'll show up, wandering around all lost and hurt. I'll have a head wound. I'll say you attacked me. That you ran off. Cops will search for you. They won't find you. Because by then? I'll have killed you. Shoved your body into a body bag. And buried you."

Joel shook his head.

Dane came back to his side. "Would you like for me to cut your throat? Is that the best way? This isn't about pain for me. Really. I have no reason for you to suffer. The others—they had to pay for what they'd done. An eye for an eye, you understand?"

No, he did not—

Laughter. "Sure, you understand. You killed the man who came after you. If anyone gets me, it's you."

Joel twisted his mouth. He pulled back his lips. Worked that stupid tape. Got it loose enough to rasp... "I'm...g-gonna...kill you..."

"I'm afraid that will be quite impossible. You'll be dead soon. I'll make sure of that. I learned from the mistakes of your last attacker. When you go in the ground, I guarantee that you will not be breathing."

***

"She can't be back here!" A woman with salt-and-pepper hair jumped into Chloe's path. "She can't be here—and neither can you!" She glared at Cedric.

He flashed his badge. "We can be anywhere."

Her mouth snapped closed.

Chloe's gaze darted around the exam rooms.

"Who are you looking for?" The woman took a step back.

Chloe's attention immediately swung to her. She scanned the ID badge. A nurse. Nancy Ferra. "Nancy, my partner came back into this area a few moments ago. Tall man, very handsome."

And over the intercom—per Cedric's orders— a page went out for Joel Landry. A page asking him to immediately check in at the ER desk.

Nancy's head tilted as her gaze jumped between Chloe and Cedric.

"The man that's being paged right now, he's the one we're looking for. Joel Landry. He's a doctor, but he wasn't wearing scrubs. He—"

"Oh, wait, do you mean Dane's friend?"

Dane. Her lungs froze. "Yes. Yes, that's exactly who I mean." Once more, she scanned the area. Didn't see Joel or Dane. "Can you tell me where they went?" Cedric already had men looking for Dane, per *her* orders. Because before they'd burst through those ER doors, she'd realized exactly why Cinnamon had been brought to that hospital.

Because Dr. Dane Ambrose works here.

Dr. Dane Ambrose...the same man who had also worked at the Serpent. The same man who could have come into contact with Donnie Adams. *I don't believe in a coincidence.*

She and Cedric hadn't wanted to page Dane, though, because they'd feared that might tip him off. But the search had started. Uniformed cops and hospital security.

"If you're looking for those two, I think they were going to the labs. At least, that's what I thought I heard them say." Nancy turned away. "I've got patients to see. Excuse me—"

"Show us exactly where you saw them go." Cedric's voice boomed with authority.

Nancy stopped. "Um, okay." She motioned down the hallway. "See that door at the end? They were going that way. Don't really know why. I mean, you can get to the labs on this floor by using that corridor, but it takes forever. The corridor leads to a wing that isn't really used anymore, so you have to cut through the old rooms. But maybe they just didn't want to deal with..." Her hands waved to indicate the packed exam area. "All of this."

Chloe was already running for the door Nancy had indicated. Her hip bumped an exam tray. She glanced down. Saw shining instruments.

A scalpel.

Don't mind if I do. She scooped it up and didn't even slow down. Chloe beat Cedric to the corridor door by seconds. She shoved open the door.

An empty hallway waited. One that branched off with way, way too many doors. And even though light spilled from the ceiling in the hallway, all of the doors appeared to lead to dark rooms. Some of the doors were open, and the darkness snaked into the hallway.

"Chloe, are you sure about this Ambrose guy being the perp?" Cedric had pulled out his gun.

"Dane knew Donnie Adams. They would have crossed paths at the Serpent. Donnie gambled there, and Dane patched up the players." Had that been when Dane noticed Donnie's ring? One night, at a game?

The Bad Deeds killings had started so recently. Something must have set off the killer. Something that had stirred up the past.

It could have been seeing Donnie. A blast from the past. Right in front of Dane. Smug, brutal Donnie still wearing that ring...

She filtered through details as quickly as she could. "The killer made sure that Gregory, Ray, and Donnie all suffered the same kind of injuries that Portia did." *And now I think he has Joel.* "But the killer doesn't want to go down for the crimes. He wants to give the cops someone else as a fall guy."

"Joel."

She'd already counted twenty different doors, and the hallway branched up ahead. "We should split up. I think..." She licked her lips. "Cedric, please help me. We have to find Joel. I need him to be okay."

"We *are* going to find him. He will be okay. You hear me, Chloe? *We have this.*" He lifted his weapon. "Let's go. That's a lot of fucking doors." And he kicked in the first one.

Chloe's gaze darted down the corridor.

***

"No one even knows to look for you." The scalpel pressed to Joel's neck. "But you have this look in your eyes, like you think the cavalry is going to break down the door at any moment." His head cocked. "Is that what it was like for you before? Did you keep thinking someone was going to save you? That if you just held out long enough, help would come?"

Dane had slapped the tape down again. Joel couldn't respond, so why did the fucker even ask the question?

Help will come. Chloe would come. He knew it. She wouldn't give up on him. She'd figure this out. When she couldn't find him in the ER, she'd start searching the hospital. She'd know something was wrong.

"Rescue is not going to happen." The scalpel cut into him. Joel felt the wet warmth of his own blood as Dane said, "But at least it will be quick and—"

"It wasn't quick for Portia."

Chloe's voice. Sweet God in heaven, Chloe's voice. Not as cool as it normally sounded. Shaking a little. Frayed at the edges. Breathless.

Joel's head turned and the scalpel nicked him even more. Chloe stood in the doorway.

"What are you doing here?" Dane demanded.

"I came for my partner. I need him, and I don't intend to let you take him away from me."

Run, Chloe! Joel tried to yell that order at her because she was standing there, no weapon on her. He knew that she sometimes kept a gun in her bag, but she hadn't brought her bag into the hospital. Weapons weren't allowed in hospitals.

Just scalpels. The place was freaking full of those.

And...actually...when his gaze dipped down to Chloe's right hand, he saw that her fingers were curled over something. He caught the fast gleam of—

She got herself a scalpel. Hell, yes, she had.

Chloe took a few quick steps forward.

"Stop!" Dane blasted.

"Why? You haven't stopped. You're making him bleed, and I can't have that."

Dane was on one side of Joel. Chloe came to the other. She casually moved her right hand so it placed along one of the straps that covered Joel's arm. He was pretty sure she began to cut into the strap.

I fucking love you.

"You're not supposed to be here," Dane managed. He seemed confused. Shaken.

He was about to be shaken a whole lot more. *As soon as I'm free...*

"You're not supposed to be here!" Dane repeated. Only this time, he was yelling.

"And Portia Strong wasn't supposed to die, was she?" Chloe's face remained expressionless as she stared straight at Dane...

And she kept sawing at the strap.

"No, no, she wasn't supposed to die." He lifted his scalpel away from Joel's throat. Pointed it at Chloe like it was a knife. "Did you figure it out? Did you realize what *they* did to her?"

"Gregory Guidry, Ray Malone, and Donnie Adams. They had to pay." She nodded. And shifted a little to the left, moving down Joel's body.

He felt tension on the strap over his thigh. She was cutting it now.

Dane hadn't even noticed what she was doing. He was too busy nodding. "They had to pay!" he echoed. "It was their fault. Do you know what they did to her? Chloe, *they paralyzed her!* She was running away from them. Those three bastards were taunting her. Chasing her. They did that to her. And they got away with it. For years and years. Everyone forgot about her. Everyone, but me."

"Then Donnie walked into your path. He brought the past back, didn't he?" She'd moved to another strap. Dane's avid focus was on her face. He didn't even notice the careful motion of her hands. She was cutting on the side of the exam table—so careful. So sneaky.

"I was working at the Serpent. Got freaking med school bills to pay, so I had to take those side jobs. Guy like Donnie…how the fuck did he ever get into a game? But one night, he was there. Still wearing that stupid ring. Still acting like *he* was the big man on campus! I'd been watching you. Watching King. You two did what you wanted. You followed your own rules. I figured it was time for me to do the same. Time for me to punish the guilty."

"So you started to hunt. Only you didn't start with Donnie."

"No. Not him. Gregory had to pay first. He was the ringleader."

"Of course. The quarterback in high school. The leader of the pack."

"You take out the leader, and the rest fall."

Joel thought most of the straps had been cut. He waited for his moment to attack.

"I only did to them," Dane's voice roughened, "what they did to her!"

Chloe's breath expelled in a soft sigh. "It was Gregory's letterman jacket buried over her face, wasn't it?"

"Yes, yes, I had to cover her up. I had to cover her up after—"

"After what you'd done." Chloe nodded. "Yes, I understand. You felt guilty. You'd hurt her, and you wanted to take it all back, but it was too late. You showed remorse when you covered Portia up and you buried her—"

"*No!*" Dane yelled. He loomed over the exam table and gripped the scalpel even tighter, as if he'd lunge and stab Chloe with it.

Not happening.

"They killed her!" Spittle flew from Dane's mouth. "Not me! They killed—"

And the bastard did lunge across the exam table. He went for Chloe with his scalpel.

Joel roared and shot up. He grabbed Dane and threw the bastard as hard as he could. The scalpel sliced over Joel's arm, blood sprayed, and Dane thudded into the wall.

CHAPTER THIRTY-ONE

Chloe yanked off the tape that covered Joel's mouth. "Are you okay?" she asked him, voice shaking.

"I will be." He tore away the loose restraint straps still over him. Jumped off the table and took the scalpel from her.

All right, if he could move that quickly, then Joel was okay. She was able to breathe again.

Dane was on his feet. He gripped his weapon. Staggered forward. "I didn't hurt Portia—"

"Yes, you did!" Chloe retorted grimly. Did he think he could lie now? Not happening. "It's the only scenario that makes sense."

"No!"

"Yes!" How dare he—

"Chloe..." Joel warned as he stood protectively before her. "We've got a crazy doc with a scalpel. Let's try to not send him into a killing fury."

It was way too late for that. Surely Joel saw that? After all, he'd just been strapped to the exam table. And he was the one with blood dripping from a head wound and from his neck. *That's why I have to keep talking and keep Dane focused on me. I don't want Joel injured again.* She moved to Joel's side. "You must have killed her," Chloe told Dane. "How else would you have known which area of her spine was injured? Only the killer would have known. Her killer. The man who put a jacket over her face because he felt too guilty looking at her. Only *her* killer because he was the one who put her body in the ground and hid her away. Gregory, Ray, and Donnie might have been bastards, but they weren't killers. They didn't break Portia's spine and bury her. But..."

Dane's breath was heaving. His eyes—*so wild. Angry.*

"But they were taking her away from you," Chloe concluded. "That's what they were doing, weren't they?"

"I loved her."

Another part of the story. Another reason why you covered her face when you buried her. "You wanted Portia. You grew up in this city. Spent your whole life here. But you didn't go to her school. In fact, you're younger than she is so...did you live in the same neighborhood?" Chloe was considering and discarding possibilities as fast as she could. "You went to a private school. You told me that once. That's why you weren't at Portia's school. She was older, at a different school. A beautiful girl. You wanted her to like you, but she didn't."

The quarterback.

"Oh, no." Chloe exhaled. "She fell for Gregory, didn't she?"

"Portia had been kicked around her whole life!" Spittle flew from his mouth. "I kept telling her that she deserved better! I would see bruises on her that Gregory had left. *Bruises!* I told her that he was trouble. I told her he wasn't worth her time. So he could toss a football? Big deal. I could play baseball! I was the best homerun hitter on the team."

"Oh, yeah," Joel growled as he tried to pull Chloe behind him once more. "I'm sure you were a fucking slugger. Still are."

Dane's stare whipped to him. "They were going to run away together. Can you believe that? She'd been in foster care her whole life. I knew she wanted a family. We met—shit, met running at that park one day. We didn't live in the same neighborhood. She lived in a rundown hole. She deserved better. So much better. I knew it from the first time I met her in that park."

The park where you buried her? Chloe was certain it was one and the same. The burial site would have held special meaning for Dane.

"She talked to me all the time about her dreams. I understood her. I got her. I *loved* her. But then that last day—that last morning—we met for our run, and she told me—she was wearing his fucking jacket and she said this stupid stuff about how she thought Gregory was going to marry her. They were going to graduate, get married, and move far away. I..." He looked down at the scalpel. "I had baseball practice later that day. I'd brought my bat along. I reached for it. I don't even know why. I did, though. I grabbed the bat, and...she was suddenly looking at me like she was scared. Scared of me."

"You chased her." But he hadn't *just* chased her. "You hit her," Chloe added.

He flinched. Looked up. He was about three feet away from her and Joel, and he still had his scalpel. Joel's blood was on the edge of that instrument.

"I chased her. I told her not to run from me. She did. She looked back—and she was so *scared*. Of me!"

"Well, sure, dumbass," Joel snarled. "You were chasing her with a damn bat!"

Dane broke. Chloe saw it happen. He let out a wild roar and leapt at Joel.

"Stop! Police!" Cedric yelled from the doorway.

But Dane didn't stop. He swung out with the scalpel.

Cedric fired. The bullet slammed into Dane's shoulder. It wrenched him back, but he surged forward again.

Surged forward—only to step right into the scalpel that Joel had just shoved toward Dane's stomach. The scalpel cut into him, and Dane screamed. He didn't back down. Didn't stop. He sliced out at Joel with his weapon, but Joel kicked him. Sent Dane scrambling back against the wall once more.

"I said stop!" Cedric bellowed.

Joel was going in for another attack. Chloe grabbed him and wrenched him out of the line of fire.

Cedric shot again. This time, the bullet sank into Dane's chest. His eyes widened. Some of the wild rage and desperation faded from his gaze. He looked down at his body even as he dropped the scalpel. "Pay...back?"

"Damn straight, it is," Joel assured him grimly.

Dane collapsed on the floor.

***

"I heard it all," Cedric told Agent Richardson flatly. "Chloe and I had a plan. She was going to head in and distract the guy. I was going to wait for the perfect moment and rush in for the arrest. I was also going to hear his confession. And I did."

Richardson was sweating. Joel also noticed the FBI agent hadn't met Chloe's stare since coming into the exam room.

Another room. Only *this* time, Joel wasn't strapped down to the table. But he had basically chained Chloe to his side.

She'd insisted that he get his arm stitched up. Like he'd even noticed that wound. And she'd wanted someone to examine his throat. He'd reminded the woman—twice—that he was a doctor, but Chloe had been adamant.

He'd been just as adamant that she stay at his side.

He'd also had his head checked out. A concussion, yes, but no skull fractures.

She tried to sidle away from him as the nurse finished up the stitches on his arm—

"No." Joel immediately pulled her back. "You know the rule. Not more than two feet until my heart rate calms down again."

Her head turned toward him. "Your heart rate is perfectly fine." With her free hand, she waved toward the nurse. "Nancy checked it a moment ago. She assured me you were good."

"He is good," Nancy agreed without looking up.

"See?" Chloe challenged.

"Not more than two feet." If he'd had his way, she would have been sitting in his lap. His hands would have been wrapped around her. And he would have been completely satisfied that she was safe.

"Joel..." Chloe sighed his name. "The bad guy is dead."

"Yes." Now Richardson seemed a little more assertive as his neck stretched. "He's dead and you—"

"I told the perpetrator to stop. I identified myself as a police officer." Cedric positioned his body on Chloe's other side. "He didn't stop. I shot him in the shoulder, and he still attacked with the scalpel. I warned him a second time. That man wasn't going to listen. He was out for blood. My second shot was to the heart." His voice was emotionless. "He died quickly. And I can assure you with one hundred percent certainty that Dane Ambrose was the Bad Deeds killer."

Richardson swallowed. "Because you and Chloe had a plan. You went in there together, and you both got the confession."

"It's what we do." Cedric shrugged. "Case closed."

Richardson stormed for the door. But stopped. Glanced back. "My profile wasn't completely off," he said as his eyes slid back to Chloe. "Dane Ambrose was the right age. He was intelligent. He wanted to punish the ones he blamed."

"The one he wanted to punish the most was himself."

"How do you figure that?" The question seemed as if it had been pulled from Richardson.

"Because he wanted me to stop him. Because he told Coreen Miller that he wanted me to come and get him. Dane knew that I hunted killers. He knew—deep down—what he was doing was wrong. He wanted to be stopped. And the way he kept attacking even after Cedric told him to stop..." Her words trailed away.

Death by cop? Joel suspected that had been the case.

"He wanted to be stopped," Chloe concluded. "And he was."

Richardson ran a hand through his hair. "Detective Coleman, I'll expect you at my side when we do the press conference."

"Ah...as to that..." Cedric rolled back his shoulders. "You can be at *my* side. Better check in with your boss. Something tells me that he's going to find out exactly how all of this went down. And he'll know all about how you were outside the hospital, trying to arrest Chloe's brother, when the real bad guy was attempting to kill another man."

Richardson flinched. "Chloe..." Richardson's voice had gone hoarse. "Did you already call him?"

"No, but he is on my contact list."

Richardson grabbed his phone and rushed out.

"Not gonna do him any good," Cedric murmured. "I think that special agent is burning far too many bridges."

Joel realized that Chloe was staring steadily at Cedric.

Cedric just shrugged.

"There." Nancy gave Joel's arm a pat. "All done." She collected her supplies. Hurried off to the next patient.

Chloe lifted a brow at Cedric.

"What am I missing?" Joel wanted to know.

"The detective just lied," Chloe informed him.

He had? Joel let go of Chloe's hand long enough to pull on the t-shirt that had been provided to him. Plain white. V neck. His bloody shirt had been taken into evidence.

"The plan *wasn't* for Cedric to stay outside and listen."

Joel stood up. Caught Chloe's hand again. "It wasn't?"

"The plan was to split up. Which we did. Because there were dozens of rooms down there." She inched closer to him. "Because I knew we had to find you fast." Her head tipped back as she looked up at Joel. "There were too many places to search and not enough time. We split up."

"And you came in armed with just a scalpel?" It had been so much better for his nerves when he'd thought that she had a cop on her six.

"I would have come in with nothing at all if it meant Dane would be distracted and you'd survive."

Breathe. She's all right. Breathe. "He was going to kill you, Chloe. He lunged across that table—"

"And you stopped him," Chloe reminded Joel.

"Because you cut through my straps!"

She smiled. "I think that means we make a pretty good team."

He wanted her mouth. Joel bent his head to kiss—

"Right. So, I have things to do. Press conferences to give—once the reporters crawl out of bed. Paperwork to file. Crime scenes to check. You know, important detective stuff."

Joel kept one hand twined with Chloe's and offered the other to Cedric. "Thank you," he told him sincerely. "You saved our lives tonight."

Cedric shook his hand. Held on. "Why didn't you take my advice?"

"What advice?"

"When I told you to forget Chloe on that very first day. Why didn't you listen to me?"

"Because it was already too late." He looked back at Chloe. His Chloe. "I was hooked."

"I think you were more than hooked. I think you were in love." Cedric let go of Joel's hand. "Welcome to the team. Can't wait to see what kind of case we work next time."

Next time?

Whistling, Cedric strolled from the room.

Joel didn't move. He couldn't look away from Chloe's bright gaze. "Next time?"

She nodded. "There's always a next time."

"Should that scare me?"

"*Are* you scared?"

His head was lowering. "Baby, there's only one thing in this world that scares me." And that was the truth. He'd thought that he feared being helpless again. But he'd been strapped down. Been promised death. And yet...

He'd just been afraid for her. Worried that he couldn't protect *her*.

"What scares you?" Chloe asked.

"The idea of losing you." Truth. She'd changed everything for him. There was no going back.

Forget Chloe?

Hell, no, that option had never been on the table. Never had. Never would be.

His mouth took hers.

CHAPTER THIRTY-TWO

Almost twenty-four hours later…

"Joel, do you want to talk about it?"

He was stripping off her clothing. One piece at a time. Kissing her.

"Joel…?"

The last twenty-four hours had been a whirlwind. After the events at the hospital, she'd just wanted to slip away with him. But slipping away hadn't been possible. Not with a dead doctor to deal with. Not with a serial killer being zipped into a body bag.

Their escape from the limelight had been delayed.

Cedric had done his press conference. Chloe and Joel had needed to answer questions. So many questions. She'd had to go back to see Ruben. Had to talk about Portia.

Had to even deal with Richardson more.

But it was over. The cops were handling things. She and Joel were finally clear.

And since she'd forced him to get yet *another* checkup before going back to their place, she also knew that he now had the all-clear to resume normal activities, all post-concussion as he was.

His mouth slowly lifted from hers. "Do I want to talk? Baby, I want *you*."

And she wanted him. She'd needed him desperately, and she'd tried to stay close to him since the attack.

"I nearly went insane." He stilled. Glanced up at her. "When he went across that table with his scalpel...when he went at *you*." He put his hands down on the mattress, moving them to either side of her body. Caging her. He kept his weight off her, though, and his mouth came down on Chloe's in a warm, passionate kiss. "Can't lose you," he rasped against her mouth.

You won't.

He was already naked. She could feel the heavy length of his arousal pushing against her. "We have to be careful," Chloe told him even as she bit his lower lip. "I don't...want to hurt...your arm. Or your head. Maybe we should stop—"

"God, no. Stopping will hurt a million times more." He ditched the rest of her clothing. "I'm a doctor. Trust me. My head's fine. So is my arm. My neck. Everything. Besides, you heard me get the all clear."

Yes, she had. "Joel..."

He spread her legs. Pushed his cock at the entrance to her body.

But he didn't thrust inside of her.

A feverish intensity had been fueling him—and her—ever since they'd walked into Joel's home. His eyes had glittered. Tension had rolled from him. And as soon as the door had shut behind them, she'd known they wouldn't make it long before they were fucking.

"I don't ever want to hurt you, Joel." She meant it. With all of her being. Joel mattered so much to her. Chloe would never forget what it had been like to search for him. To throw open door after door after door...and find empty rooms. To know that Joel was somewhere, and he needed her.

And she hadn't been able to get to him.

She'd known—with cold, brutal clarity—that if Dane had killed him, she would make sure that Dane died, too.

A savage realization. She didn't want to be that person. That person scared her. But...when it came to Joel...

I will protect him at all costs.

His tongue thrust into her mouth. His fingers slid over the curve of her breast. He teased her nipple. Pulled her out of the darkness of her own mind and back into the moment with him.

Joel isn't dead. I opened the right door. I saw him.

And Dane had still died.

"I want you so much," Joel breathed. "Will never have enough of you."

She'd never get enough of him, either. Her hand slipped between them. Her fingers curled around the length of his cock. Stroked. Pumped.

Another kiss. Deep. Sensual. She arched up to him.

He spread her wider.

Sank into her.

There was no more talking. The need was too intense. Her hips surged toward each thrust of his body. They strained together. Her nails started to rake over his arms—

No, his wound!

He caught her wrists. Pinned them to the bed. Put his mouth to her throat. Kissed her.

Thrust.

Her eyes squeezed shut as the orgasm rocked through her. Her legs clamped around his hips, and she held onto him with all of her might.

He licked her neck. Sucked sensually. Her eyes opened as his head lifted, and Chloe was staring at him when he came. Pleasure flashed across his face. His body jerked. She just tightened around him even more.

His ragged breathing slowed down. So did hers. He was back to propping up on his hands as he stared down at her. She licked her lips. This was one of those important moments. She should say something meaningful. Something... "I want to sleep with you."

"Chloe, baby, you just did." His grin flashed. "But I am more than ready to go again—"

"No, I mean sleep. I want to sleep with you tonight. In this bed. In your arms. Is...is that okay?"

His expression softened. "It's more than okay."

"I might wake up. Scream." Only fair to warn him. "And if I should punch out—"

"I can defend myself, don't worry." He feathered a kiss over her cheek, and she felt him getting thicker inside of her. "But if you don't mind," Joel murmured. "How about we put off sleeping a little while?"

He wanted to go again? Chloe smiled at him. "I'm not even a little bit tired."

"Me, either..."

***

She hated hospitals. Chloe marched smartly down the corridor and ignored the sting of the antiseptic smell in her nose. When she reached the patient's room, she gave a friendly wave to the cop stationed at the door.

He recognized her and motioned Chloe inside. After giving him a quick smile, she headed for her target.

Cinnamon—Coreen—was propped up in bed. A large bandage was wrapped around her head. When she saw Chloe, her eyes widened with alarm. "Please! I'm so sorry! I was scared out of my mind, and Dane made me say—"

"He offered you money to turn on Joel, didn't he?" Crisp. Cold.

Miserably, Coreen nodded.

"How did you meet Dane?"

"Donnie...one night, he beat me up pretty badly. Dane patched me up. Said it wasn't right. That someone should stop him." A shuddering breath. "Then he did. He stopped Donnie. I-I saw him that night in the alley. I recognized Dane, but he was helping me! How could I turn on him when he was helping me? Or at least, I thought he was...and I...God, I am so sorry!"

"You'll have to tell the police everything."

A nod. "I'll...go to jail."

Chloe cocked her head. "Probably not. See what sort of deal they will give you." She studied the other woman. "Cedric has your bag."

"My...what?"

"Your bag, you know, the one with all of the money in it? Cedric has it. You wanted to run, didn't you?"

"I just wanted to go someplace and be somebody new."

"You don't have to go to a new place to be someone new. You can be someone new right here." She put her card—with her address—on the tray next to the bed. "After you talk to the police, if you want help with that new life, come to me." She'd gotten her questions answered.

And she really did hate hospitals.

Her heels tapped as she made her way for the door.

"Why would you help me? I lied about your boyfriend."

Chloe considered the question. "I'm not the kind of person who wants payback. That kind of thinking just leads to a circle of pain that never ends." *If Joel had been killed*...No, she wouldn't think of that. Joel hadn't been killed. He was alive and safe, and she intended to keep him that way, thank you very much. Chloe looked over her shoulder. "I want something different. Sounds like you do, too."

A tear trickled down Coreen's cheek. "Yes."

"Then let's just see what we can make happen, shall we? Be sure you ask for Detective Coleman when you speak with the police. He's the best detective on the force."

With that, Chloe made her exit. She wasted no time leaving the hospital. She'd slipped away from the house first thing that morning. Joel didn't know that she was gone. But...

If she didn't get back soon, he would.

Dane Ambrose.

She'd thought that he'd gone to Miami. Shortly before she'd started the investigation into Gregory Guidry's murder, she'd heard of Dane's departure. Now she realized that the Miami job had been a trick. A ruse to provide him with an alibi, at least for the first two killings. By the time he'd gotten around to eliminating Donnie Adams, he'd been letting people know he was back in New Orleans.

Probably because he'd felt safe then. Or because...

Come and get me.

He'd been ready for things to end.

It was Judith Key's death that bothered Chloe. The three men had been obvious targets. Dane hadn't wanted to blame himself for Portia's murder, so he'd taken out the rage he felt on them. But Judith?

That was why he didn't paralyze her. He hit her with his bat. Then stabbed her. But he didn't kill her at the scene. Maybe he couldn't, not like that. Or maybe they'd interrupted him. But Chloe did think he had done something to Judith in the hospital. Perhaps that air bubble in her IV, as she'd suspected before. Ruben would help her find out when he completed his autopsy. Ruben tended to be very good with details.

But why go after Judith?

Chloe was afraid that she might have led Dane to Judith. If he'd been watching her...and she knew that he probably had...he might have seen her go to Judith. He'd gotten Judith to tell him what Chloe wanted. And once he'd confronted Judith, perhaps there had been no going back for him?

Come and get me.

They had gotten the bastard. He wouldn't be hurting anyone else. And Portia? She wouldn't be tossed into an unmarked grave. Chloe and Cedric were making arrangements for her. They were planning a big procession for her. They even had the brass band scheduled for the second line. It seemed fitting that Portia have the special New Orleans tradition. Her funeral procession would be something special. She deserved that.

The hospital's doors opened for her. Chloe took a deep breath as she stepped outside. She made her way to—

"Would you like a ride? I know you took a taxi this morning, but I thought you might enjoy going back with me." Joel straddled his motorcycle. Smiled at her.

Her breath caught.

He was so different, now. The shadows didn't haunt his eyes. His smile was wide and warm. His gaze gleamed. Looking at him, you'd never know the man had faced death so recently.

If she hadn't known better, Chloe would have believed that the encounter with a killer had actually energized Joel. But she *did* know better. He wasn't looking so fit and good because of what had happened.

But because of what he'd realized.

Joel knows there is more to this life than darkness. He'd survived, and he'd fought to protect her. Chloe had told him that he would love her.

She knew now that he already did.

Just as she loved him. With every bit of her being. She loved him more than she'd ever thought it was possible to love someone.

"You thought I didn't notice when you slipped out of bed?" He offered her a helmet.

She took it. Held it in her hands. "I tried to be quiet."

"I heard you tip-toeing."

"Why didn't you say something?"

"Figured you were tying up some loose ends."

Yes.

"I tailed you, though, in case you needed help." His head turned as he studied the parking lot. "Also, I don't know where your crazy ex is, so there's that."

"Is he a problem for you?" Why was she even asking? Morgan was a problem for everyone. She slid the helmet onto her head.

"Nothing we can't handle." He caught her hand. Brought it to his lips. "Am I right?"

"I think we can handle anything."

His face had gone tender. "You still have secrets, don't you?"

Her heart squeezed. "One day, you'll know every secret that I have." Her words were a promise.

Another kiss to her hand. "Good. I look forward to that day. Until then, I think I'll just have one hell of a time figuring them out." He let her hand go. Tapped the helmet. "Make sure it's strapped on well. You know we both like to go fast…"

Yes, they did.

She checked the strap. Slid in place behind him. He revved the engine. She held on tight.

Fast.

That was how everything had been since she'd met Joel. She'd intended to pull him into her world, but he'd wound up making her fall for him. Fall so very fast. Now they were tangled together, and there was no going back. She didn't want to go back. She wanted Joel. She wanted a partner— a real one—who understood her.

Fast. That was how things would keep coming at them. More cases. More criminals. Enemies in the dark.

But they'd be ready. They'd face the threats out there.

Every single one.

The killers who hunted in the streets had better be prepared.

Because we're coming for you.

The End

Want to see what's coming next in the "Death and Moonlight" world? Well...turn the page for an early look at SAVE ME FROM THE DARK.

SAVE ME FROM THE DARK

"You have to tell him." Reese seemed uncharacteristically determined. "It can't go on this way." He gave a firm nod.

Chloe exhaled slowly. "I have told Joel." And it had been a major step for her. "I told Joel that I think I love him." *Love.* A four letter word that she didn't use often. But everything with Joel was different. Even the way she felt. She wanted to—

"No! Jeez, no, I am not talking about how you feel about the guy." A wince. "But if you really *do* love him, don't you think that is all the more reason to tell the man the truth?"

The truth. A weight seemed to settle in the pit of her stomach. "I want to protect him."

His hands curled around her shoulders. "I get that. I do, Chloe. But this is huge. Life-altering. Joel is going to lose his shit when he finds out."

"Why do you think I haven't told him?" Because the last thing she wanted was for, um, Joel to lose his shit.

"He deserves to know." Reese gazed into her eyes. "You know it."

"It will wreck him." Everything was different now.

"Yes, well, it's kind of wrecking information, don't you think?"

"Reese..." He didn't understand. She didn't have proof yet. She didn't—

I can't hurt Joel. I can't.

"You have to tell him." His hold tightened on her. "You have to tell Joel that when he crawled out of that fucking hole he'd been buried in...when Joel killed the man he found waiting for him—*that* bastard wasn't the sick SOB who'd tortured Joel for hours on end. You have to tell Joel that he killed the wrong man. The real sadistic prick is still out there. You have to tell him—"

"What?" Joel's voice. Ragged. Gruff.

Stunned.

Stay tuned. SAVE ME FROM THE DARK will be available in early 2021.

A NOTE FROM THE AUTHOR

Thank you so much for reading STEP INTO MY WEB!

Chloe and Joel were two characters who slipped into my head, and I just could not get them out! Chloe's entire life is all about secrets—keeping her own and discovering the secrets that other people possess. But once she meets Joel, everything changes for her. Chloe and Joel have more stories to tell...and I hope you'll follow their adventures in SAVE ME FROM THE DARK when it is released in 2021.

If you'd like to stay updated on my releases and sales, please join my newsletter list.

https://cynthiaeden.com/newsletter/

Again, thank you for reading STEP INTO MY WEB.

Best,
Cynthia Eden
cynthiaeden.com

ABOUT THE AUTHOR

Cynthia Eden is a *New York Times*, *USA Today*, *Digital Book World*, and *IndieReader* best-seller.

Cynthia writes sexy tales of contemporary romance, romantic suspense, and paranormal romance. Since she began writing full-time in 2005, Cynthia has written over one hundred novels and novellas.

Cynthia lives along the Alabama Gulf Coast. She loves romance novels, horror movies, and chocolate.

For More Information
- *cynthiaeden.com*
- *facebook.com/cynthiaedenfanpage*

HER OTHER WORKS

Wilde Ways

- Protecting Piper (Book 1)
- Guarding Gwen (Book 2)
- Before Ben (Book 3)
- The Heart You Break (Book 4)
- Fighting For Her (Book 5)
- Ghost Of A Chance (Book 6)
- Crossing The Line (Book 7)
- Counting On Cole (Book 8)
- Chase After Me (Book 9)
- Say I Do (Book 10)

Dark Sins

- Don't Trust A Killer (Book 1)
- Don't Love A Liar (Book 2)

Lazarus Rising

- Never Let Go (Book One)
- Keep Me Close (Book Two)
- Stay With Me (Book Three)
- Run To Me (Book Four)
- Lie Close To Me (Book Five)
- Hold On Tight (Book Six)
- Lazarus Rising Volume One (Books 1 to 3)

- Lazarus Rising Volume Two (Books 4 to 6)

Dark Obsession Series

- Watch Me (Book 1)
- Want Me (Book 2)
- Need Me (Book 3)
- Beware Of Me (Book 4)
- Only For Me (Books 1 to 4)

Mine Series

- Mine To Take (Book 1)
- Mine To Keep (Book 2)
- Mine To Hold (Book 3)
- Mine To Crave (Book 4)
- Mine To Have (Book 5)
- Mine To Protect (Book 6)
- Mine Box Set Volume 1 (Books 1-3)
- Mine Box Set Volume 2 (Books 4-6)

Bad Things

- The Devil In Disguise (Book 1)
- On The Prowl (Book 2)
- Undead Or Alive (Book 3)
- Broken Angel (Book 4)
- Heart Of Stone (Book 5)
- Tempted By Fate (Book 6)
- Wicked And Wild (Book 7)
- Saint Or Sinner (Book 8)
- Bad Things Volume One (Books 1 to 3)
- Bad Things Volume Two (Books 4 to 6)
- Bad Things Deluxe Box Set (Books 1 to 6)

Bite Series

- Forbidden Bite (Bite Book 1)
- Mating Bite (Bite Book 2)

Blood and Moonlight Series

- Bite The Dust (Book 1)
- Better Off Undead (Book 2)
- Bitter Blood (Book 3)
- Blood and Moonlight (The Complete Series)

Purgatory Series

- The Wolf Within (Book 1)
- Marked By The Vampire (Book 2)
- Charming The Beast (Book 3)
- Deal with the Devil (Book 4)
- The Beasts Inside (Books 1 to 4)

Bound Series

- Bound By Blood (Book 1)
- Bound In Darkness (Book 2)
- Bound In Sin (Book 3)
- Bound By The Night (Book 4)
- Bound in Death (Book 5)
- Forever Bound (Books 1 to 4)

Other Romantic Suspense

- Never Gonna Happen
- One Hot Holiday
- Secret Admirer
- First Taste of Darkness
- Sinful Secrets
- Until Death
- Christmas With A Spy

CPSIA information can be obtained
at www.ICGtesting.com
Printed in the USA
LVHW080552161120
671807LV00044B/1288